LEGENDARY COMICS YA

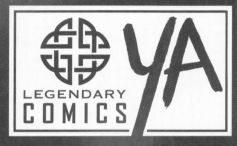

TRA

GIC

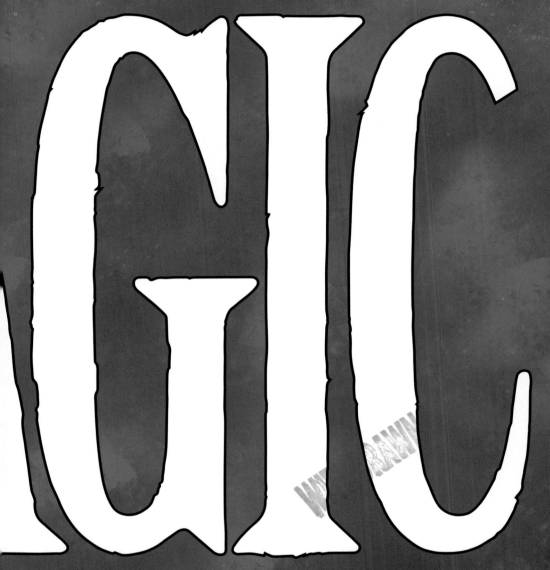

Volume One

Creator & Writer
DANA MELE

Cover Inks & Interior Art
VALENTINA PINTI

Cover Colors & Interior Colors
CHIARA DI FRANCIA

Lettering
COMICRAFT'S
JIMMY BETANCOURT

Design
COMICRAFT'S
TYLER SMITH

Editor
NIKITA KANNEKANTI

Logo
KATIE AGUILAR

Special Thanks
LEGENDARY MARKETING
LEGENDARY PUBLICITY

 LEGENDARY

LEGENDARY COMICS

JOSHUA GRODE Chief Executive Officer	**RONALD HOHAUSER** Chief Financial Officer	**KRISTINA HOLLIMAN** SVP, Business Affairs & Operations	**ROBERT NAPTON** SVP and Publisher
MARY PARENT Vice Chairman of Worldwide Production	**BARNABY LEGG** Chief Creative Marketing Executive	**REBECCA RUSH** Director, Business & Legal Affairs	**NIKITA KANNEKANTI** Senior Editor
CHRIS ALBRECHT Managing Director, Legendary Television	**MIKE ROSS** EVP, Business & Legal Affairs	**BAYAN LAIRD** SVP, Business & Legal Affairs	**SARA HASKELL** Director, Publishing Marketing & Sales

Chapter One
TRAGIC

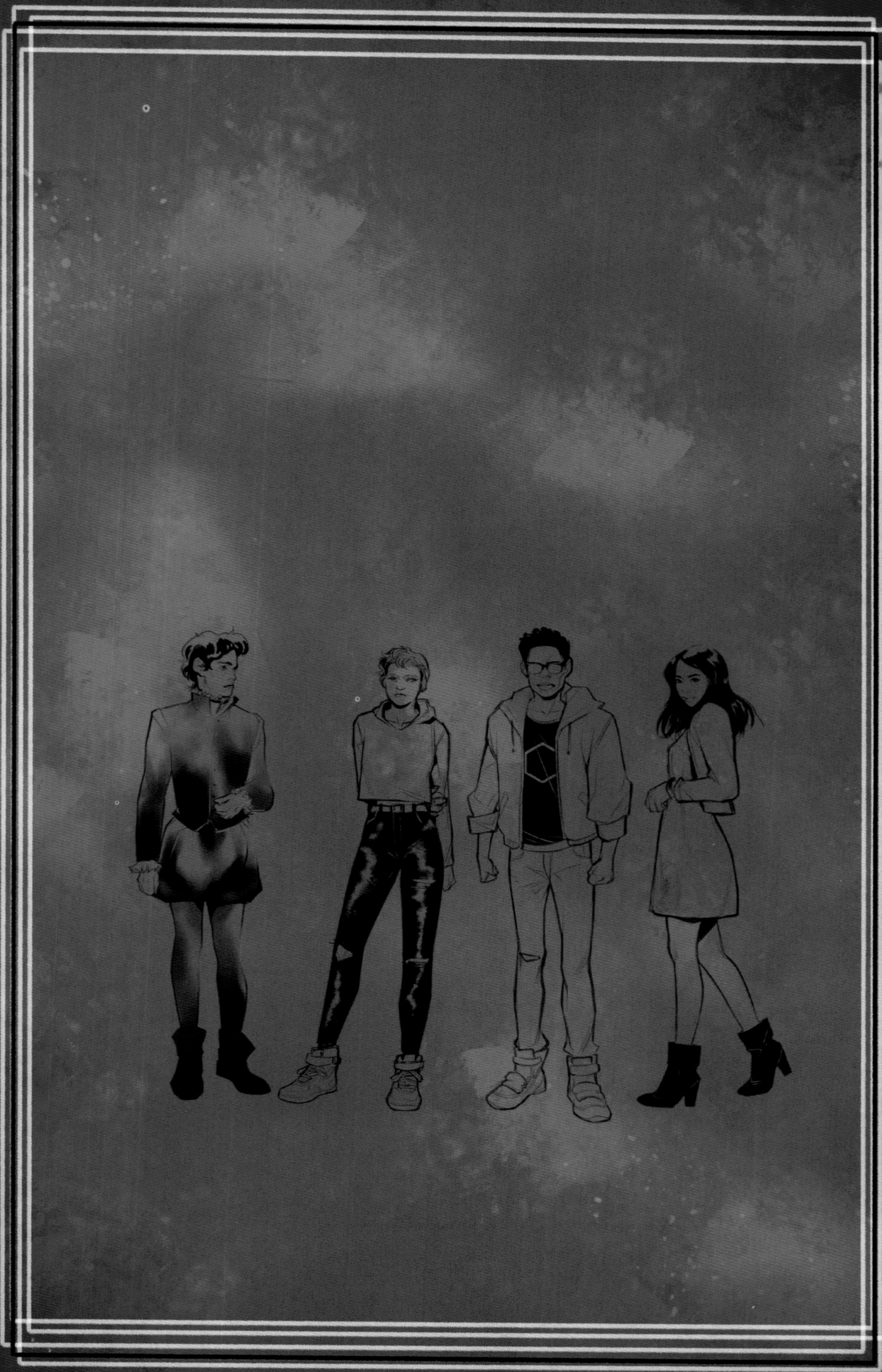

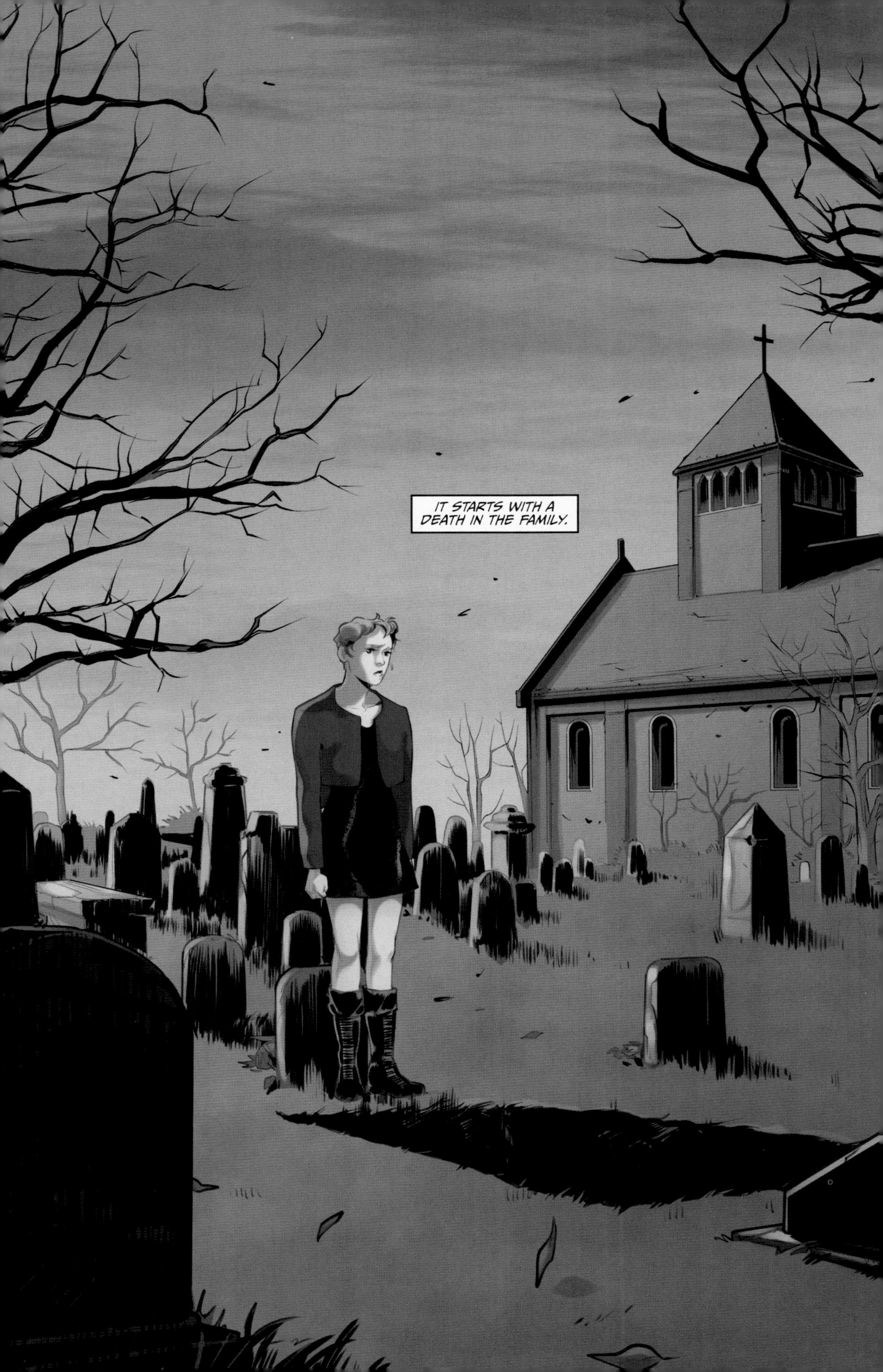
IT STARTS WITH A DEATH IN THE FAMILY.

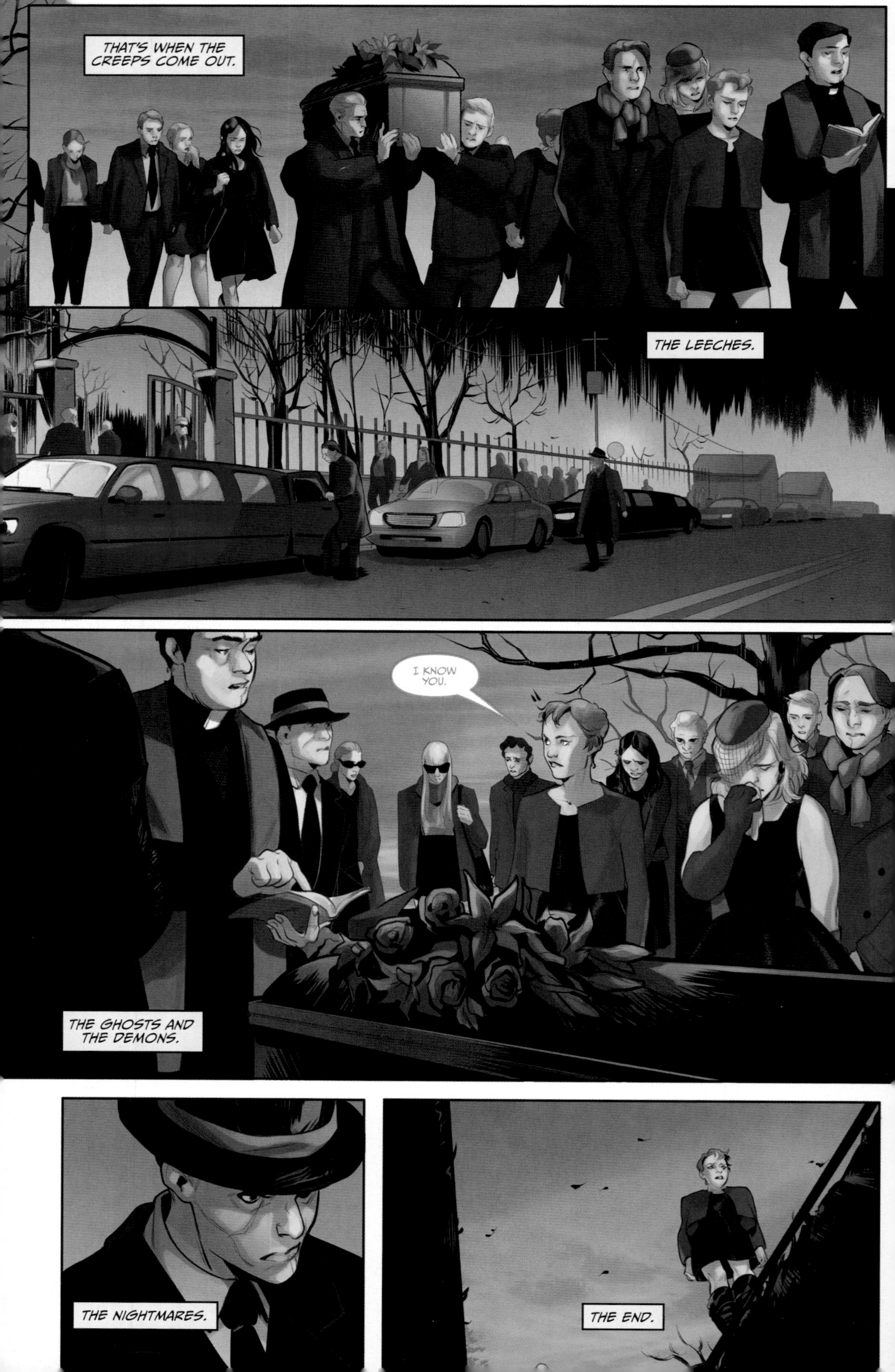
THAT'S WHEN THE CREEPS COME OUT.
THE LEECHES.
I KNOW YOU.
THE GHOSTS AND THE DEMONS.
THE NIGHTMARES.
THE END.

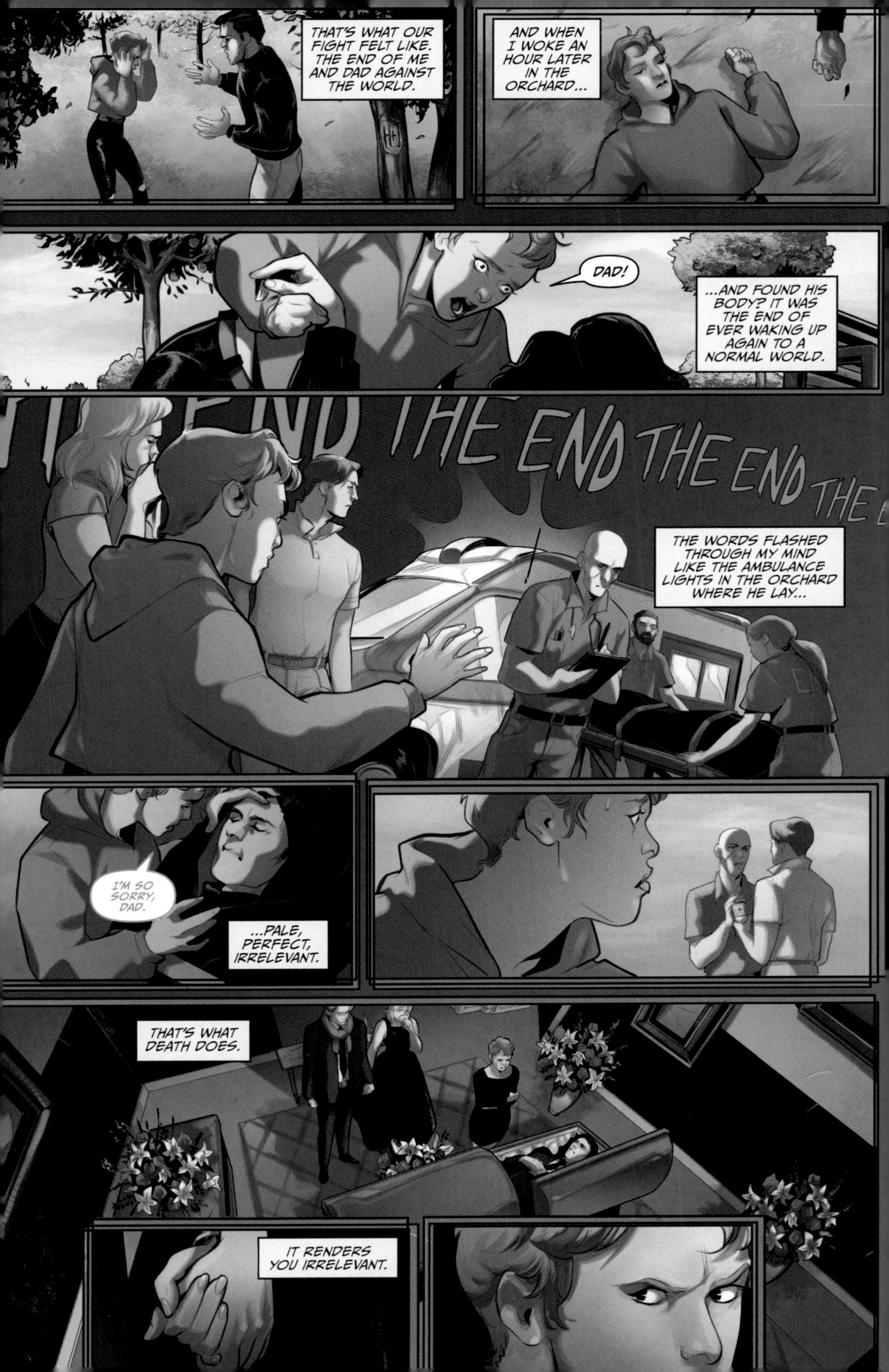
THAT'S WHAT OUR FIGHT FELT LIKE. THE END OF ME AND DAD AGAINST THE WORLD.
AND WHEN I WOKE AN HOUR LATER IN THE ORCHARD...
DAD!
...AND FOUND HIS BODY? IT WAS THE END OF EVER WAKING UP AGAIN TO A NORMAL WORLD.
THE END THE END THE END
THE WORDS FLASHED THROUGH MY MIND LIKE THE AMBULANCE LIGHTS IN THE ORCHARD WHERE HE LAY...
I'M SO SORRY, DAD.
...PALE, PERFECT, IRRELEVANT.
THAT'S WHAT DEATH DOES.
IT RENDERS YOU IRRELEVANT.

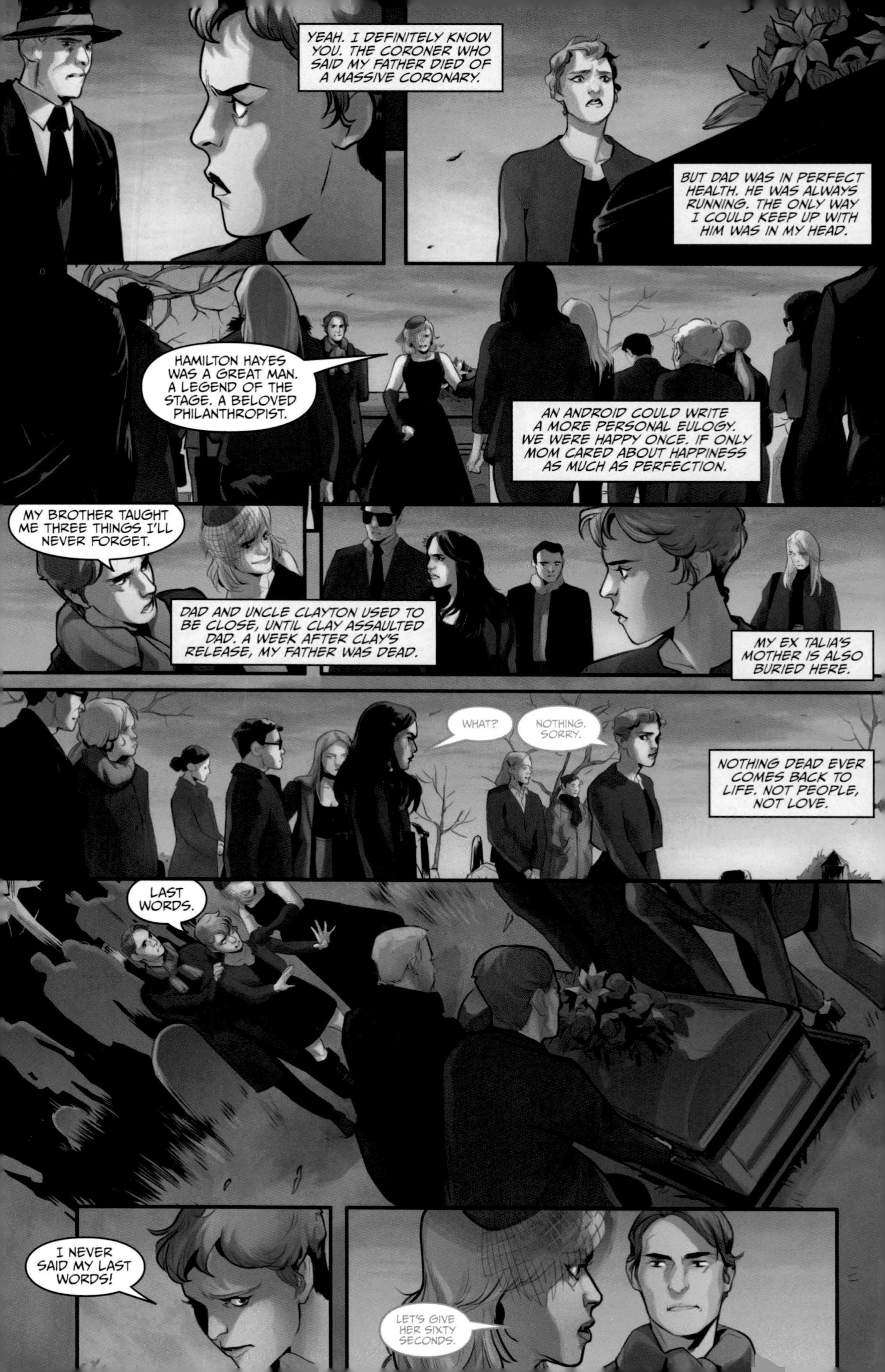
YEAH. I DEFINITELY KNOW YOU. THE CORONER WHO SAID MY FATHER DIED OF A MASSIVE CORONARY.
BUT DAD WAS IN PERFECT HEALTH. HE WAS ALWAYS RUNNING. THE ONLY WAY I COULD KEEP UP WITH HIM WAS IN MY HEAD.
HAMILTON HAYES WAS A GREAT MAN. A LEGEND OF THE STAGE. A BELOVED PHILANTHROPIST.
AN ANDROID COULD WRITE A MORE PERSONAL EULOGY. WE WERE HAPPY ONCE. IF ONLY MOM CARED ABOUT HAPPINESS AS MUCH AS PERFECTION.
MY BROTHER TAUGHT ME THREE THINGS I'LL NEVER FORGET.
DAD AND UNCLE CLAYTON USED TO BE CLOSE, UNTIL CLAY ASSAULTED DAD. A WEEK AFTER CLAY'S RELEASE, MY FATHER WAS DEAD.
MY EX TALIA'S MOTHER IS ALSO BURIED HERE.
WHAT?
NOTHING. SORRY.
NOTHING DEAD EVER COMES BACK TO LIFE. NOT PEOPLE, NOT LOVE.
LAST WORDS.
I NEVER SAID MY LAST WORDS!
LET'S GIVE HER SIXTY SECONDS.

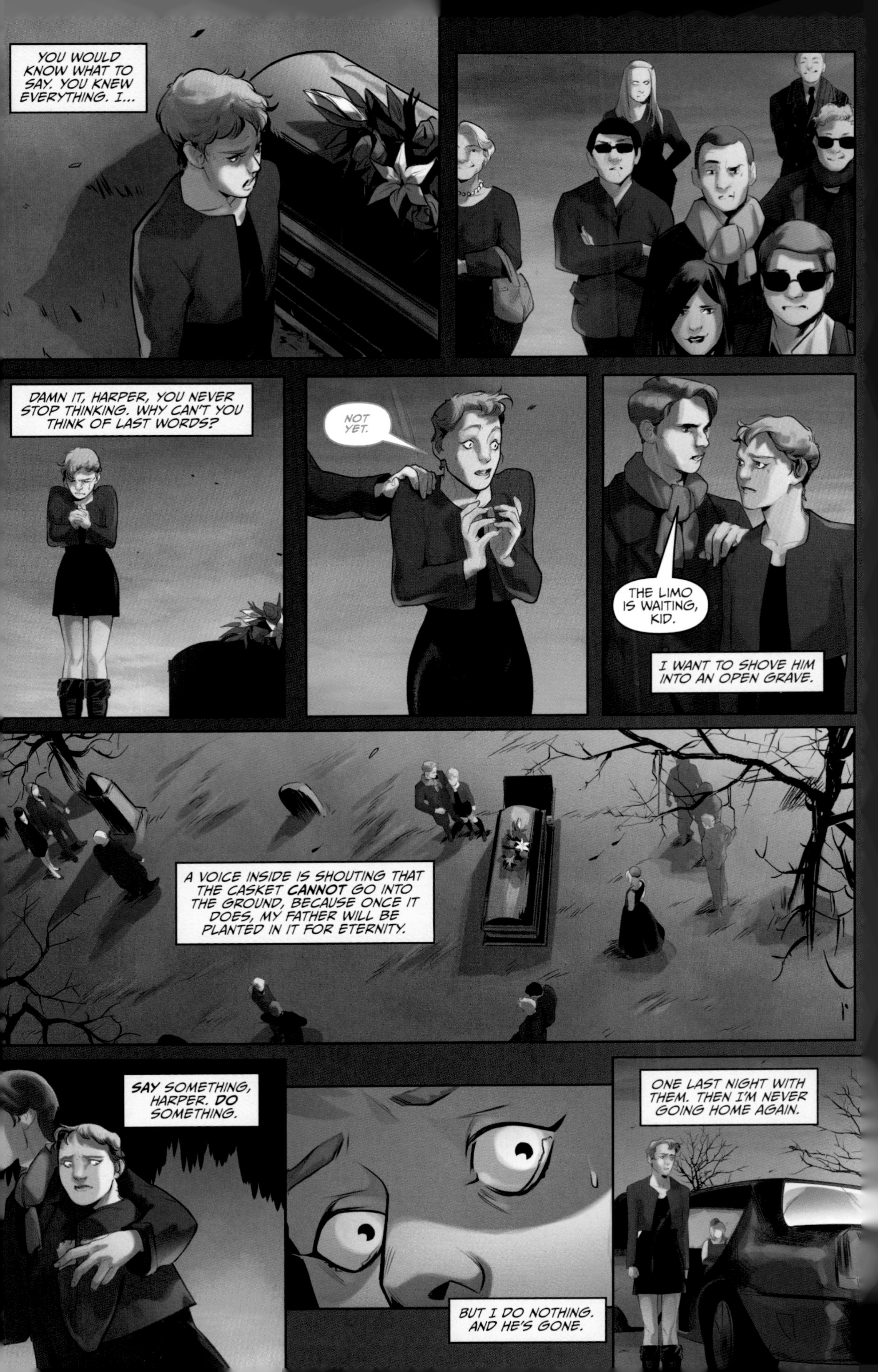
YOU WOULD KNOW WHAT TO SAY. YOU KNEW EVERYTHING. I...
DAMN IT, HARPER, YOU NEVER STOP THINKING. WHY CAN'T YOU THINK OF LAST WORDS?
NOT YET.
THE LIMO IS WAITING, KID.
I WANT TO SHOVE HIM INTO AN OPEN GRAVE.
A VOICE INSIDE IS SHOUTING THAT THE CASKET CANNOT GO INTO THE GROUND, BECAUSE ONCE IT DOES, MY FATHER WILL BE PLANTED IN IT FOR ETERNITY.
SAY SOMETHING, HARPER. DO SOMETHING.
BUT I DO NOTHING. AND HE'S GONE.
ONE LAST NIGHT WITH THEM. THEN I'M NEVER GOING HOME AGAIN.

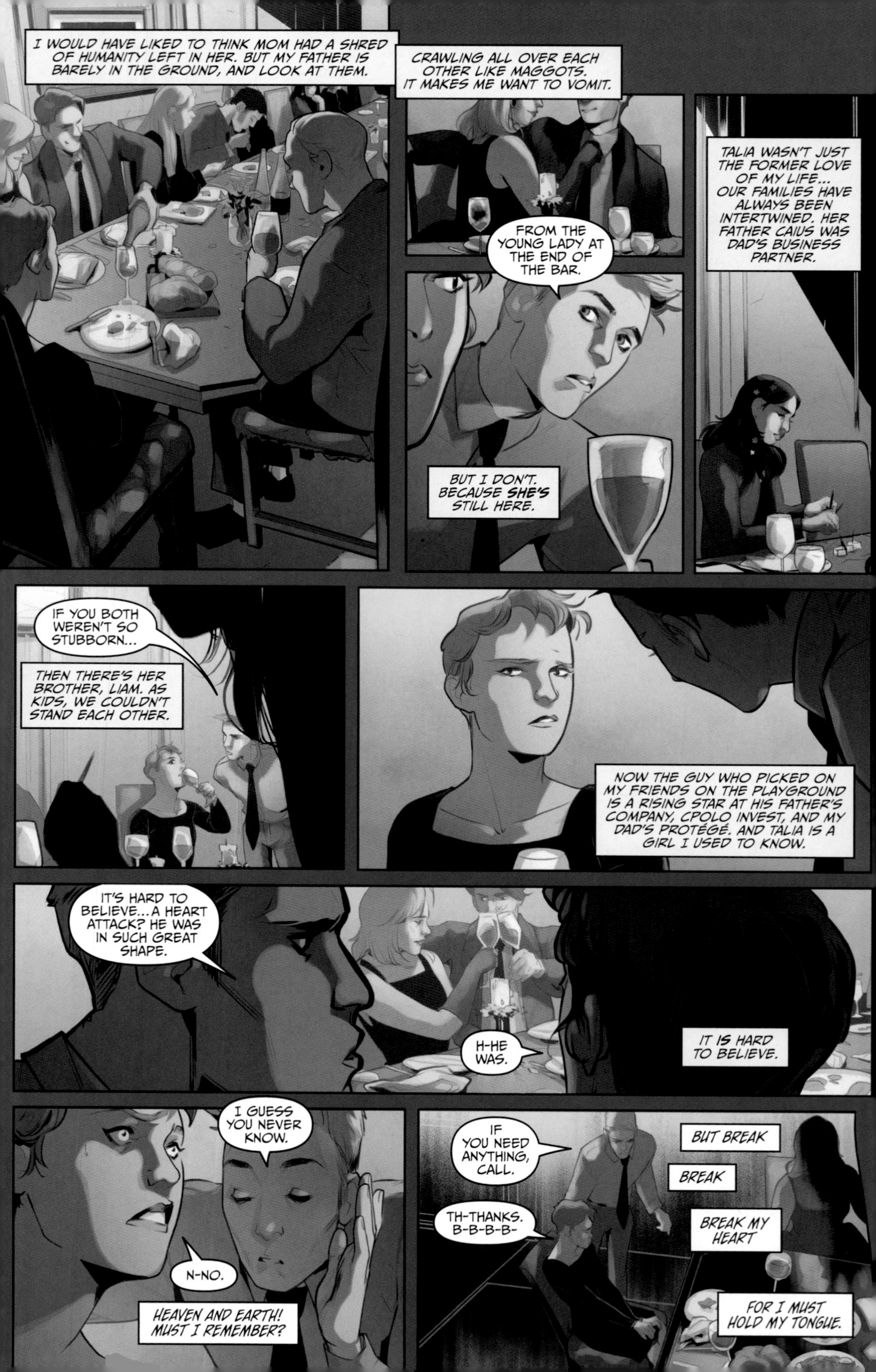
I WOULD HAVE LIKED TO THINK MOM HAD A SHRED OF HUMANITY LEFT IN HER. BUT MY FATHER IS BARELY IN THE GROUND, AND LOOK AT THEM.
CRAWLING ALL OVER EACH OTHER LIKE MAGGOTS. IT MAKES ME WANT TO VOMIT.
FROM THE YOUNG LADY AT THE END OF THE BAR.
BUT I DON'T. BECAUSE SHE'S STILL HERE.
TALIA WASN'T JUST THE FORMER LOVE OF MY LIFE... OUR FAMILIES HAVE ALWAYS BEEN INTERTWINED. HER FATHER CAIUS WAS DAD'S BUSINESS PARTNER.
IF YOU BOTH WEREN'T SO STUBBORN...
THEN THERE'S HER BROTHER, LIAM. AS KIDS, WE COULDN'T STAND EACH OTHER.
NOW THE GUY WHO PICKED ON MY FRIENDS ON THE PLAYGROUND IS A RISING STAR AT HIS FATHER'S COMPANY, CPOLO INVEST, AND MY DAD'S PROTÉGÉ. AND TALIA IS A GIRL I USED TO KNOW.
IT'S HARD TO BELIEVE... A HEART ATTACK? HE WAS IN SUCH GREAT SHAPE.
H-HE WAS.
IT IS HARD TO BELIEVE.
I GUESS YOU NEVER KNOW.
N-NO.
HEAVEN AND EARTH! MUST I REMEMBER?
IF YOU NEED ANYTHING, CALL.
TH-THANKS. B-B-B-B-
BUT BREAK
BREAK
BREAK MY HEART
FOR I MUST HOLD MY TONGUE.

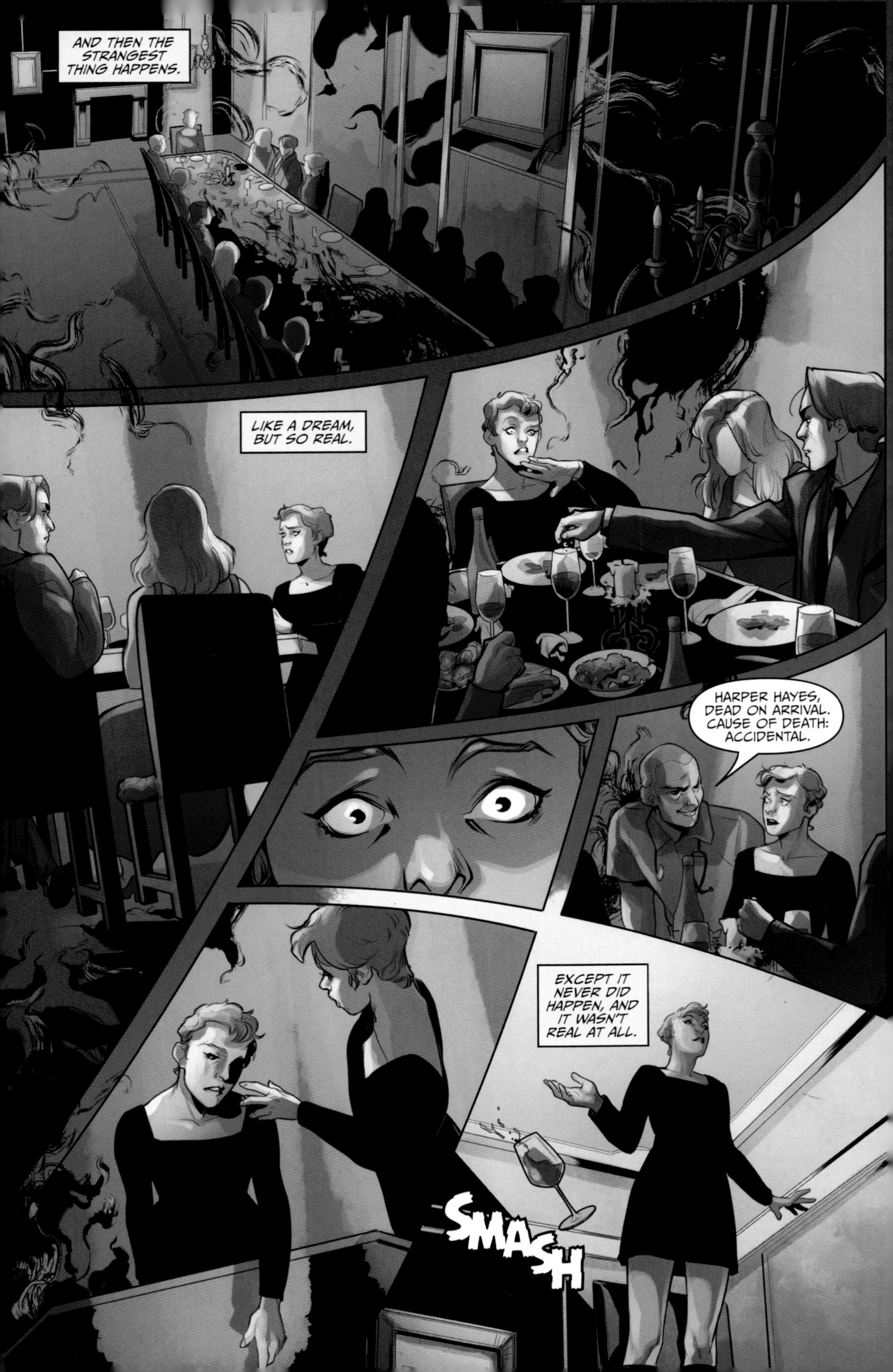
AND THEN THE STRANGEST THING HAPPENS.
LIKE A DREAM, BUT SO REAL.
HARPER HAYES, DEAD ON ARRIVAL. CAUSE OF DEATH: ACCIDENTAL.
EXCEPT IT NEVER DID HAPPEN, AND IT WASN'T REAL AT ALL.
SMASH

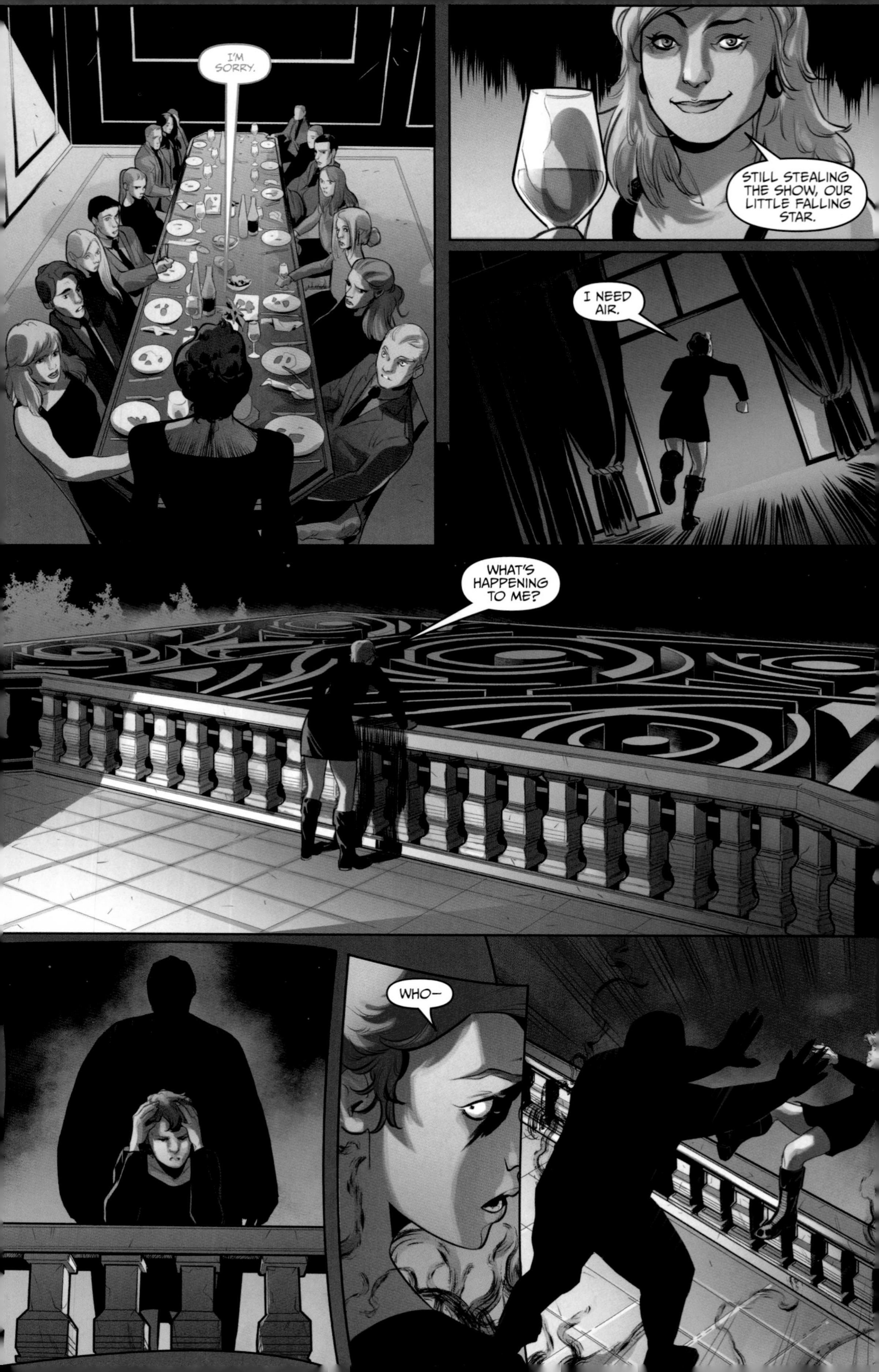

I'M SORRY.
STILL STEALING THE SHOW, OUR LITTLE FALLING STAR.
I NEED AIR.
WHAT'S HAPPENING TO ME?
WHO–

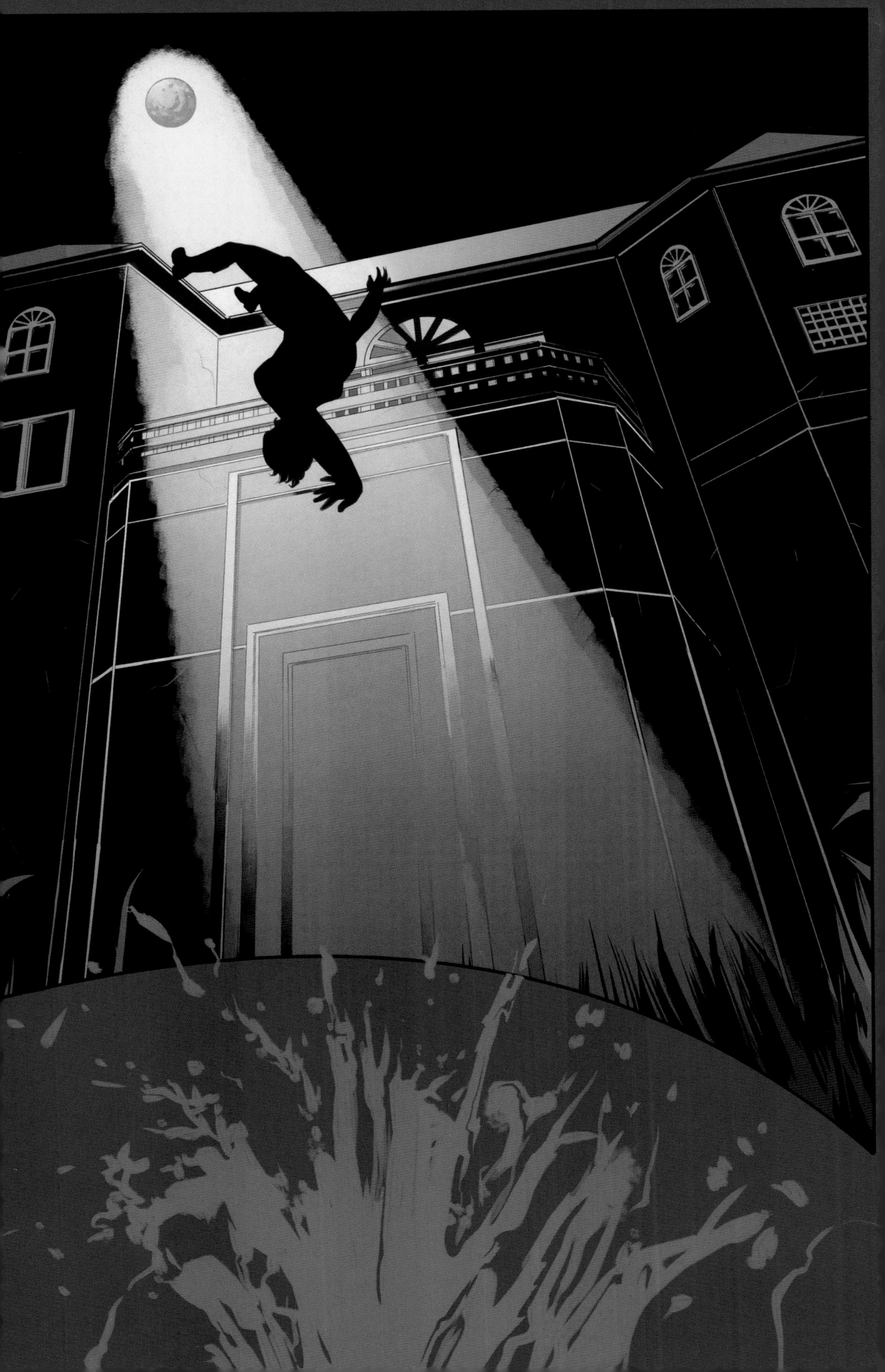

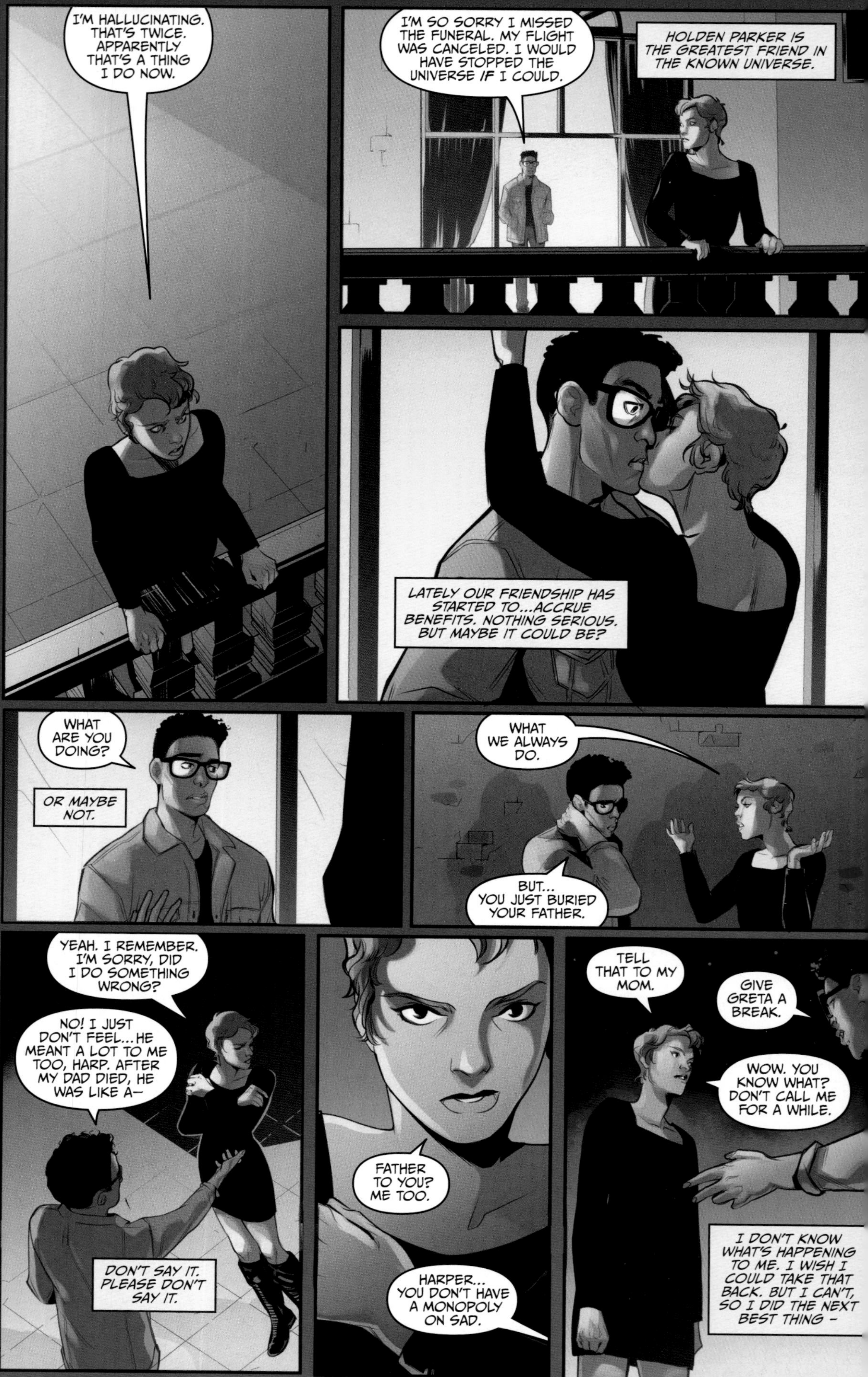
I'M HALLUCINATING. THAT'S TWICE. APPARENTLY THAT'S A THING I DO NOW.
I'M SO SORRY I MISSED THE FUNERAL. MY FLIGHT WAS CANCELED. I WOULD HAVE STOPPED THE UNIVERSE IF I COULD.
HOLDEN PARKER IS THE GREATEST FRIEND IN THE KNOWN UNIVERSE.
LATELY OUR FRIENDSHIP HAS STARTED TO...ACCRUE BENEFITS. NOTHING SERIOUS. BUT MAYBE IT COULD BE?
WHAT ARE YOU DOING?
OR MAYBE NOT.
WHAT WE ALWAYS DO.
BUT... YOU JUST BURIED YOUR FATHER.
YEAH. I REMEMBER. I'M SORRY, DID I DO SOMETHING WRONG?
NO! I JUST DON'T FEEL...HE MEANT A LOT TO ME TOO, HARP. AFTER MY DAD DIED, HE WAS LIKE A—
DON'T SAY IT. PLEASE DON'T SAY IT.
FATHER TO YOU? ME TOO.
HARPER... YOU DON'T HAVE A MONOPOLY ON SAD.
TELL THAT TO MY MOM.
GIVE GRETA A BREAK.
WOW. YOU KNOW WHAT? DON'T CALL ME FOR A WHILE.
I DON'T KNOW WHAT'S HAPPENING TO ME. I WISH I COULD TAKE THAT BACK. BUT I CAN'T, SO I DID THE NEXT BEST THING –

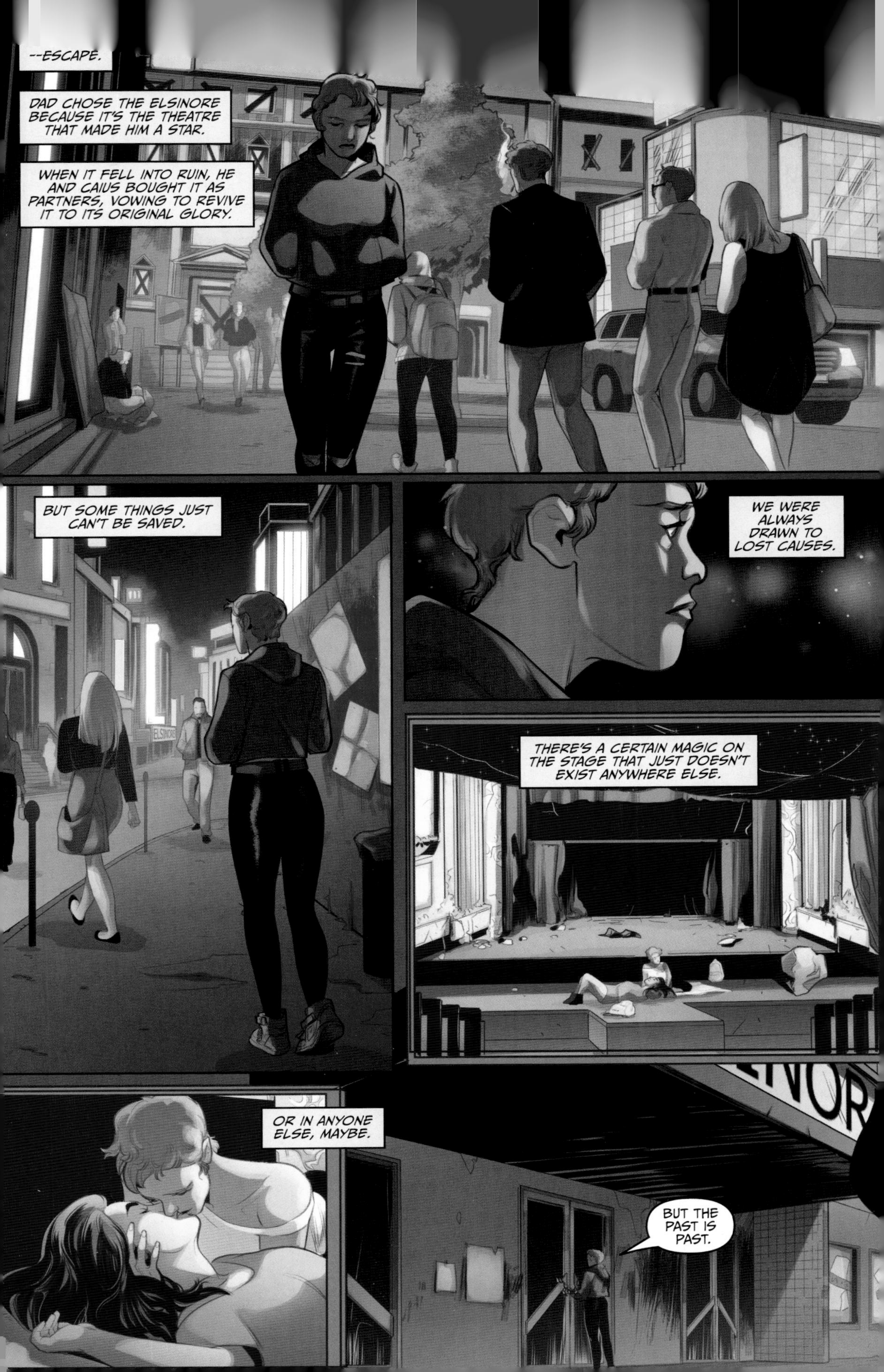
--ESCAPE.
DAD CHOSE THE ELSINORE BECAUSE IT'S THE THEATRE THAT MADE HIM A STAR.
WHEN IT FELL INTO RUIN, HE AND CAIUS BOUGHT IT AS PARTNERS, VOWING TO REVIVE IT TO ITS ORIGINAL GLORY.
BUT SOME THINGS JUST CAN'T BE SAVED.
ELSINORE
WE WERE ALWAYS DRAWN TO LOST CAUSES.
THERE'S A CERTAIN MAGIC ON THE STAGE THAT JUST DOESN'T EXIST ANYWHERE ELSE.
OR IN ANYONE ELSE, MAYBE.
LSINOR
BUT THE PAST IS PAST.

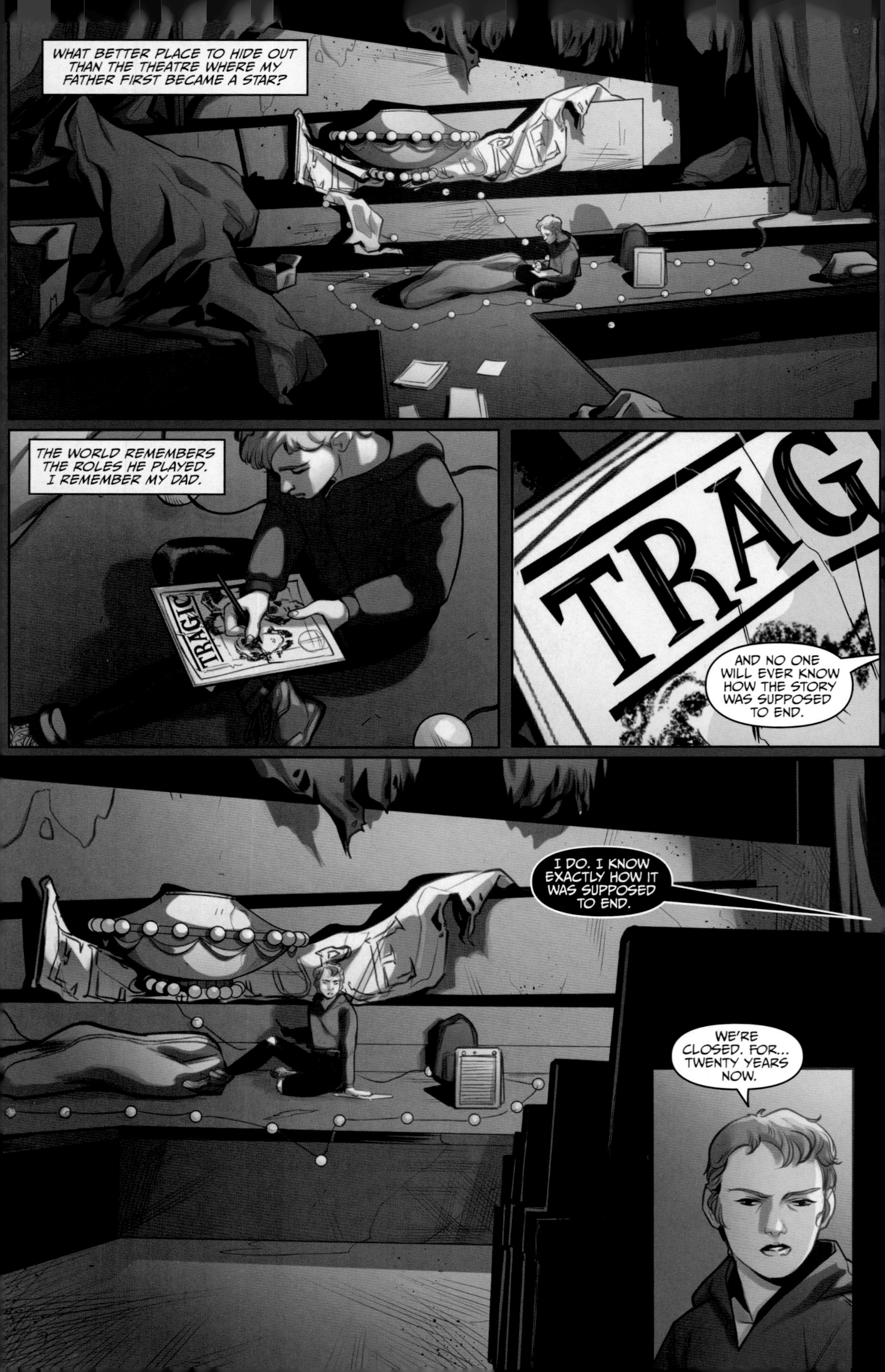
WHAT BETTER PLACE TO HIDE OUT THAN THE THEATRE WHERE MY FATHER FIRST BECAME A STAR?
THE WORLD REMEMBERS THE ROLES HE PLAYED. I REMEMBER MY DAD.
TRAGIC
TRAG
AND NO ONE WILL EVER KNOW HOW THE STORY WAS SUPPOSED TO END.
I DO. I KNOW EXACTLY HOW IT WAS SUPPOSED TO END.
WE'RE CLOSED. FOR... TWENTY YEARS NOW.

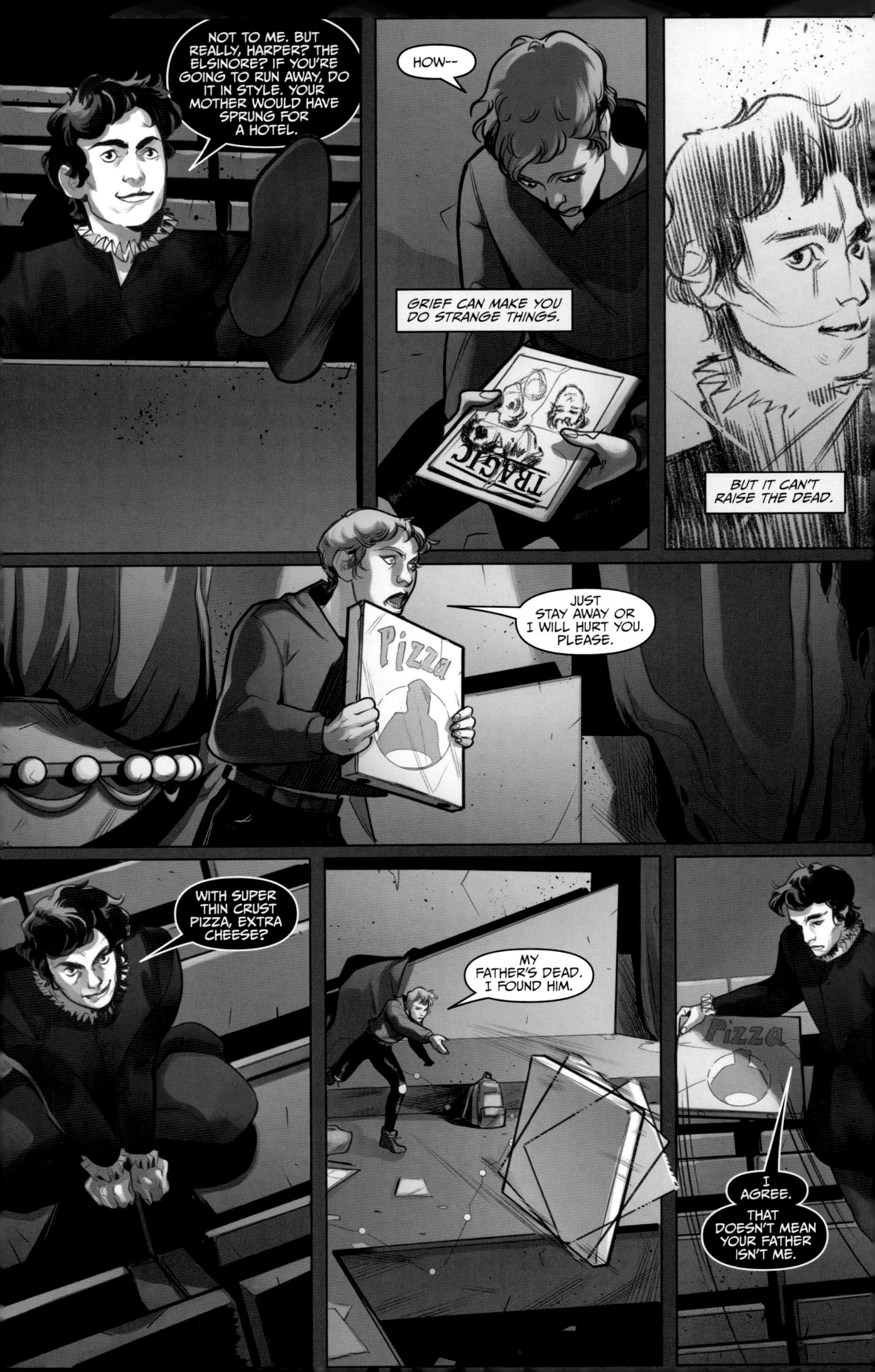
NOT TO ME. BUT REALLY, HARPER? THE ELSINORE? IF YOU'RE GOING TO RUN AWAY, DO IT IN STYLE. YOUR MOTHER WOULD HAVE SPRUNG FOR A HOTEL.
HOW--
GRIEF CAN MAKE YOU DO STRANGE THINGS.
TRAGIC
BUT IT CAN'T RAISE THE DEAD.
JUST STAY AWAY OR I WILL HURT YOU. PLEASE.
Pizza
WITH SUPER THIN CRUST PIZZA, EXTRA CHEESE?
MY FATHER'S DEAD. I FOUND HIM.
Pizza
I AGREE.
THAT DOESN'T MEAN YOUR FATHER ISN'T ME.

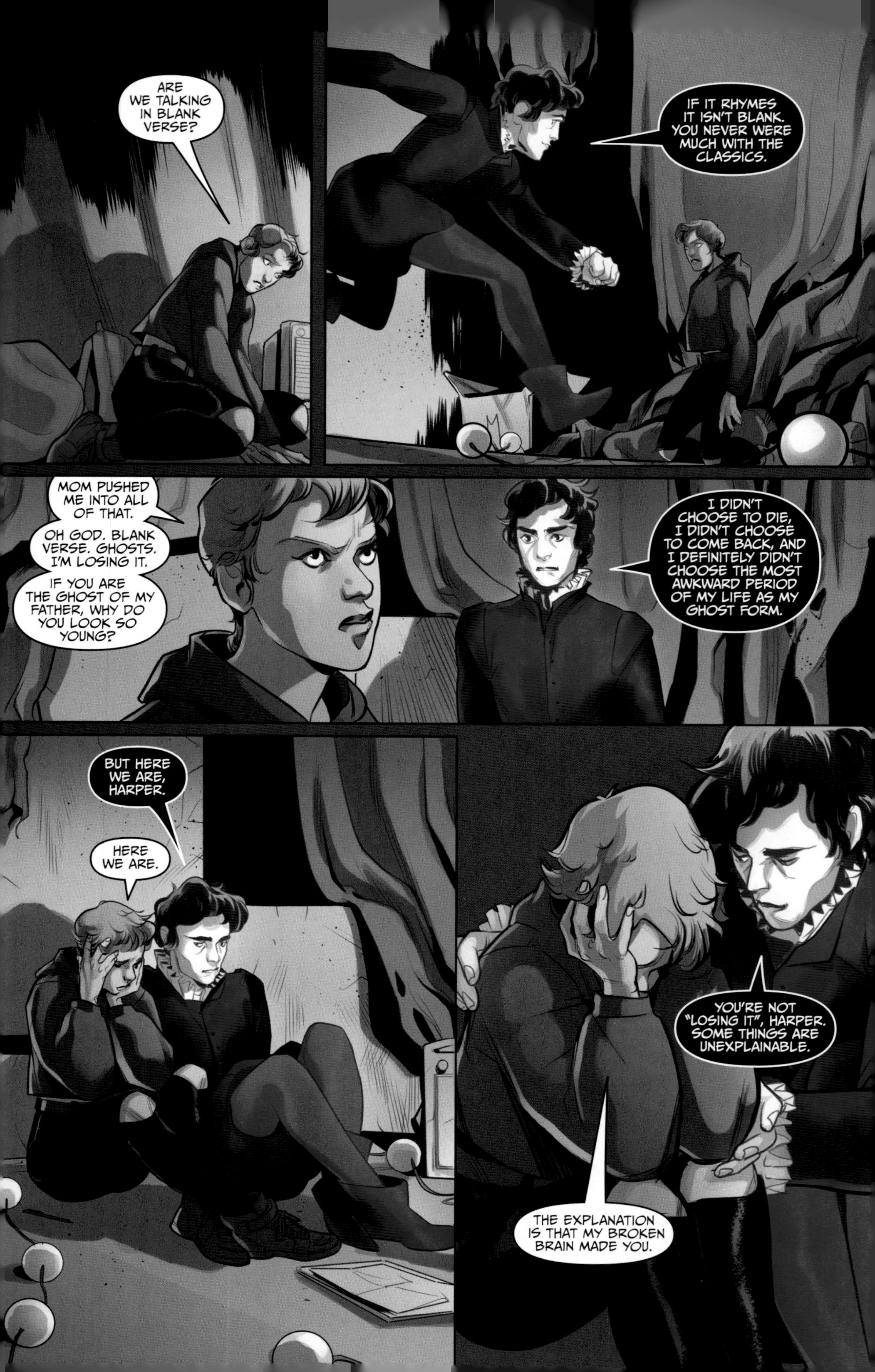
ARE WE TALKING IN BLANK VERSE?
IF IT RHYMES IT ISN'T BLANK. YOU NEVER WERE MUCH WITH THE CLASSICS.
MOM PUSHED ME INTO ALL OF THAT.
OH GOD. BLANK VERSE. GHOSTS. I'M LOSING IT.
IF YOU ARE THE GHOST OF MY FATHER, WHY DO YOU LOOK SO YOUNG?
I DIDN'T CHOOSE TO DIE, I DIDN'T CHOOSE TO COME BACK, AND I DEFINITELY DIDN'T CHOOSE THE MOST AWKWARD PERIOD OF MY LIFE AS MY GHOST FORM.
BUT HERE WE ARE, HARPER.
HERE WE ARE.
YOU'RE NOT "LOSING IT", HARPER. SOME THINGS ARE UNEXPLAINABLE.
THE EXPLANATION IS THAT MY BROKEN BRAIN MADE YOU.

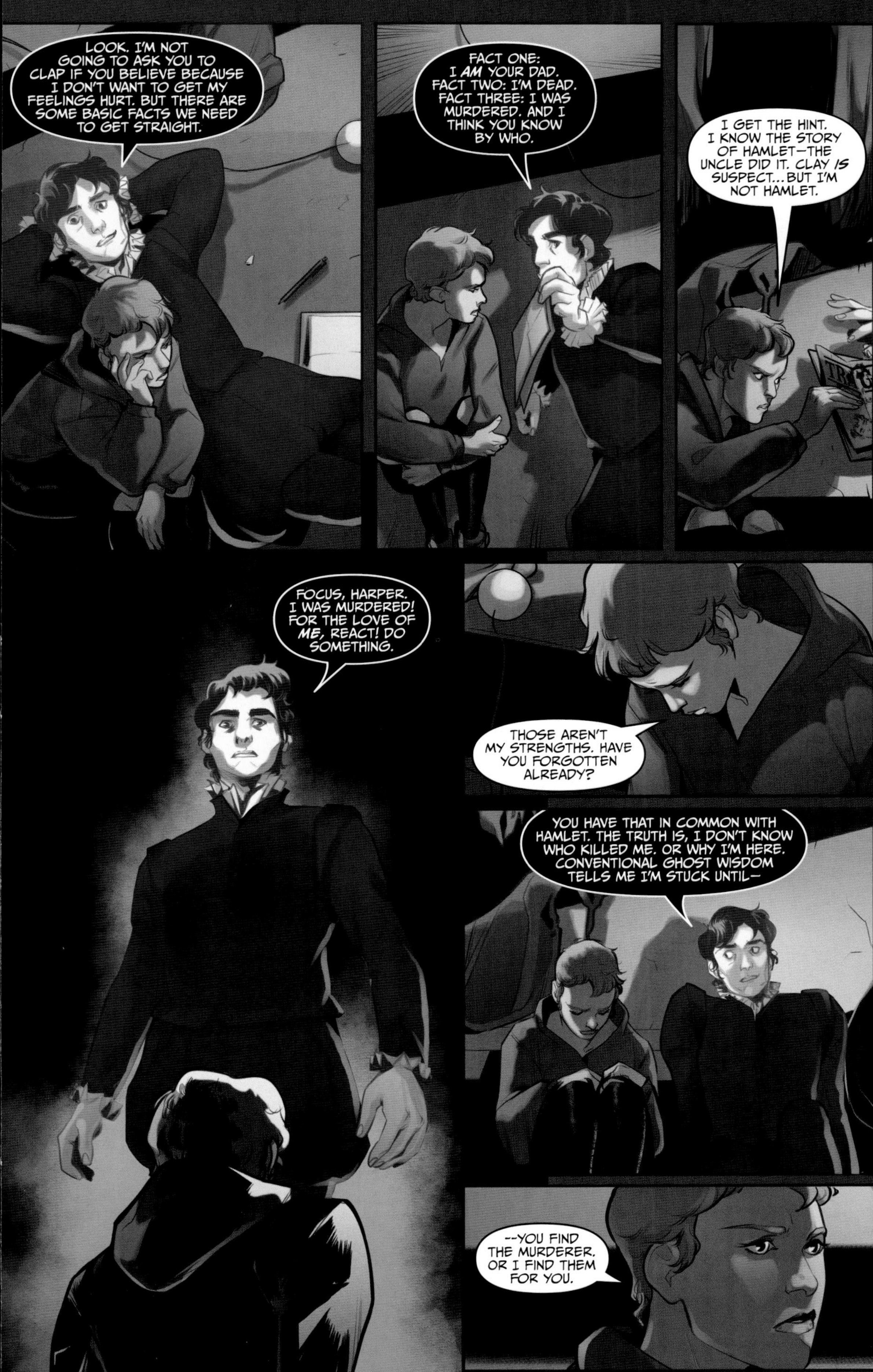

LOOK. I'M NOT GOING TO ASK YOU TO CLAP IF YOU BELIEVE BECAUSE I DON'T WANT TO GET MY FEELINGS HURT. BUT THERE ARE SOME BASIC FACTS WE NEED TO GET STRAIGHT.
FACT ONE: I *AM* YOUR DAD. FACT TWO: I'M DEAD. FACT THREE: I WAS MURDERED. AND I THINK YOU KNOW BY WHO.
I GET THE HINT. I KNOW THE STORY OF HAMLET—THE UNCLE DID IT. CLAY *IS* SUSPECT... BUT I'M NOT HAMLET.
FOCUS, HARPER. I WAS MURDERED! FOR THE LOVE OF *ME*, REACT! DO SOMETHING.
THOSE AREN'T MY STRENGTHS. HAVE YOU FORGOTTEN ALREADY?
YOU HAVE THAT IN COMMON WITH HAMLET. THE TRUTH IS, I DON'T KNOW WHO KILLED ME. OR WHY I'M HERE. CONVENTIONAL GHOST WISDOM TELLS ME I'M STUCK UNTIL—
--YOU FIND THE MURDERER. OR I FIND THEM FOR YOU.

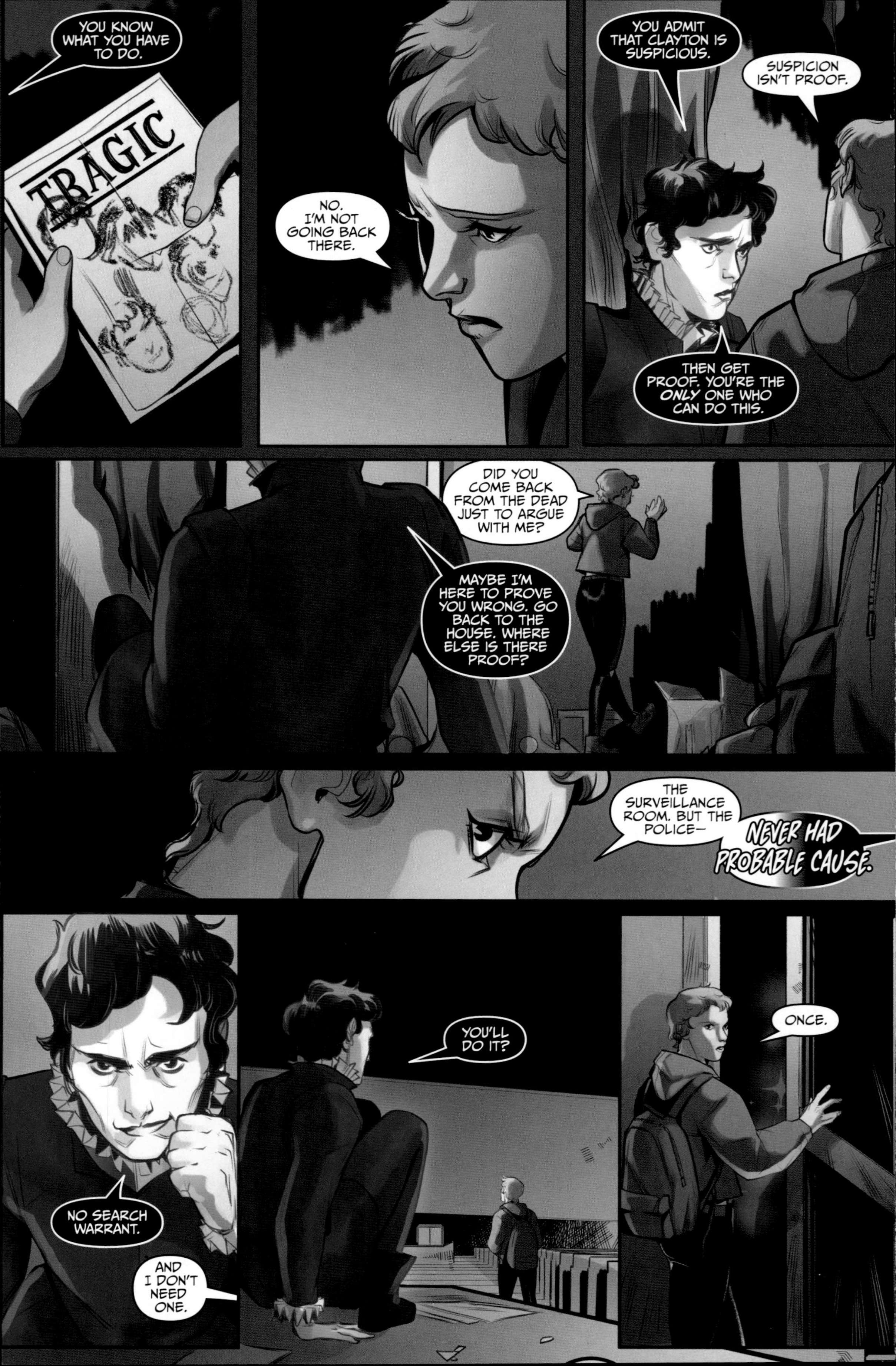
YOU KNOW WHAT YOU HAVE TO DO.
TRAGIC
NO. I'M NOT GOING BACK THERE.
YOU ADMIT THAT CLAYTON IS SUSPICIOUS.
SUSPICION ISN'T PROOF.
THEN GET PROOF. YOU'RE THE *ONLY* ONE WHO CAN DO THIS.
DID YOU COME BACK FROM THE DEAD JUST TO ARGUE WITH ME?
MAYBE I'M HERE TO PROVE YOU WRONG. GO BACK TO THE HOUSE. WHERE ELSE IS THERE PROOF?
THE SURVEILLANCE ROOM. BUT THE POLICE—
NEVER HAD PROBABLE CAUSE.
NO SEARCH WARRANT.
AND I DON'T NEED ONE.
YOU'LL DO IT?
ONCE.

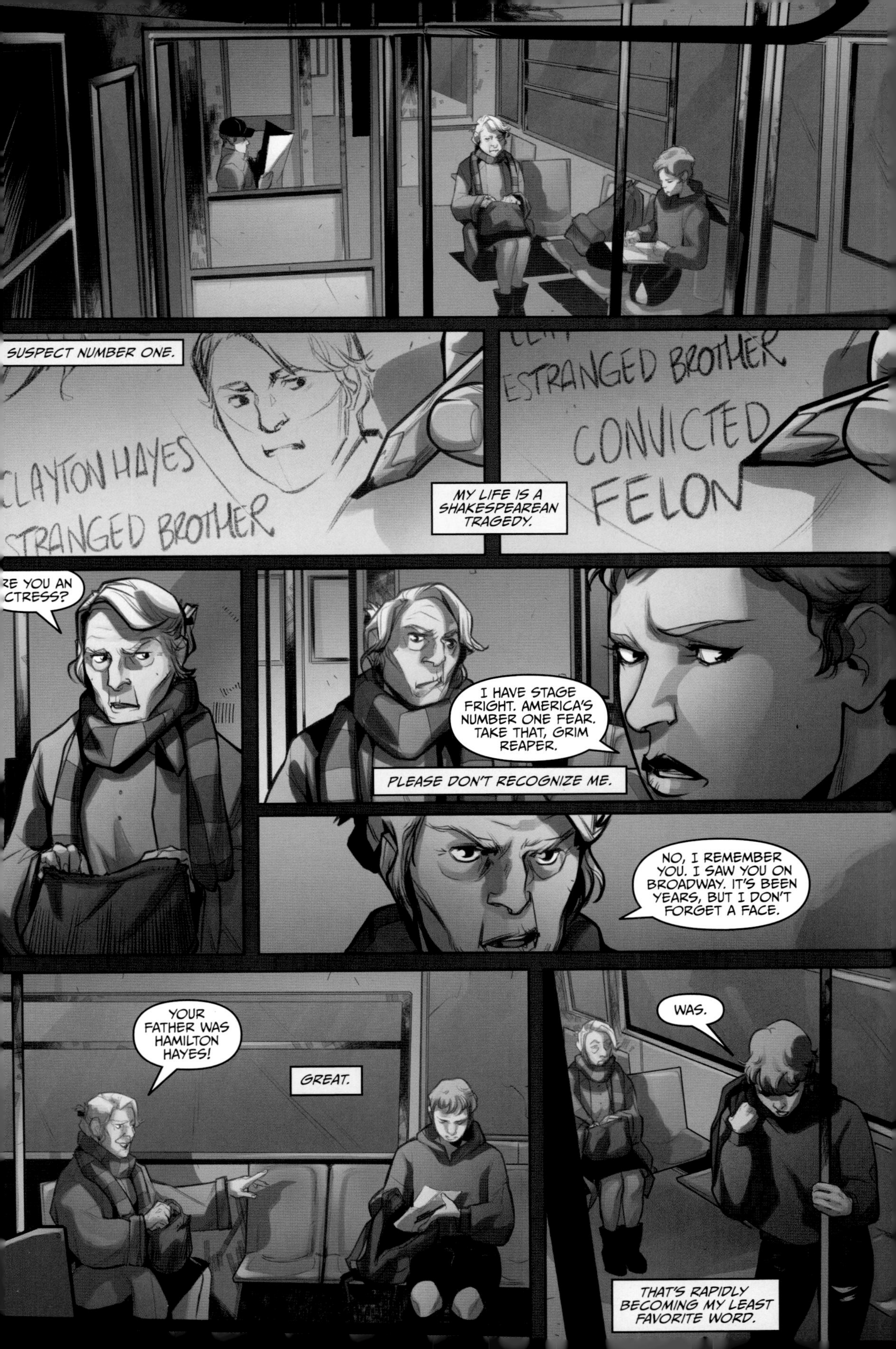
SUSPECT NUMBER ONE.
CLAYTON HAYES
STRANGED BROTHER
MY LIFE IS A SHAKESPEAREAN TRAGEDY.
ESTRANGED BROTHER
CONVICTED FELON
RE YOU AN CTRESS?
I HAVE STAGE FRIGHT. AMERICA'S NUMBER ONE FEAR. TAKE THAT, GRIM REAPER.
PLEASE DON'T RECOGNIZE ME.
NO, I REMEMBER YOU. I SAW YOU ON BROADWAY. IT'S BEEN YEARS, BUT I DON'T FORGET A FACE.
YOUR FATHER WAS HAMILTON HAYES!
GREAT.
WAS.
THAT'S RAPIDLY BECOMING MY LEAST FAVORITE WORD.

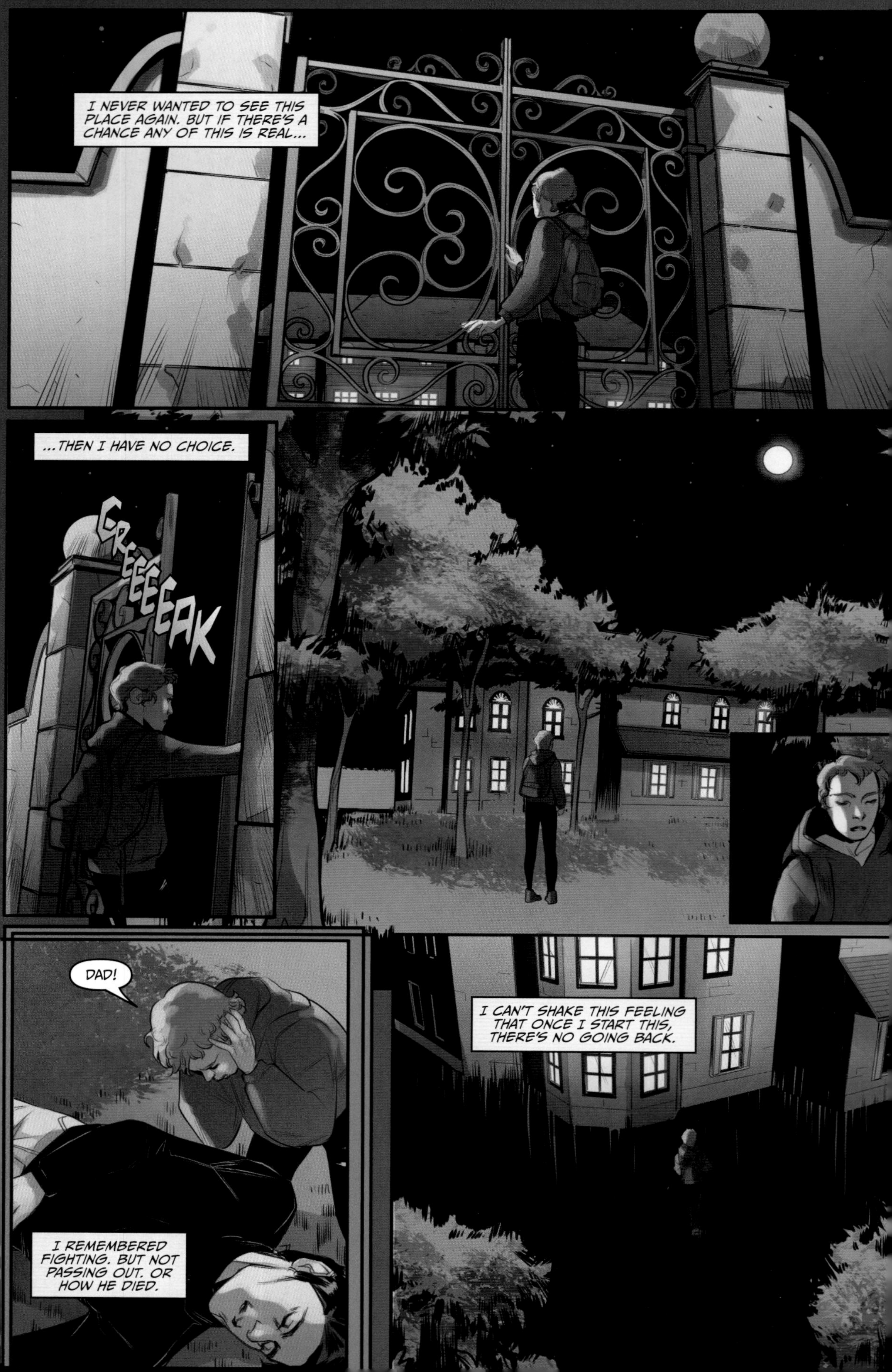
I NEVER WANTED TO SEE THIS PLACE AGAIN. BUT IF THERE'S A CHANCE ANY OF THIS IS REAL...
...THEN I HAVE NO CHOICE.
GREEEEEAK
DAD!
I REMEMBERED FIGHTING. BUT NOT PASSING OUT. OR HOW HE DIED.
I CAN'T SHAKE THIS FEELING THAT ONCE I START THIS, THERE'S NO GOING BACK.

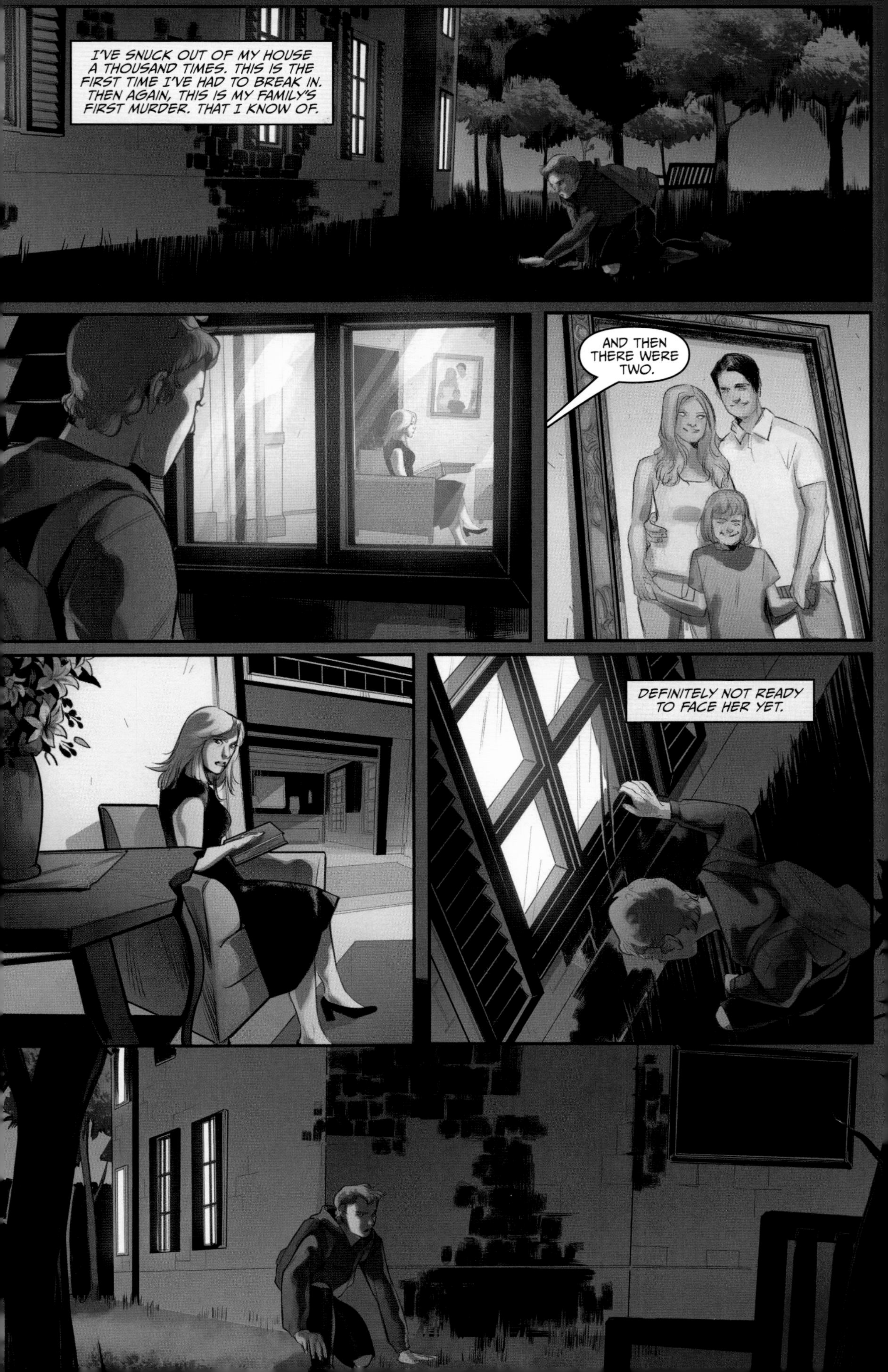
I'VE SNUCK OUT OF MY HOUSE A THOUSAND TIMES. THIS IS THE FIRST TIME I'VE HAD TO BREAK IN. THEN AGAIN, THIS IS MY FAMILY'S FIRST MURDER. THAT I KNOW OF.
AND THEN THERE WERE TWO.
DEFINITELY NOT READY TO FACE HER YET.

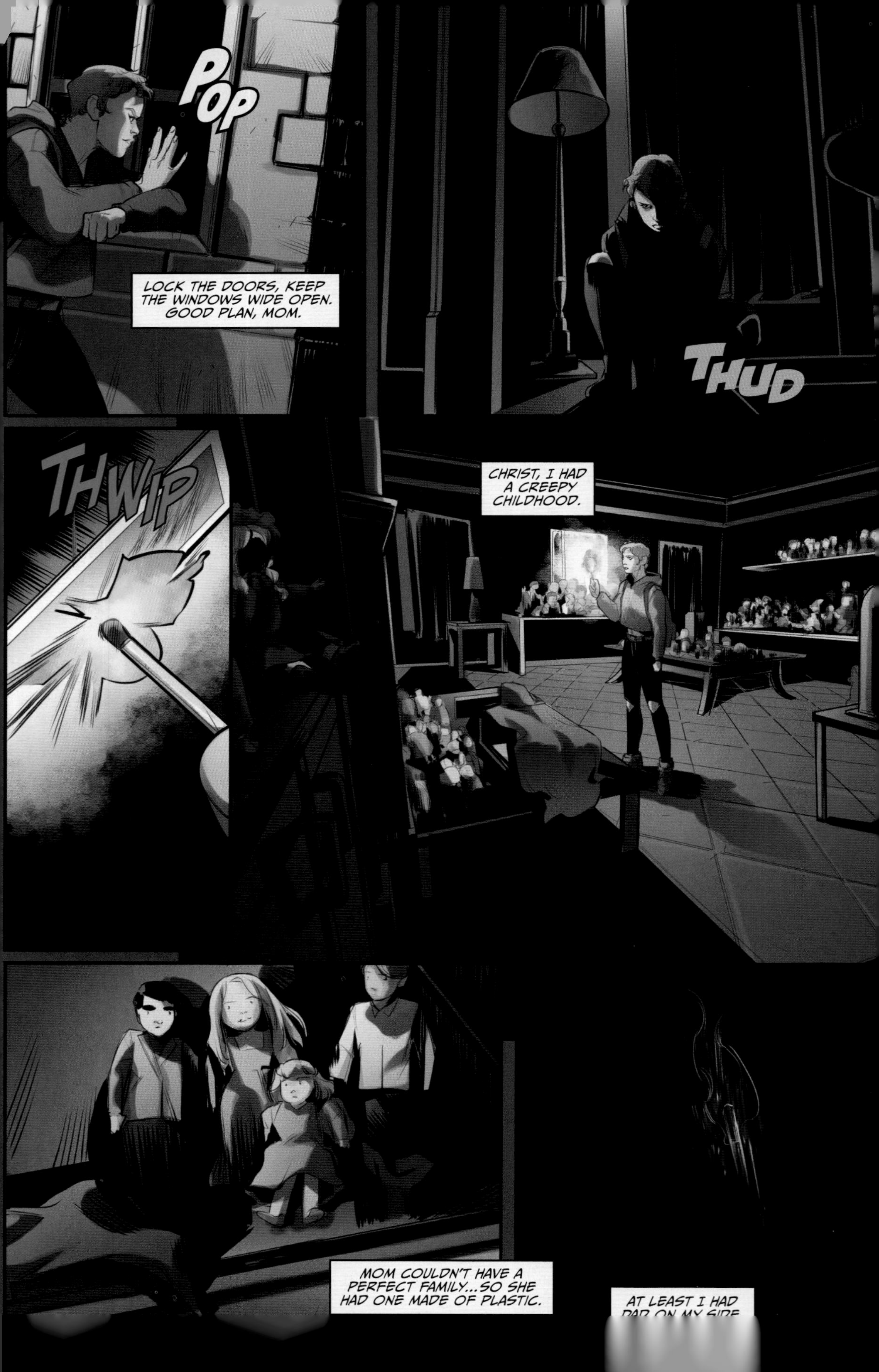
POP
LOCK THE DOORS, KEEP THE WINDOWS WIDE OPEN. GOOD PLAN, MOM.
THUD
THWIP
CHRIST, I HAD A CREEPY CHILDHOOD.
MOM COULDN'T HAVE A PERFECT FAMILY...SO SHE HAD ONE MADE OF PLASTIC.
AT LEAST I HAD

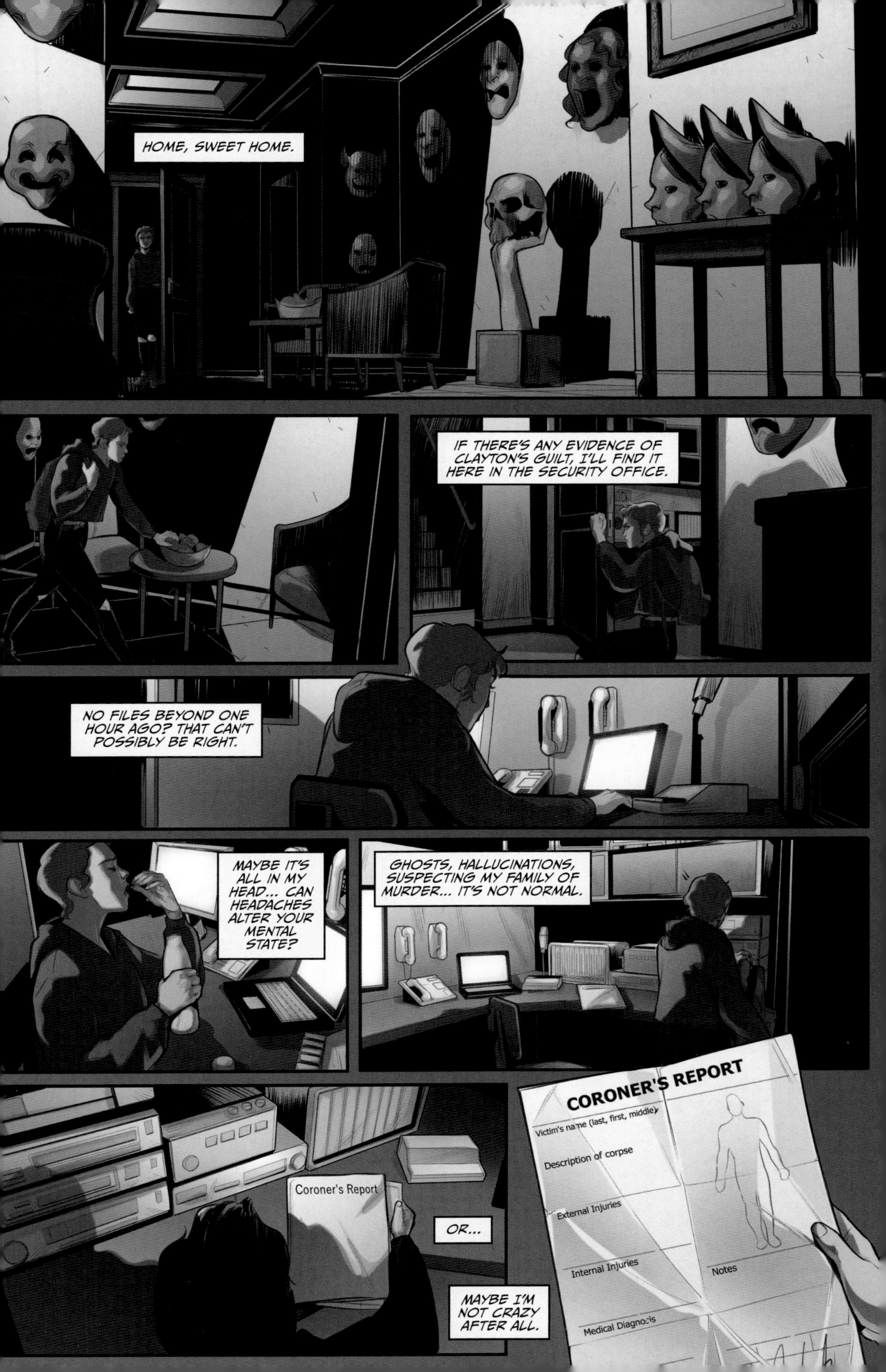
HOME, SWEET HOME.
IF THERE'S ANY EVIDENCE OF CLAYTON'S GUILT, I'LL FIND IT HERE IN THE SECURITY OFFICE.
NO FILES BEYOND ONE HOUR AGO? THAT CAN'T POSSIBLY BE RIGHT.
MAYBE IT'S ALL IN MY HEAD... CAN HEADACHES ALTER YOUR MENTAL STATE?
GHOSTS, HALLUCINATIONS, SUSPECTING MY FAMILY OF MURDER... IT'S NOT NORMAL.
Coroner's Report
OR...
MAYBE I'M NOT CRAZY AFTER ALL.
CORONER'S REPORT
Victim's name (last, first, middle)
Description of corpse
External Injuries
Internal Injuries
Notes
Medical Diagnosis

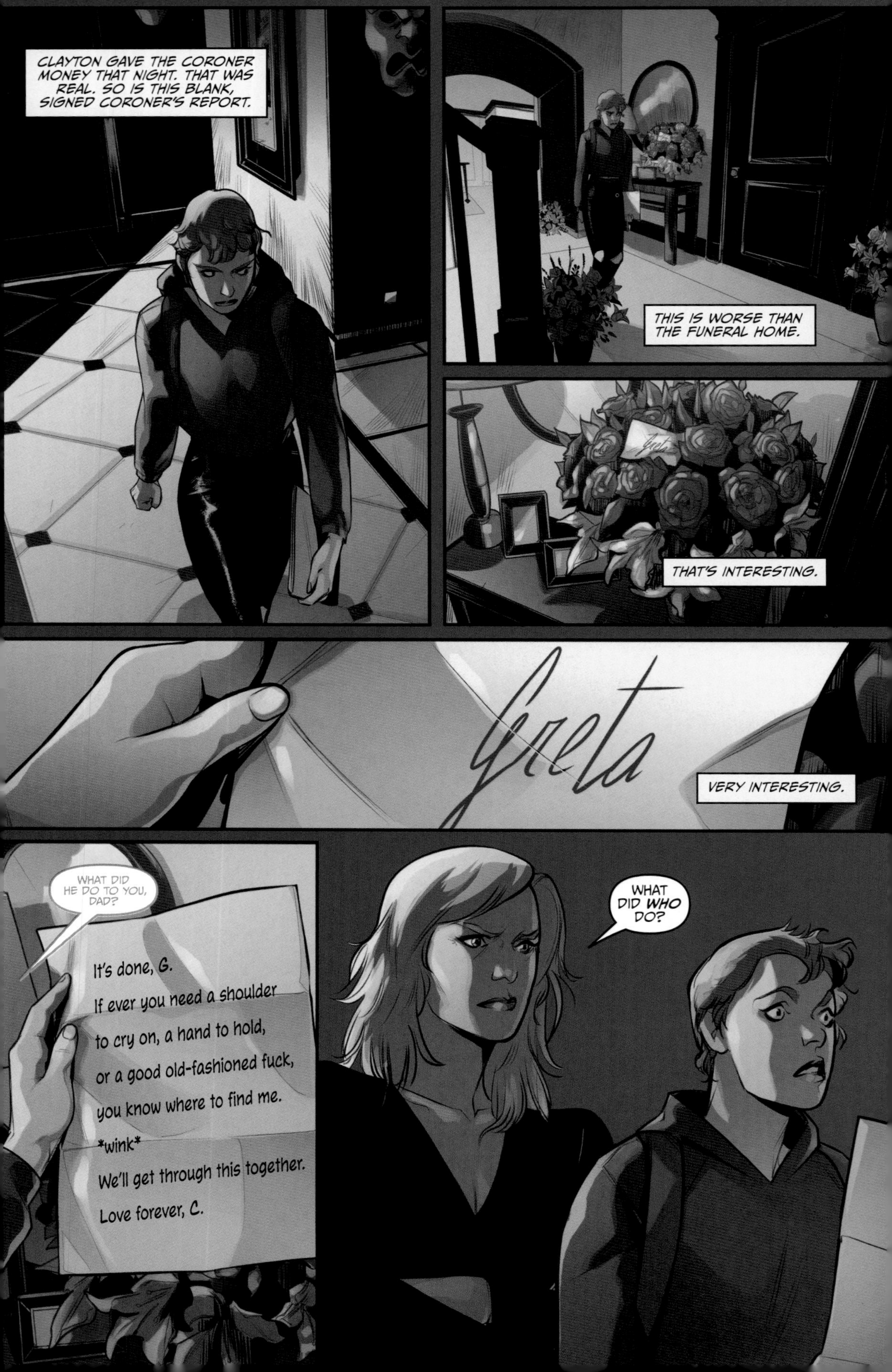
CLAYTON GAVE THE CORONER MONEY THAT NIGHT. THAT WAS REAL. SO IS THIS BLANK, SIGNED CORONER'S REPORT.
THIS IS WORSE THAN THE FUNERAL HOME.
THAT'S INTERESTING.
Greta
VERY INTERESTING.
WHAT DID HE DO TO YOU, DAD?
It's done, G.
If ever you need a shoulder
to cry on, a hand to hold,
or a good old-fashioned fuck,
you know where to find me.
wink
We'll get through this together.
Love forever, C.
WHAT DID WHO DO?

Chapter Two
ROTTEN

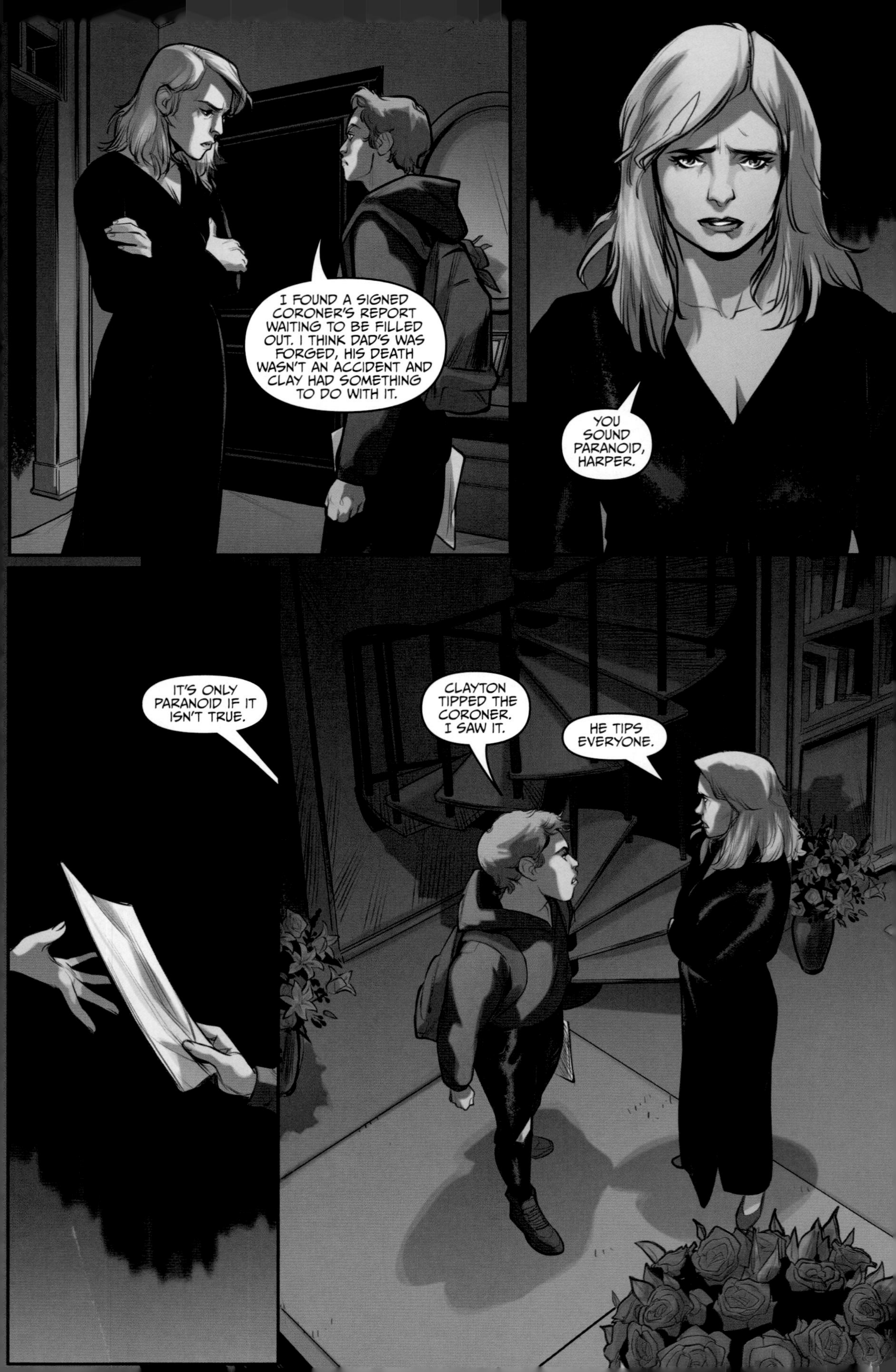
I FOUND A SIGNED CORONER'S REPORT WAITING TO BE FILLED OUT. I THINK DAD'S WAS FORGED, HIS DEATH WASN'T AN ACCIDENT AND CLAY HAD SOMETHING TO DO WITH IT.
YOU SOUND PARANOID, HARPER.
IT'S ONLY PARANOID IF IT ISN'T TRUE.
CLAYTON TIPPED THE CORONER. I SAW IT.
HE TIPS EVERYONE.

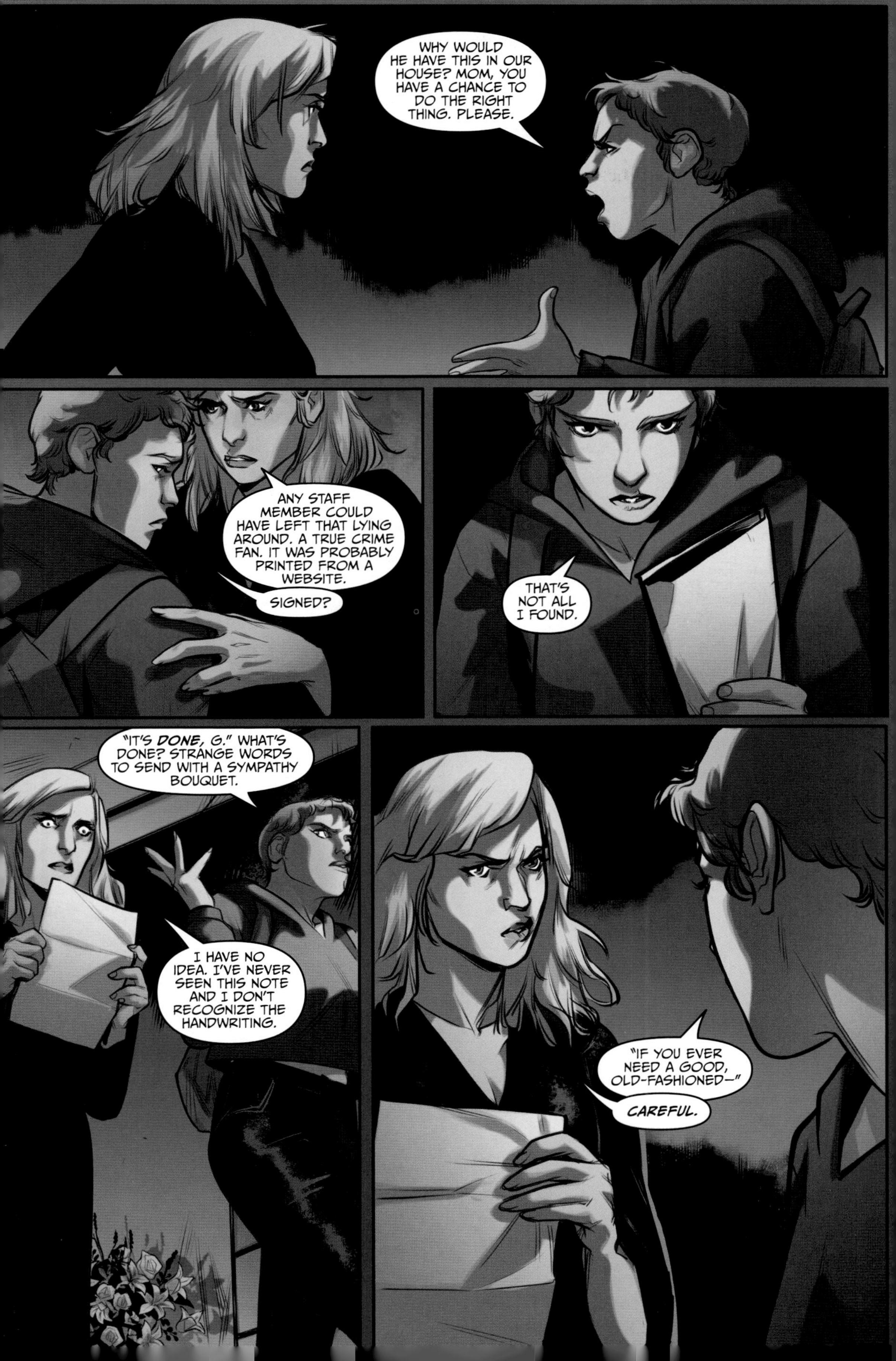
WHY WOULD HE HAVE THIS IN OUR HOUSE? MOM, YOU HAVE A CHANCE TO DO THE RIGHT THING. PLEASE.
ANY STAFF MEMBER COULD HAVE LEFT THAT LYING AROUND. A TRUE CRIME FAN. IT WAS PROBABLY PRINTED FROM A WEBSITE.
SIGNED?
THAT'S NOT ALL I FOUND.
"IT'S *DONE*, G." WHAT'S DONE? STRANGE WORDS TO SEND WITH A SYMPATHY BOUQUET.
I HAVE NO IDEA. I'VE NEVER SEEN THIS NOTE AND I DON'T RECOGNIZE THE HANDWRITING.
"IF YOU EVER NEED A GOOD, OLD-FASHIONED—"
CAREFUL.

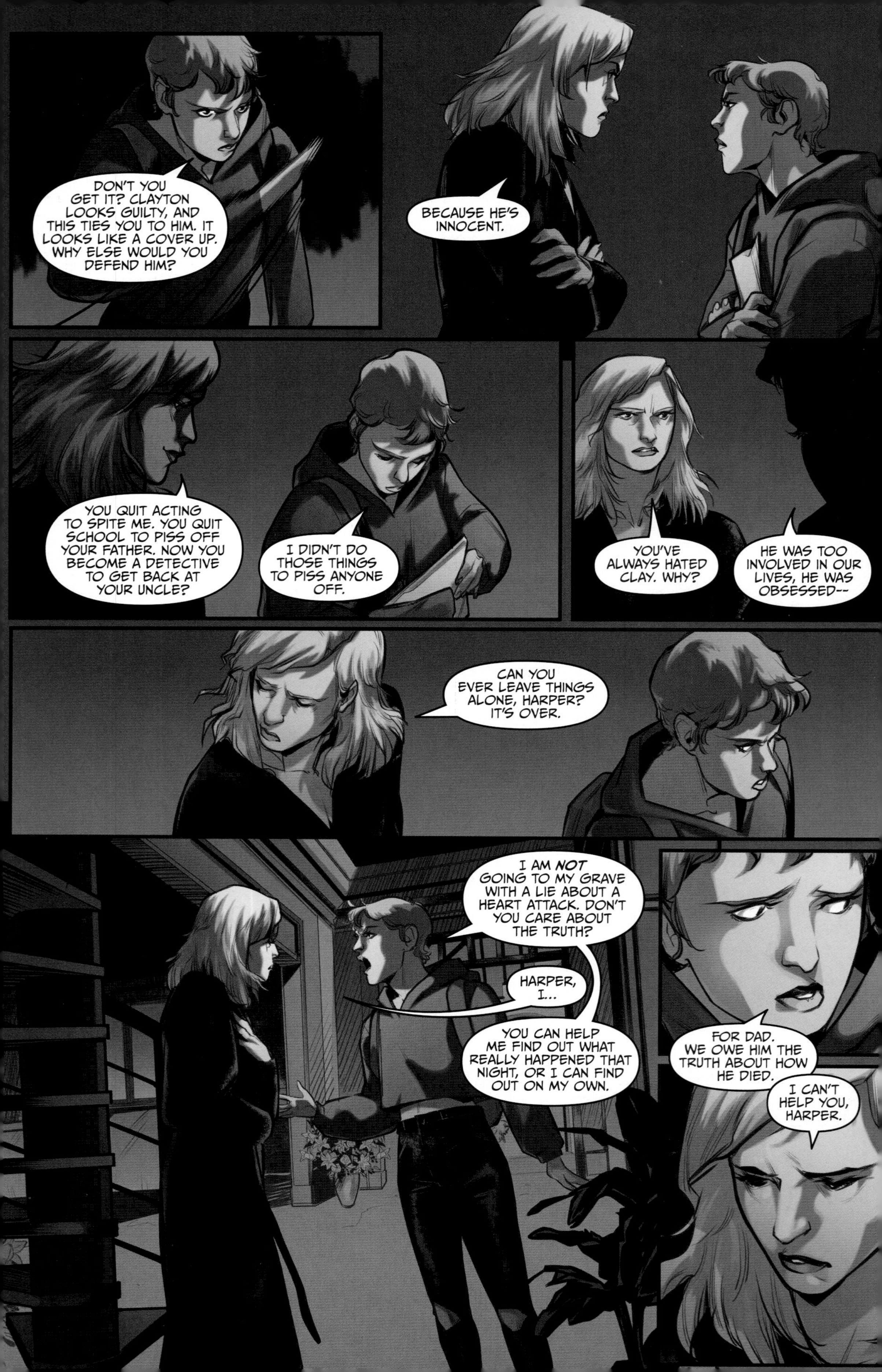
DON'T YOU GET IT? CLAYTON LOOKS GUILTY, AND THIS TIES YOU TO HIM. IT LOOKS LIKE A COVER UP. WHY ELSE WOULD YOU DEFEND HIM?
BECAUSE HE'S INNOCENT.
YOU QUIT ACTING TO SPITE ME. YOU QUIT SCHOOL TO PISS OFF YOUR FATHER. NOW YOU BECOME A DETECTIVE TO GET BACK AT YOUR UNCLE?
I DIDN'T DO THOSE THINGS TO PISS ANYONE OFF.
YOU'VE ALWAYS HATED CLAY. WHY?
HE WAS TOO INVOLVED IN OUR LIVES, HE WAS OBSESSED--
CAN YOU EVER LEAVE THINGS ALONE, HARPER? IT'S OVER.
I AM ***NOT*** GOING TO MY GRAVE WITH A LIE ABOUT A HEART ATTACK. DON'T YOU CARE ABOUT THE TRUTH?
HARPER, I...
YOU CAN HELP ME FIND OUT WHAT REALLY HAPPENED THAT NIGHT, OR I CAN FIND OUT ON MY OWN.
FOR DAD. WE OWE HIM THE TRUTH ABOUT HOW HE DIED.
I CAN'T HELP YOU, HARPER.

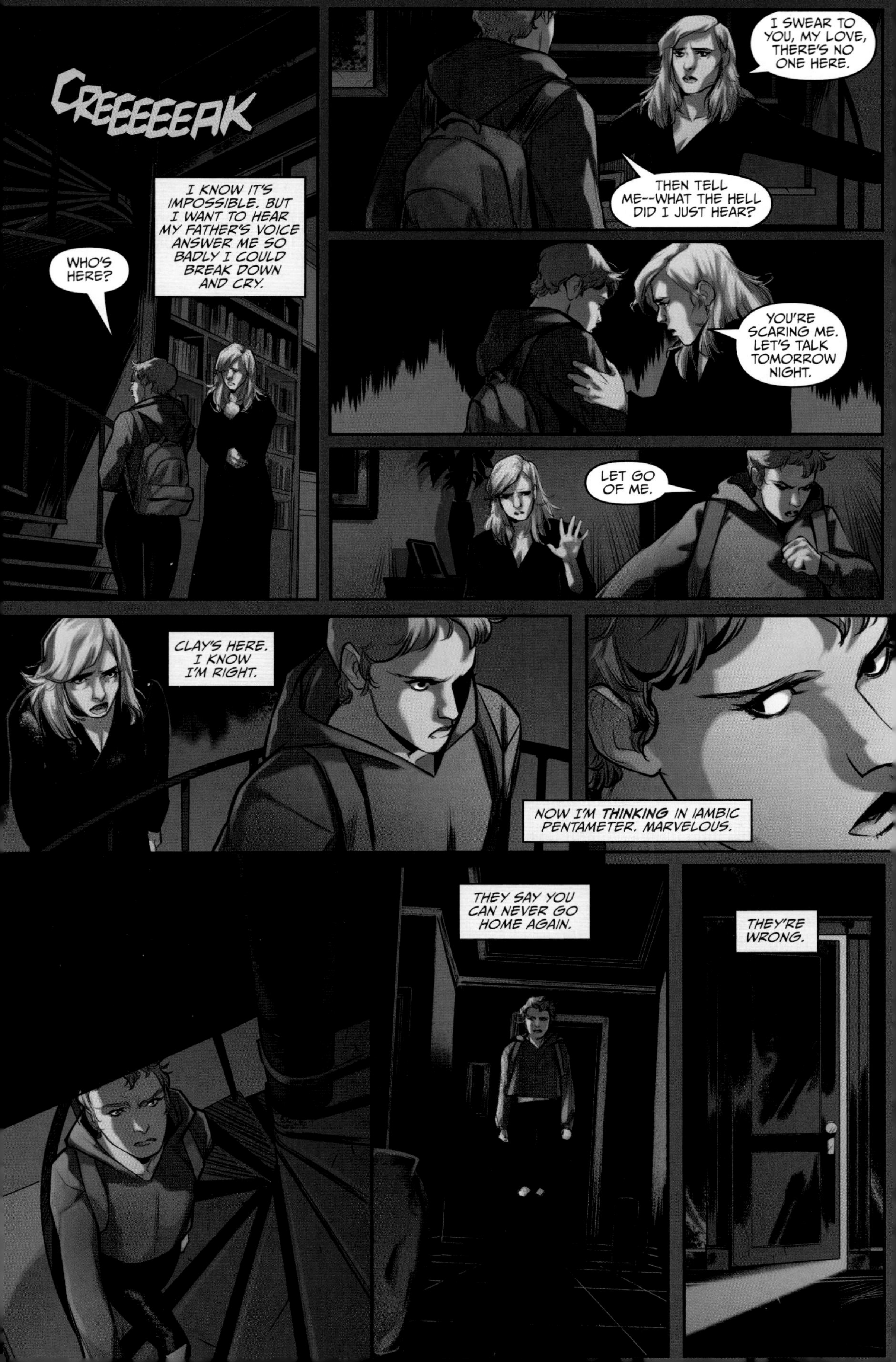
CREEEEEEAK
I KNOW IT'S IMPOSSIBLE. BUT I WANT TO HEAR MY FATHER'S VOICE ANSWER ME SO BADLY I COULD BREAK DOWN AND CRY.
WHO'S HERE?
I SWEAR TO YOU, MY LOVE, THERE'S NO ONE HERE.
THEN TELL ME--WHAT THE HELL DID I JUST HEAR?
YOU'RE SCARING ME. LET'S TALK TOMORROW NIGHT.
LET GO OF ME.
CLAY'S HERE. I KNOW I'M RIGHT.
NOW I'M THINKING IN IAMBIC PENTAMETER. MARVELOUS.
THEY SAY YOU CAN NEVER GO HOME AGAIN.
THEY'RE WRONG.

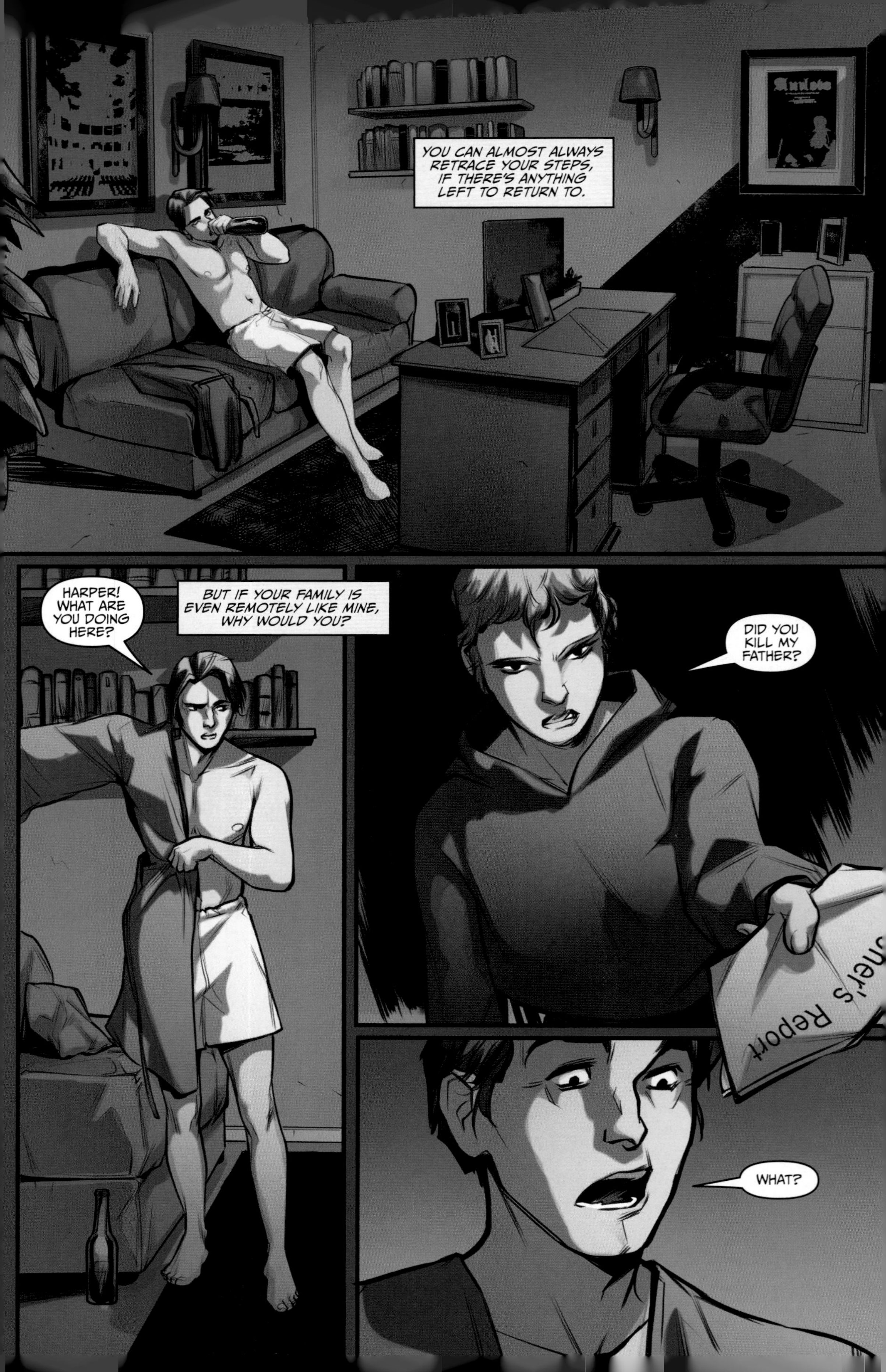
YOU CAN ALMOST ALWAYS RETRACE YOUR STEPS, IF THERE'S ANYTHING LEFT TO RETURN TO.
HARPER! WHAT ARE YOU DOING HERE?
BUT IF YOUR FAMILY IS EVEN REMOTELY LIKE MINE, WHY WOULD YOU?
DID YOU KILL MY FATHER?
ner's Report
WHAT?

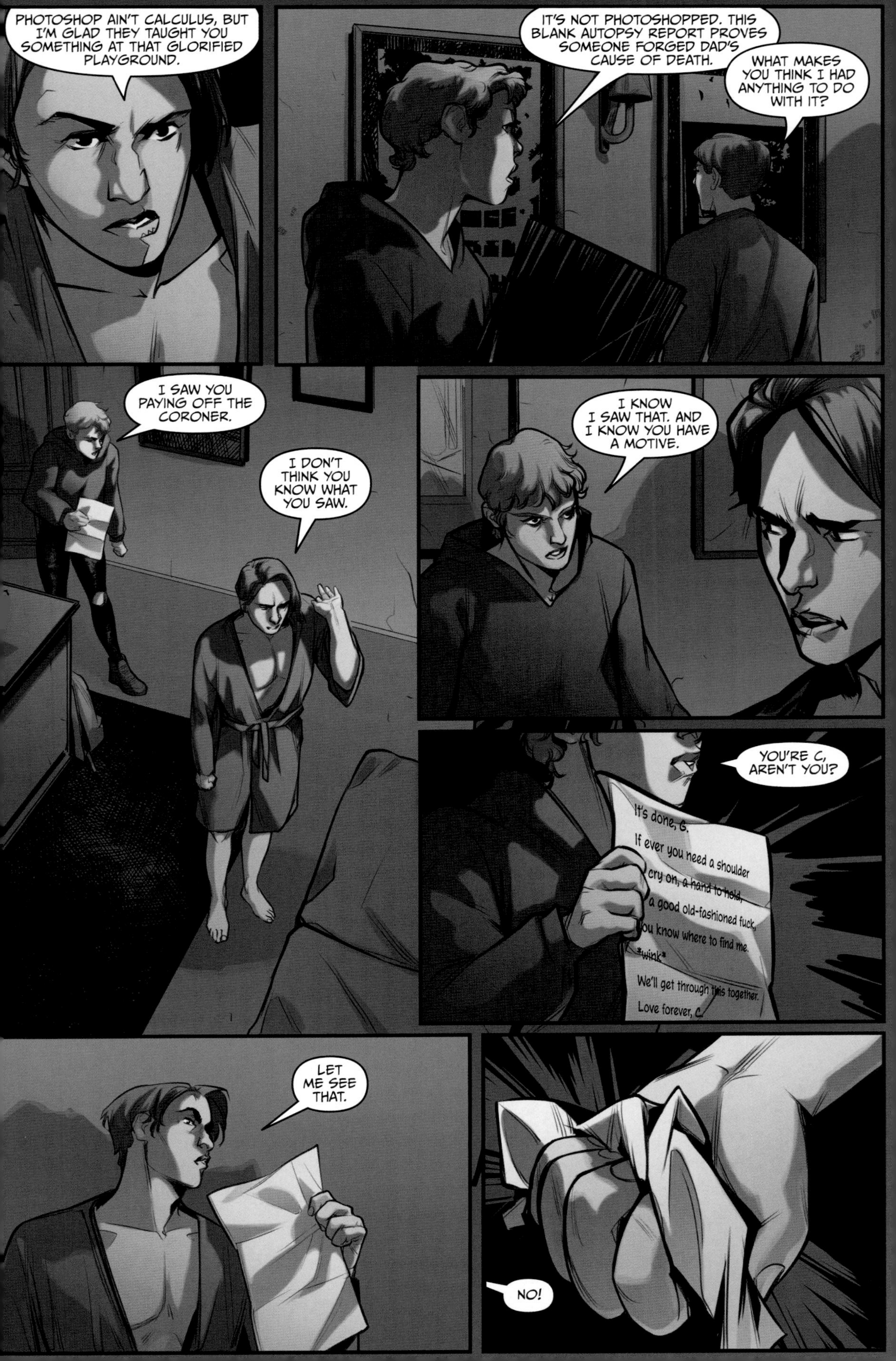
PHOTOSHOP AIN'T CALCULUS, BUT I'M GLAD THEY TAUGHT YOU SOMETHING AT THAT GLORIFIED PLAYGROUND.
IT'S NOT PHOTOSHOPPED. THIS BLANK AUTOPSY REPORT PROVES SOMEONE FORGED DAD'S CAUSE OF DEATH.
WHAT MAKES YOU THINK I HAD ANYTHING TO DO WITH IT?
I SAW YOU PAYING OFF THE CORONER.
I DON'T THINK YOU KNOW WHAT YOU SAW.
I KNOW I SAW THAT. AND I KNOW YOU HAVE A MOTIVE.
YOU'RE C, AREN'T YOU?
It's done, G.
If ever you need a shoulder
cry on, a hand to hold,
a good old-fashioned fuck,
ou know where to find me.
wink
We'll get through this together.
Love forever, C.
LET ME SEE THAT.
NO!

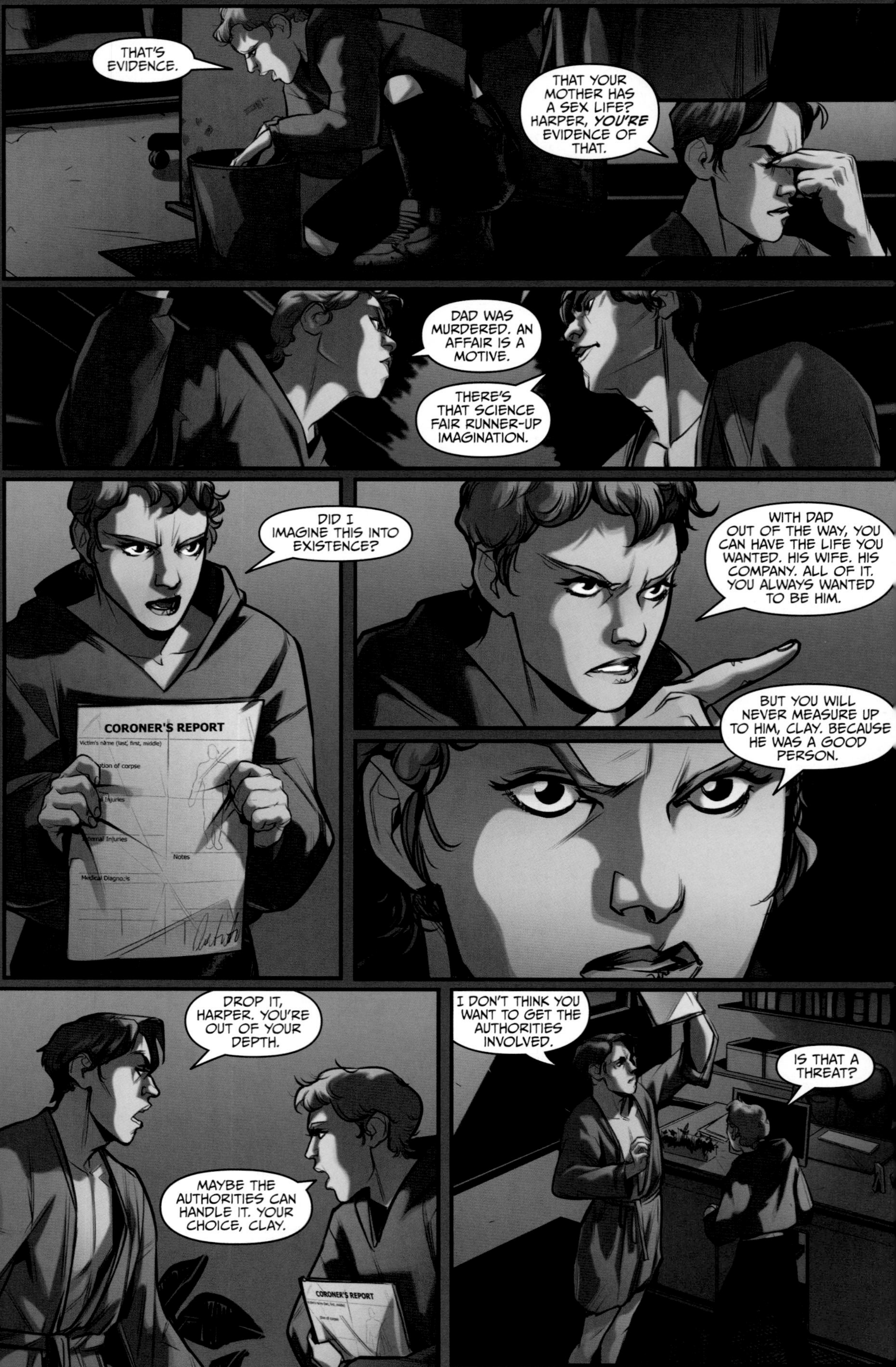
THAT'S EVIDENCE.
THAT YOUR MOTHER HAS A SEX LIFE? HARPER, YOU'RE EVIDENCE OF THAT.
DAD WAS MURDERED. AN AFFAIR IS A MOTIVE.
THERE'S THAT SCIENCE FAIR RUNNER-UP IMAGINATION.
DID I IMAGINE THIS INTO EXISTENCE?
CORONER'S REPORT
WITH DAD OUT OF THE WAY, YOU CAN HAVE THE LIFE YOU WANTED. HIS WIFE. HIS COMPANY. ALL OF IT. YOU ALWAYS WANTED TO BE HIM.
BUT YOU WILL NEVER MEASURE UP TO HIM, CLAY. BECAUSE HE WAS A GOOD PERSON.
DROP IT, HARPER. YOU'RE OUT OF YOUR DEPTH.
MAYBE THE AUTHORITIES CAN HANDLE IT. YOUR CHOICE, CLAY.
CORONER'S REPORT
I DON'T THINK YOU WANT TO GET THE AUTHORITIES INVOLVED.
IS THAT A THREAT?

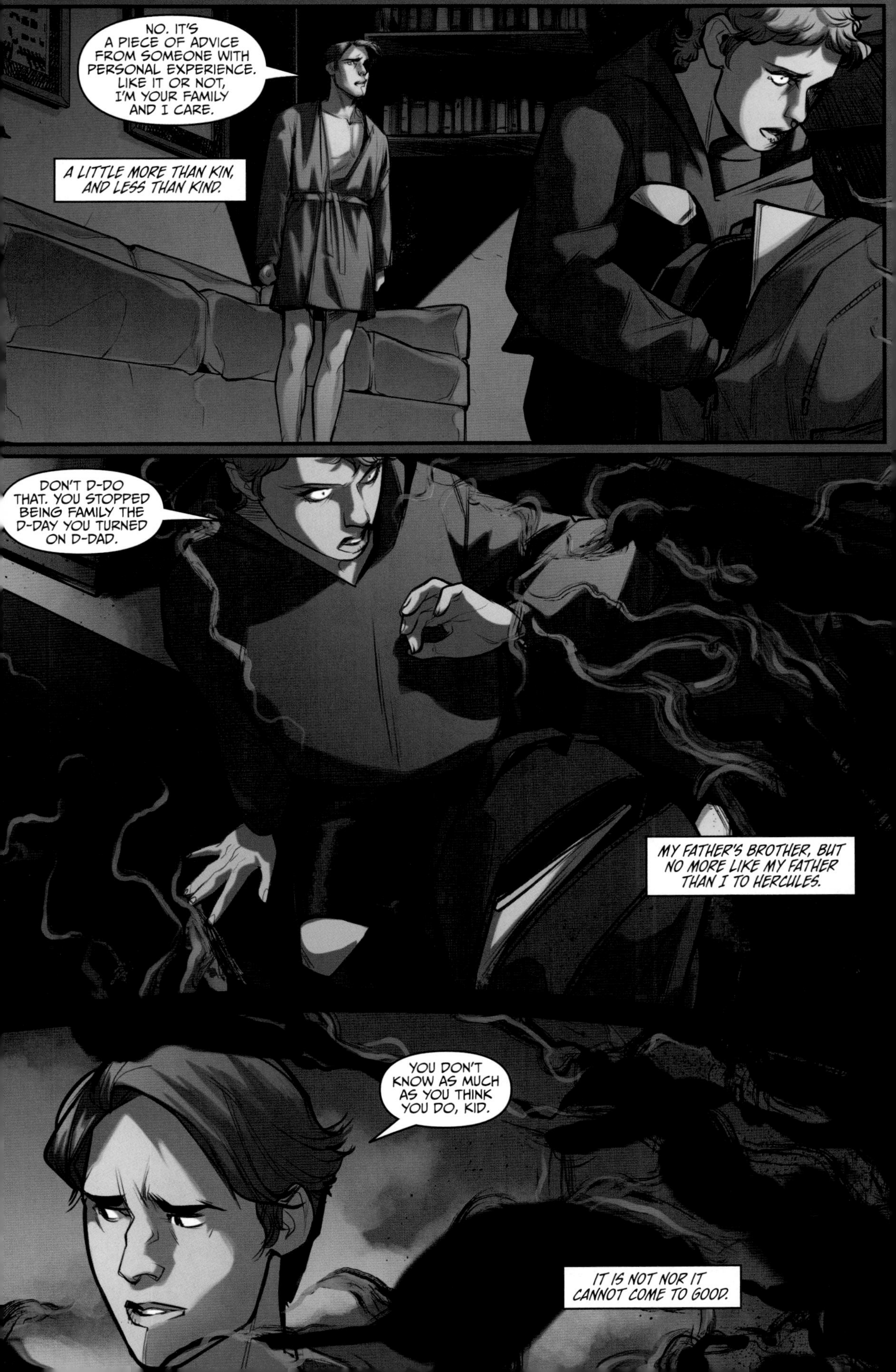
NO. IT'S A PIECE OF ADVICE FROM SOMEONE WITH PERSONAL EXPERIENCE. LIKE IT OR NOT, I'M YOUR FAMILY AND I CARE.
A LITTLE MORE THAN KIN, AND LESS THAN KIND.
DON'T D-DO THAT. YOU STOPPED BEING FAMILY THE D-DAY YOU TURNED ON D-DAD.
MY FATHER'S BROTHER, BUT NO MORE LIKE MY FATHER THAN I TO HERCULES.
YOU DON'T KNOW AS MUCH AS YOU THINK YOU DO, KID.
IT IS NOT NOR IT CANNOT COME TO GOOD.

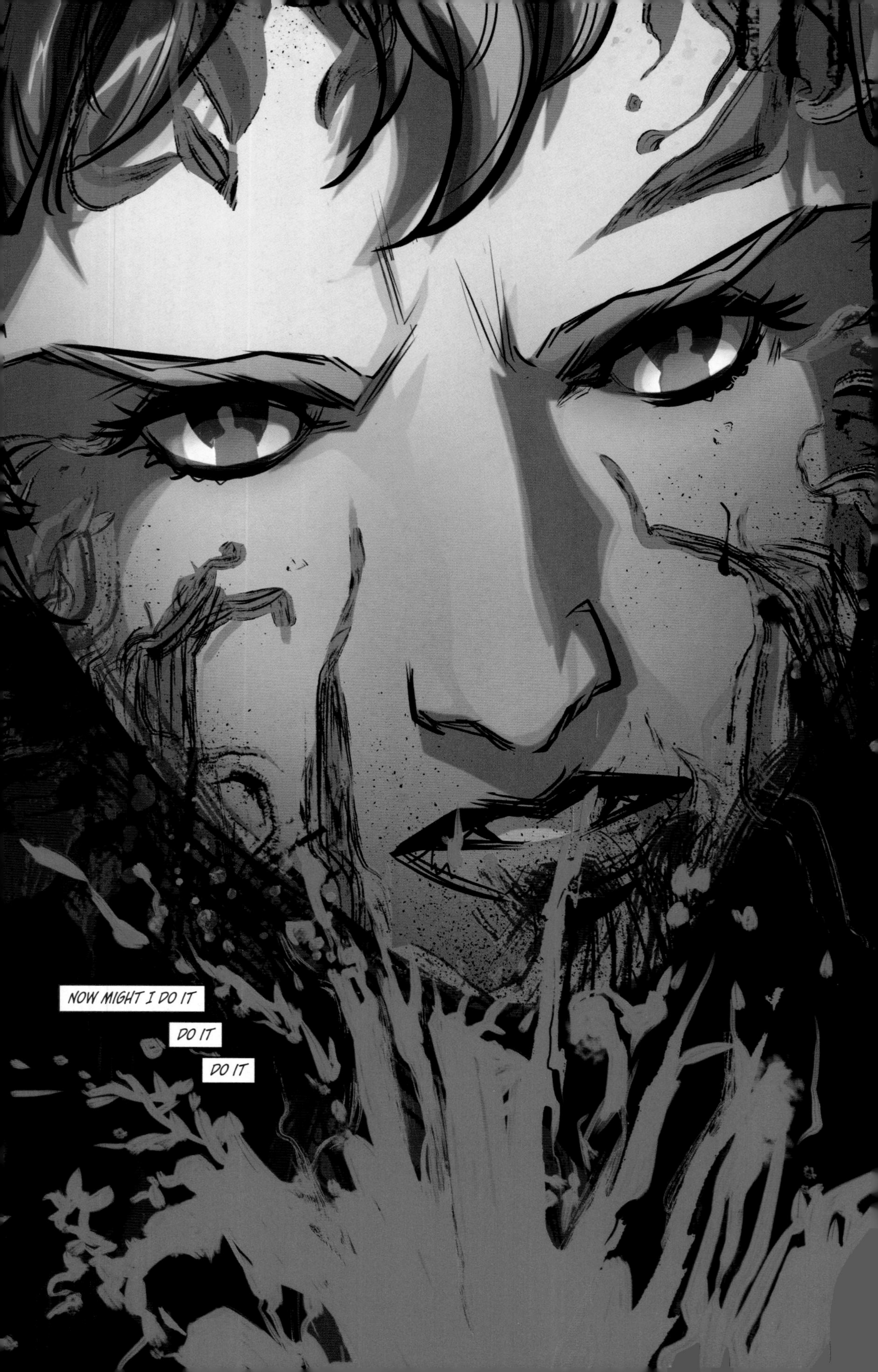
NOW MIGHT I DO IT
DO IT
DO IT

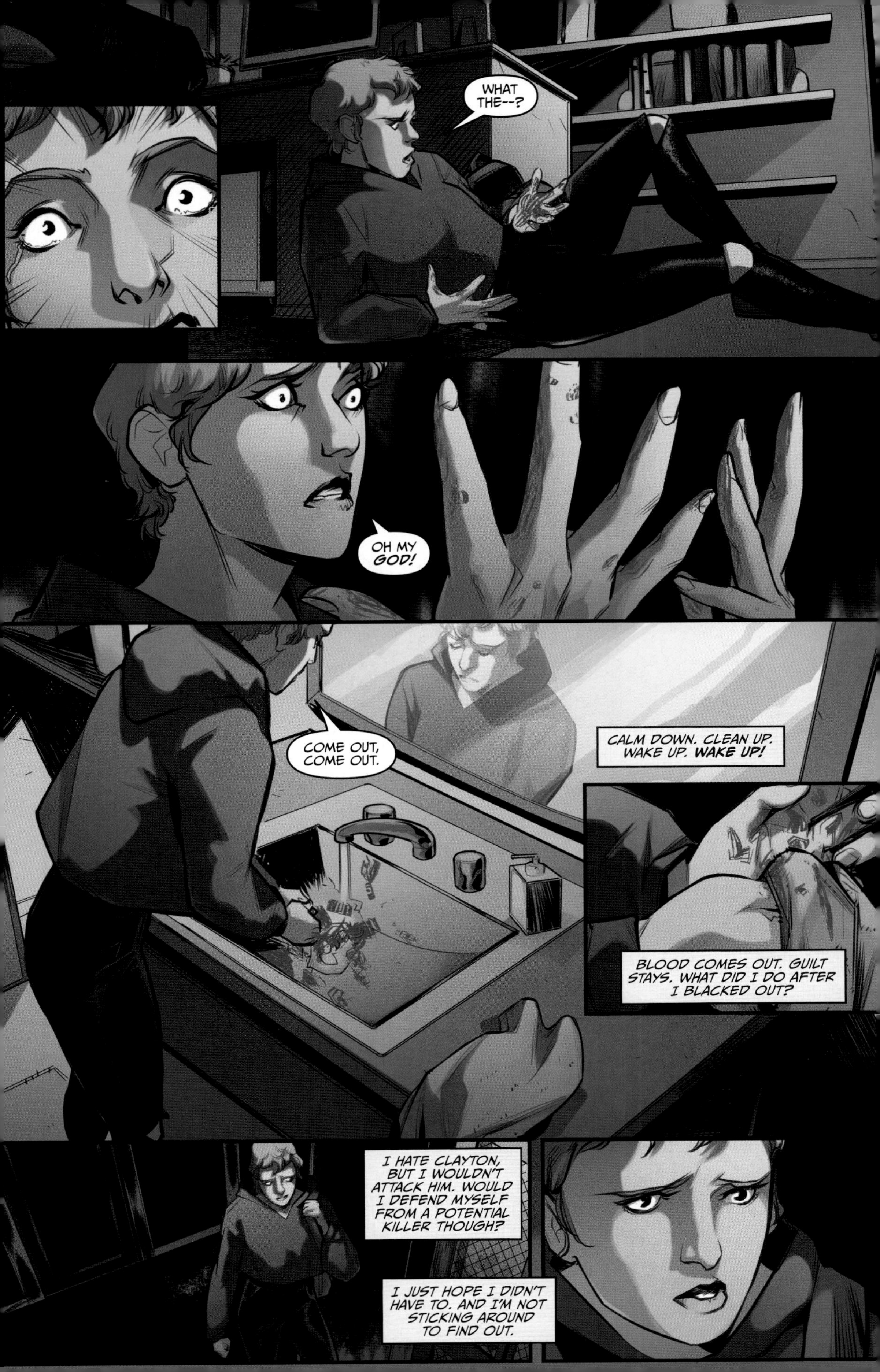
WHAT THE--?
OH MY GOD!
COME OUT, COME OUT.
CALM DOWN. CLEAN UP. WAKE UP. WAKE UP!
BLOOD COMES OUT. GUILT STAYS. WHAT DID I DO AFTER I BLACKED OUT?
I HATE CLAYTON, BUT I WOULDN'T ATTACK HIM. WOULD I DEFEND MYSELF FROM A POTENTIAL KILLER THOUGH?
I JUST HOPE I DIDN'T HAVE TO. AND I'M NOT STICKING AROUND TO FIND OUT.

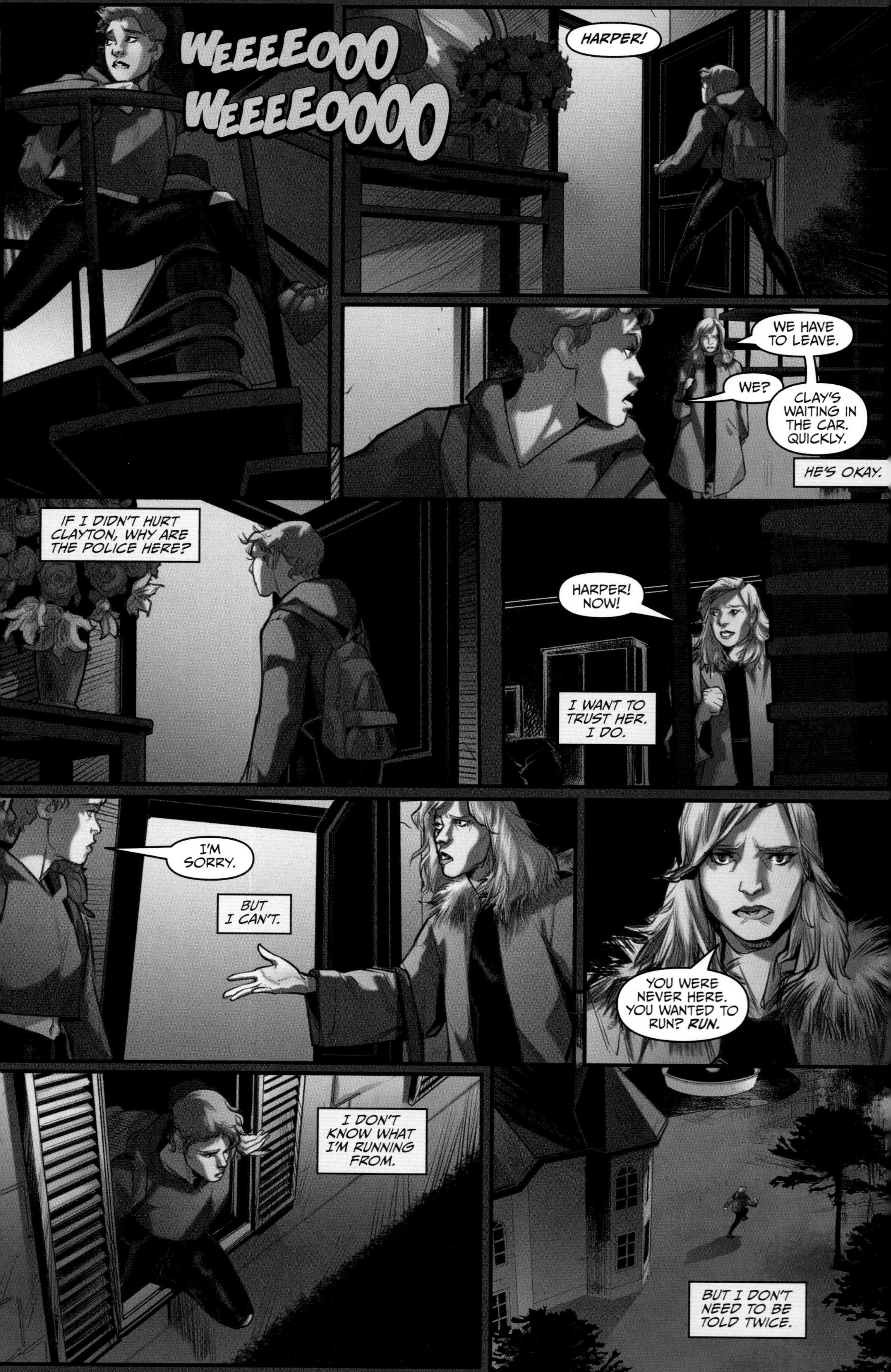
WEEEEOOO
WEEEEOOOO
HARPER!
WE HAVE TO LEAVE.
WE?
CLAY'S WAITING IN THE CAR. QUICKLY.
HE'S OKAY.
IF I DIDN'T HURT CLAYTON, WHY ARE THE POLICE HERE?
HARPER! NOW!
I WANT TO TRUST HER. I DO.
I'M SORRY.
BUT I CAN'T.
YOU WERE NEVER HERE. YOU WANTED TO RUN? RUN.
I DON'T KNOW WHAT I'M RUNNING FROM.
BUT I DON'T NEED TO BE TOLD TWICE.

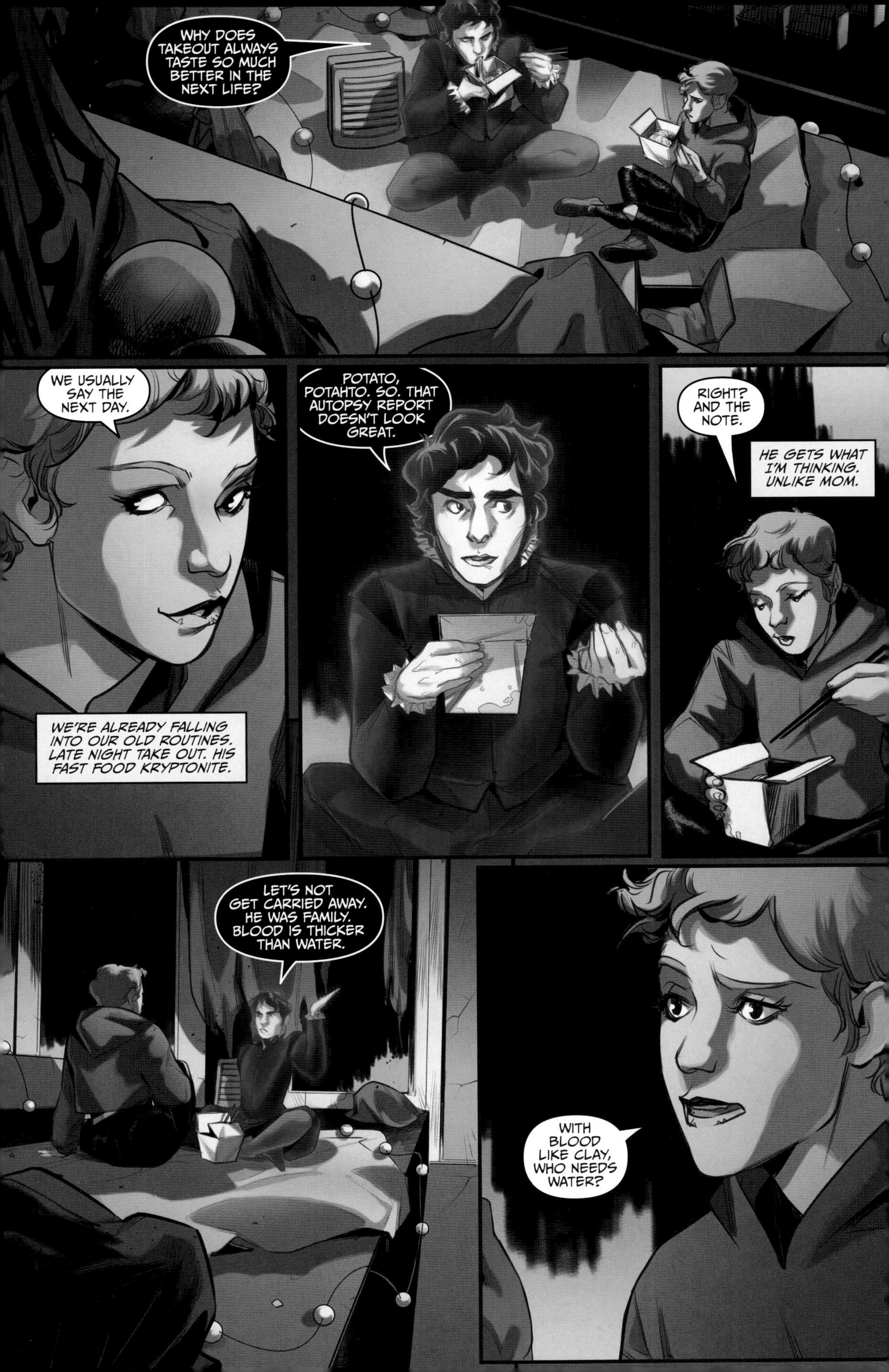
WHY DOES TAKEOUT ALWAYS TASTE SO MUCH BETTER IN THE NEXT LIFE?
WE USUALLY SAY THE NEXT DAY.
WE'RE ALREADY FALLING INTO OUR OLD ROUTINES. LATE NIGHT TAKE OUT. HIS FAST FOOD KRYPTONITE.
POTATO, POTAHTO. SO. THAT AUTOPSY REPORT DOESN'T LOOK GREAT.
RIGHT? AND THE NOTE.
HE GETS WHAT I'M THINKING. UNLIKE MOM.
LET'S NOT GET CARRIED AWAY. HE WAS FAMILY. BLOOD IS THICKER THAN WATER.
WITH BLOOD LIKE CLAY, WHO NEEDS WATER?

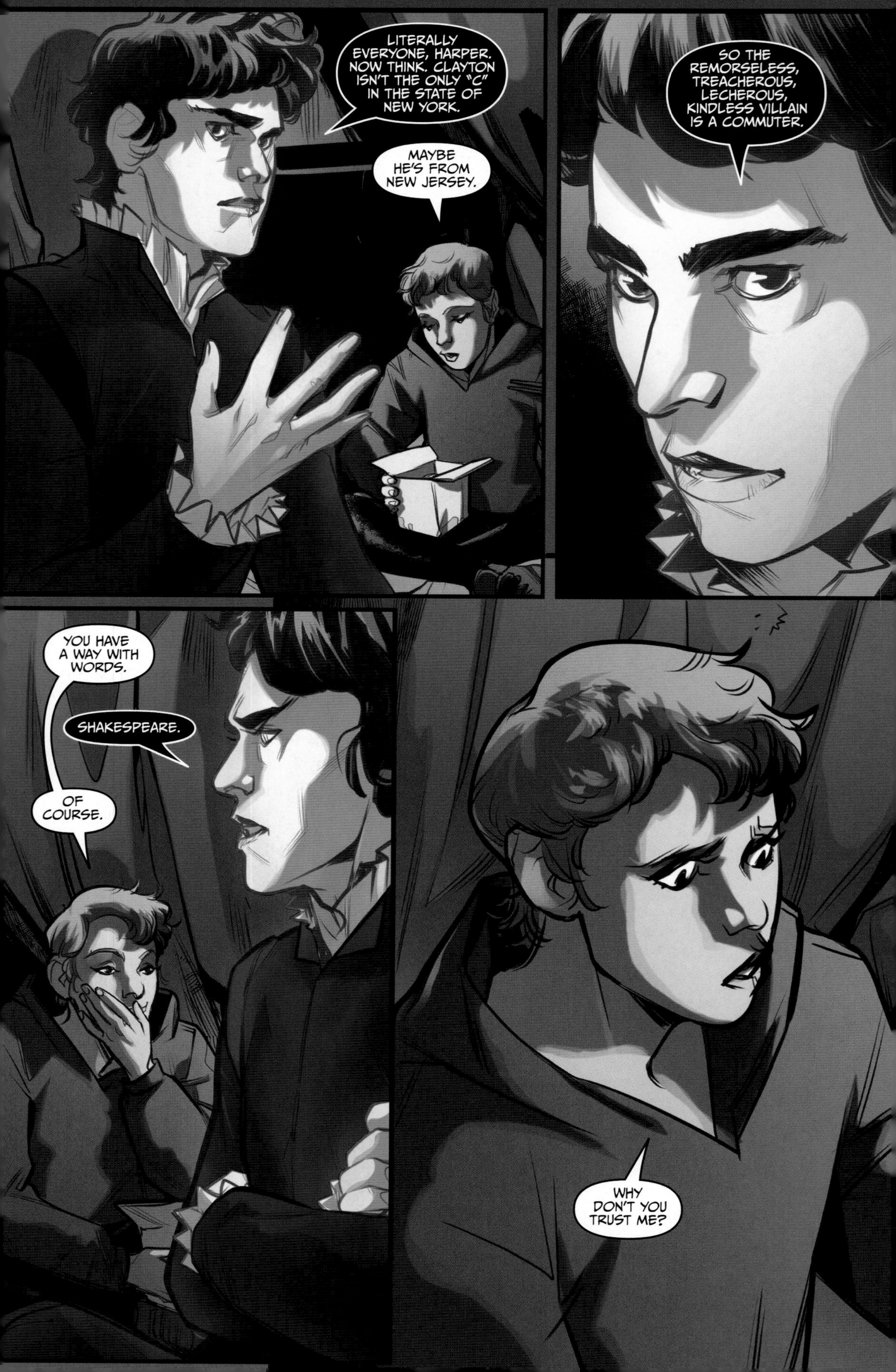
LITERALLY EVERYONE, HARPER. NOW THINK. CLAYTON ISN'T THE ONLY "C" IN THE STATE OF NEW YORK.
MAYBE HE'S FROM NEW JERSEY.
SO THE REMORSELESS, TREACHEROUS, LECHEROUS, KINDLESS VILLAIN IS A COMMUTER.
YOU HAVE A WAY WITH WORDS.
SHAKESPEARE.
OF COURSE.
WHY DON'T YOU TRUST ME?

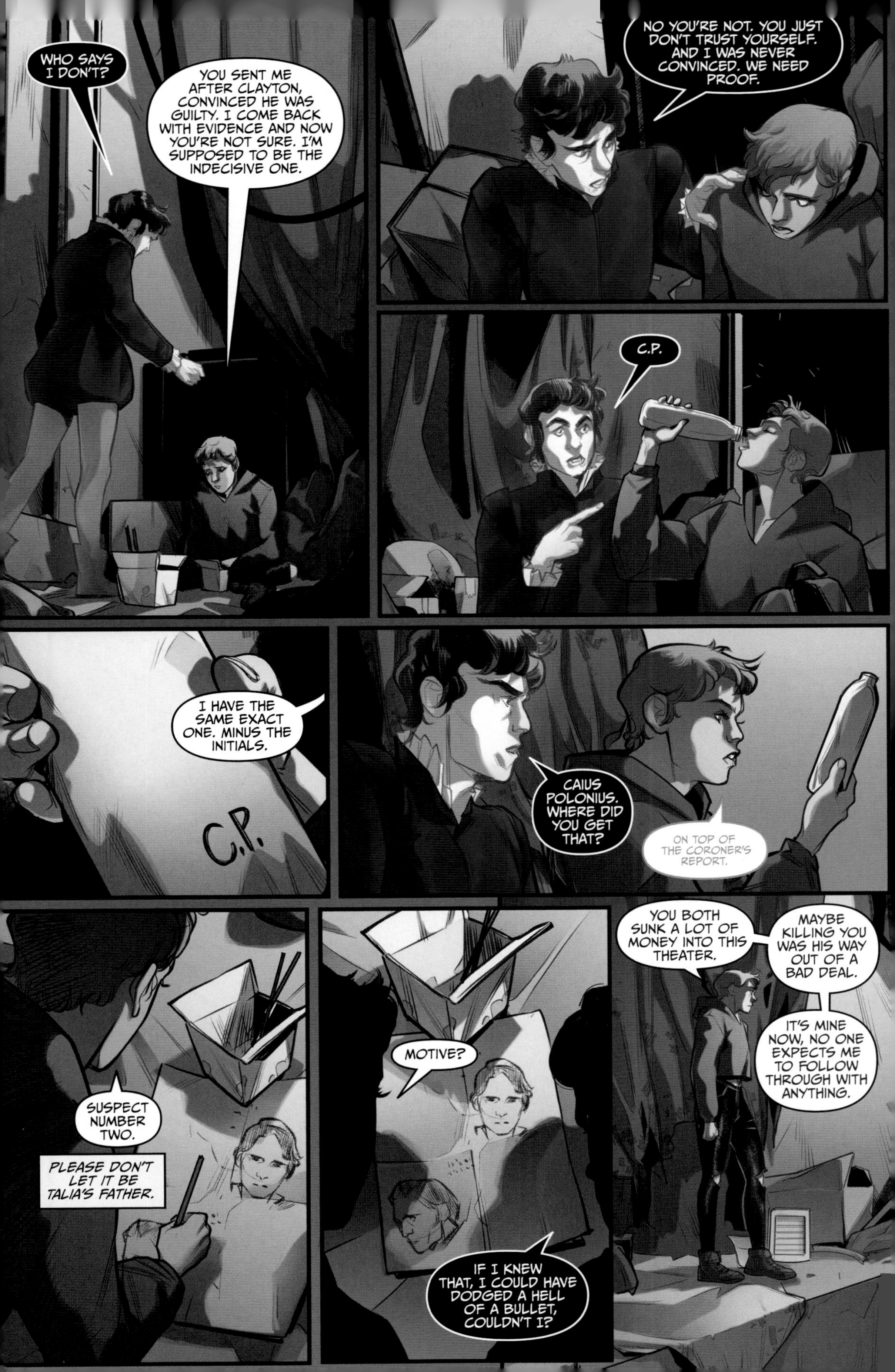
WHO SAYS I DON'T?
YOU SENT ME AFTER CLAYTON, CONVINCED HE WAS GUILTY. I COME BACK WITH EVIDENCE AND NOW YOU'RE NOT SURE. I'M SUPPOSED TO BE THE INDECISIVE ONE.
NO YOU'RE NOT. YOU JUST DON'T TRUST YOURSELF. AND I WAS NEVER CONVINCED. WE NEED PROOF.
C.P.
I HAVE THE SAME EXACT ONE. MINUS THE INITIALS.
C.P.
CAIUS POLONIUS. WHERE DID YOU GET THAT?
ON TOP OF THE CORONER'S REPORT.
SUSPECT NUMBER TWO.
PLEASE DON'T LET IT BE TALIA'S FATHER.
MOTIVE?
IF I KNEW THAT, I COULD HAVE DODGED A HELL OF A BULLET, COULDN'T I?
YOU BOTH SUNK A LOT OF MONEY INTO THIS THEATER.
MAYBE KILLING YOU WAS HIS WAY OUT OF A BAD DEAL.
IT'S MINE NOW, NO ONE EXPECTS ME TO FOLLOW THROUGH WITH ANYTHING.

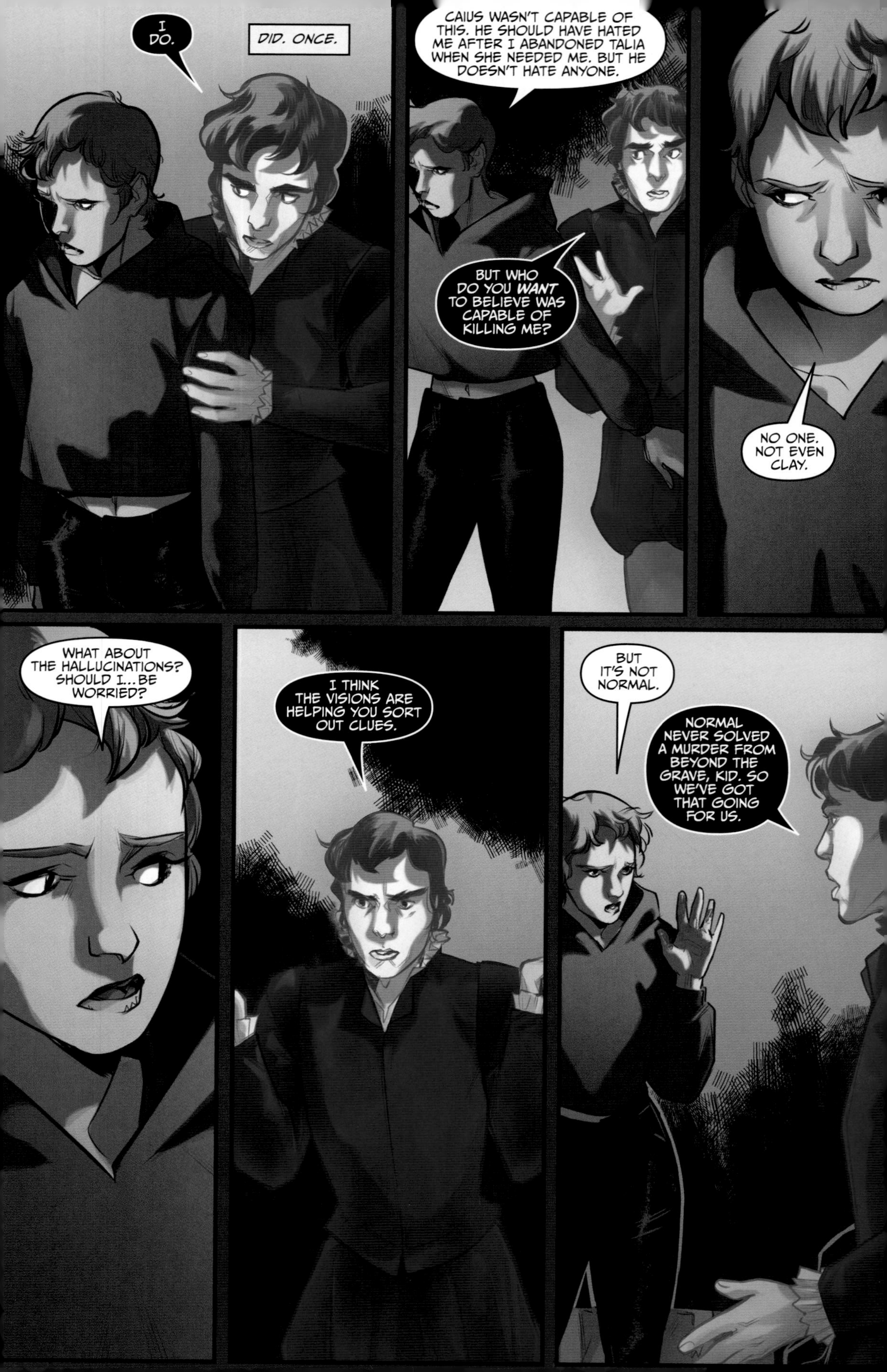
I DO.
DID. ONCE.
CAIUS WASN'T CAPABLE OF THIS. HE SHOULD HAVE HATED ME AFTER I ABANDONED TALIA WHEN SHE NEEDED ME. BUT HE DOESN'T HATE ANYONE.
BUT WHO DO YOU *WANT* TO BELIEVE WAS CAPABLE OF KILLING ME?
NO ONE. NOT EVEN CLAY.
WHAT ABOUT THE HALLUCINATIONS? SHOULD I... BE WORRIED?
I THINK THE VISIONS ARE HELPING YOU SORT OUT CLUES.
BUT IT'S NOT NORMAL.
NORMAL NEVER SOLVED A MURDER FROM BEYOND THE GRAVE, KID. SO WE'VE GOT THAT GOING FOR US.

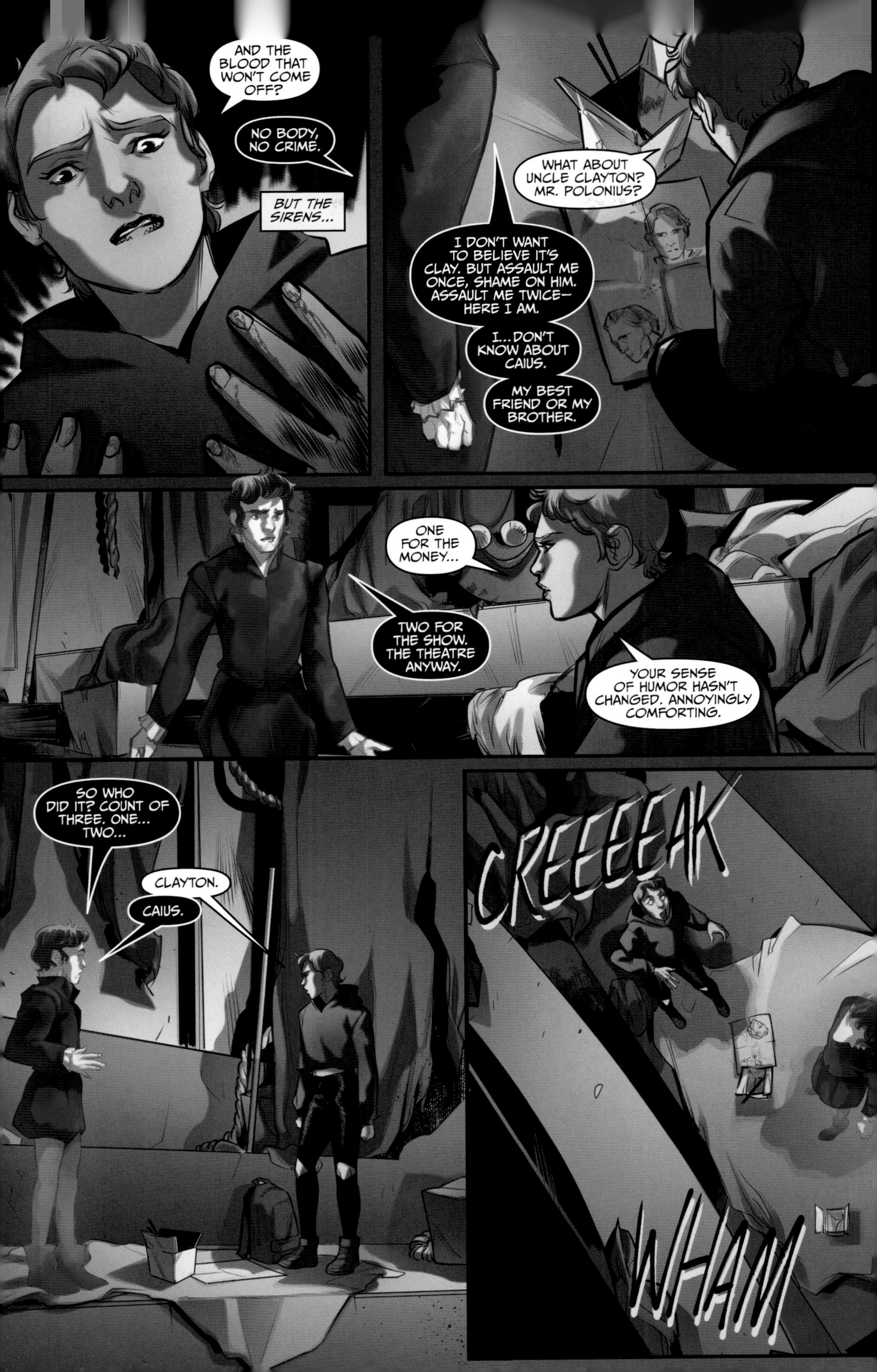
AND THE BLOOD THAT WON'T COME OFF?
NO BODY, NO CRIME.
BUT THE SIRENS...
WHAT ABOUT UNCLE CLAYTON? MR. POLONIUS?
I DON'T WANT TO BELIEVE IT'S CLAY. BUT ASSAULT ME ONCE, SHAME ON HIM. ASSAULT ME TWICE— HERE I AM.
I...DON'T KNOW ABOUT CAIUS.
MY BEST FRIEND OR MY BROTHER.
ONE FOR THE MONEY...
TWO FOR THE SHOW. THE THEATRE ANYWAY.
YOUR SENSE OF HUMOR HASN'T CHANGED. ANNOYINGLY COMFORTING.
SO WHO DID IT? COUNT OF THREE. ONE... TWO...
CLAYTON.
CAIUS.
CREEEEAK
WHAM

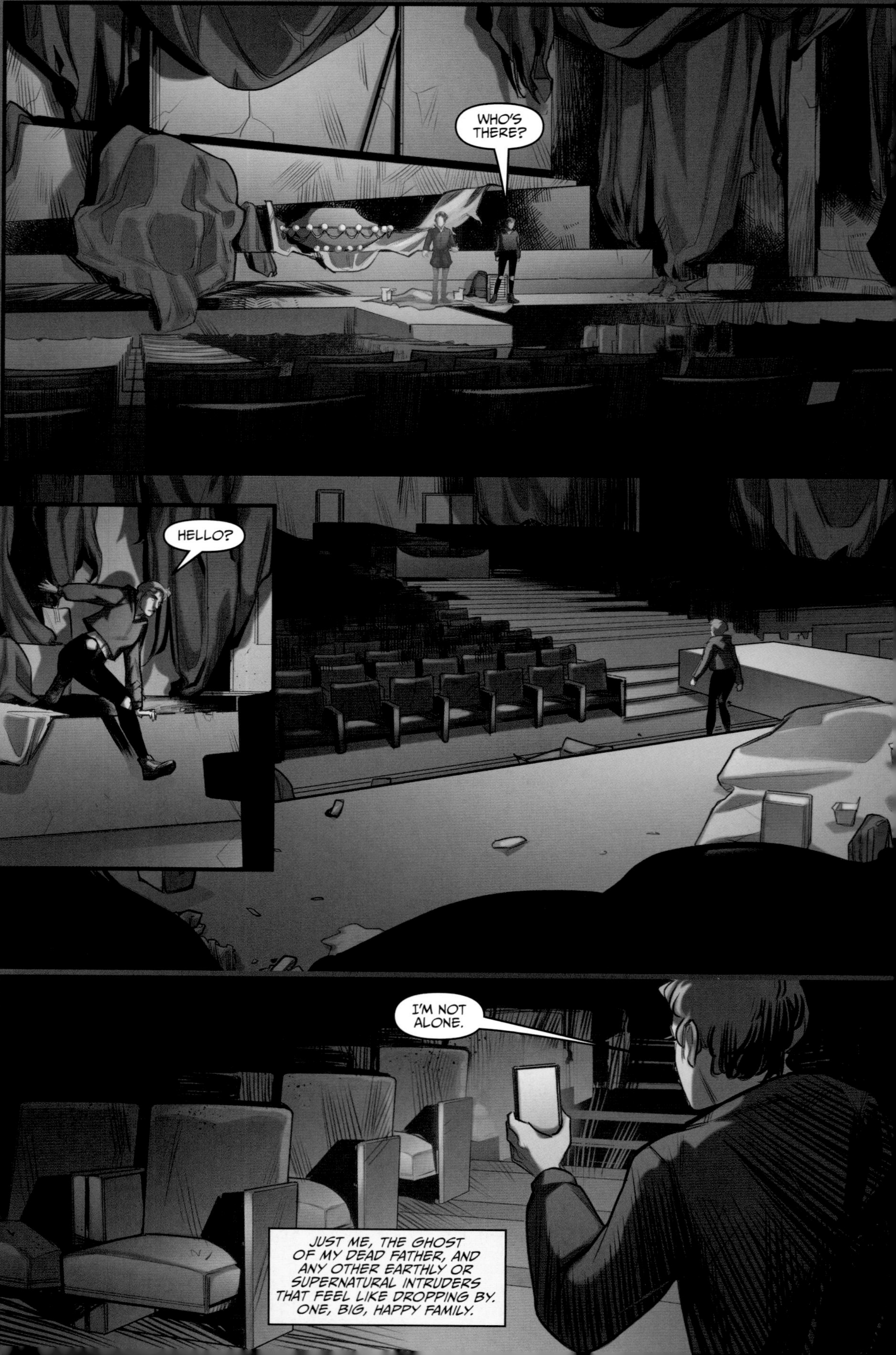
WHO'S THERE?
HELLO?
I'M NOT ALONE.
JUST ME, THE GHOST OF MY DEAD FATHER, AND ANY OTHER EARTHLY OR SUPERNATURAL INTRUDERS THAT FEEL LIKE DROPPING BY. ONE, BIG, HAPPY FAMILY.

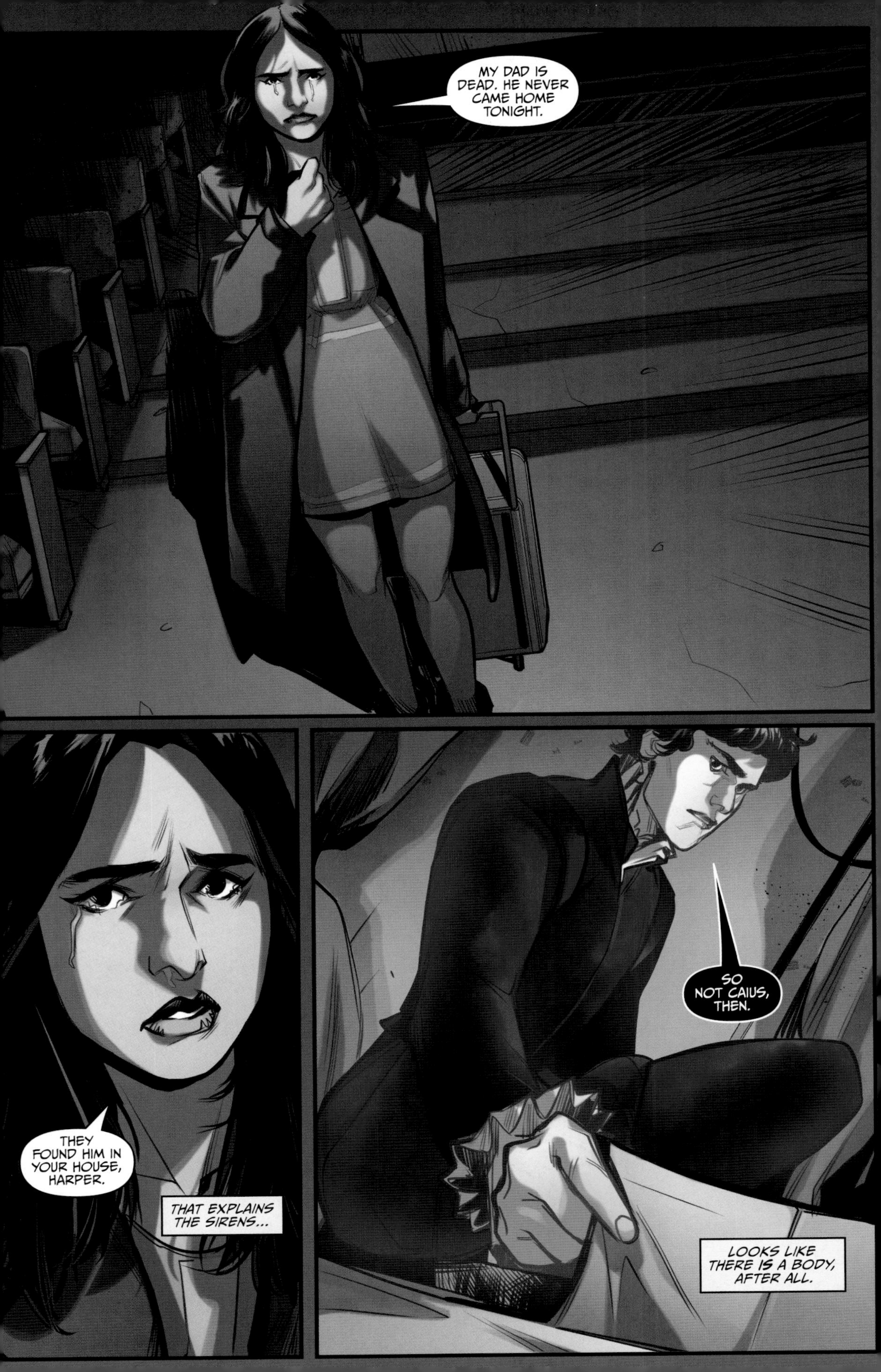

MY DAD IS DEAD. HE NEVER CAME HOME TONIGHT.
THEY FOUND HIM IN YOUR HOUSE, HARPER.
THAT EXPLAINS THE SIRENS...
SO NOT CAIUS, THEN.
LOOKS LIKE THERE IS A BODY, AFTER ALL.

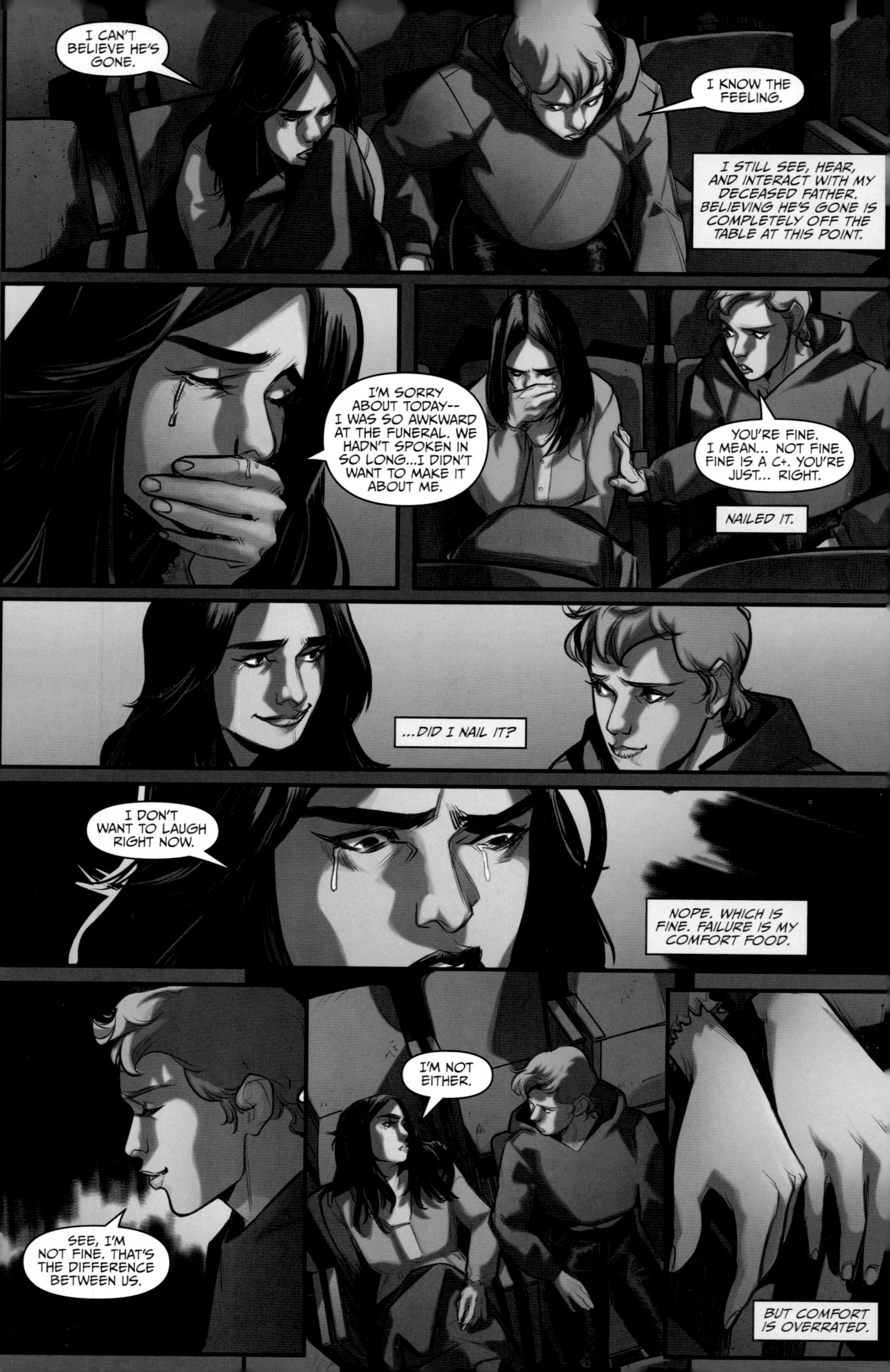
I CAN'T BELIEVE HE'S GONE.
I KNOW THE FEELING.
I STILL SEE, HEAR, AND INTERACT WITH MY DECEASED FATHER. BELIEVING HE'S GONE IS COMPLETELY OFF THE TABLE AT THIS POINT.
I'M SORRY ABOUT TODAY-- I WAS SO AWKWARD AT THE FUNERAL. WE HADN'T SPOKEN IN SO LONG...I DIDN'T WANT TO MAKE IT ABOUT ME.
YOU'RE FINE. I MEAN... NOT FINE. FINE IS A C+. YOU'RE JUST... RIGHT.
NAILED IT.
...DID I NAIL IT?
I DON'T WANT TO LAUGH RIGHT NOW.
NOPE. WHICH IS FINE. FAILURE IS MY COMFORT FOOD.
SEE, I'M NOT FINE. THAT'S THE DIFFERENCE BETWEEN US.
I'M NOT EITHER.
BUT COMFORT IS OVERRATED.

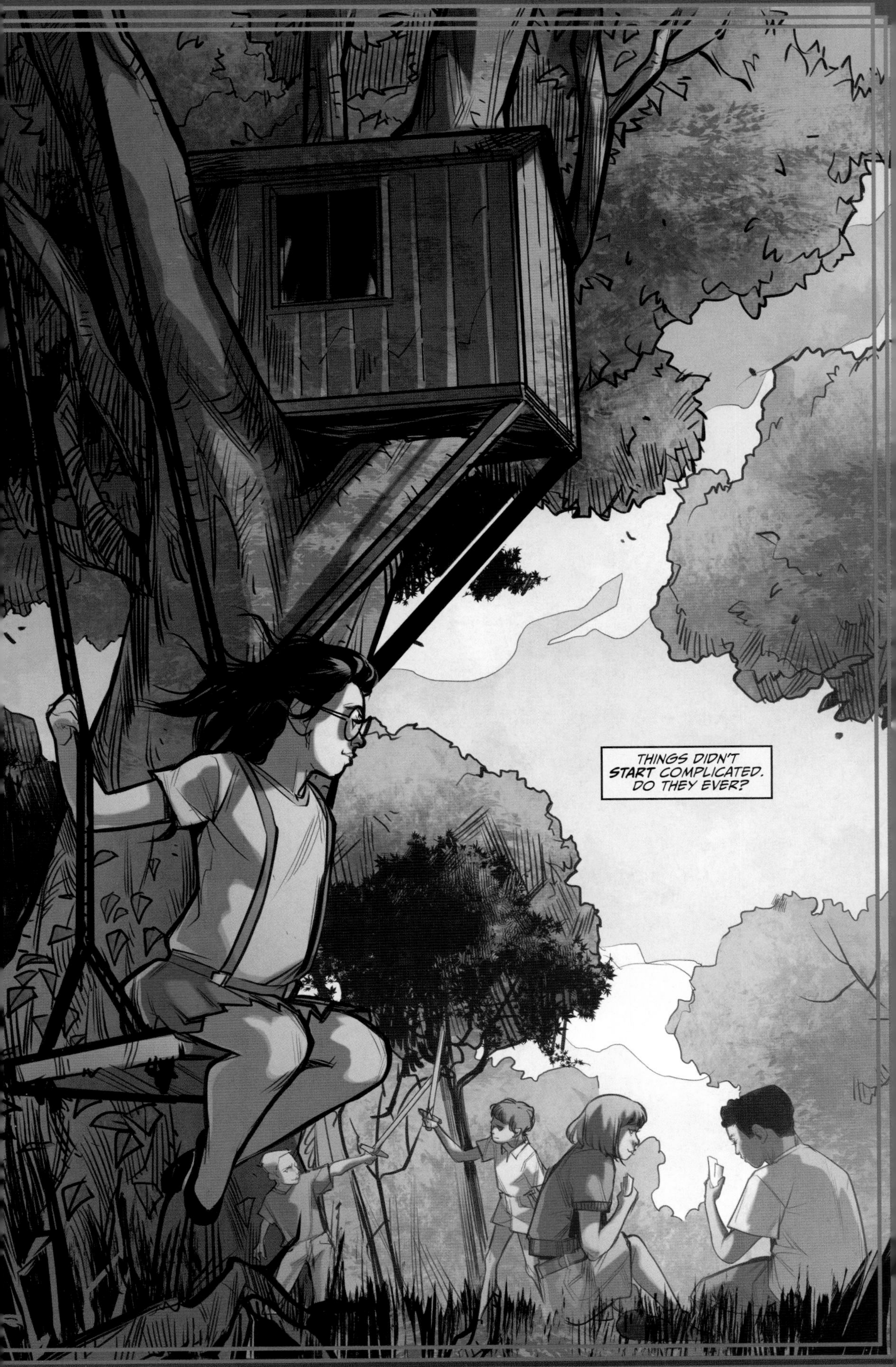
THINGS DIDN'T START COMPLICATED. DO THEY EVER?

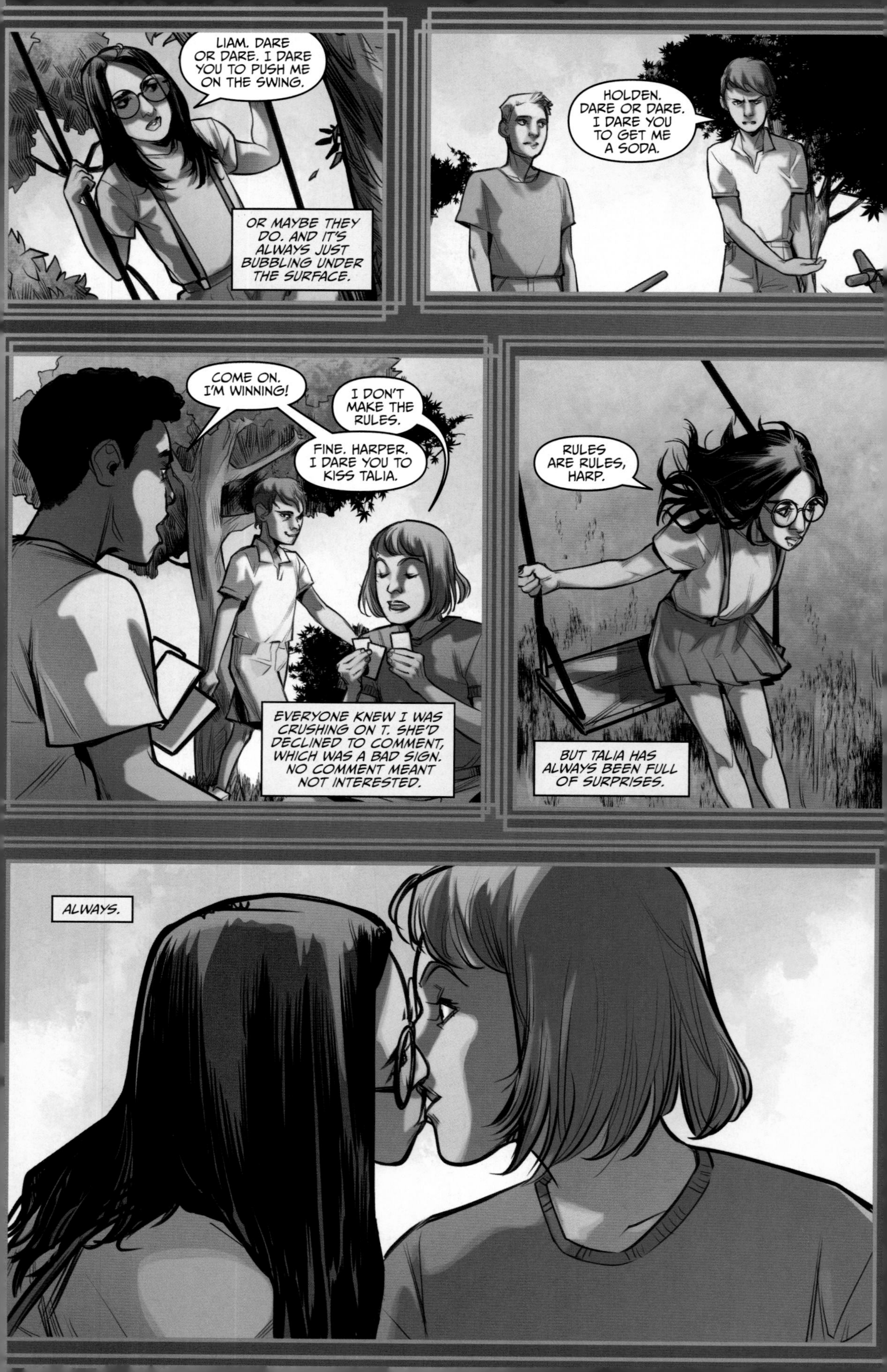
LIAM. DARE OR DARE. I DARE YOU TO PUSH ME ON THE SWING.
OR MAYBE THEY DO. AND IT'S ALWAYS JUST BUBBLING UNDER THE SURFACE.
HOLDEN. DARE OR DARE. I DARE YOU TO GET ME A SODA.
COME ON. I'M WINNING!
I DON'T MAKE THE RULES.
FINE. HARPER. I DARE YOU TO KISS TALIA.
EVERYONE KNEW I WAS CRUSHING ON T. SHE'D DECLINED TO COMMENT, WHICH WAS A BAD SIGN. NO COMMENT MEANT NOT INTERESTED.
RULES ARE RULES, HARP.
BUT TALIA HAS ALWAYS BEEN FULL OF SURPRISES.
ALWAYS.

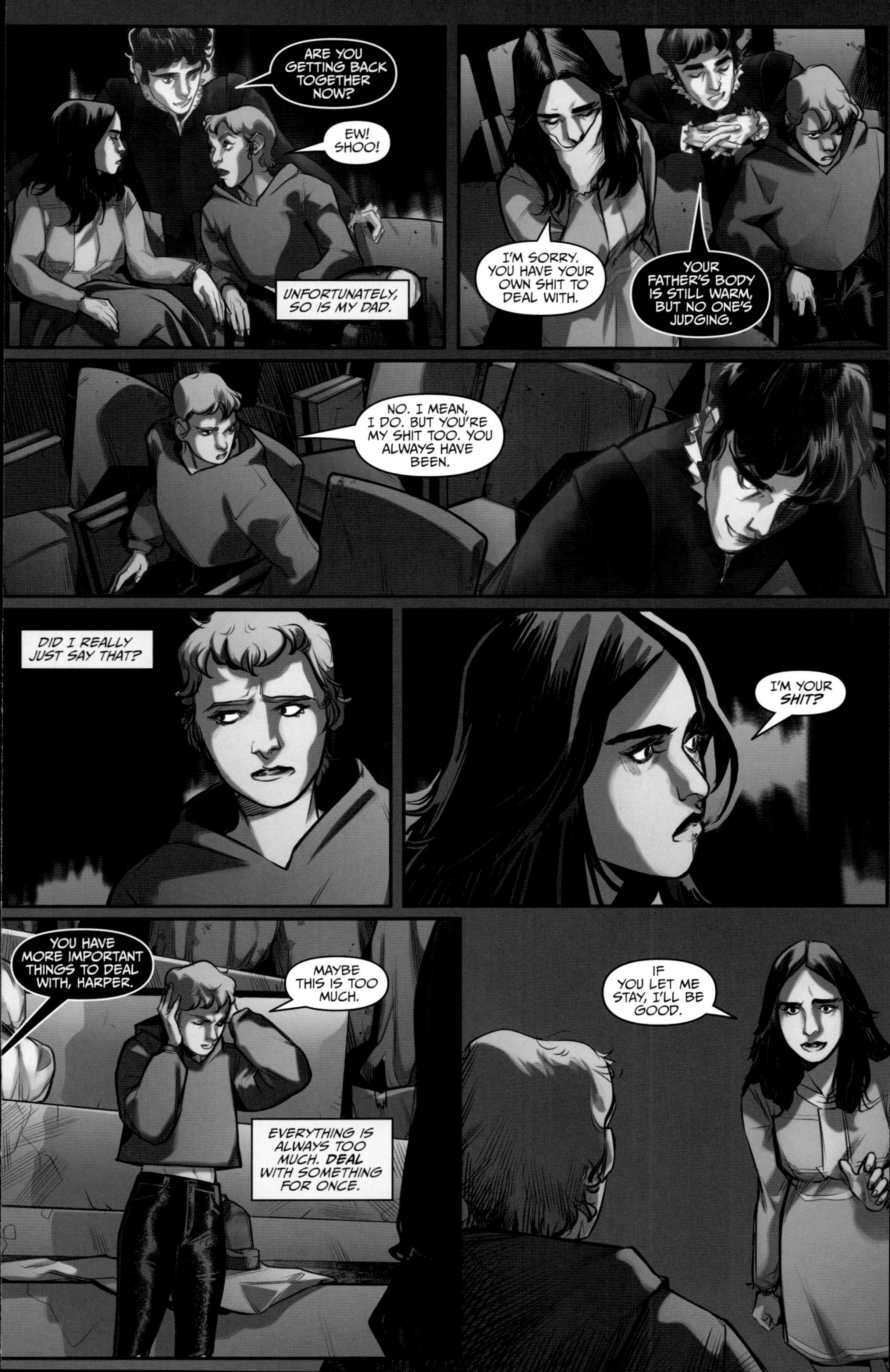
ARE YOU GETTING BACK TOGETHER NOW?
EW! SHOO!
UNFORTUNATELY, SO IS MY DAD.
I'M SORRY. YOU HAVE YOUR OWN SHIT TO DEAL WITH.
YOUR FATHER'S BODY IS STILL WARM, BUT NO ONE'S JUDGING.
NO. I MEAN, I DO. BUT YOU'RE MY SHIT TOO. YOU ALWAYS HAVE BEEN.
DID I REALLY JUST SAY THAT?
I'M YOUR SHIT?
YOU HAVE MORE IMPORTANT THINGS TO DEAL WITH, HARPER.
MAYBE THIS IS TOO MUCH.
EVERYTHING IS ALWAYS TOO MUCH. DEAL WITH SOMETHING FOR ONCE.
IF YOU LET ME STAY, I'LL BE GOOD.

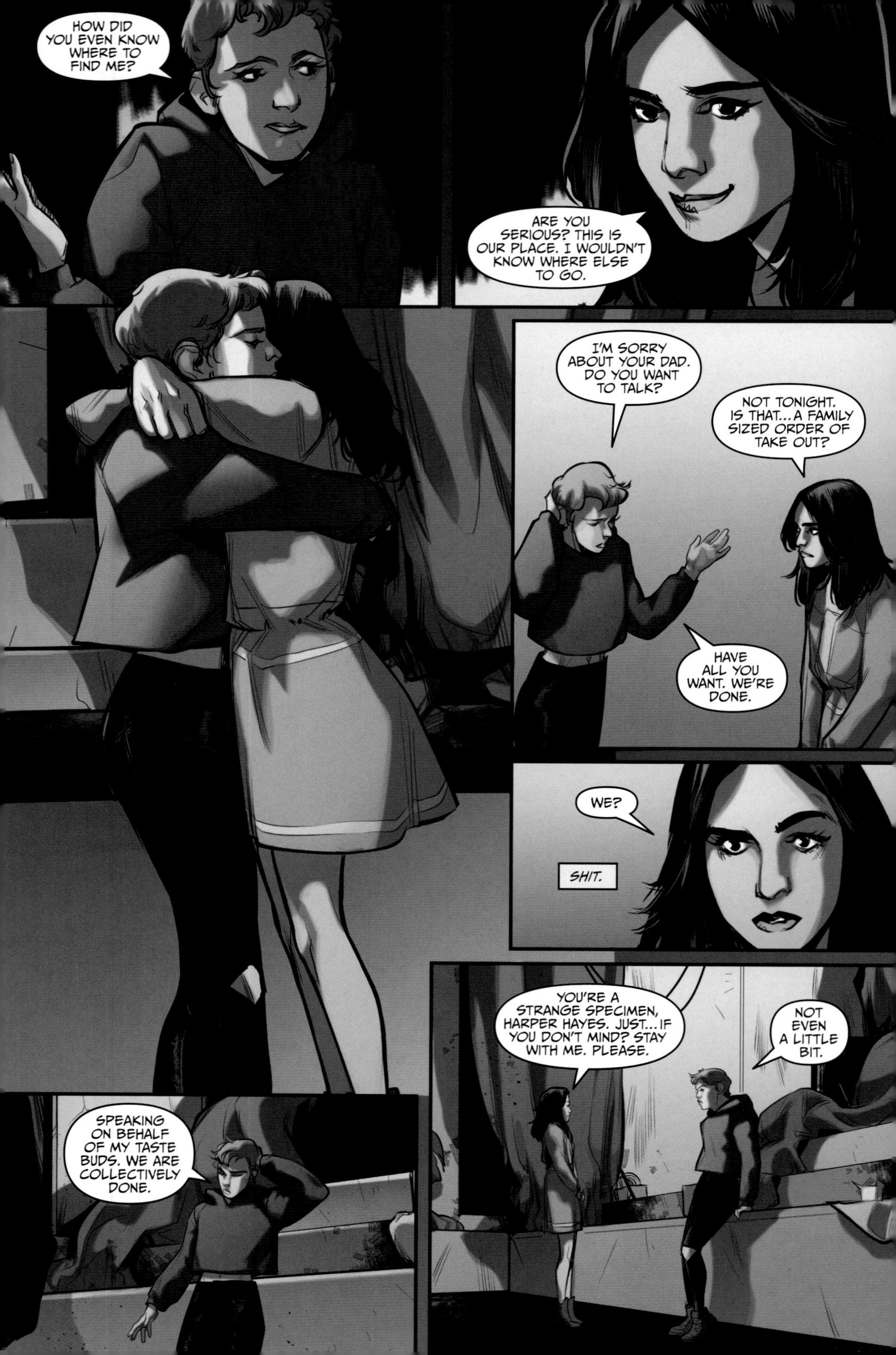
HOW DID YOU EVEN KNOW WHERE TO FIND ME?
ARE YOU SERIOUS? THIS IS OUR PLACE. I WOULDN'T KNOW WHERE ELSE TO GO.
I'M SORRY ABOUT YOUR DAD. DO YOU WANT TO TALK?
NOT TONIGHT. IS THAT... A FAMILY SIZED ORDER OF TAKE OUT?
HAVE ALL YOU WANT. WE'RE DONE.
WE?
SHIT.
SPEAKING ON BEHALF OF MY TASTE BUDS. WE ARE COLLECTIVELY DONE.
YOU'RE A STRANGE SPECIMEN, HARPER HAYES. JUST... IF YOU DON'T MIND? STAY WITH ME. PLEASE.
NOT EVEN A LITTLE BIT.

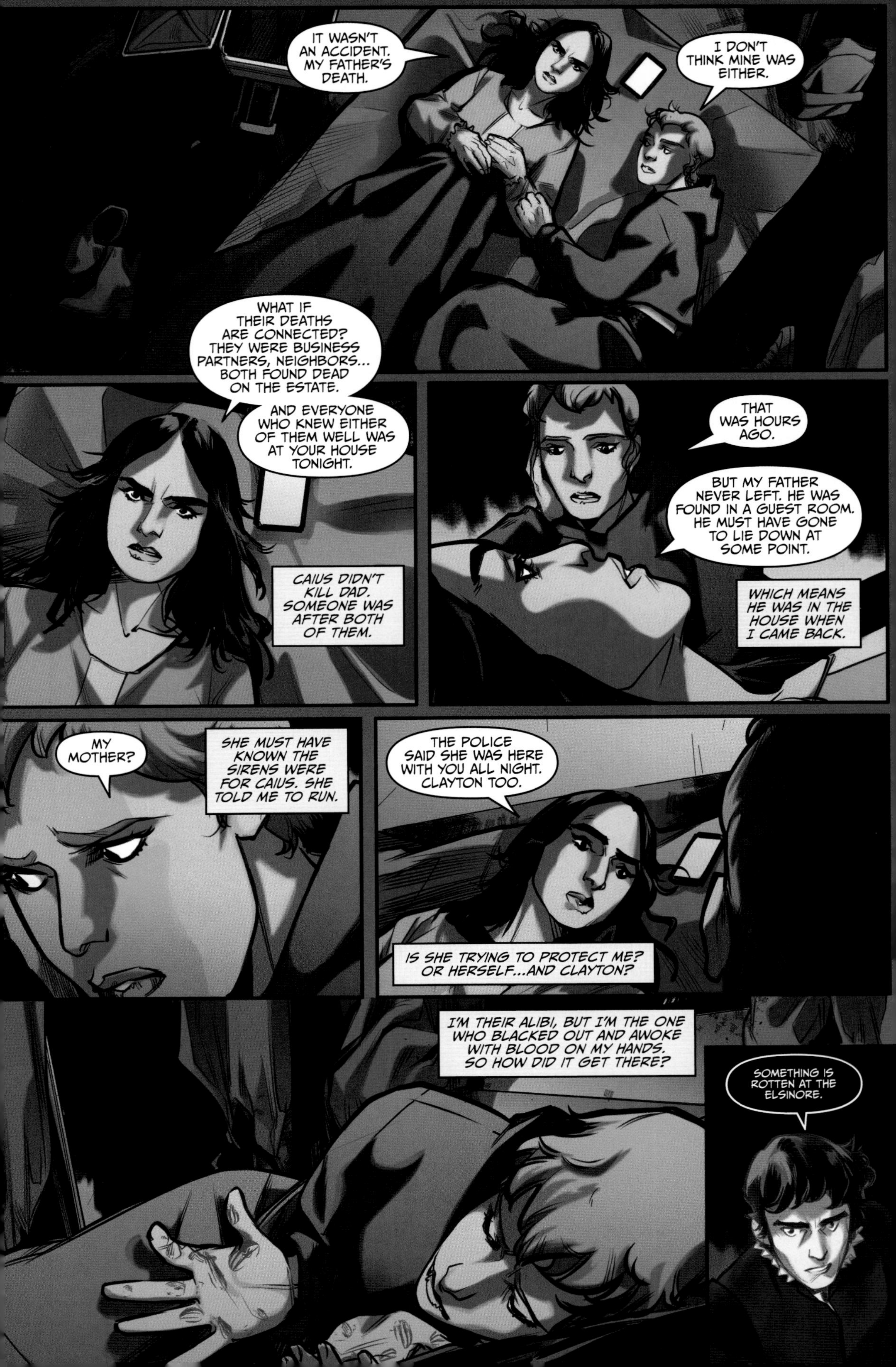
IT WASN'T AN ACCIDENT. MY FATHER'S DEATH.
I DON'T THINK MINE WAS EITHER.
WHAT IF THEIR DEATHS ARE CONNECTED? THEY WERE BUSINESS PARTNERS, NEIGHBORS... BOTH FOUND DEAD ON THE ESTATE.
AND EVERYONE WHO KNEW EITHER OF THEM WELL WAS AT YOUR HOUSE TONIGHT.
CAIUS DIDN'T KILL DAD. SOMEONE WAS AFTER BOTH OF THEM.
THAT WAS HOURS AGO.
BUT MY FATHER NEVER LEFT. HE WAS FOUND IN A GUEST ROOM. HE MUST HAVE GONE TO LIE DOWN AT SOME POINT.
WHICH MEANS HE WAS IN THE HOUSE WHEN I CAME BACK.
MY MOTHER?
SHE MUST HAVE KNOWN THE SIRENS WERE FOR CAIUS. SHE TOLD ME TO RUN.
THE POLICE SAID SHE WAS HERE WITH YOU ALL NIGHT. CLAYTON TOO.
IS SHE TRYING TO PROTECT ME? OR HERSELF...AND CLAYTON?
I'M THEIR ALIBI, BUT I'M THE ONE WHO BLACKED OUT AND AWOKE WITH BLOOD ON MY HANDS. SO HOW DID IT GET THERE?
SOMETHING IS ROTTEN AT THE ELSINORE.

Chapter Three

WHAT
A PIECE
OF WORK

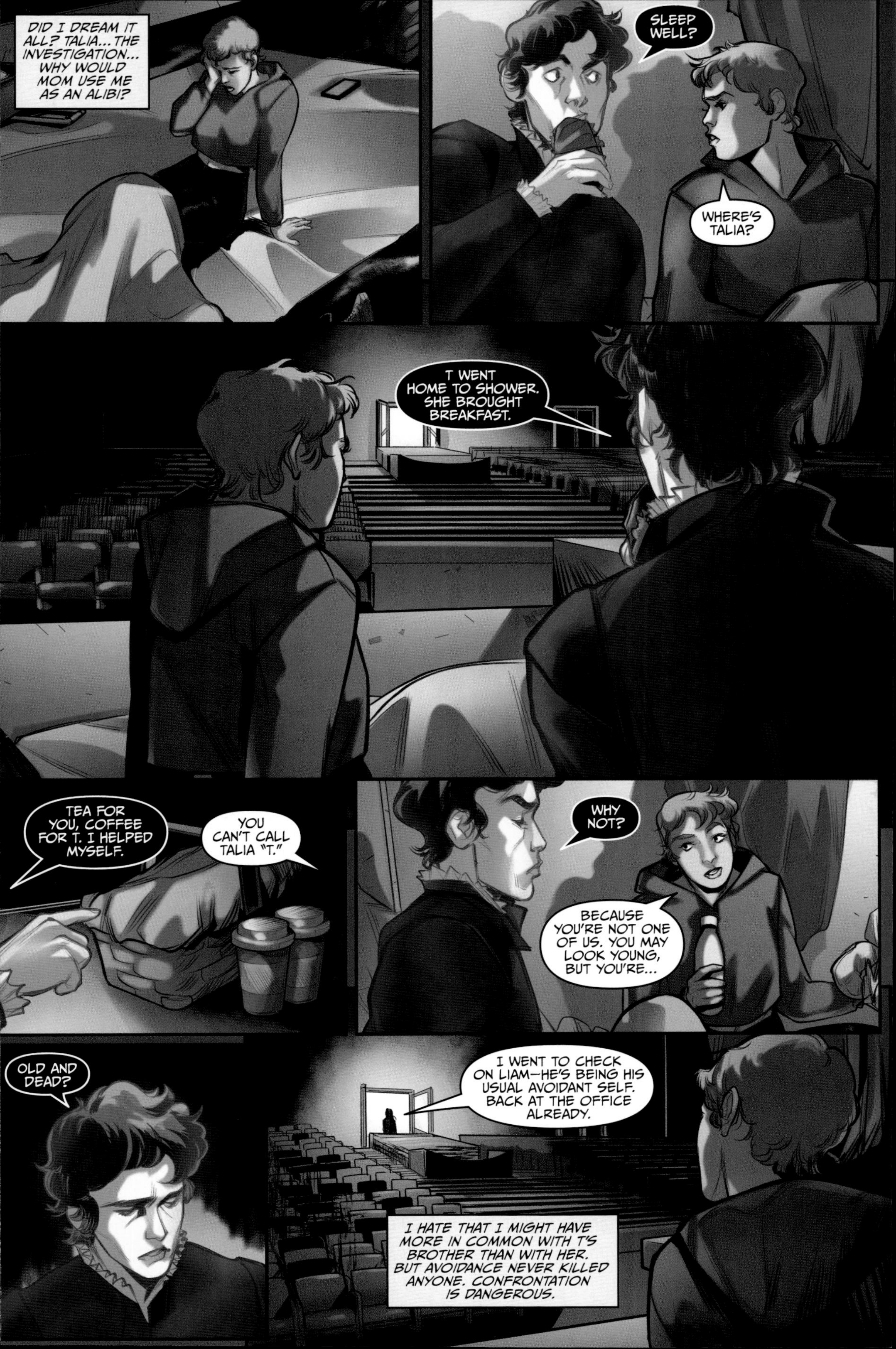
DID I DREAM IT ALL? TALIA... THE INVESTIGATION... WHY WOULD MOM USE ME AS AN ALIBI?
SLEEP WELL?
WHERE'S TALIA?
T WENT HOME TO SHOWER. SHE BROUGHT BREAKFAST.
TEA FOR YOU, COFFEE FOR T. I HELPED MYSELF.
YOU CAN'T CALL TALIA "T."
WHY NOT?
BECAUSE YOU'RE NOT ONE OF US. YOU MAY LOOK YOUNG, BUT YOU'RE...
OLD AND DEAD?
I WENT TO CHECK ON LIAM—HE'S BEING HIS USUAL AVOIDANT SELF. BACK AT THE OFFICE ALREADY.
I HATE THAT I MIGHT HAVE MORE IN COMMON WITH T'S BROTHER THAN WITH HER. BUT AVOIDANCE NEVER KILLED ANYONE. CONFRONTATION IS DANGEROUS.

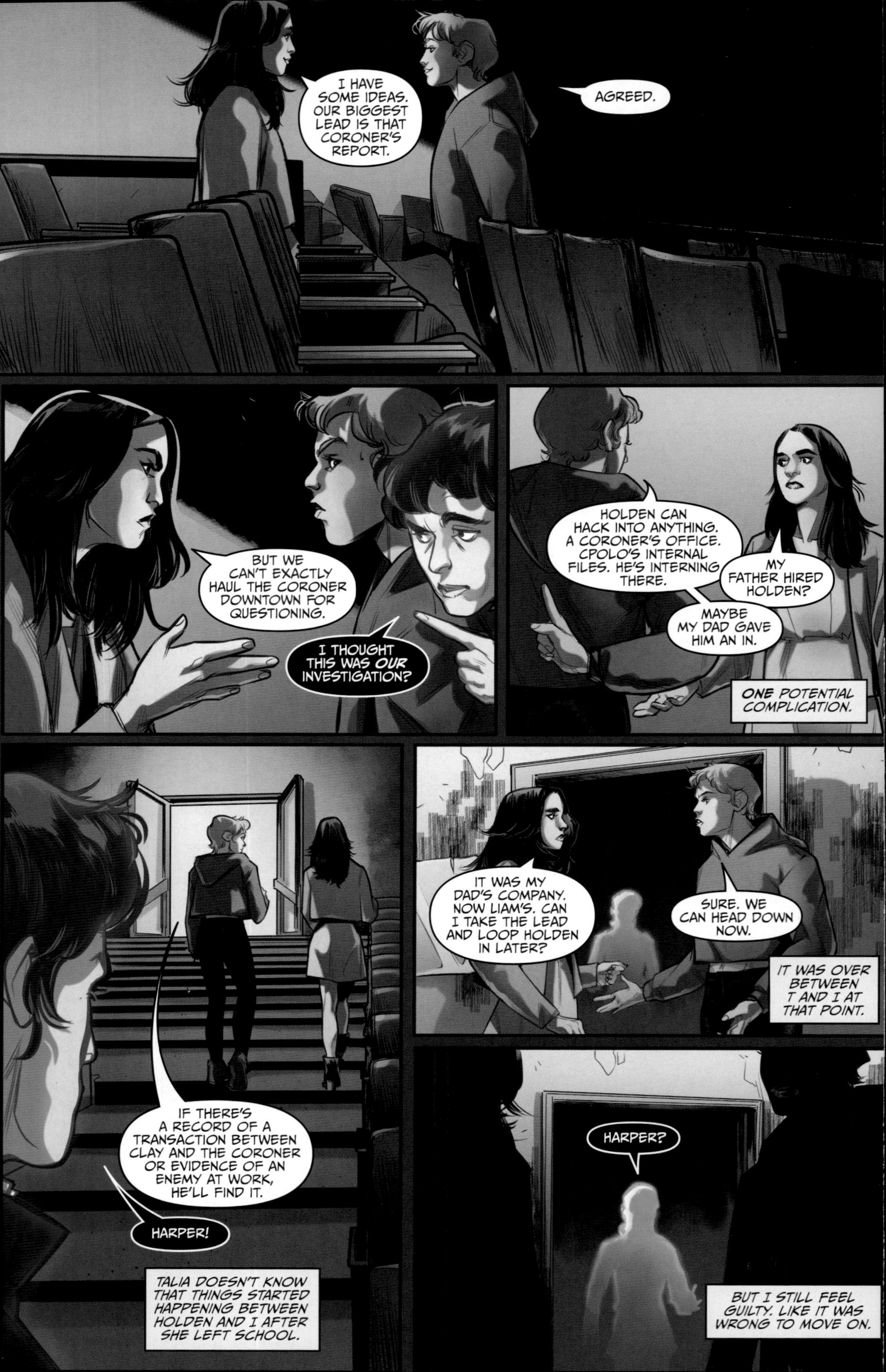
I HAVE SOME IDEAS. OUR BIGGEST LEAD IS THAT CORONER'S REPORT.
AGREED.
BUT WE CAN'T EXACTLY HAUL THE CORONER DOWNTOWN FOR QUESTIONING.
I THOUGHT THIS WAS *OUR* INVESTIGATION?
HOLDEN CAN HACK INTO ANYTHING. A CORONER'S OFFICE. CPOLO'S INTERNAL FILES. HE'S INTERNING THERE.
MY FATHER HIRED HOLDEN?
MAYBE MY DAD GAVE HIM AN IN.
ONE POTENTIAL COMPLICATION.
IF THERE'S A RECORD OF A TRANSACTION BETWEEN CLAY AND THE CORONER OR EVIDENCE OF AN ENEMY AT WORK, HE'LL FIND IT.
HARPER!
TALIA DOESN'T KNOW THAT THINGS STARTED HAPPENING BETWEEN HOLDEN AND I AFTER SHE LEFT SCHOOL.
IT WAS MY DAD'S COMPANY. NOW LIAM'S. CAN I TAKE THE LEAD AND LOOP HOLDEN IN LATER?
SURE. WE CAN HEAD DOWN NOW.
IT WAS OVER BETWEEN T AND I AT THAT POINT.
HARPER?
BUT I STILL FEEL GUILTY. LIKE IT WAS WRONG TO MOVE ON.

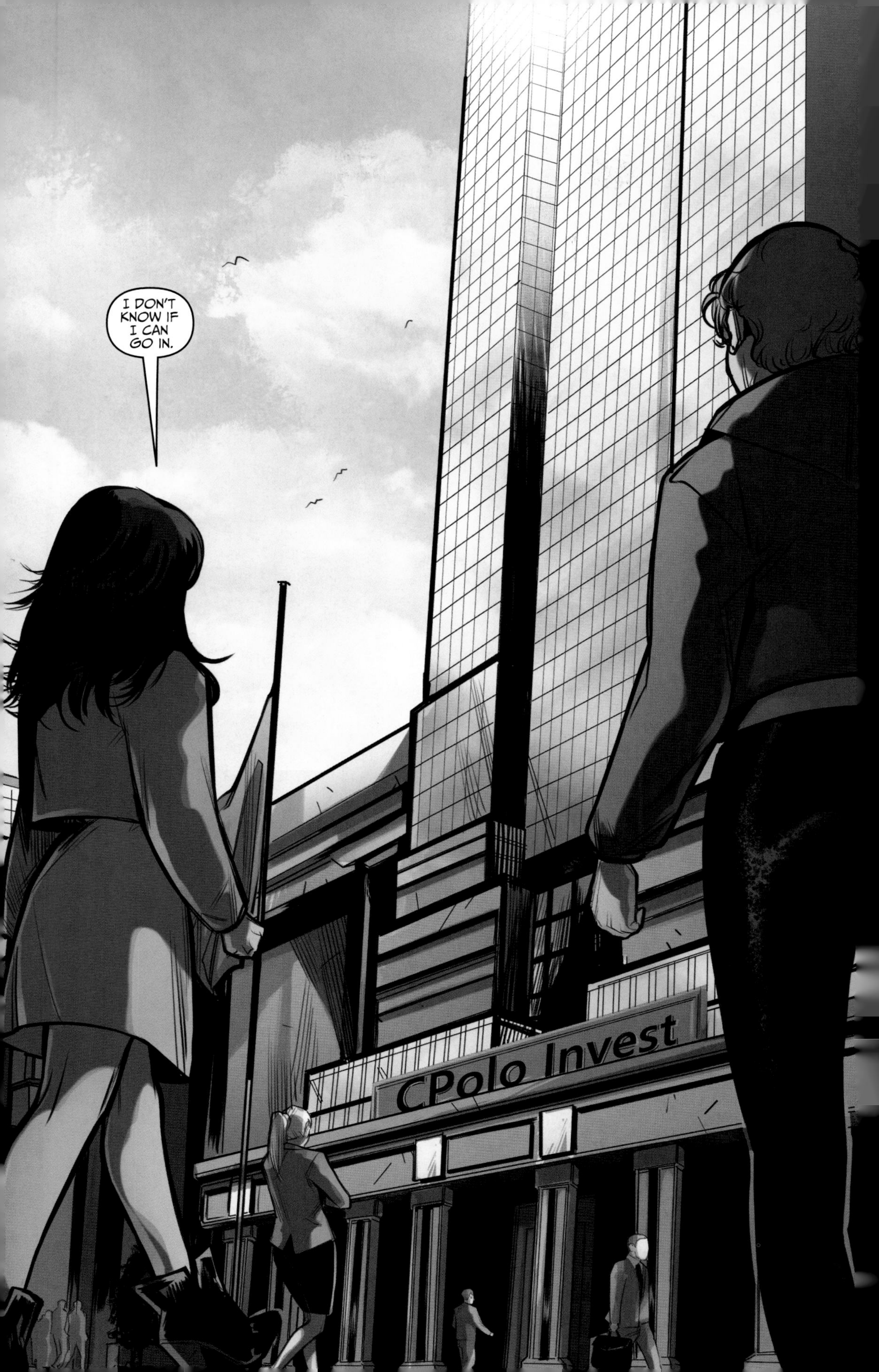
I DON'T KNOW IF I CAN GO IN.
CPolo Invest

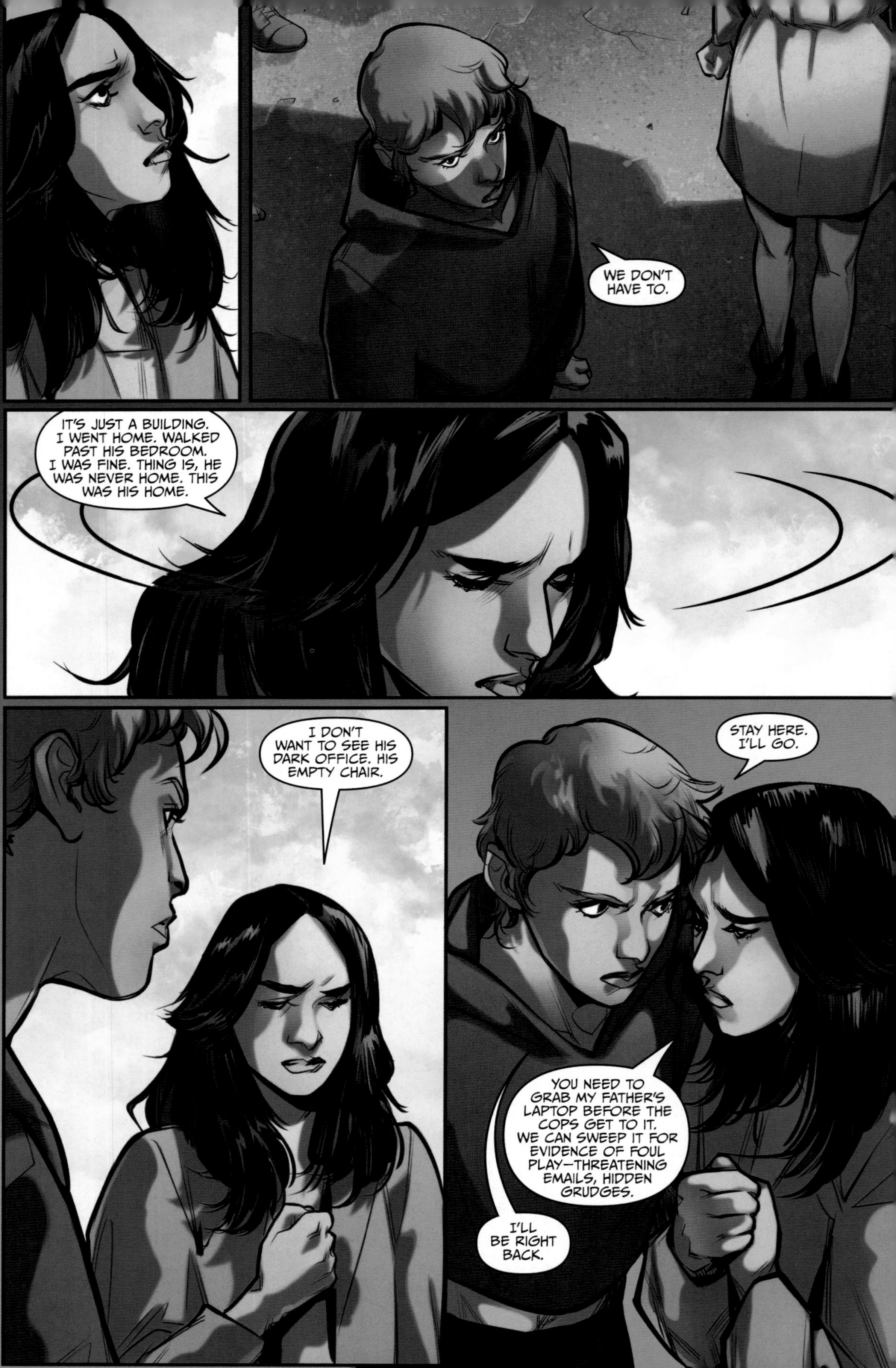
WE DON'T HAVE TO.
IT'S JUST A BUILDING. I WENT HOME. WALKED PAST HIS BEDROOM. I WAS FINE. THING IS, HE WAS NEVER HOME. THIS WAS HIS HOME.
I DON'T WANT TO SEE HIS DARK OFFICE. HIS EMPTY CHAIR.
STAY HERE. I'LL GO.
YOU NEED TO GRAB MY FATHER'S LAPTOP BEFORE THE COPS GET TO IT. WE CAN SWEEP IT FOR EVIDENCE OF FOUL PLAY—THREATENING EMAILS, HIDDEN GRUDGES.
I'LL BE RIGHT BACK.

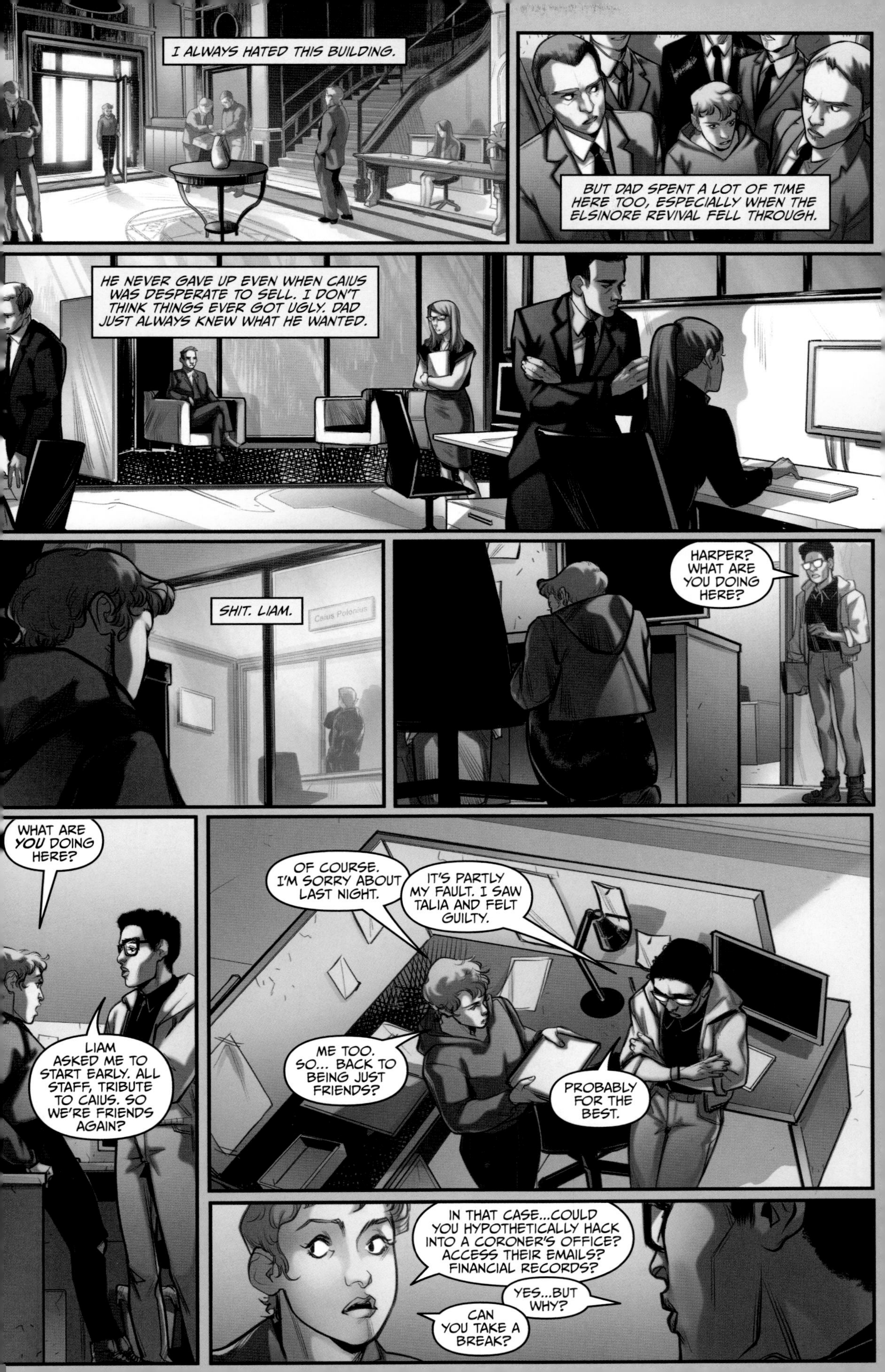
I ALWAYS HATED THIS BUILDING.
BUT DAD SPENT A LOT OF TIME HERE TOO, ESPECIALLY WHEN THE ELSINORE REVIVAL FELL THROUGH.
HE NEVER GAVE UP EVEN WHEN CAIUS WAS DESPERATE TO SELL. I DON'T THINK THINGS EVER GOT UGLY. DAD JUST ALWAYS KNEW WHAT HE WANTED.
SHIT. LIAM.
Caius Polonius
HARPER? WHAT ARE YOU DOING HERE?
WHAT ARE *YOU* DOING HERE?
LIAM ASKED ME TO START EARLY. ALL STAFF, TRIBUTE TO CAIUS. SO WE'RE FRIENDS AGAIN?
OF COURSE. I'M SORRY ABOUT LAST NIGHT.
IT'S PARTLY MY FAULT. I SAW TALIA AND FELT GUILTY.
ME TOO. SO... BACK TO BEING JUST FRIENDS?
PROBABLY FOR THE BEST.
IN THAT CASE...COULD YOU HYPOTHETICALLY HACK INTO A CORONER'S OFFICE? ACCESS THEIR EMAILS? FINANCIAL RECORDS?
YES...BUT WHY?
CAN YOU TAKE A BREAK?

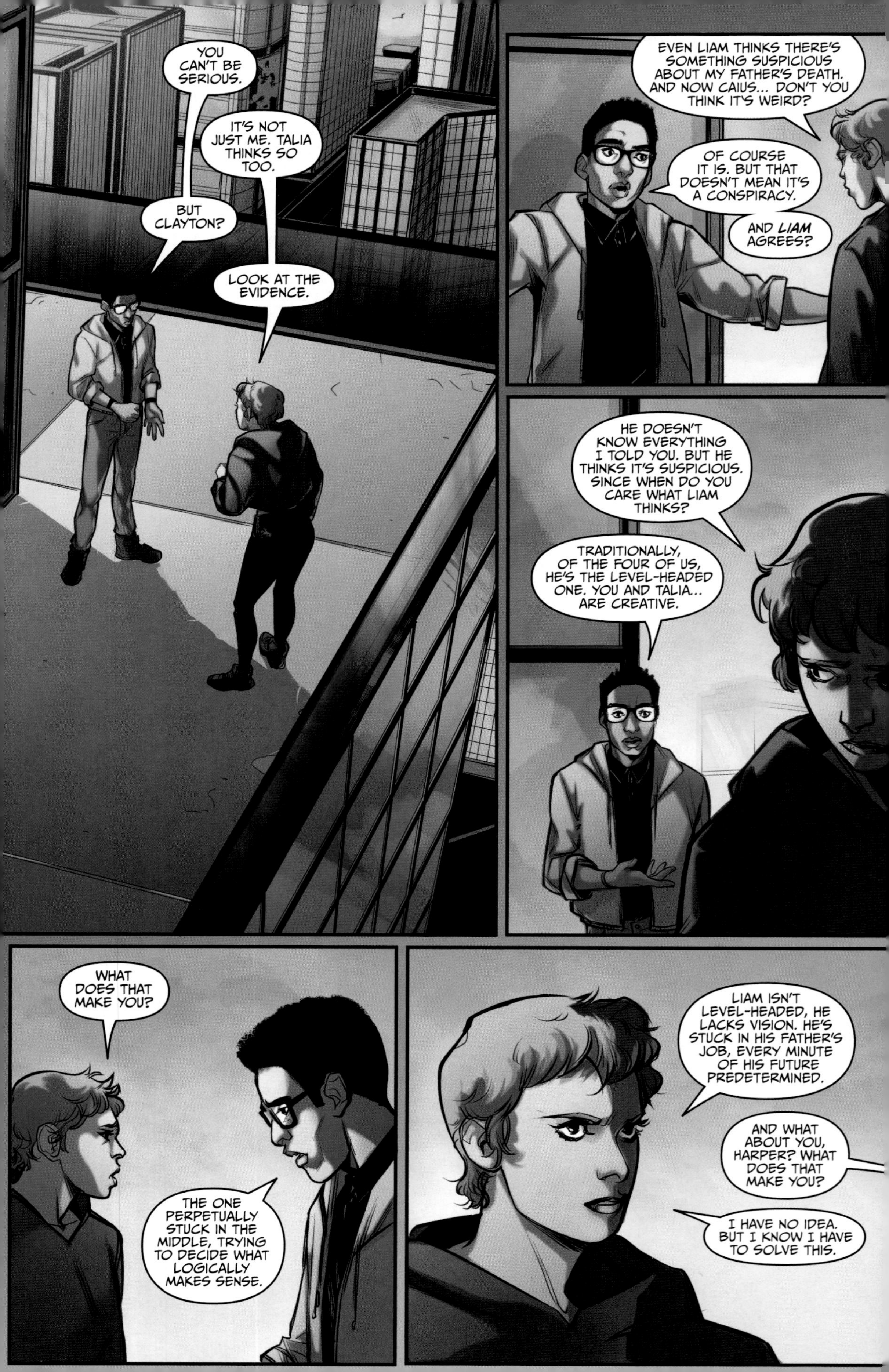
YOU CAN'T BE SERIOUS.
IT'S NOT JUST ME. TALIA THINKS SO TOO.
BUT CLAYTON?
LOOK AT THE EVIDENCE.
EVEN LIAM THINKS THERE'S SOMETHING SUSPICIOUS ABOUT MY FATHER'S DEATH. AND NOW CAIUS... DON'T YOU THINK IT'S WEIRD?
OF COURSE IT IS. BUT THAT DOESN'T MEAN IT'S A CONSPIRACY.
AND *LIAM* AGREES?
HE DOESN'T KNOW EVERYTHING I TOLD YOU. BUT HE THINKS IT'S SUSPICIOUS. SINCE WHEN DO YOU CARE WHAT LIAM THINKS?
TRADITIONALLY, OF THE FOUR OF US, HE'S THE LEVEL-HEADED ONE. YOU AND TALIA... ARE CREATIVE.
WHAT DOES THAT MAKE YOU?
THE ONE PERPETUALLY STUCK IN THE MIDDLE, TRYING TO DECIDE WHAT LOGICALLY MAKES SENSE.
LIAM ISN'T LEVEL-HEADED, HE LACKS VISION. HE'S STUCK IN HIS FATHER'S JOB, EVERY MINUTE OF HIS FUTURE PREDETERMINED.
AND WHAT ABOUT YOU, HARPER? WHAT DOES THAT MAKE YOU?
I HAVE NO IDEA. BUT I KNOW I HAVE TO SOLVE THIS.

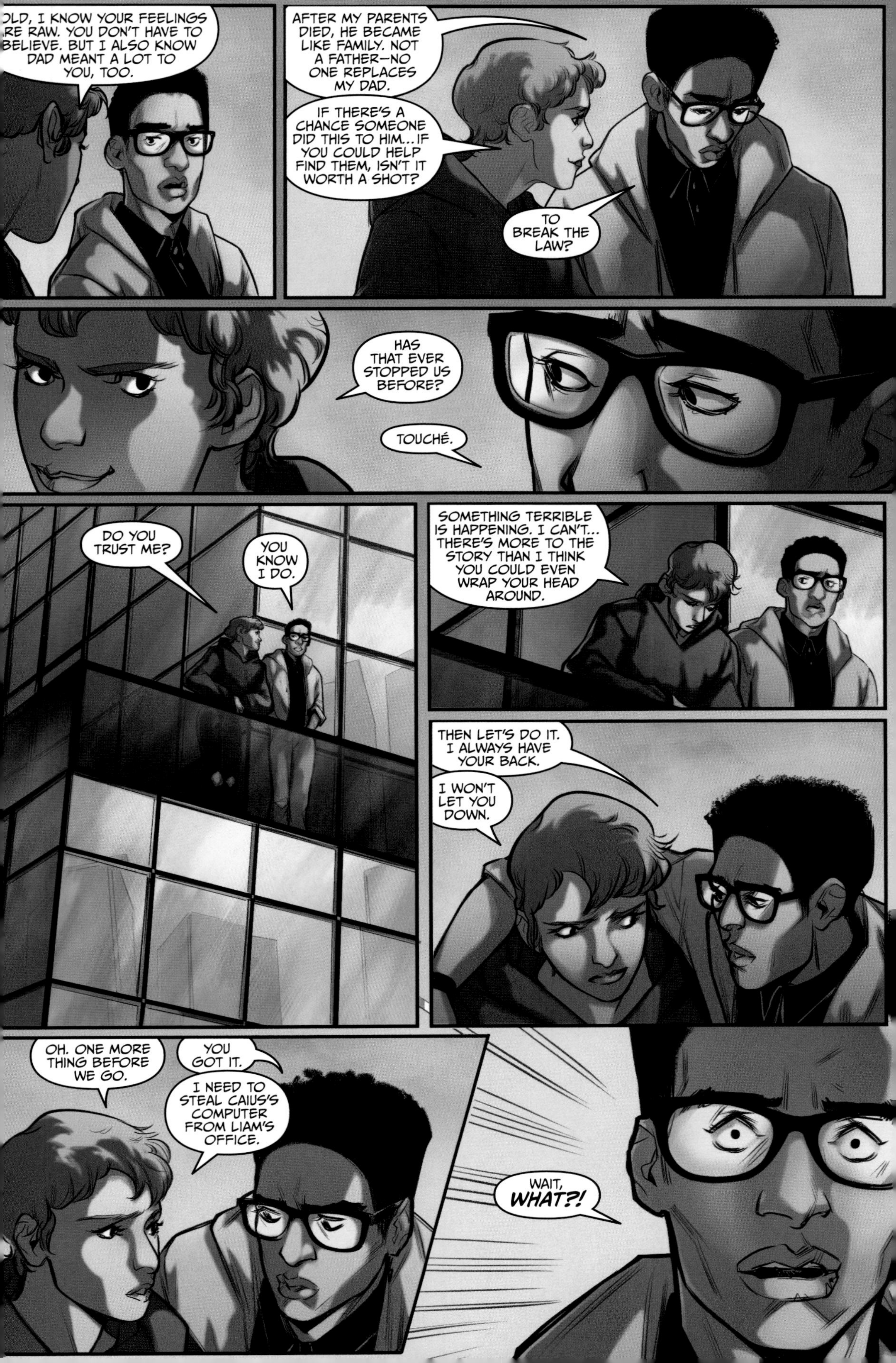

OLD, I KNOW YOUR FEELINGS
RE RAW. YOU DON'T HAVE TO
BELIEVE. BUT I ALSO KNOW
DAD MEANT A LOT TO
YOU, TOO.
AFTER MY PARENTS DIED, HE BECAME LIKE FAMILY. NOT A FATHER—NO ONE REPLACES MY DAD.
IF THERE'S A CHANCE SOMEONE DID THIS TO HIM...IF YOU COULD HELP FIND THEM, ISN'T IT WORTH A SHOT?
TO BREAK THE LAW?
HAS THAT EVER STOPPED US BEFORE?
TOUCHÉ.
DO YOU TRUST ME?
YOU KNOW I DO.
SOMETHING TERRIBLE IS HAPPENING. I CAN'T... THERE'S MORE TO THE STORY THAN I THINK YOU COULD EVEN WRAP YOUR HEAD AROUND.
THEN LET'S DO IT. I ALWAYS HAVE YOUR BACK.
I WON'T LET YOU DOWN.
OH. ONE MORE THING BEFORE WE GO.
YOU GOT IT.
I NEED TO STEAL CAIUS'S COMPUTER FROM LIAM'S OFFICE.
WAIT, *WHAT?!*

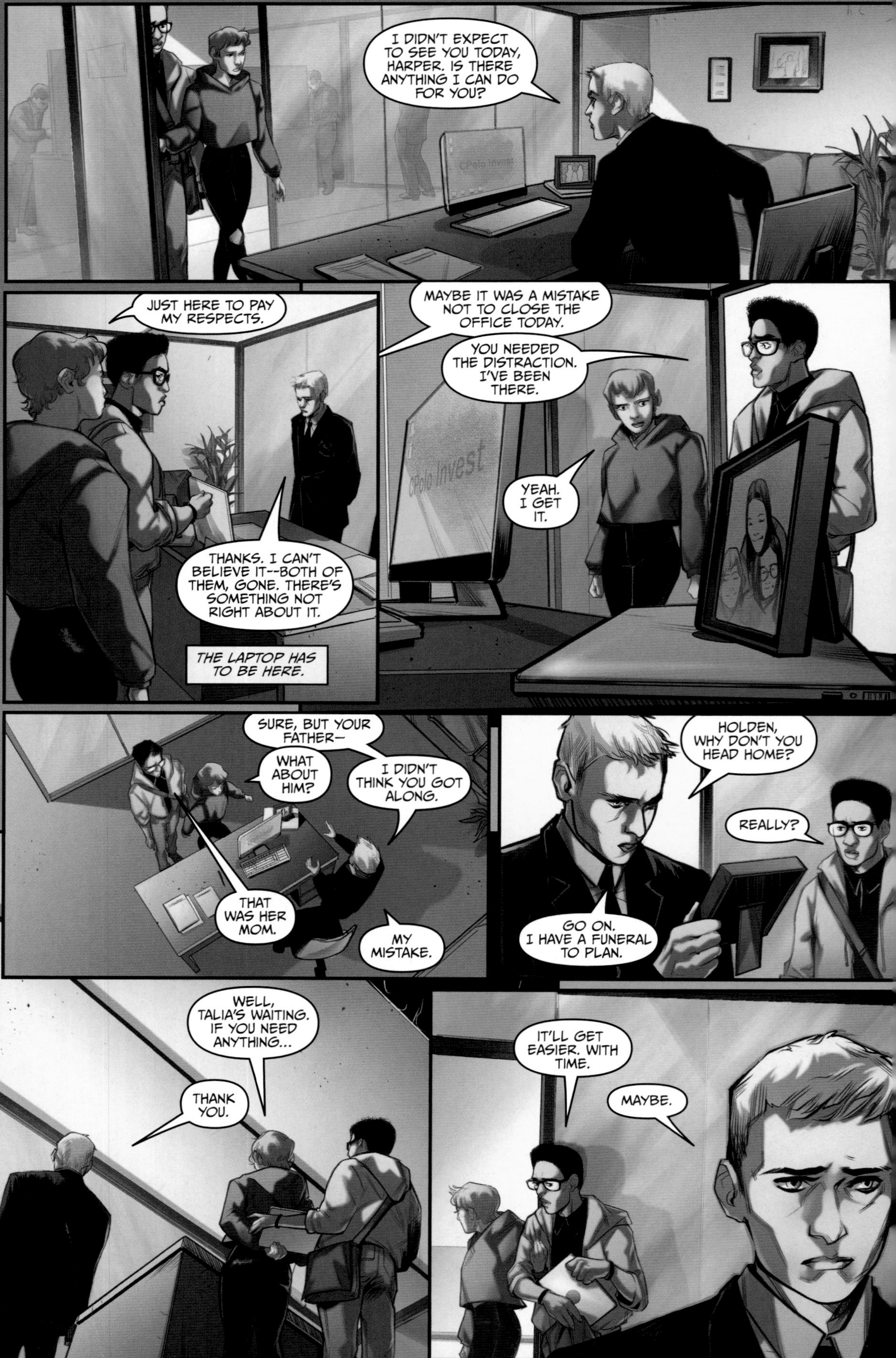
I DIDN'T EXPECT TO SEE YOU TODAY, HARPER. IS THERE ANYTHING I CAN DO FOR YOU?
JUST HERE TO PAY MY RESPECTS.
THANKS. I CAN'T BELIEVE IT--BOTH OF THEM, GONE. THERE'S SOMETHING NOT RIGHT ABOUT IT.
THE LAPTOP HAS TO BE HERE.
MAYBE IT WAS A MISTAKE NOT TO CLOSE THE OFFICE TODAY.
YOU NEEDED THE DISTRACTION. I'VE BEEN THERE.
YEAH. I GET IT.
SURE, BUT YOUR FATHER—
WHAT ABOUT HIM?
I DIDN'T THINK YOU GOT ALONG.
THAT WAS HER MOM.
MY MISTAKE.
HOLDEN, WHY DON'T YOU HEAD HOME?
REALLY?
GO ON. I HAVE A FUNERAL TO PLAN.
WELL, TALIA'S WAITING. IF YOU NEED ANYTHING...
THANK YOU.
IT'LL GET EASIER. WITH TIME.
MAYBE.

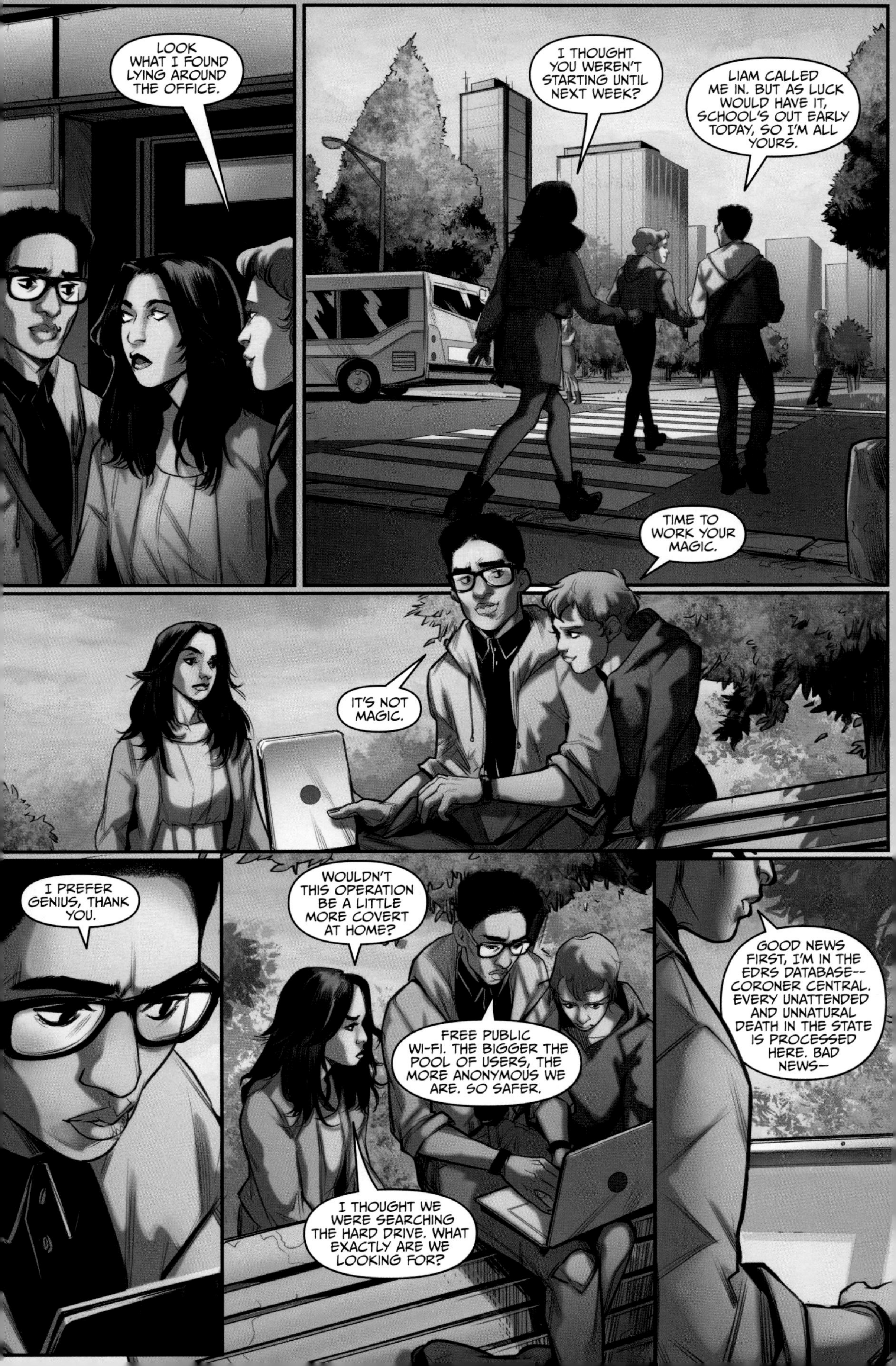
LOOK WHAT I FOUND LYING AROUND THE OFFICE.
I THOUGHT YOU WEREN'T STARTING UNTIL NEXT WEEK?
LIAM CALLED ME IN. BUT AS LUCK WOULD HAVE IT, SCHOOL'S OUT EARLY TODAY, SO I'M ALL YOURS.
TIME TO WORK YOUR MAGIC.
IT'S NOT MAGIC.
I PREFER GENIUS, THANK YOU.
WOULDN'T THIS OPERATION BE A LITTLE MORE COVERT AT HOME?
FREE PUBLIC WI-FI. THE BIGGER THE POOL OF USERS, THE MORE ANONYMOUS WE ARE. SO SAFER.
I THOUGHT WE WERE SEARCHING THE HARD DRIVE. WHAT EXACTLY ARE WE LOOKING FOR?
GOOD NEWS FIRST, I'M IN THE EDRS DATABASE--CORONER CENTRAL. EVERY UNATTENDED AND UNNATURAL DEATH IN THE STATE IS PROCESSED HERE. BAD NEWS—

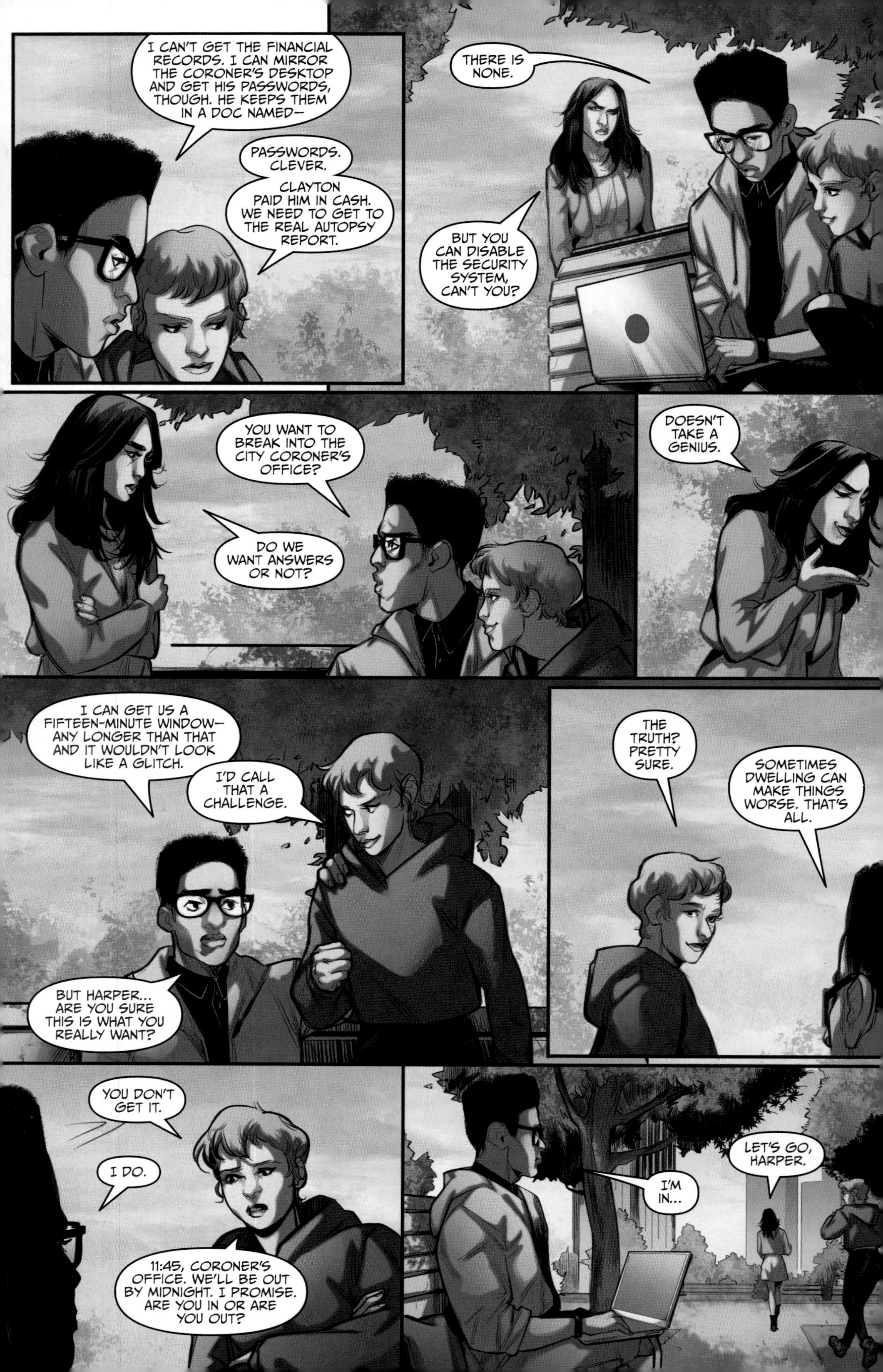

I CAN'T GET THE FINANCIAL RECORDS. I CAN MIRROR THE CORONER'S DESKTOP AND GET HIS PASSWORDS, THOUGH. HE KEEPS THEM IN A DOC NAMED—
PASSWORDS. CLEVER.
CLAYTON PAID HIM IN CASH. WE NEED TO GET TO THE REAL AUTOPSY REPORT.
THERE IS NONE.
BUT YOU CAN DISABLE THE SECURITY SYSTEM, CAN'T YOU?
YOU WANT TO BREAK INTO THE CITY CORONER'S OFFICE?
DO WE WANT ANSWERS OR NOT?
DOESN'T TAKE A GENIUS.
I CAN GET US A FIFTEEN-MINUTE WINDOW— ANY LONGER THAN THAT AND IT WOULDN'T LOOK LIKE A GLITCH.
I'D CALL THAT A CHALLENGE.
BUT HARPER... ARE YOU SURE THIS IS WHAT YOU REALLY WANT?
THE TRUTH? PRETTY SURE.
SOMETIMES DWELLING CAN MAKE THINGS WORSE. THAT'S ALL.
YOU DON'T GET IT.
I DO.
11:45, CORONER'S OFFICE. WE'LL BE OUT BY MIDNIGHT. I PROMISE. ARE YOU IN OR ARE YOU OUT?
I'M IN...
LET'S GO, HARPER.

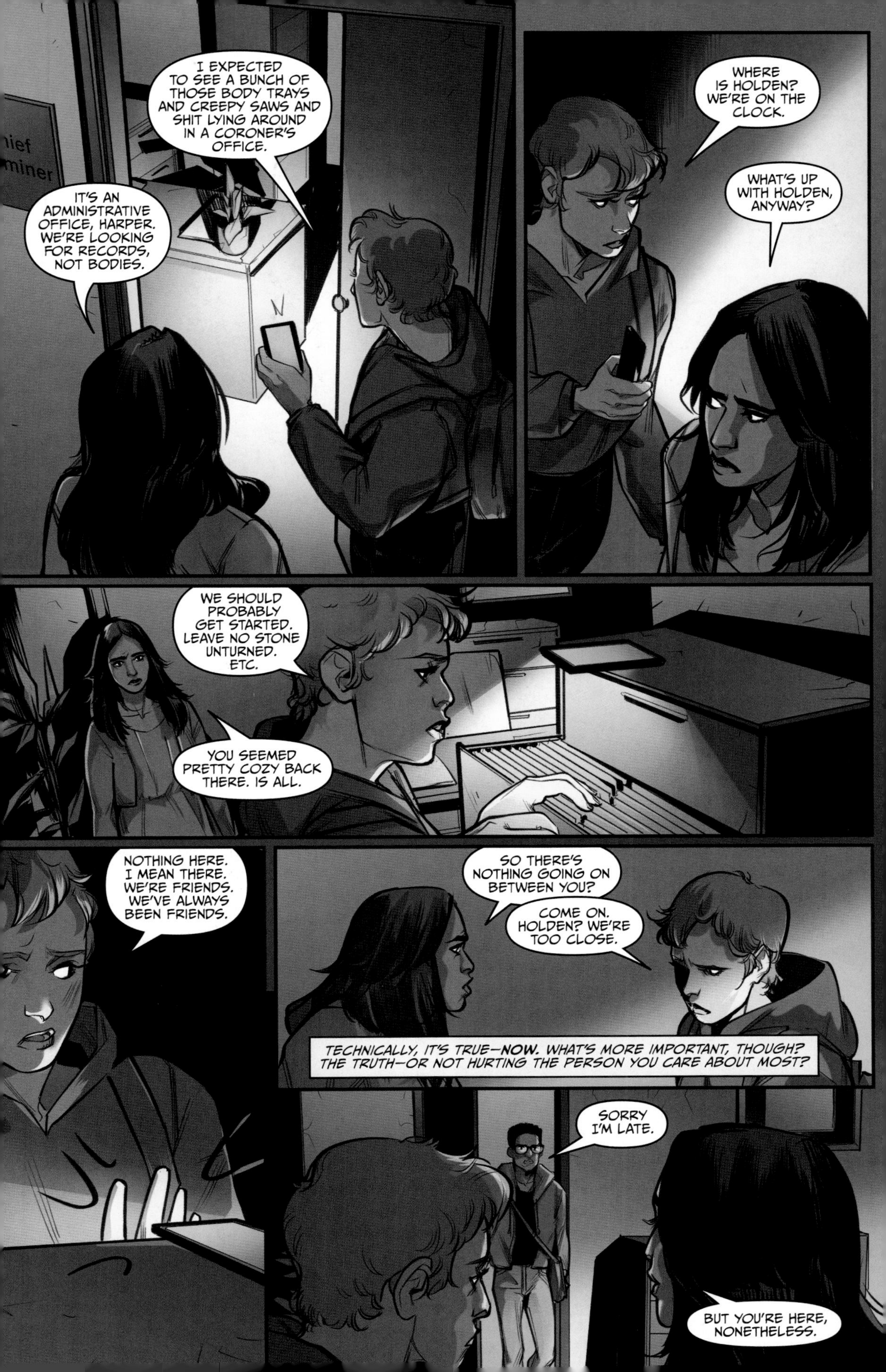

ief
miner
I EXPECTED TO SEE A BUNCH OF THOSE BODY TRAYS AND CREEPY SAWS AND SHIT LYING AROUND IN A CORONER'S OFFICE.
IT'S AN ADMINISTRATIVE OFFICE, HARPER. WE'RE LOOKING FOR RECORDS, NOT BODIES.
WHERE IS HOLDEN? WE'RE ON THE CLOCK.
WHAT'S UP WITH HOLDEN, ANYWAY?
WE SHOULD PROBABLY GET STARTED. LEAVE NO STONE UNTURNED. ETC.
YOU SEEMED PRETTY COZY BACK THERE. IS ALL.
NOTHING HERE. I MEAN THERE. WE'RE FRIENDS. WE'VE ALWAYS BEEN FRIENDS.
SO THERE'S NOTHING GOING ON BETWEEN YOU?
COME ON. HOLDEN? WE'RE TOO CLOSE.
TECHNICALLY, IT'S TRUE—NOW. WHAT'S MORE IMPORTANT, THOUGH? THE TRUTH—OR NOT HURTING THE PERSON YOU CARE ABOUT MOST?
SORRY I'M LATE.
BUT YOU'RE HERE, NONETHELESS.

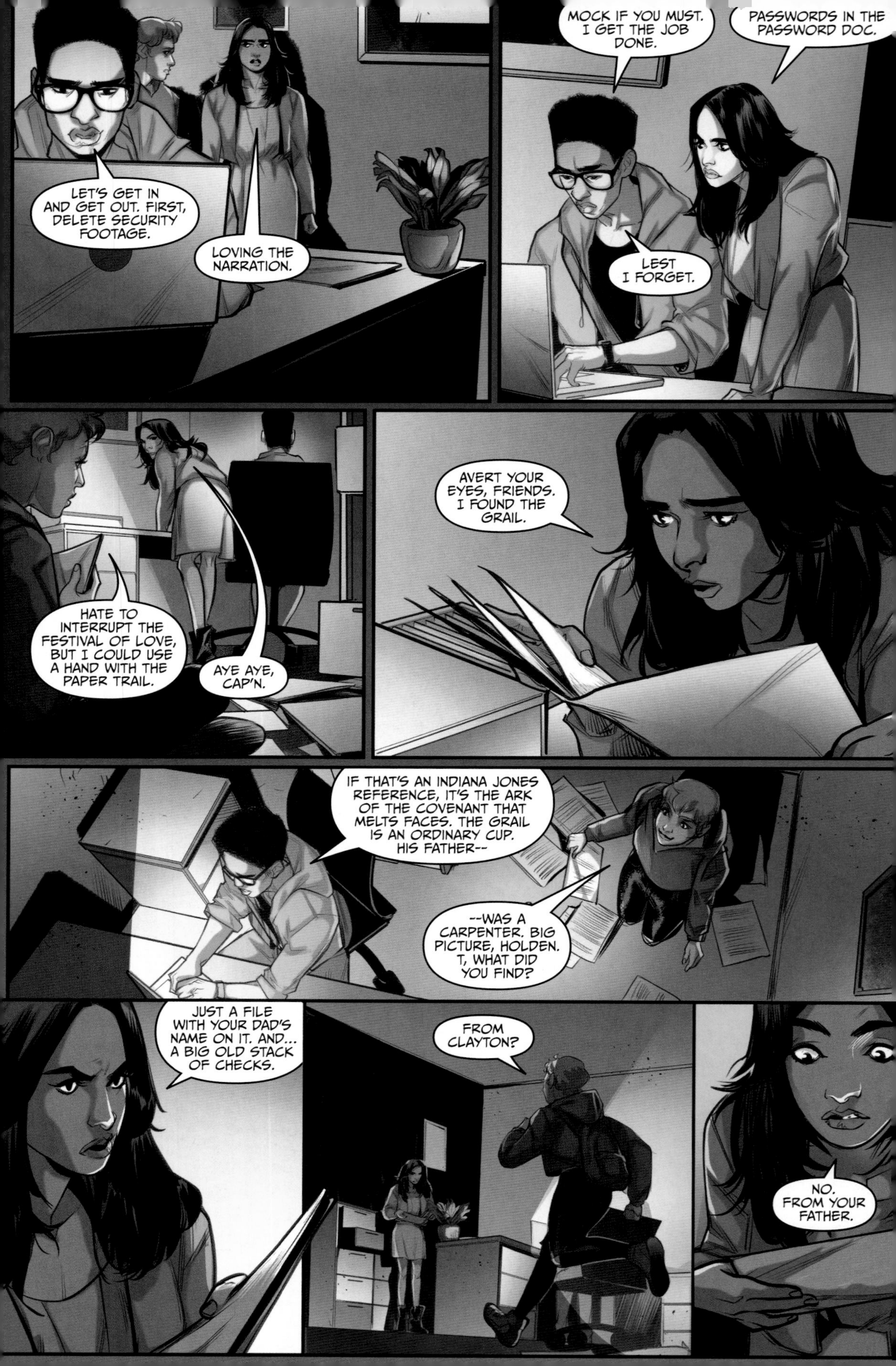
LET'S GET IN AND GET OUT. FIRST, DELETE SECURITY FOOTAGE.
LOVING THE NARRATION.
MOCK IF YOU MUST. I GET THE JOB DONE.
PASSWORDS IN THE PASSWORD DOC.
LEST I FORGET.
HATE TO INTERRUPT THE FESTIVAL OF LOVE, BUT I COULD USE A HAND WITH THE PAPER TRAIL.
AYE AYE, CAP'N.
AVERT YOUR EYES, FRIENDS. I FOUND THE GRAIL.
IF THAT'S AN INDIANA JONES REFERENCE, IT'S THE ARK OF THE COVENANT THAT MELTS FACES. THE GRAIL IS AN ORDINARY CUP. HIS FATHER--
--WAS A CARPENTER. BIG PICTURE, HOLDEN. T, WHAT DID YOU FIND?
JUST A FILE WITH YOUR DAD'S NAME ON IT. AND... A BIG OLD STACK OF CHECKS.
FROM CLAYTON?
NO. FROM YOUR FATHER.

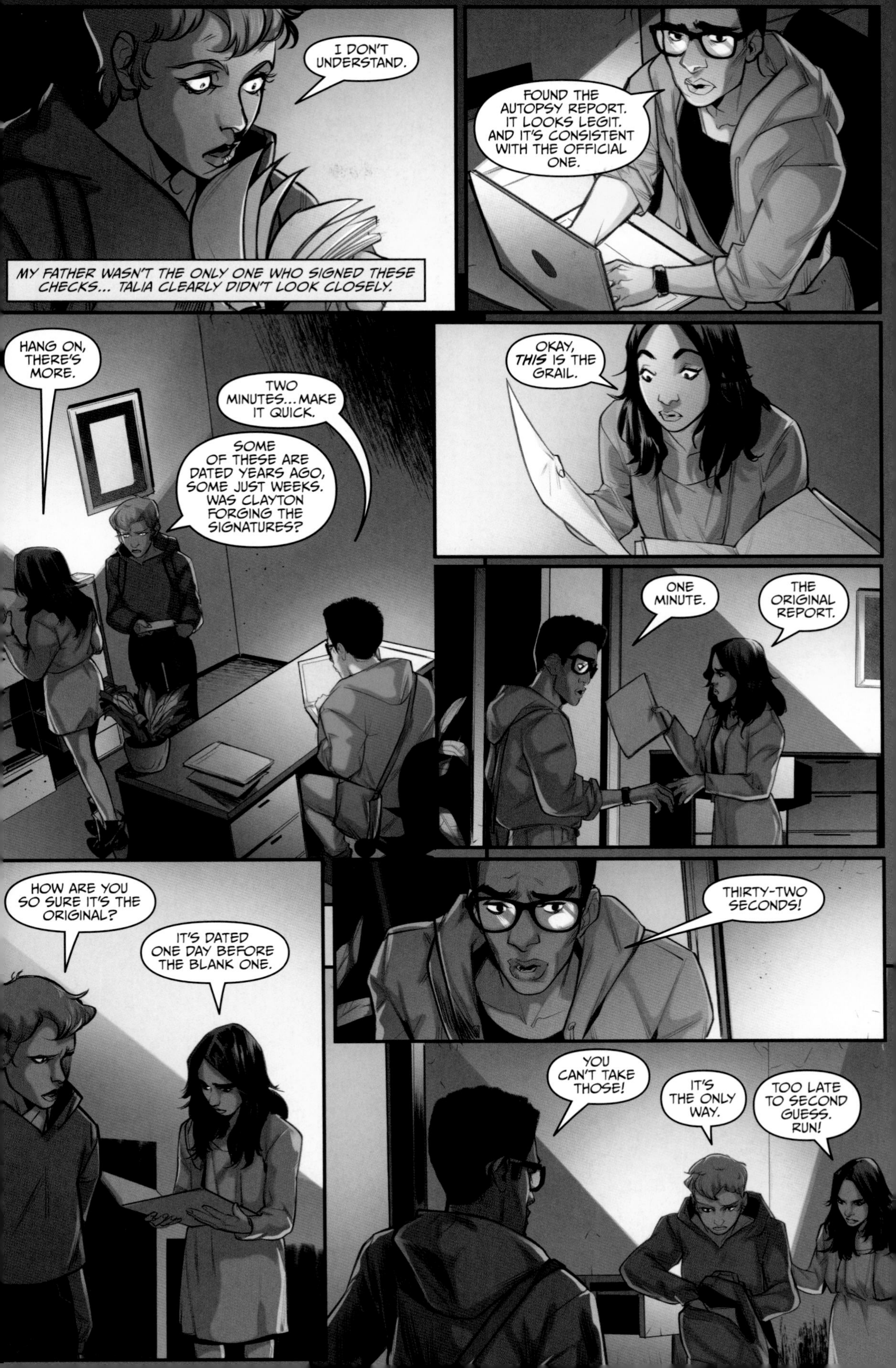
I DON'T UNDERSTAND.
MY FATHER WASN'T THE ONLY ONE WHO SIGNED THESE CHECKS... TALIA CLEARLY DIDN'T LOOK CLOSELY.
FOUND THE AUTOPSY REPORT. IT LOOKS LEGIT. AND IT'S CONSISTENT WITH THE OFFICIAL ONE.
HANG ON, THERE'S MORE.
TWO MINUTES...MAKE IT QUICK.
SOME OF THESE ARE DATED YEARS AGO, SOME JUST WEEKS. WAS CLAYTON FORGING THE SIGNATURES?
OKAY, THIS IS THE GRAIL.
ONE MINUTE.
THE ORIGINAL REPORT.
HOW ARE YOU SO SURE IT'S THE ORIGINAL?
IT'S DATED ONE DAY BEFORE THE BLANK ONE.
THIRTY-TWO SECONDS!
YOU CAN'T TAKE THOSE!
IT'S THE ONLY WAY.
TOO LATE TO SECOND GUESS. RUN!

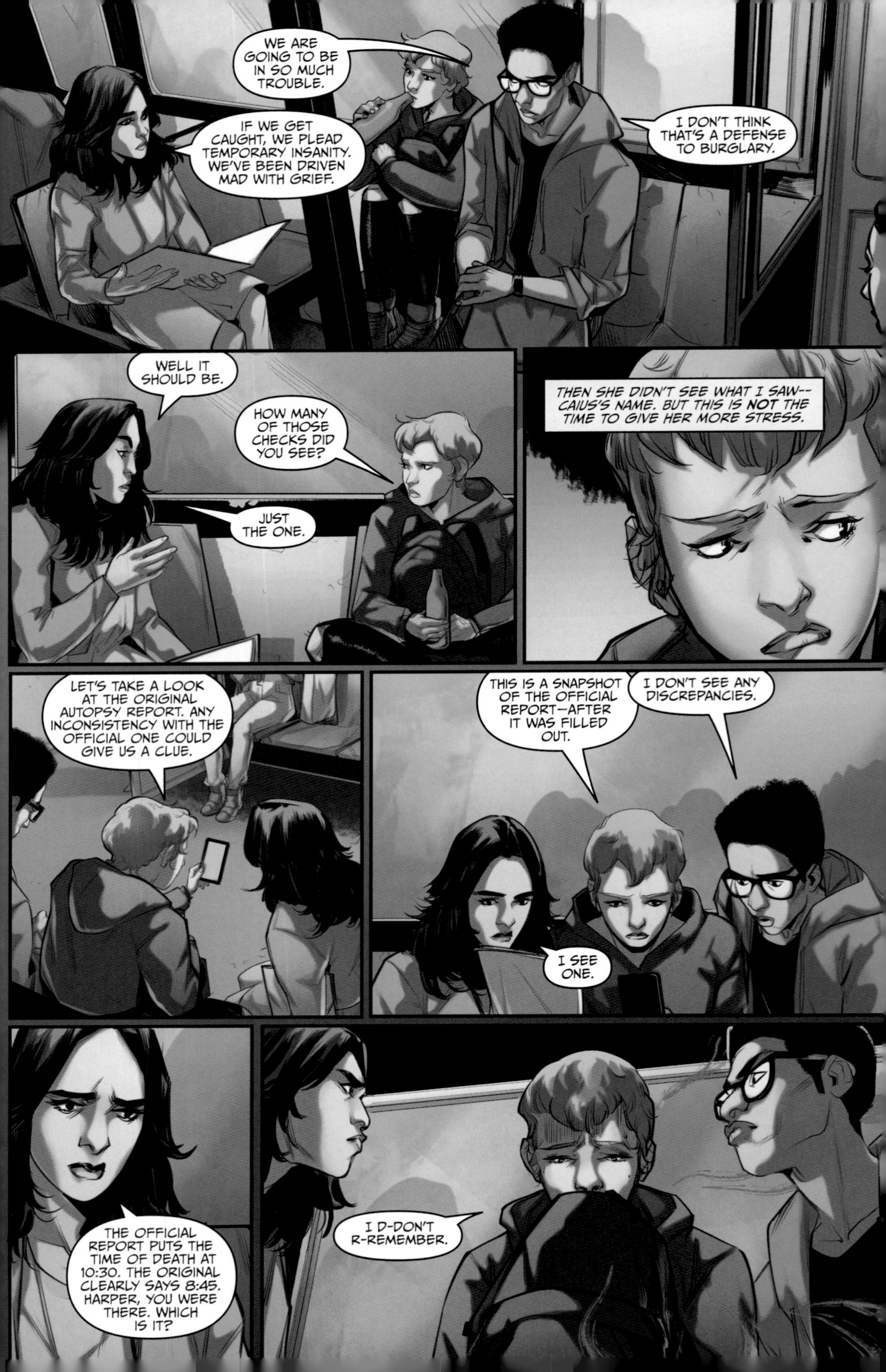
WE ARE GOING TO BE IN SO MUCH TROUBLE.
IF WE GET CAUGHT, WE PLEAD TEMPORARY INSANITY. WE'VE BEEN DRIVEN MAD WITH GRIEF.
I DON'T THINK THAT'S A DEFENSE TO BURGLARY.
WELL IT SHOULD BE.
HOW MANY OF THOSE CHECKS DID YOU SEE?
JUST THE ONE.
THEN SHE DIDN'T SEE WHAT I SAW-- CAIUS'S NAME. BUT THIS IS NOT THE TIME TO GIVE HER MORE STRESS.
LET'S TAKE A LOOK AT THE ORIGINAL AUTOPSY REPORT. ANY INCONSISTENCY WITH THE OFFICIAL ONE COULD GIVE US A CLUE.
THIS IS A SNAPSHOT OF THE OFFICIAL REPORT—AFTER IT WAS FILLED OUT.
I DON'T SEE ANY DISCREPANCIES.
I SEE ONE.
THE OFFICIAL REPORT PUTS THE TIME OF DEATH AT 10:30. THE ORIGINAL CLEARLY SAYS 8:45. HARPER, YOU WERE THERE. WHICH IS IT?
I D-DON'T R-REMEMBER.

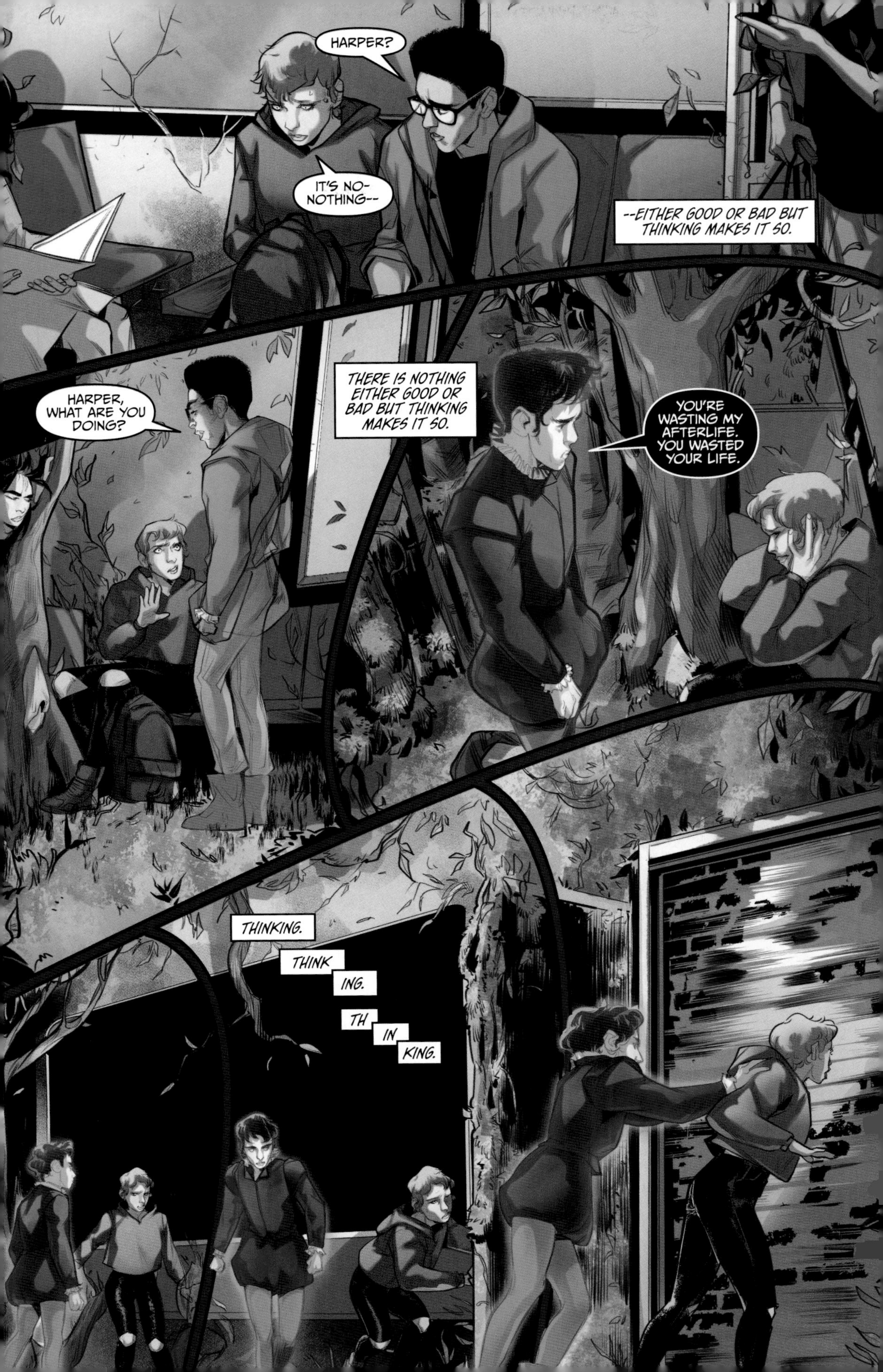
HARPER?
IT'S NO-NOTHING--
--EITHER GOOD OR BAD BUT THINKING MAKES IT SO.
HARPER, WHAT ARE YOU DOING?
THERE IS NOTHING EITHER GOOD OR BAD BUT THINKING MAKES IT SO.
YOU'RE WASTING MY AFTERLIFE. YOU WASTED YOUR LIFE.
THINKING.
THINK
ING.
TH
IN
KING.

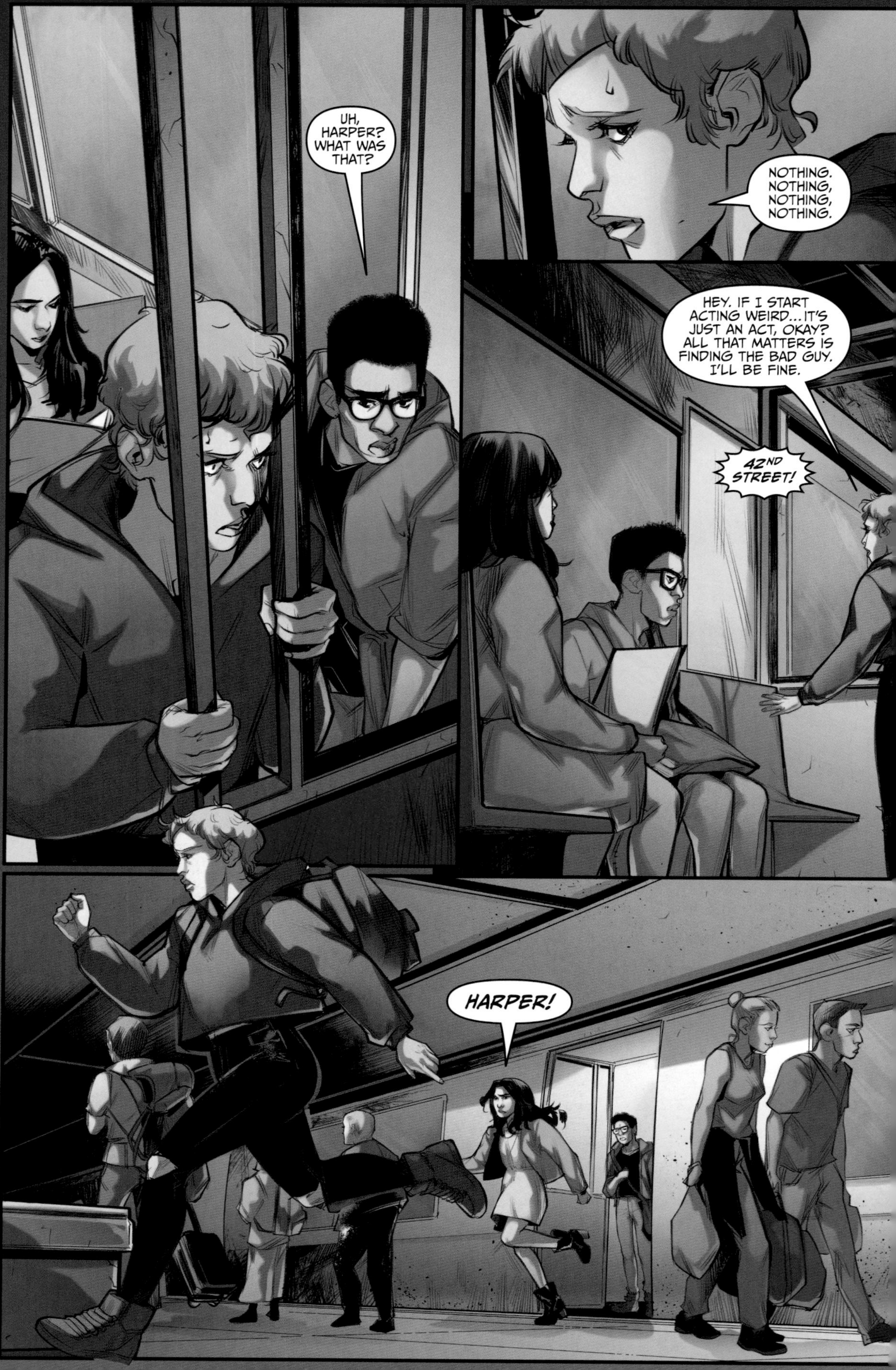
UH, HARPER? WHAT WAS THAT?
NOTHING. NOTHING, NOTHING, NOTHING.
HEY. IF I START ACTING WEIRD...IT'S JUST AN ACT, OKAY? ALL THAT MATTERS IS FINDING THE BAD GUY. I'LL BE FINE.
42ND STREET!
HARPER!

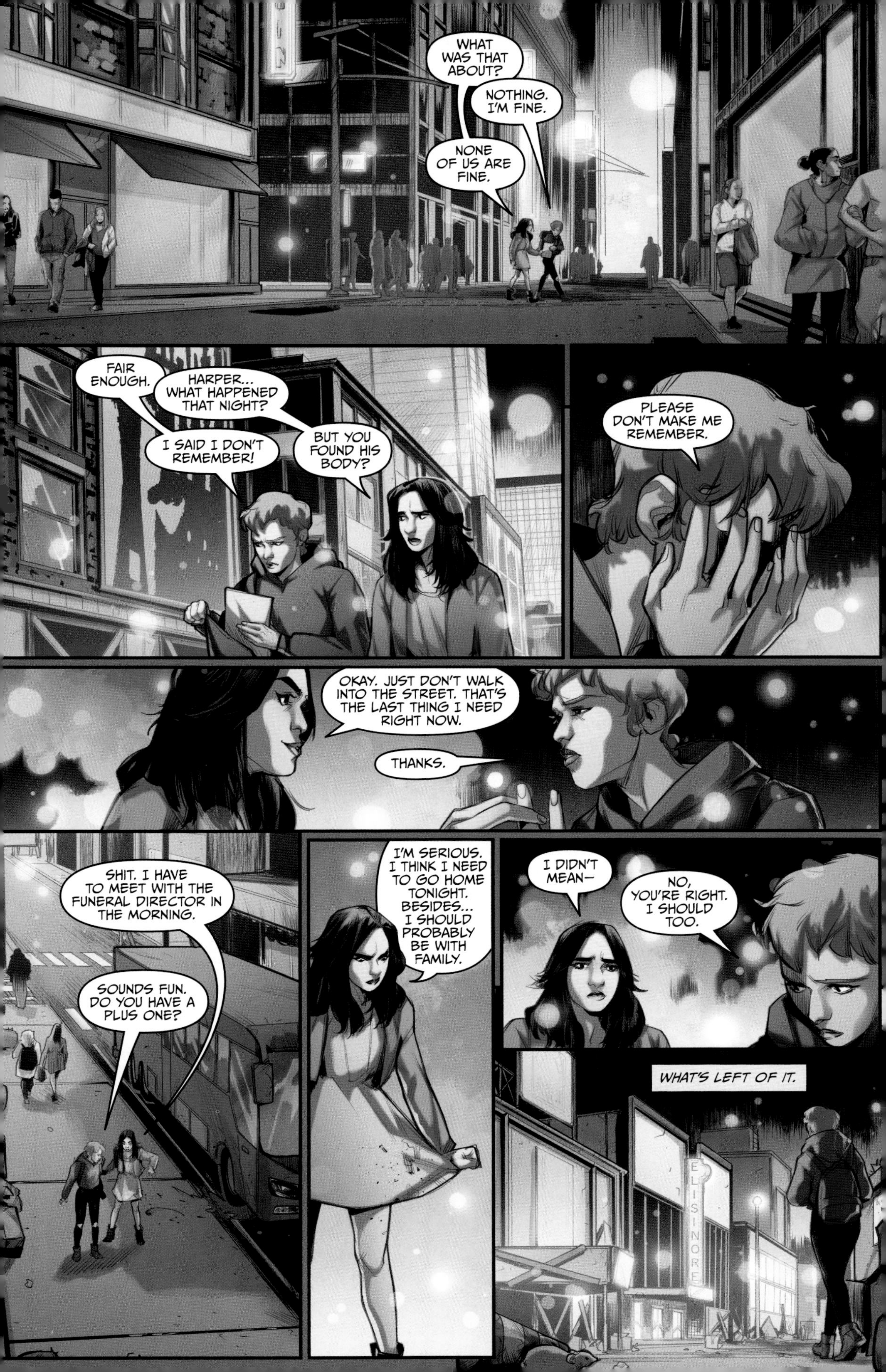
WHAT WAS THAT ABOUT?
NOTHING. I'M FINE.
NONE OF US ARE FINE.
FAIR ENOUGH.
HARPER... WHAT HAPPENED THAT NIGHT?
I SAID I DON'T REMEMBER!
BUT YOU FOUND HIS BODY?
PLEASE DON'T MAKE ME REMEMBER.
OKAY. JUST DON'T WALK INTO THE STREET. THAT'S THE LAST THING I NEED RIGHT NOW.
THANKS.
SHIT. I HAVE TO MEET WITH THE FUNERAL DIRECTOR IN THE MORNING.
SOUNDS FUN. DO YOU HAVE A PLUS ONE?
I'M SERIOUS. I THINK I NEED TO GO HOME TONIGHT. BESIDES... I SHOULD PROBABLY BE WITH FAMILY.
I DIDN'T MEAN—
NO, YOU'RE RIGHT. I SHOULD TOO.
WHAT'S LEFT OF IT.
ELSINORE

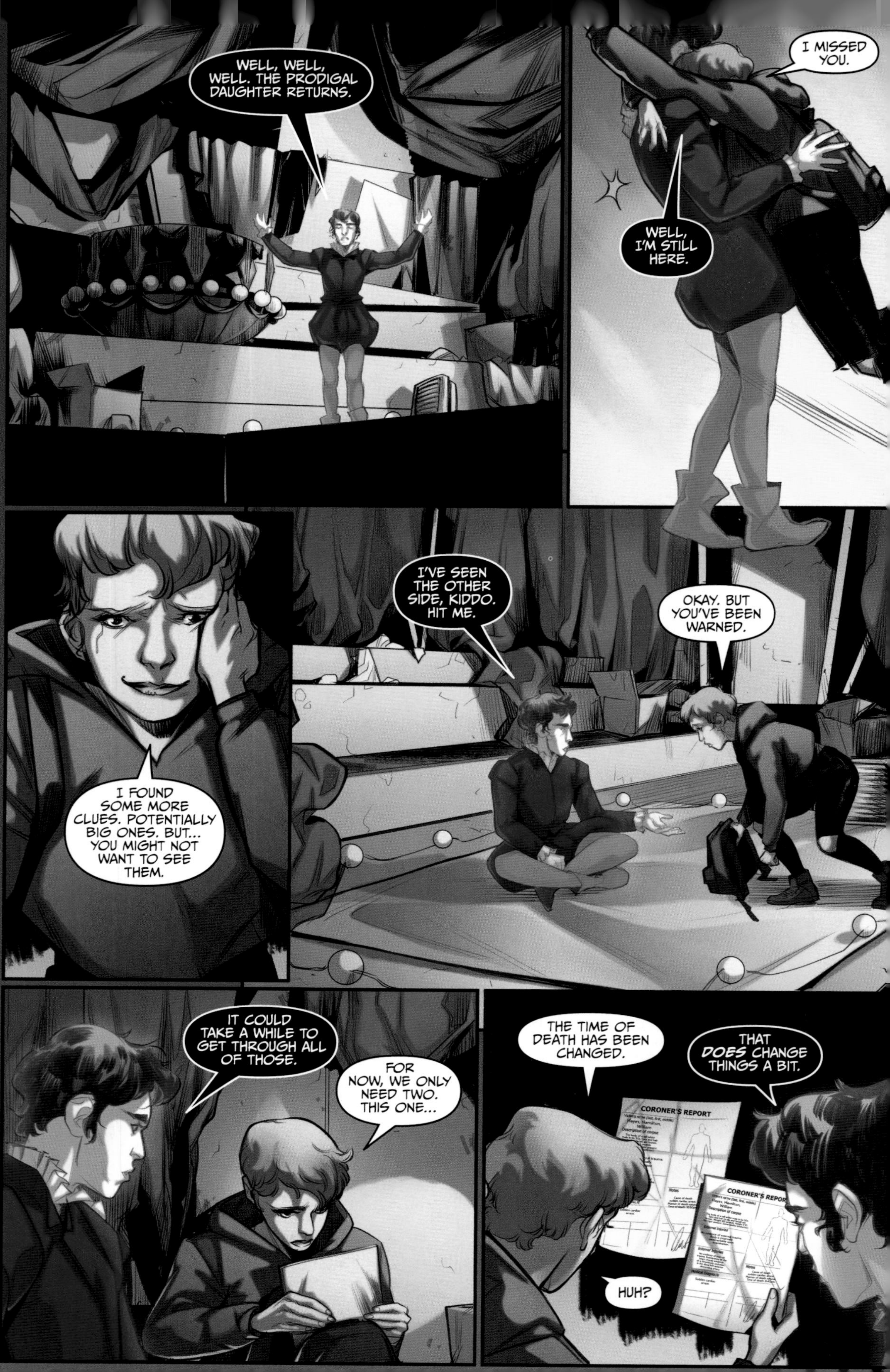
WELL, WELL, WELL. THE PRODIGAL DAUGHTER RETURNS.
I MISSED YOU.
WELL, I'M STILL HERE.
I FOUND SOME MORE CLUES. POTENTIALLY BIG ONES. BUT... YOU MIGHT NOT WANT TO SEE THEM.
I'VE SEEN THE OTHER SIDE, KIDDO. HIT ME.
OKAY. BUT YOU'VE BEEN WARNED.
IT COULD TAKE A WHILE TO GET THROUGH ALL OF THOSE.
FOR NOW, WE ONLY NEED TWO. THIS ONE...
THE TIME OF DEATH HAS BEEN CHANGED.
HUH?
THAT DOES CHANGE THINGS A BIT.
CORONER'S REPORT
CORONER'S REPORT

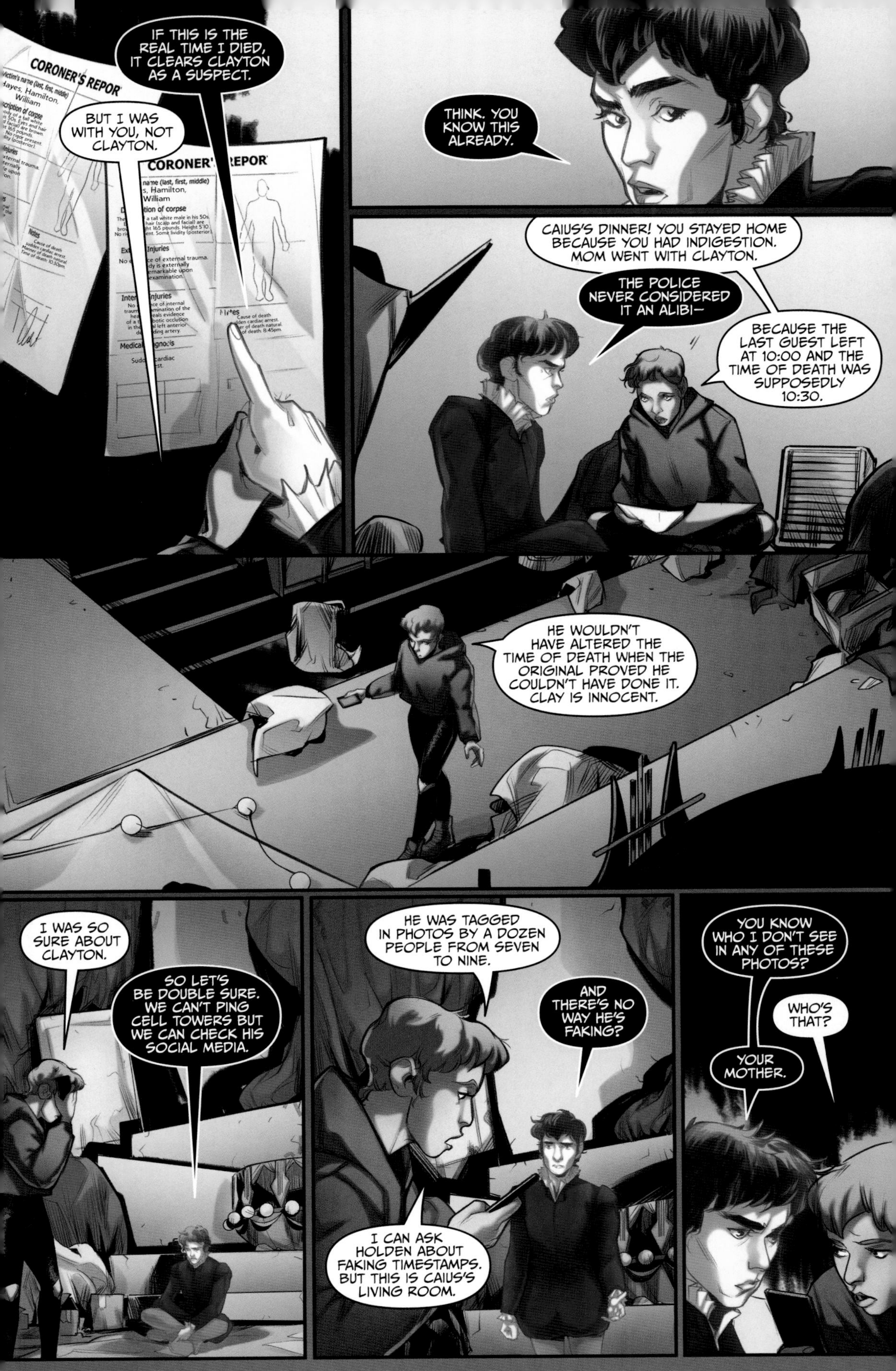
CORONER'S REPOR
Hayes, Hamilton, William
IF THIS IS THE REAL TIME I DIED, IT CLEARS CLAYTON AS A SUSPECT.
BUT I WAS WITH YOU, NOT CLAYTON.
CORONER'S REPOR
Cause of death
Sudden cardiac arrest
THINK. YOU KNOW THIS ALREADY.
CAIUS'S DINNER! YOU STAYED HOME BECAUSE YOU HAD INDIGESTION. MOM WENT WITH CLAYTON.
THE POLICE NEVER CONSIDERED IT AN ALIBI—
BECAUSE THE LAST GUEST LEFT AT 10:00 AND THE TIME OF DEATH WAS SUPPOSEDLY 10:30.
HE WOULDN'T HAVE ALTERED THE TIME OF DEATH WHEN THE ORIGINAL PROVED HE COULDN'T HAVE DONE IT. CLAY IS INNOCENT.
I WAS SO SURE ABOUT CLAYTON.
SO LET'S BE DOUBLE SURE. WE CAN'T PING CELL TOWERS BUT WE CAN CHECK HIS SOCIAL MEDIA.
HE WAS TAGGED IN PHOTOS BY A DOZEN PEOPLE FROM SEVEN TO NINE.
AND THERE'S NO WAY HE'S FAKING?
I CAN ASK HOLDEN ABOUT FAKING TIMESTAMPS. BUT THIS IS CAIUS'S LIVING ROOM.
YOU KNOW WHO I DON'T SEE IN ANY OF THESE PHOTOS?
WHO'S THAT?
YOUR MOTHER.

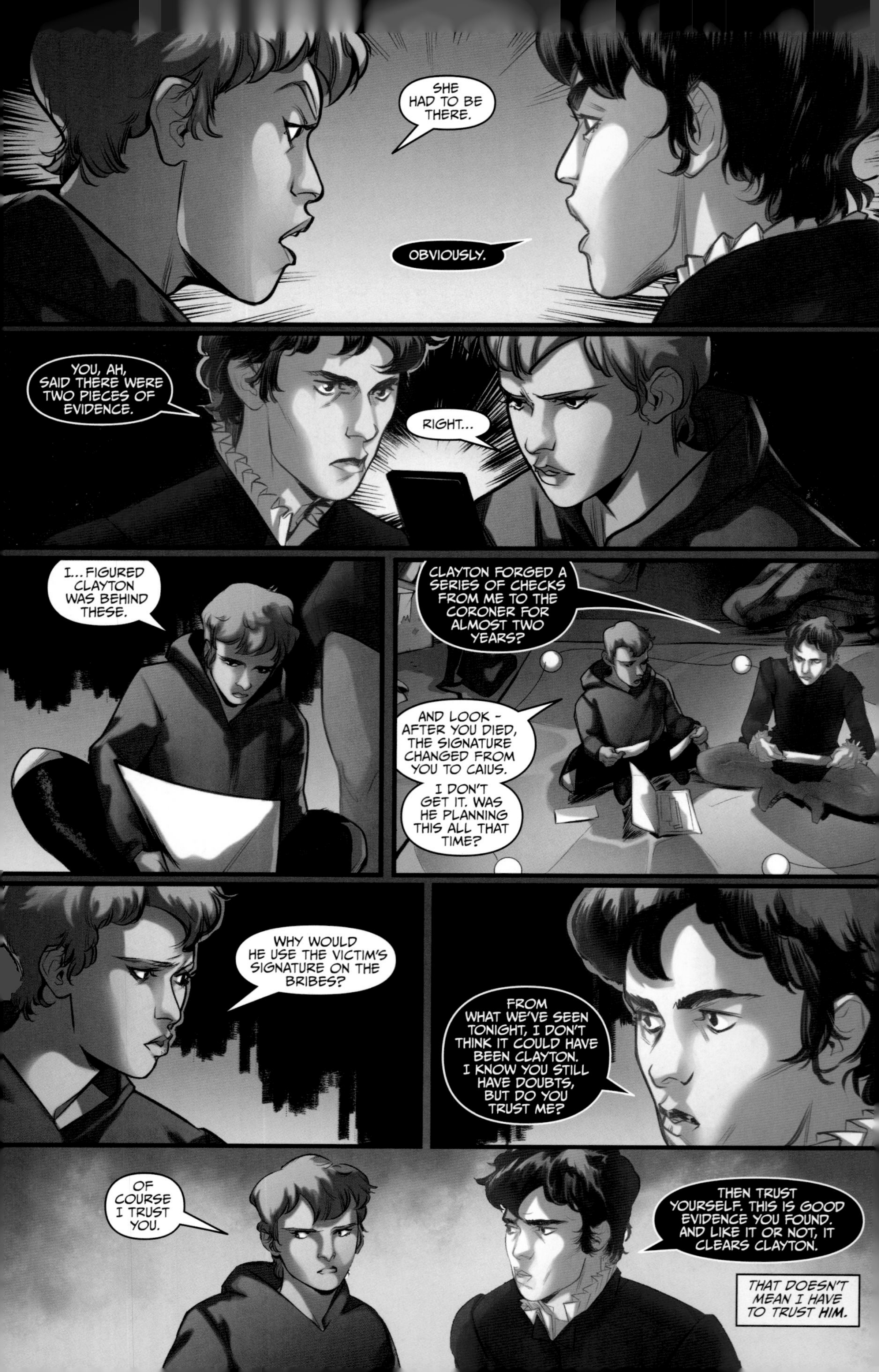
SHE HAD TO BE THERE.
OBVIOUSLY.
YOU, AH, SAID THERE WERE TWO PIECES OF EVIDENCE.
RIGHT...
I...FIGURED CLAYTON WAS BEHIND THESE.
CLAYTON FORGED A SERIES OF CHECKS FROM ME TO THE CORONER FOR ALMOST TWO YEARS?
AND LOOK - AFTER YOU DIED, THE SIGNATURE CHANGED FROM YOU TO CAIUS.
I DON'T GET IT. WAS HE PLANNING THIS ALL THAT TIME?
WHY WOULD HE USE THE VICTIM'S SIGNATURE ON THE BRIBES?
FROM WHAT WE'VE SEEN TONIGHT, I DON'T THINK IT COULD HAVE BEEN CLAYTON. I KNOW YOU STILL HAVE DOUBTS, BUT DO YOU TRUST ME?
OF COURSE I TRUST YOU.
THEN TRUST YOURSELF. THIS IS GOOD EVIDENCE YOU FOUND. AND LIKE IT OR NOT, IT CLEARS CLAYTON.
THAT DOESN'T MEAN I HAVE TO TRUST HIM.

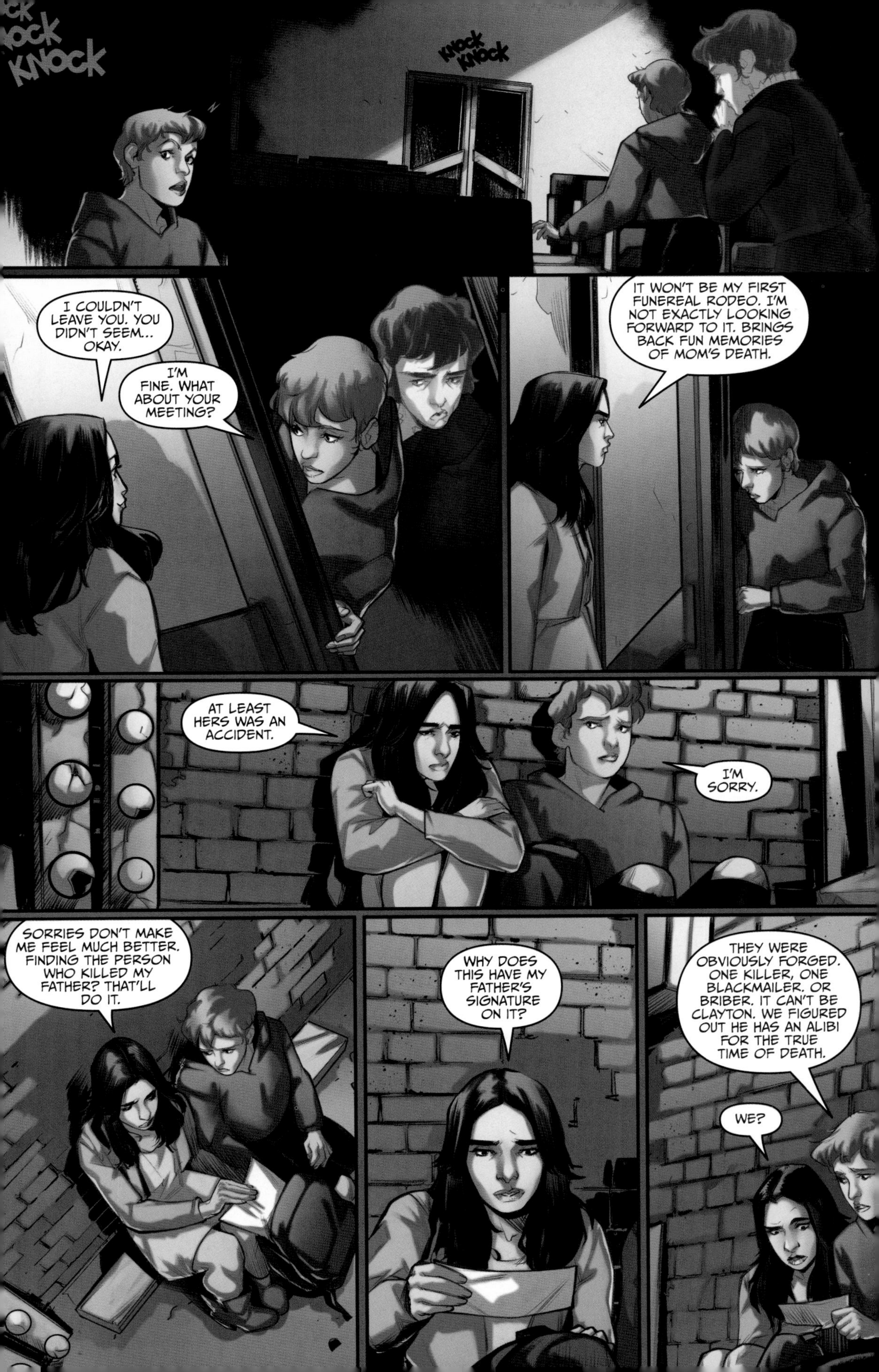
KNOCK
KNOCK
KNOCK KNOCK
I COULDN'T LEAVE YOU. YOU DIDN'T SEEM... OKAY.
I'M FINE. WHAT ABOUT YOUR MEETING?
IT WON'T BE MY FIRST FUNEREAL RODEO. I'M NOT EXACTLY LOOKING FORWARD TO IT. BRINGS BACK FUN MEMORIES OF MOM'S DEATH.
AT LEAST HERS WAS AN ACCIDENT.
I'M SORRY.
SORRIES DON'T MAKE ME FEEL MUCH BETTER. FINDING THE PERSON WHO KILLED MY FATHER? THAT'LL DO IT.
WHY DOES THIS HAVE MY FATHER'S SIGNATURE ON IT?
THEY WERE OBVIOUSLY FORGED. ONE KILLER, ONE BLACKMAILER. OR BRIBER. IT CAN'T BE CLAYTON. WE FIGURED OUT HE HAS AN ALIBI FOR THE TRUE TIME OF DEATH.
WE?

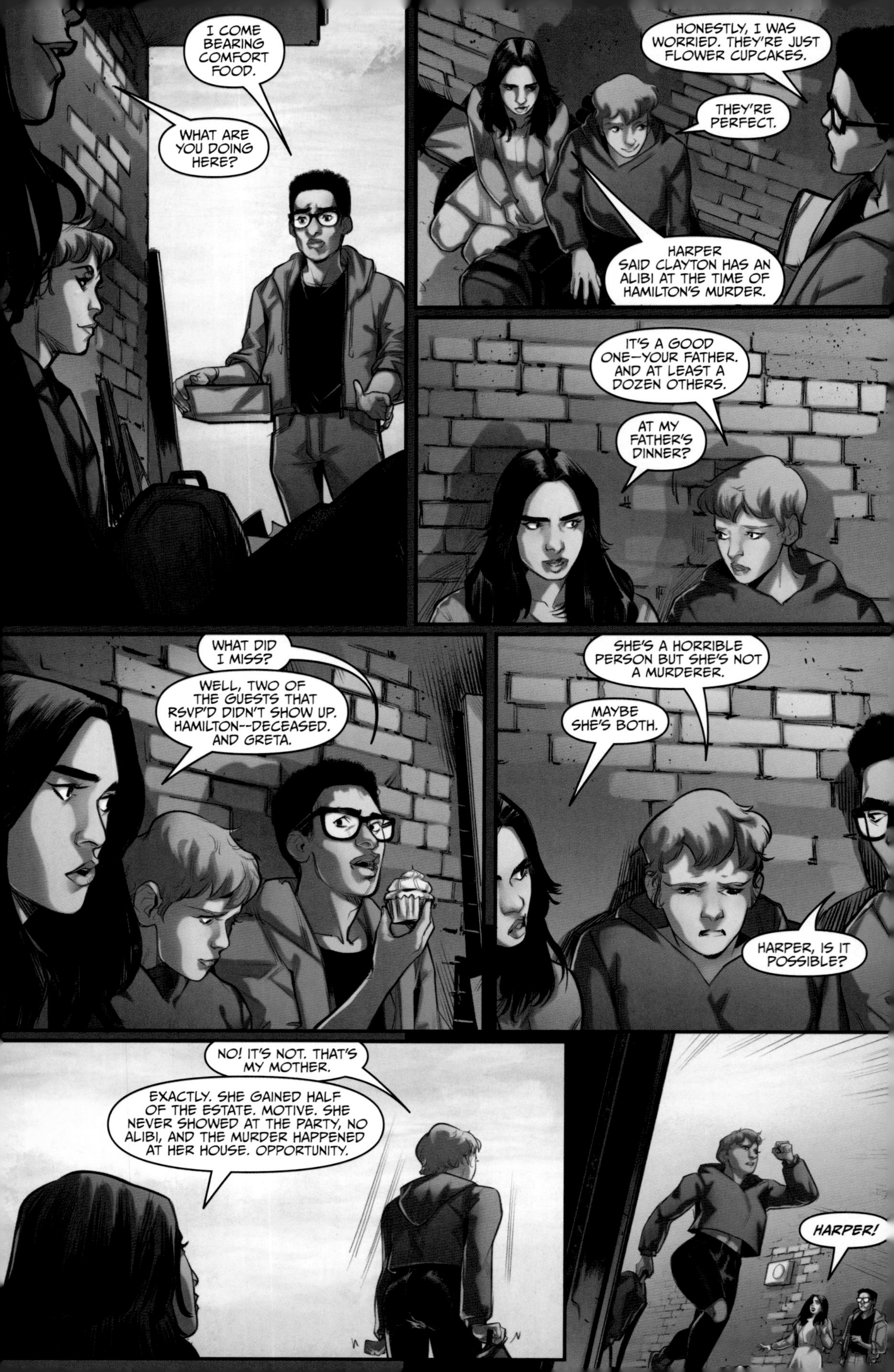
I COME BEARING COMFORT FOOD.
WHAT ARE YOU DOING HERE?
HONESTLY, I WAS WORRIED. THEY'RE JUST FLOWER CUPCAKES.
THEY'RE PERFECT.
HARPER SAID CLAYTON HAS AN ALIBI AT THE TIME OF HAMILTON'S MURDER.
IT'S A GOOD ONE—YOUR FATHER. AND AT LEAST A DOZEN OTHERS.
AT MY FATHER'S DINNER?
WHAT DID I MISS?
WELL, TWO OF THE GUESTS THAT RSVP'D DIDN'T SHOW UP. HAMILTON--DECEASED. AND GRETA.
SHE'S A HORRIBLE PERSON BUT SHE'S NOT A MURDERER.
MAYBE SHE'S BOTH.
HARPER, IS IT POSSIBLE?
NO! IT'S NOT. THAT'S MY MOTHER.
EXACTLY. SHE GAINED HALF OF THE ESTATE. MOTIVE. SHE NEVER SHOWED AT THE PARTY, NO ALIBI, AND THE MURDER HAPPENED AT HER HOUSE. OPPORTUNITY.
HARPER!

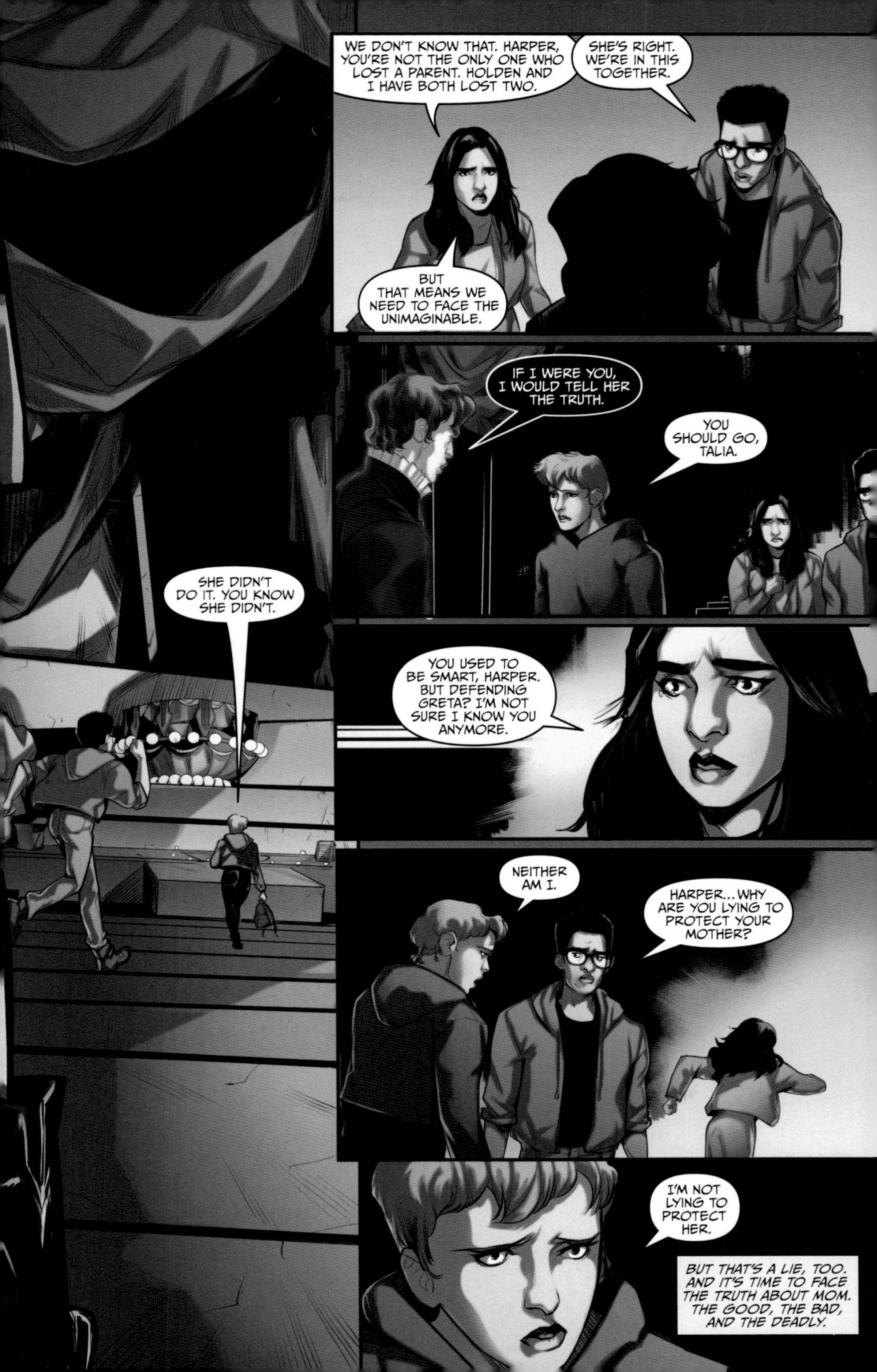
WE DON'T KNOW THAT. HARPER, YOU'RE NOT THE ONLY ONE WHO LOST A PARENT. HOLDEN AND I HAVE BOTH LOST TWO.
SHE'S RIGHT. WE'RE IN THIS TOGETHER.
BUT THAT MEANS WE NEED TO FACE THE UNIMAGINABLE.
IF I WERE YOU, I WOULD TELL HER THE TRUTH.
YOU SHOULD GO, TALIA.
SHE DIDN'T DO IT. YOU KNOW SHE DIDN'T.
YOU USED TO BE SMART, HARPER. BUT DEFENDING GRETA? I'M NOT SURE I KNOW YOU ANYMORE.
NEITHER AM I.
HARPER... WHY ARE YOU LYING TO PROTECT YOUR MOTHER?
I'M NOT LYING TO PROTECT HER.
BUT THAT'S A LIE, TOO. AND IT'S TIME TO FACE THE TRUTH ABOUT MOM. THE GOOD, THE BAD, AND THE DEADLY.

Chapter Four

AS EASY
AS LYING

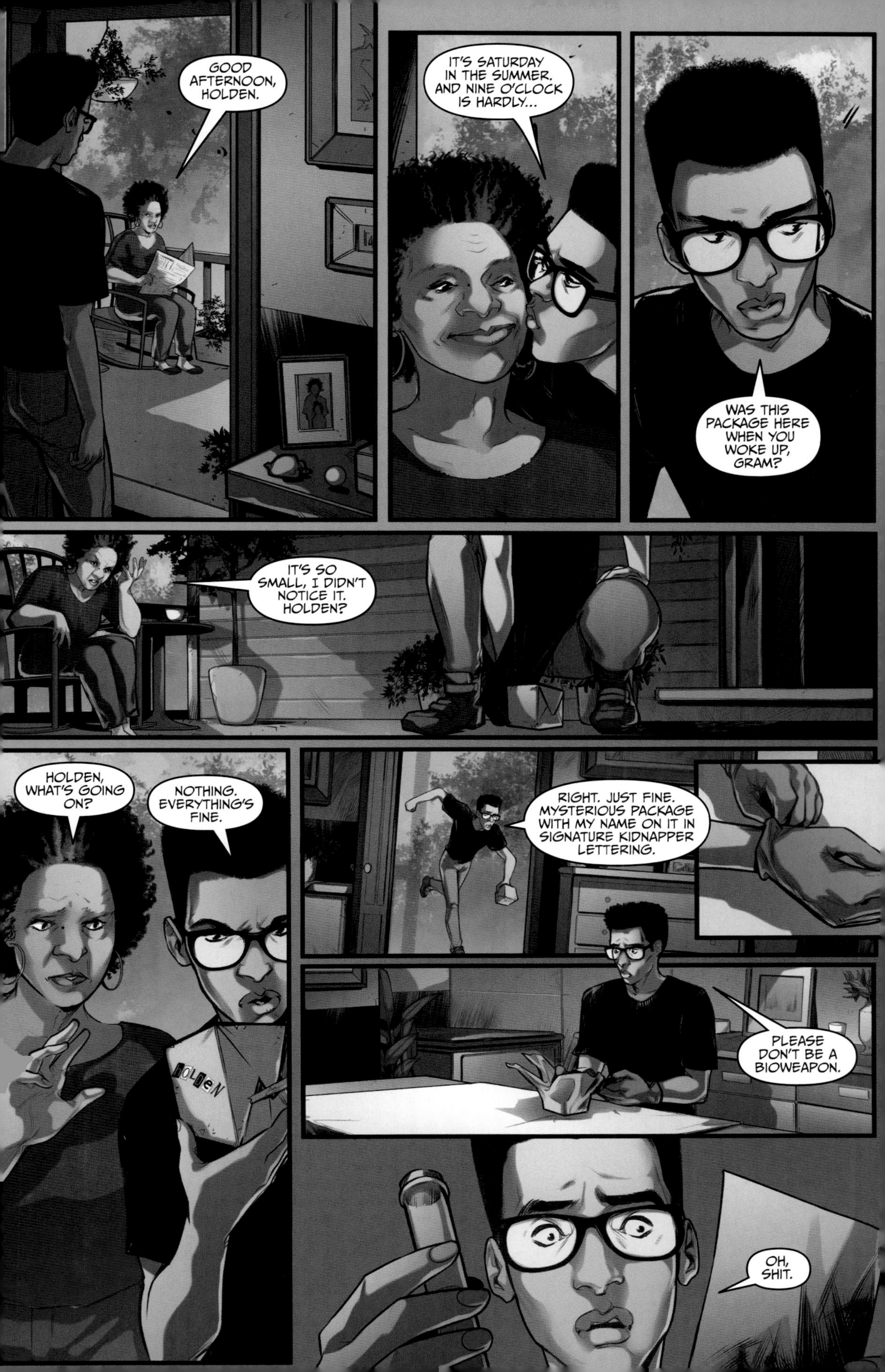
GOOD AFTERNOON, HOLDEN.
IT'S SATURDAY IN THE SUMMER. AND NINE O'CLOCK IS HARDLY...
WAS THIS PACKAGE HERE WHEN YOU WOKE UP, GRAM?
IT'S SO SMALL, I DIDN'T NOTICE IT. HOLDEN?
HOLDEN, WHAT'S GOING ON?
NOTHING. EVERYTHING'S FINE.
HOLDEN
RIGHT. JUST FINE. MYSTERIOUS PACKAGE WITH MY NAME ON IT IN SIGNATURE KIDNAPPER LETTERING.
PLEASE DON'T BE A BIOWEAPON.
OH, SHIT.

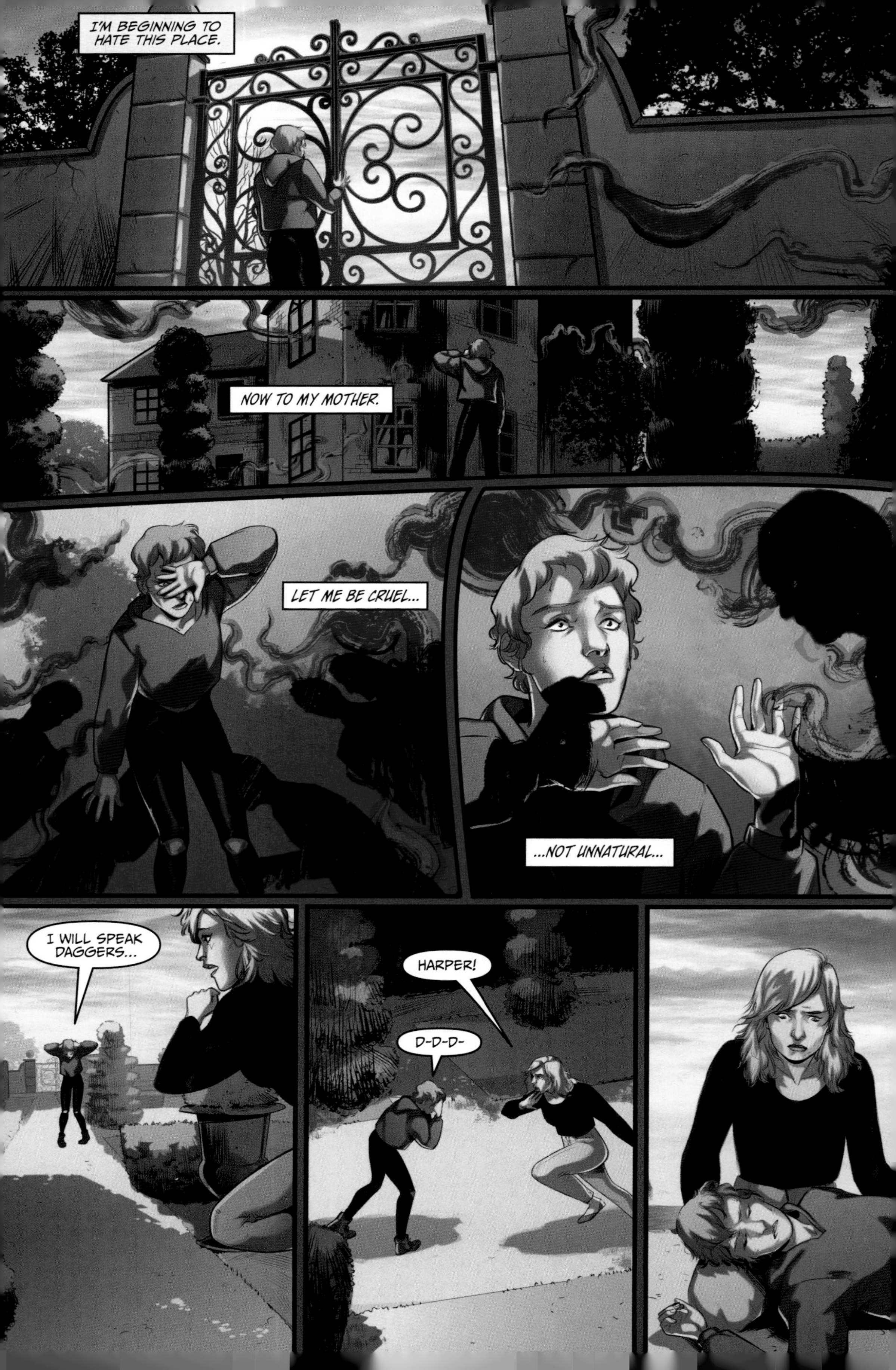
I'M BEGINNING TO HATE THIS PLACE.
NOW TO MY MOTHER.
LET ME BE CRUEL...
...NOT UNNATURAL...
I WILL SPEAK DAGGERS...
HARPER!
D-D-D-

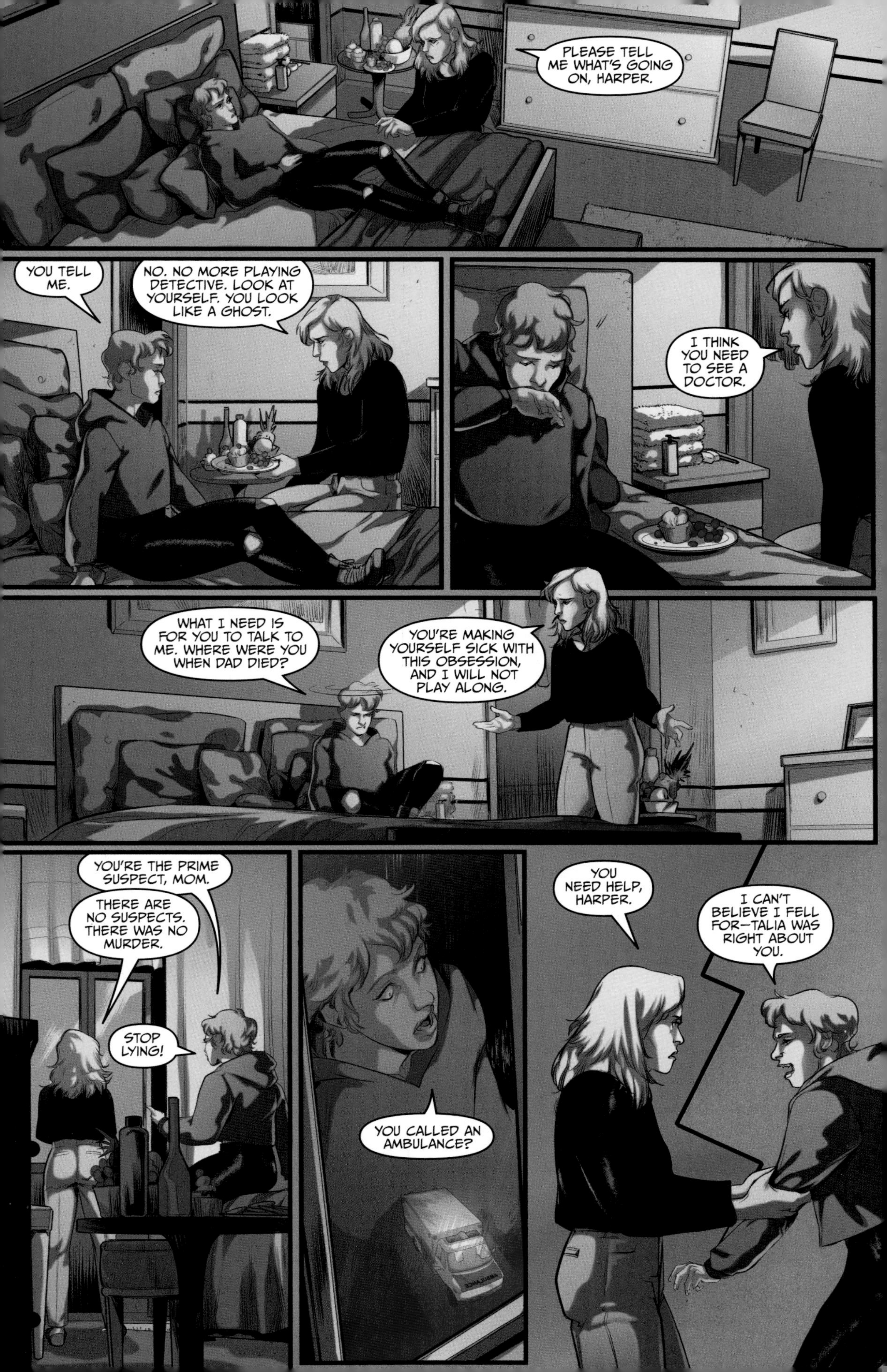
PLEASE TELL ME WHAT'S GOING ON, HARPER.
YOU TELL ME.
NO. NO MORE PLAYING DETECTIVE. LOOK AT YOURSELF. YOU LOOK LIKE A GHOST.
I THINK YOU NEED TO SEE A DOCTOR.
WHAT I NEED IS FOR YOU TO TALK TO ME. WHERE WERE YOU WHEN DAD DIED?
YOU'RE MAKING YOURSELF SICK WITH THIS OBSESSION, AND I WILL NOT PLAY ALONG.
YOU'RE THE PRIME SUSPECT, MOM.
THERE ARE NO SUSPECTS. THERE WAS NO MURDER.
STOP LYING!
YOU CALLED AN AMBULANCE?
YOU NEED HELP, HARPER.
I CAN'T BELIEVE I FELL FOR—TALIA WAS RIGHT ABOUT YOU.

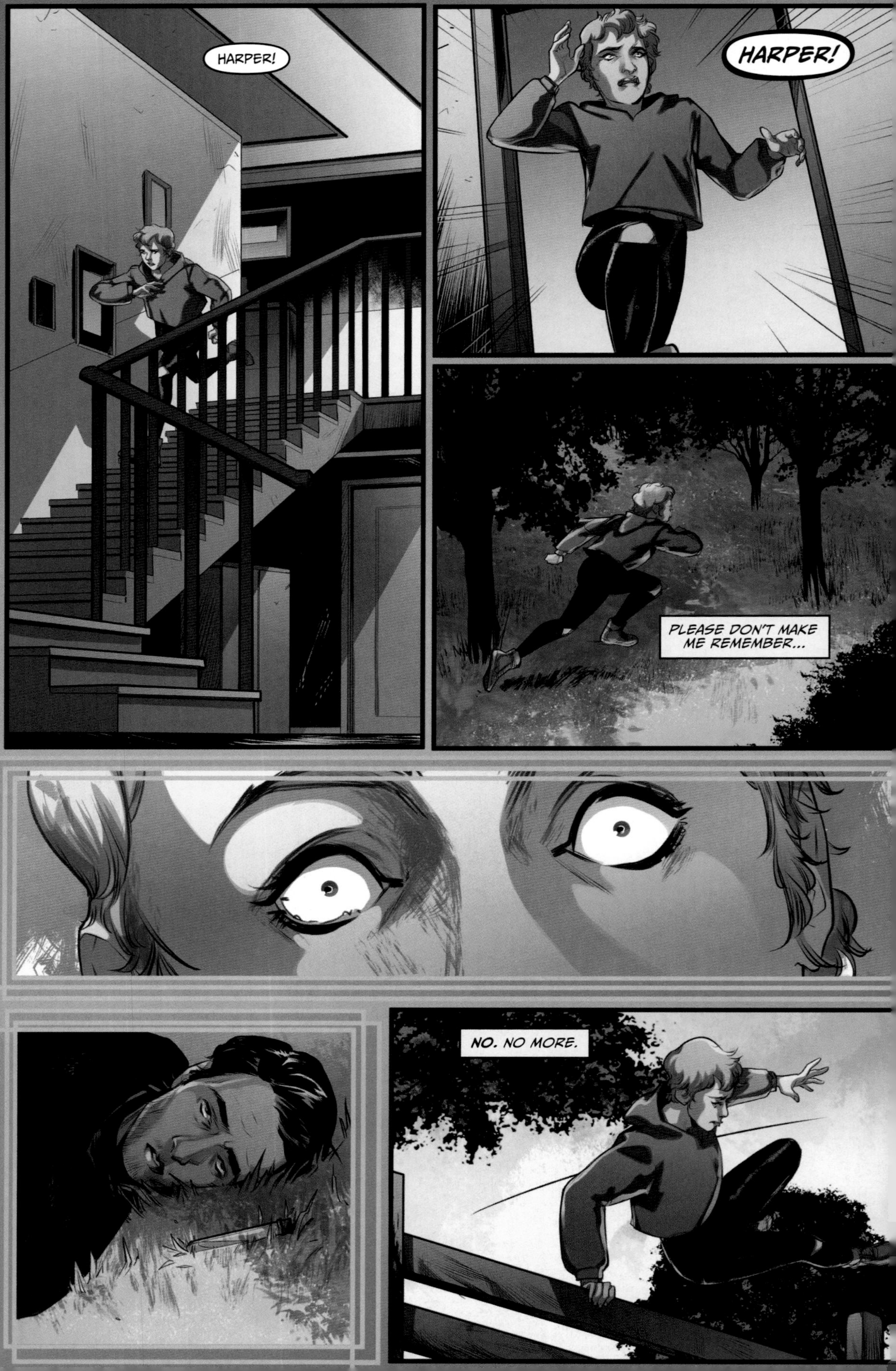
HARPER!
HARPER!
PLEASE DON'T MAKE ME REMEMBER...
NO. NO MORE.

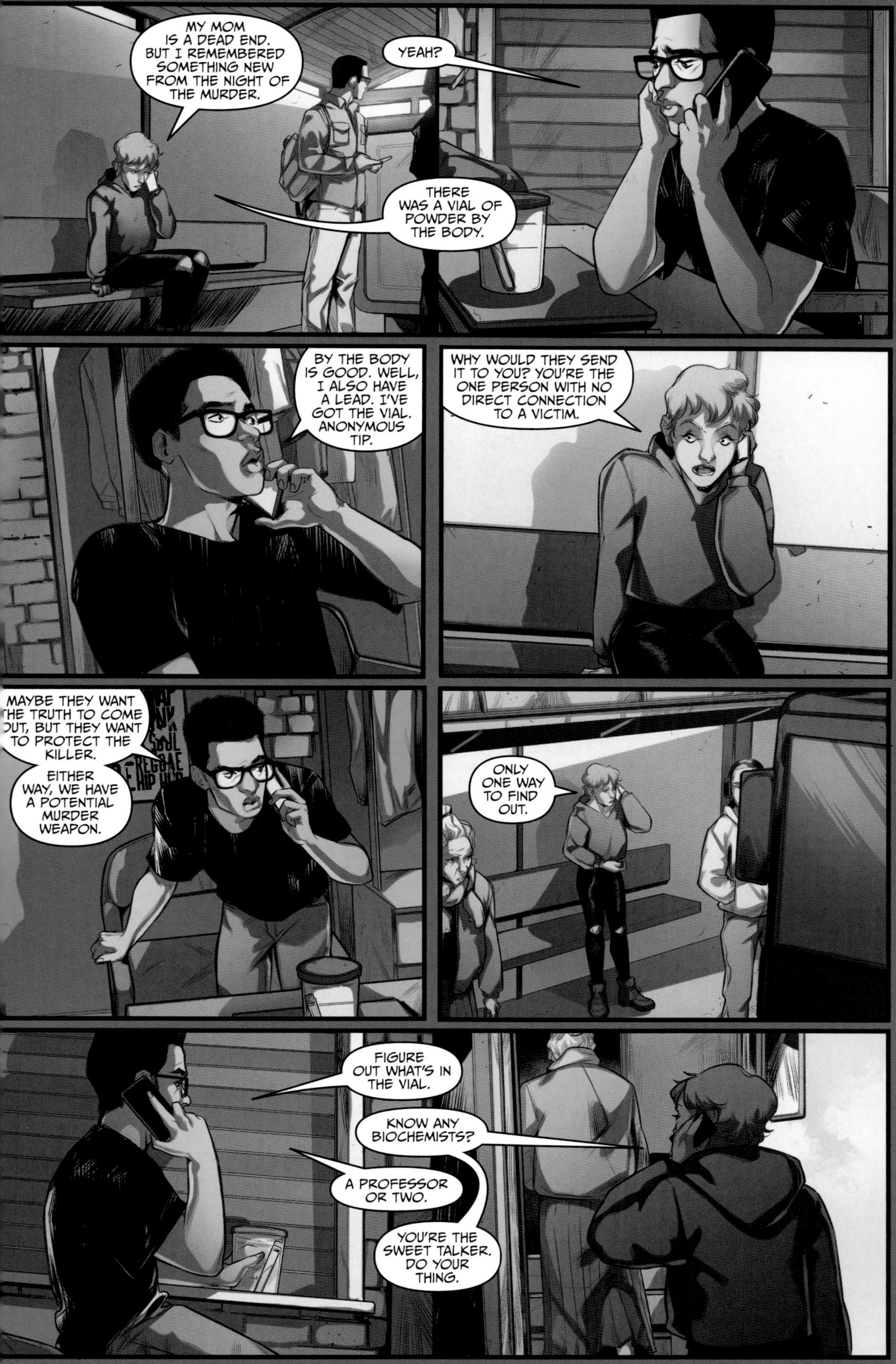
MY MOM IS A DEAD END. BUT I REMEMBERED SOMETHING NEW FROM THE NIGHT OF THE MURDER.
YEAH?
THERE WAS A VIAL OF POWDER BY THE BODY.
BY THE BODY IS GOOD. WELL, I ALSO HAVE A LEAD. I'VE GOT THE VIAL. ANONYMOUS TIP.
WHY WOULD THEY SEND IT TO YOU? YOU'RE THE ONE PERSON WITH NO DIRECT CONNECTION TO A VICTIM.
MAYBE THEY WANT THE TRUTH TO COME OUT, BUT THEY WANT TO PROTECT THE KILLER.
EITHER WAY, WE HAVE A POTENTIAL MURDER WEAPON.
ONLY ONE WAY TO FIND OUT.
FIGURE OUT WHAT'S IN THE VIAL.
KNOW ANY BIOCHEMISTS?
A PROFESSOR OR TWO.
YOU'RE THE SWEET TALKER. DO YOUR THING.

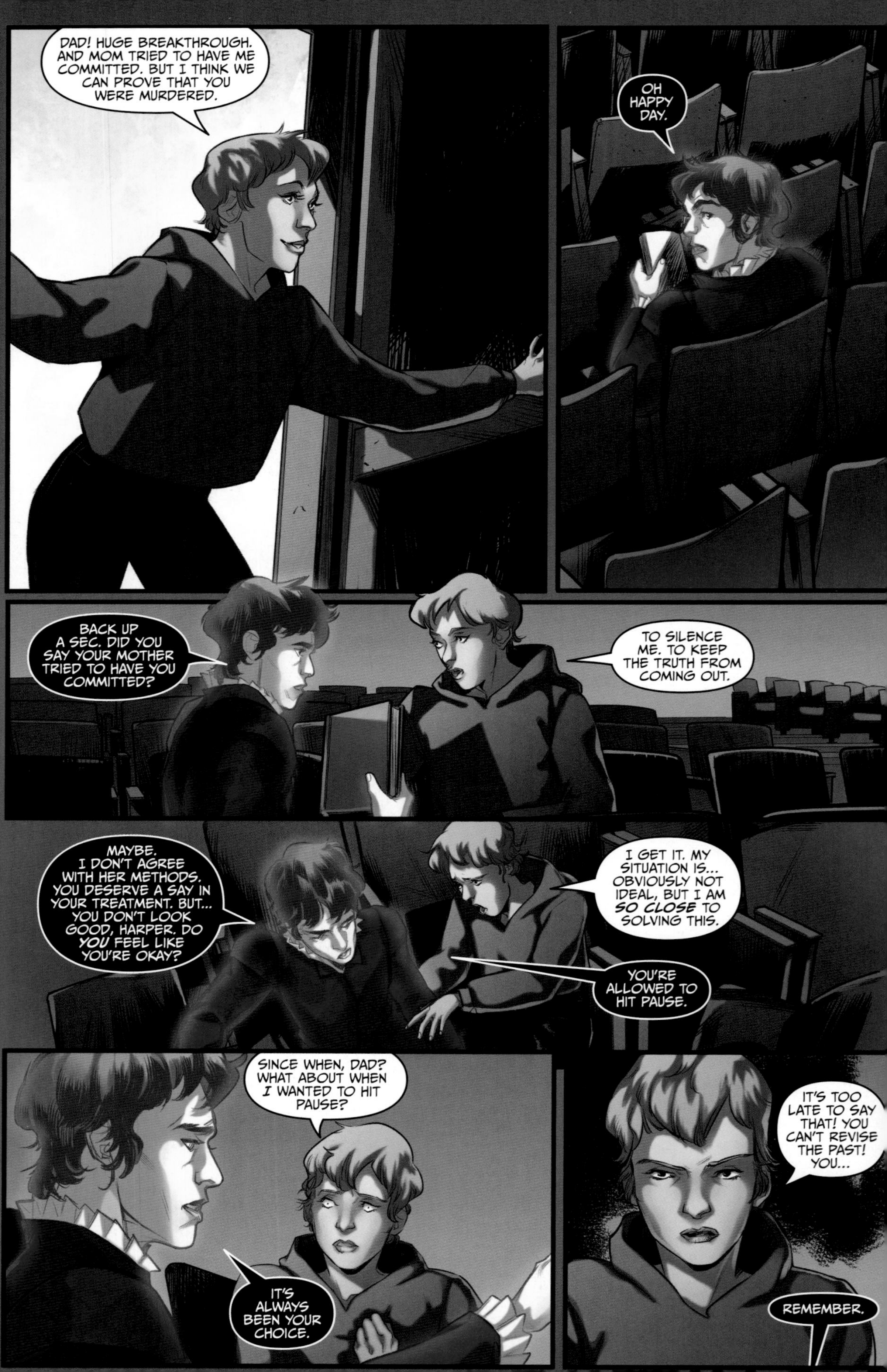

DAD! HUGE BREAKTHROUGH. AND MOM TRIED TO HAVE ME COMMITTED. BUT I THINK WE CAN PROVE THAT YOU WERE MURDERED.
OH HAPPY DAY.
BACK UP A SEC. DID YOU SAY YOUR MOTHER TRIED TO HAVE YOU COMMITTED?
TO SILENCE ME. TO KEEP THE TRUTH FROM COMING OUT.
MAYBE. I DON'T AGREE WITH HER METHODS. YOU DESERVE A SAY IN YOUR TREATMENT. BUT... YOU DON'T LOOK GOOD, HARPER. DO YOU FEEL LIKE YOU'RE OKAY?
I GET IT. MY SITUATION IS... OBVIOUSLY NOT IDEAL, BUT I AM SO CLOSE TO SOLVING THIS.
YOU'RE ALLOWED TO HIT PAUSE.
SINCE WHEN, DAD? WHAT ABOUT WHEN I WANTED TO HIT PAUSE?
IT'S ALWAYS BEEN YOUR CHOICE.
IT'S TOO LATE TO SAY THAT! YOU CAN'T REVISE THE PAST! YOU...
REMEMBER.

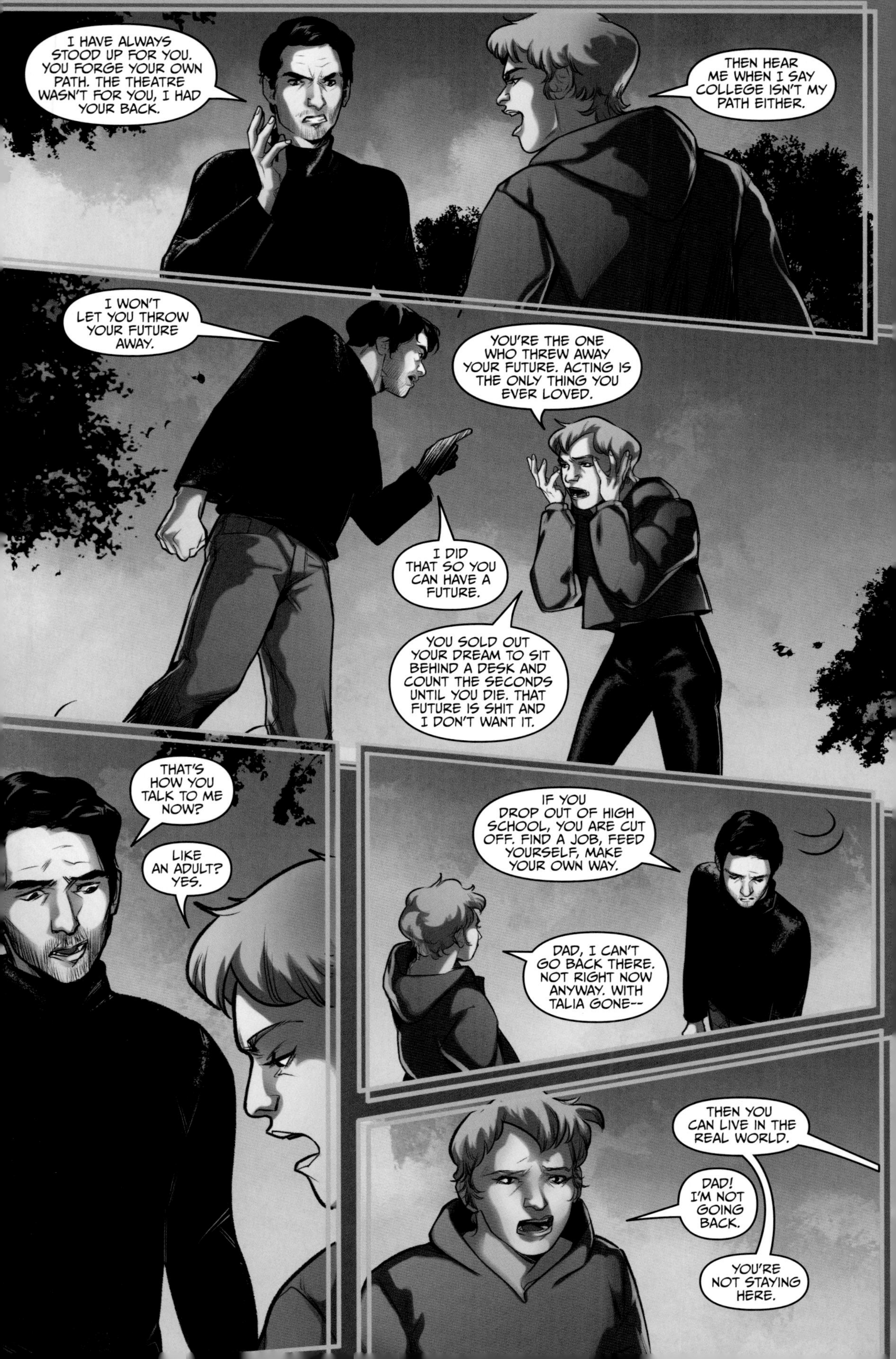
I HAVE ALWAYS STOOD UP FOR YOU. YOU FORGE YOUR OWN PATH. THE THEATRE WASN'T FOR YOU, I HAD YOUR BACK.
THEN HEAR ME WHEN I SAY COLLEGE ISN'T MY PATH EITHER.
I WON'T LET YOU THROW YOUR FUTURE AWAY.
YOU'RE THE ONE WHO THREW AWAY YOUR FUTURE. ACTING IS THE ONLY THING YOU EVER LOVED.
I DID THAT SO YOU CAN HAVE A FUTURE.
YOU SOLD OUT YOUR DREAM TO SIT BEHIND A DESK AND COUNT THE SECONDS UNTIL YOU DIE. THAT FUTURE IS SHIT AND I DON'T WANT IT.
THAT'S HOW YOU TALK TO ME NOW?
LIKE AN ADULT? YES.
IF YOU DROP OUT OF HIGH SCHOOL, YOU ARE CUT OFF. FIND A JOB, FEED YOURSELF, MAKE YOUR OWN WAY.
DAD, I CAN'T GO BACK THERE. NOT RIGHT NOW ANYWAY. WITH TALIA GONE--
THEN YOU CAN LIVE IN THE REAL WORLD.
DAD! I'M NOT GOING BACK.
YOU'RE NOT STAYING HERE.

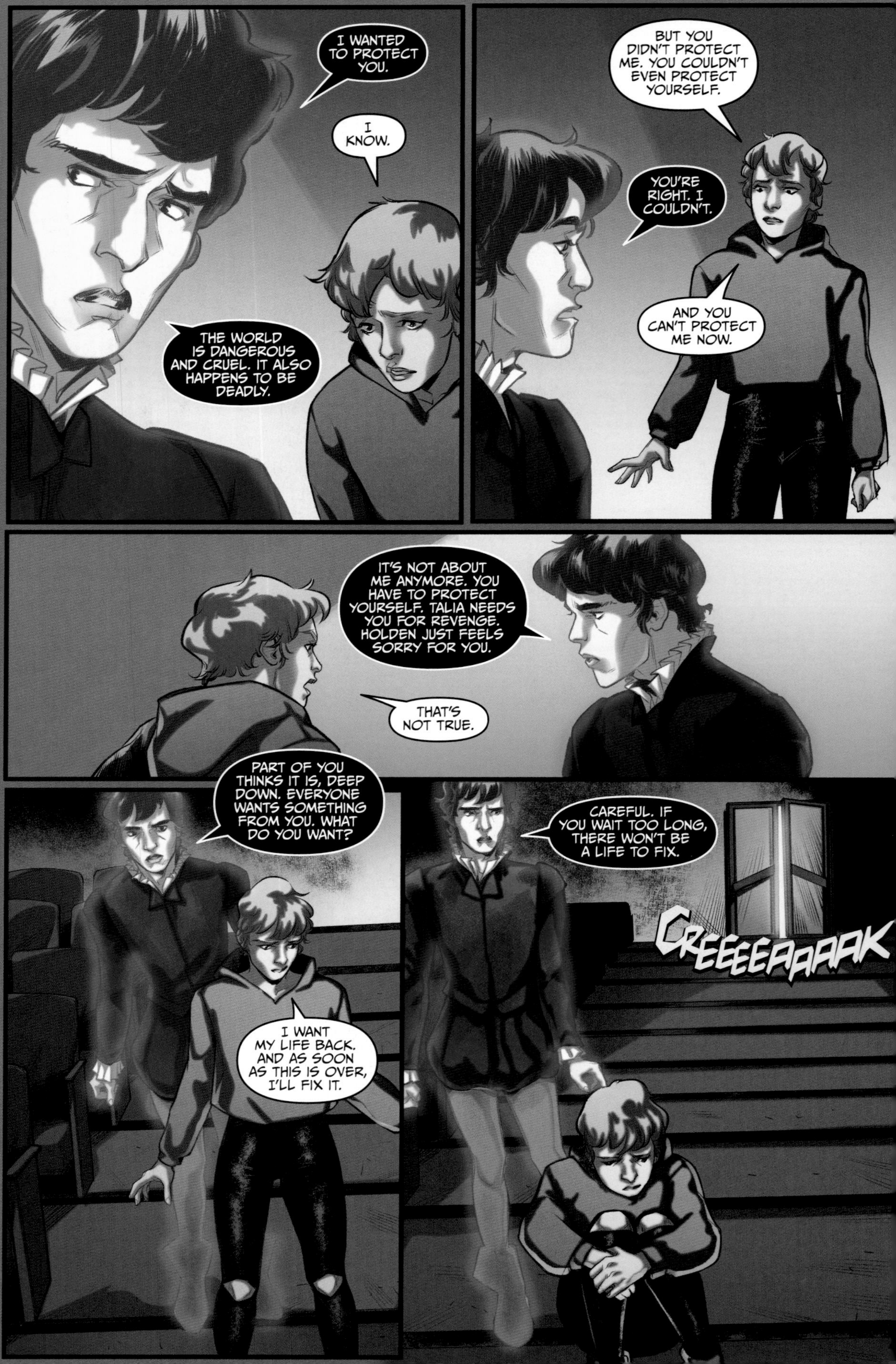
I WANTED TO PROTECT YOU.
I KNOW.
THE WORLD IS DANGEROUS AND CRUEL. IT ALSO HAPPENS TO BE DEADLY.
BUT YOU DIDN'T PROTECT ME. YOU COULDN'T EVEN PROTECT YOURSELF.
YOU'RE RIGHT. I COULDN'T.
AND YOU CAN'T PROTECT ME NOW.
IT'S NOT ABOUT ME ANYMORE. YOU HAVE TO PROTECT YOURSELF. TALIA NEEDS YOU FOR REVENGE. HOLDEN JUST FEELS SORRY FOR YOU.
THAT'S NOT TRUE.
PART OF YOU THINKS IT IS, DEEP DOWN. EVERYONE WANTS SOMETHING FROM YOU. WHAT DO YOU WANT?
I WANT MY LIFE BACK. AND AS SOON AS THIS IS OVER, I'LL FIX IT.
CAREFUL. IF YOU WAIT TOO LONG, THERE WON'T BE A LIFE TO FIX.
CREEEEAAAAK

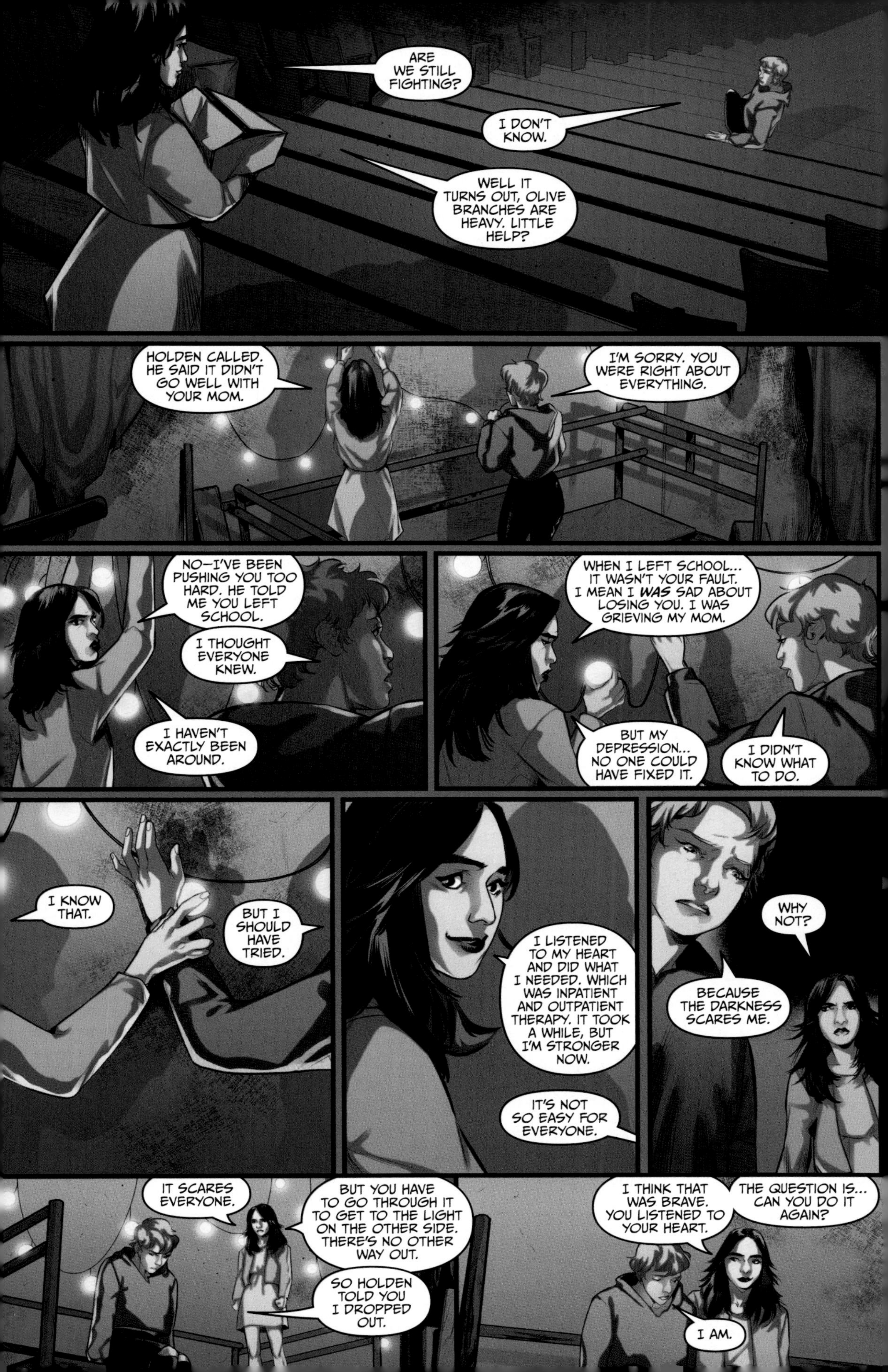
ARE WE STILL FIGHTING?
I DON'T KNOW.
WELL IT TURNS OUT, OLIVE BRANCHES ARE HEAVY. LITTLE HELP?
HOLDEN CALLED. HE SAID IT DIDN'T GO WELL WITH YOUR MOM.
I'M SORRY. YOU WERE RIGHT ABOUT EVERYTHING.
NO—I'VE BEEN PUSHING YOU TOO HARD. HE TOLD ME YOU LEFT SCHOOL.
I THOUGHT EVERYONE KNEW.
I HAVEN'T EXACTLY BEEN AROUND.
WHEN I LEFT SCHOOL... IT WASN'T YOUR FAULT. I MEAN I *WAS* SAD ABOUT LOSING YOU. I WAS GRIEVING MY MOM.
BUT MY DEPRESSION... NO ONE COULD HAVE FIXED IT.
I DIDN'T KNOW WHAT TO DO.
I KNOW THAT.
BUT I SHOULD HAVE TRIED.
I LISTENED TO MY HEART AND DID WHAT I NEEDED. WHICH WAS INPATIENT AND OUTPATIENT THERAPY. IT TOOK A WHILE, BUT I'M STRONGER NOW.
IT'S NOT SO EASY FOR EVERYONE.
WHY NOT?
BECAUSE THE DARKNESS SCARES ME.
IT SCARES EVERYONE.
BUT YOU HAVE TO GO THROUGH IT TO GET TO THE LIGHT ON THE OTHER SIDE. THERE'S NO OTHER WAY OUT.
SO HOLDEN TOLD YOU I DROPPED OUT.
I THINK THAT WAS BRAVE. YOU LISTENED TO YOUR HEART.
THE QUESTION IS... CAN YOU DO IT AGAIN?
I AM.

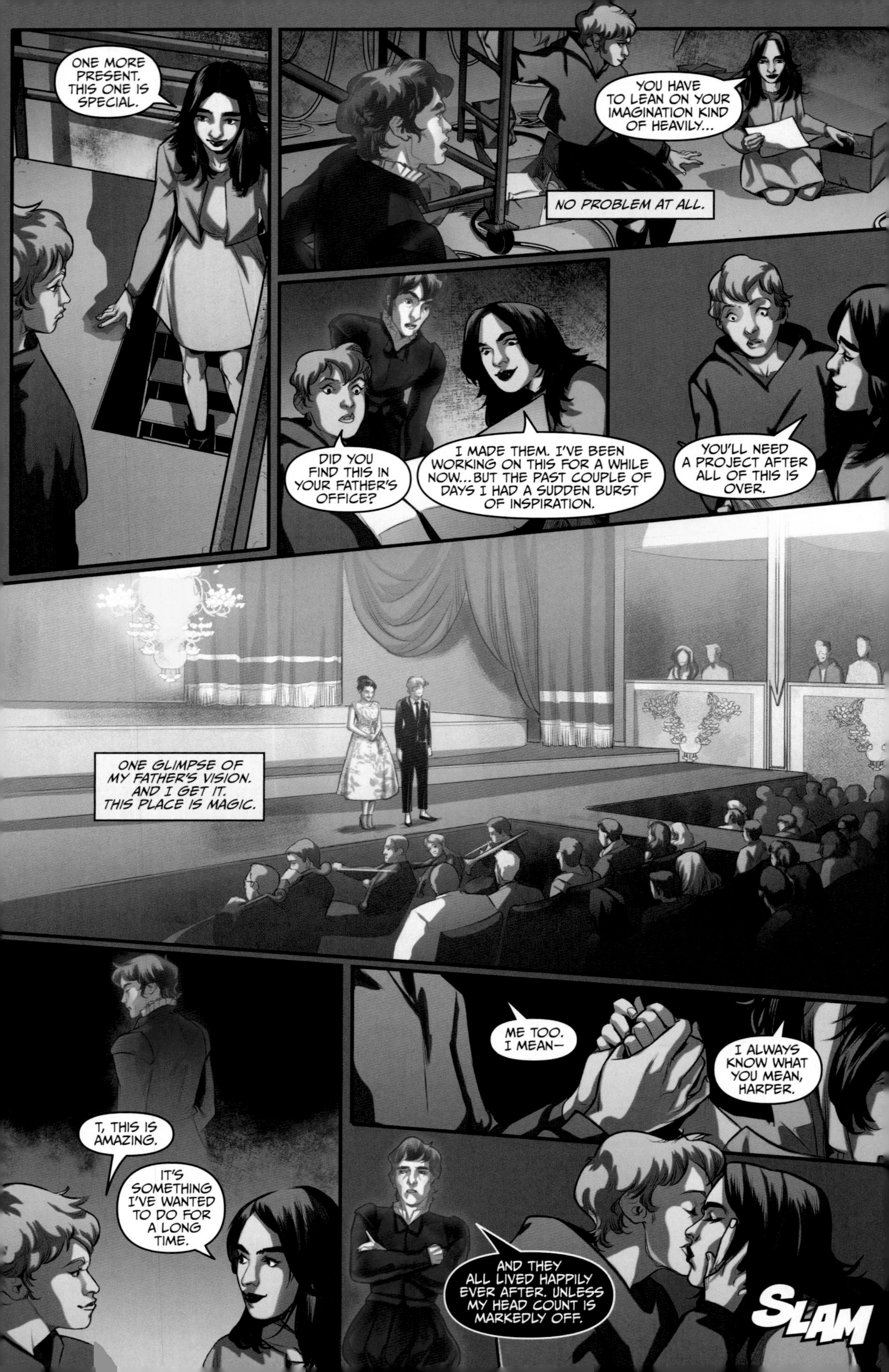
ONE MORE PRESENT. THIS ONE IS SPECIAL.
YOU HAVE TO LEAN ON YOUR IMAGINATION KIND OF HEAVILY...
NO PROBLEM AT ALL.
DID YOU FIND THIS IN YOUR FATHER'S OFFICE?
I MADE THEM. I'VE BEEN WORKING ON THIS FOR A WHILE NOW...BUT THE PAST COUPLE OF DAYS I HAD A SUDDEN BURST OF INSPIRATION.
YOU'LL NEED A PROJECT AFTER ALL OF THIS IS OVER.
ONE GLIMPSE OF MY FATHER'S VISION. AND I GET IT. THIS PLACE IS MAGIC.
T, THIS IS AMAZING.
IT'S SOMETHING I'VE WANTED TO DO FOR A LONG TIME.
ME TOO. I MEAN—
I ALWAYS KNOW WHAT YOU MEAN, HARPER.
AND THEY ALL LIVED HAPPILY EVER AFTER. UNLESS MY HEAD COUNT IS MARKEDLY OFF.
SLAM

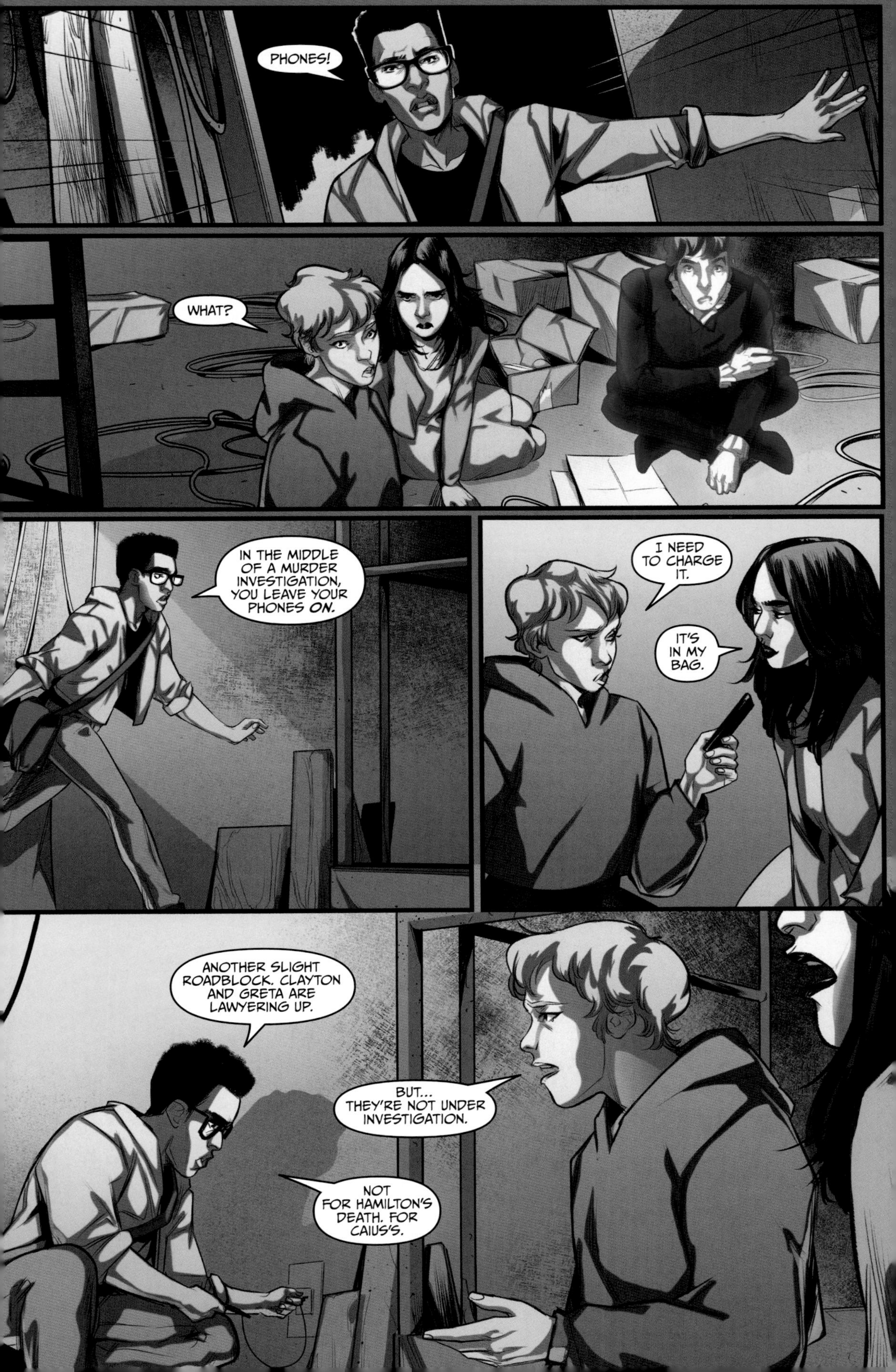
PHONES!
WHAT?
IN THE MIDDLE OF A MURDER INVESTIGATION, YOU LEAVE YOUR PHONES ON.
I NEED TO CHARGE IT.
IT'S IN MY BAG.
ANOTHER SLIGHT ROADBLOCK. CLAYTON AND GRETA ARE LAWYERING UP.
BUT... THEY'RE NOT UNDER INVESTIGATION.
NOT FOR HAMILTON'S DEATH. FOR CAIUS'S.

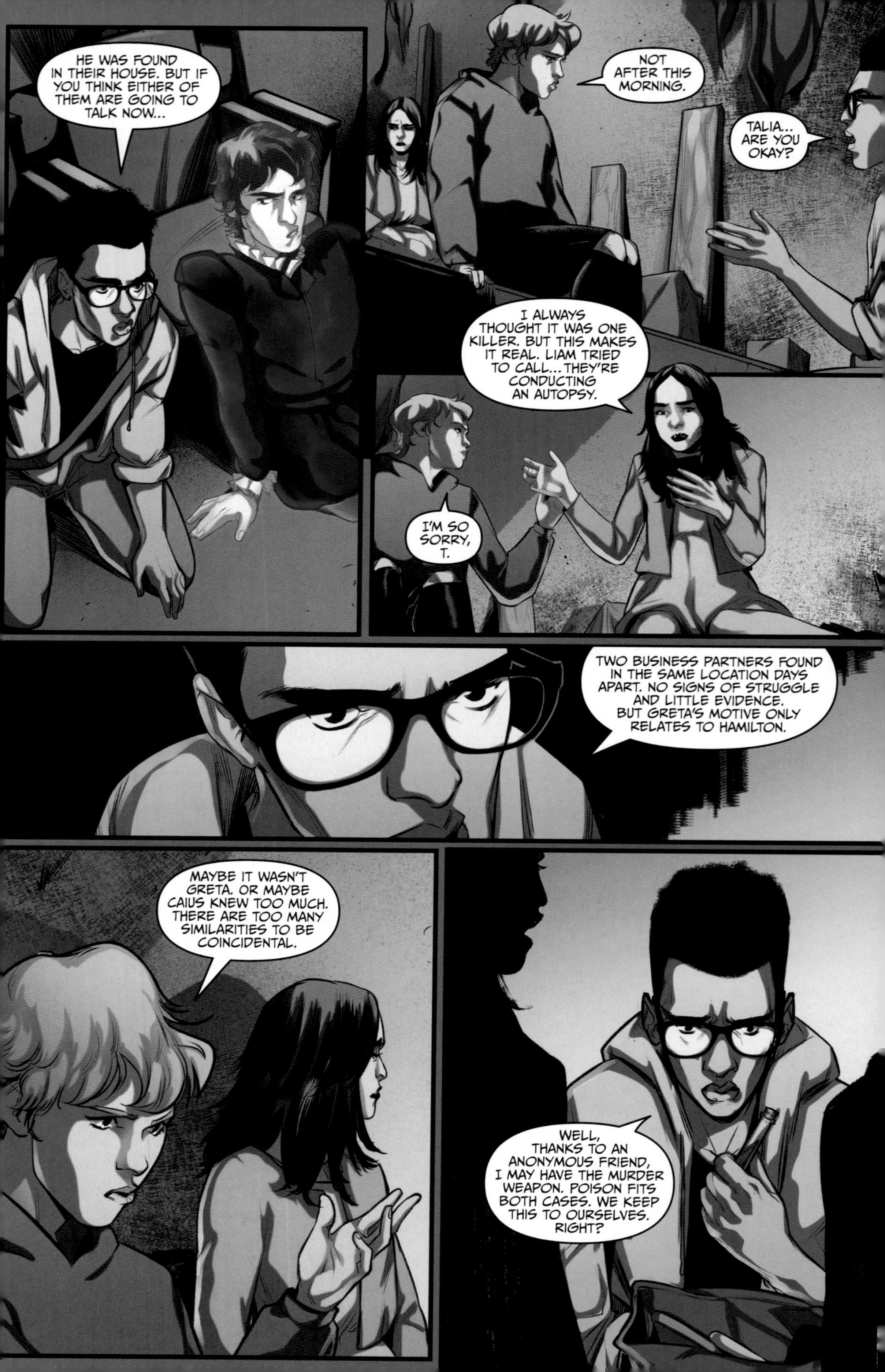
HE WAS FOUND IN THEIR HOUSE. BUT IF YOU THINK EITHER OF THEM ARE GOING TO TALK NOW...
NOT AFTER THIS MORNING.
TALIA... ARE YOU OKAY?
I ALWAYS THOUGHT IT WAS ONE KILLER. BUT THIS MAKES IT REAL. LIAM TRIED TO CALL... THEY'RE CONDUCTING AN AUTOPSY.
I'M SO SORRY, T.
TWO BUSINESS PARTNERS FOUND IN THE SAME LOCATION DAYS APART. NO SIGNS OF STRUGGLE AND LITTLE EVIDENCE. BUT GRETA'S MOTIVE ONLY RELATES TO HAMILTON.
MAYBE IT WASN'T GRETA. OR MAYBE CAIUS KNEW TOO MUCH. THERE ARE TOO MANY SIMILARITIES TO BE COINCIDENTAL.
WELL, THANKS TO AN ANONYMOUS FRIEND, I MAY HAVE THE MURDER WEAPON. POISON FITS BOTH CASES. WE KEEP THIS TO OURSELVES. RIGHT?

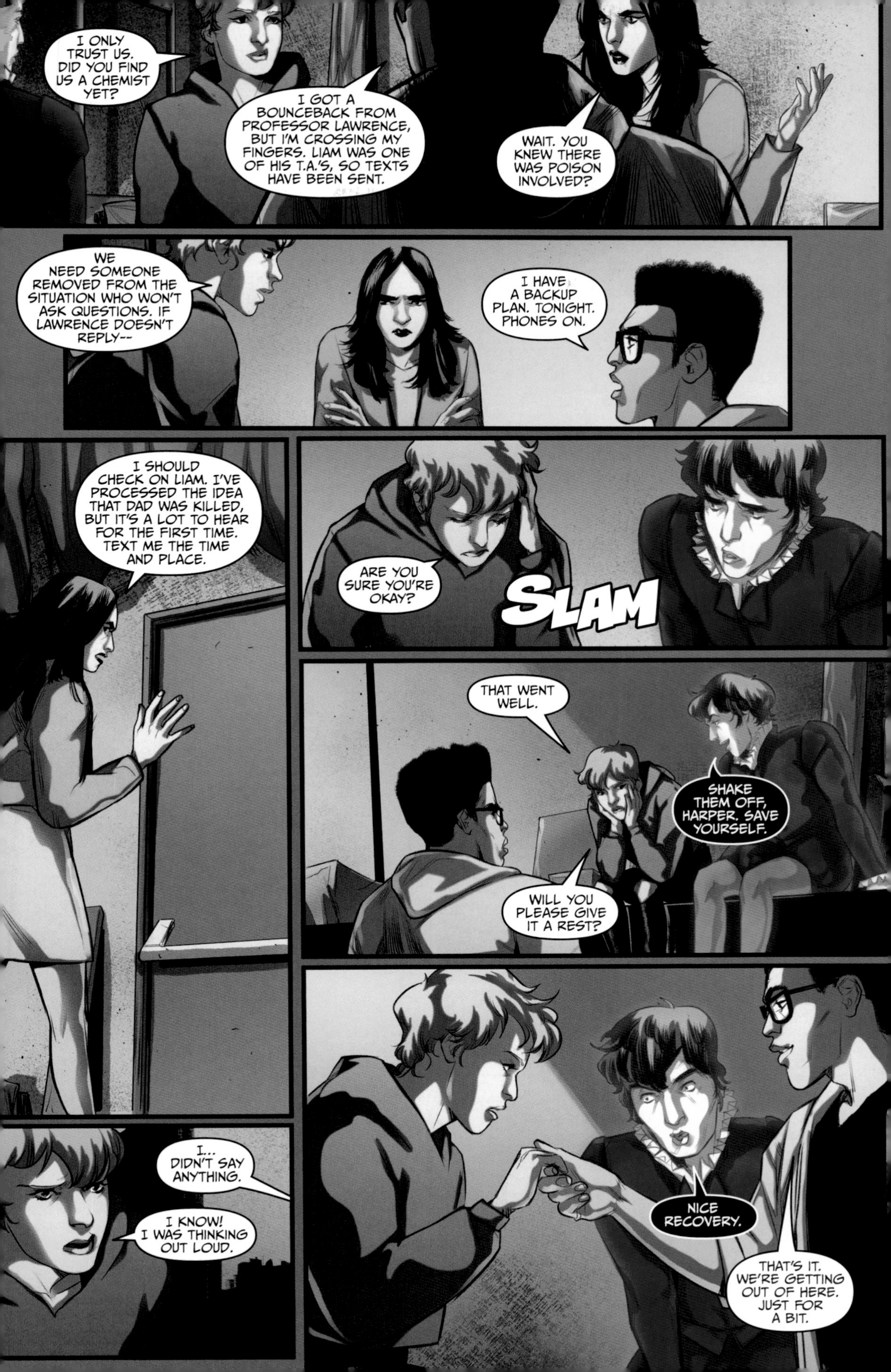
I ONLY TRUST US. DID YOU FIND US A CHEMIST YET?
I GOT A BOUNCEBACK FROM PROFESSOR LAWRENCE, BUT I'M CROSSING MY FINGERS. LIAM WAS ONE OF HIS T.A.'S, SO TEXTS HAVE BEEN SENT.
WAIT. YOU KNEW THERE WAS POISON INVOLVED?
WE NEED SOMEONE REMOVED FROM THE SITUATION WHO WON'T ASK QUESTIONS. IF LAWRENCE DOESN'T REPLY--
I HAVE A BACKUP PLAN. TONIGHT. PHONES ON.
I SHOULD CHECK ON LIAM. I'VE PROCESSED THE IDEA THAT DAD WAS KILLED, BUT IT'S A LOT TO HEAR FOR THE FIRST TIME. TEXT ME THE TIME AND PLACE.
ARE YOU SURE YOU'RE OKAY?
SLAM
THAT WENT WELL.
SHAKE THEM OFF, HARPER. SAVE YOURSELF.
WILL YOU PLEASE GIVE IT A REST?
I... DIDN'T SAY ANYTHING.
I KNOW! I WAS THINKING OUT LOUD.
NICE RECOVERY.
THAT'S IT. WE'RE GETTING OUT OF HERE. JUST FOR A BIT.

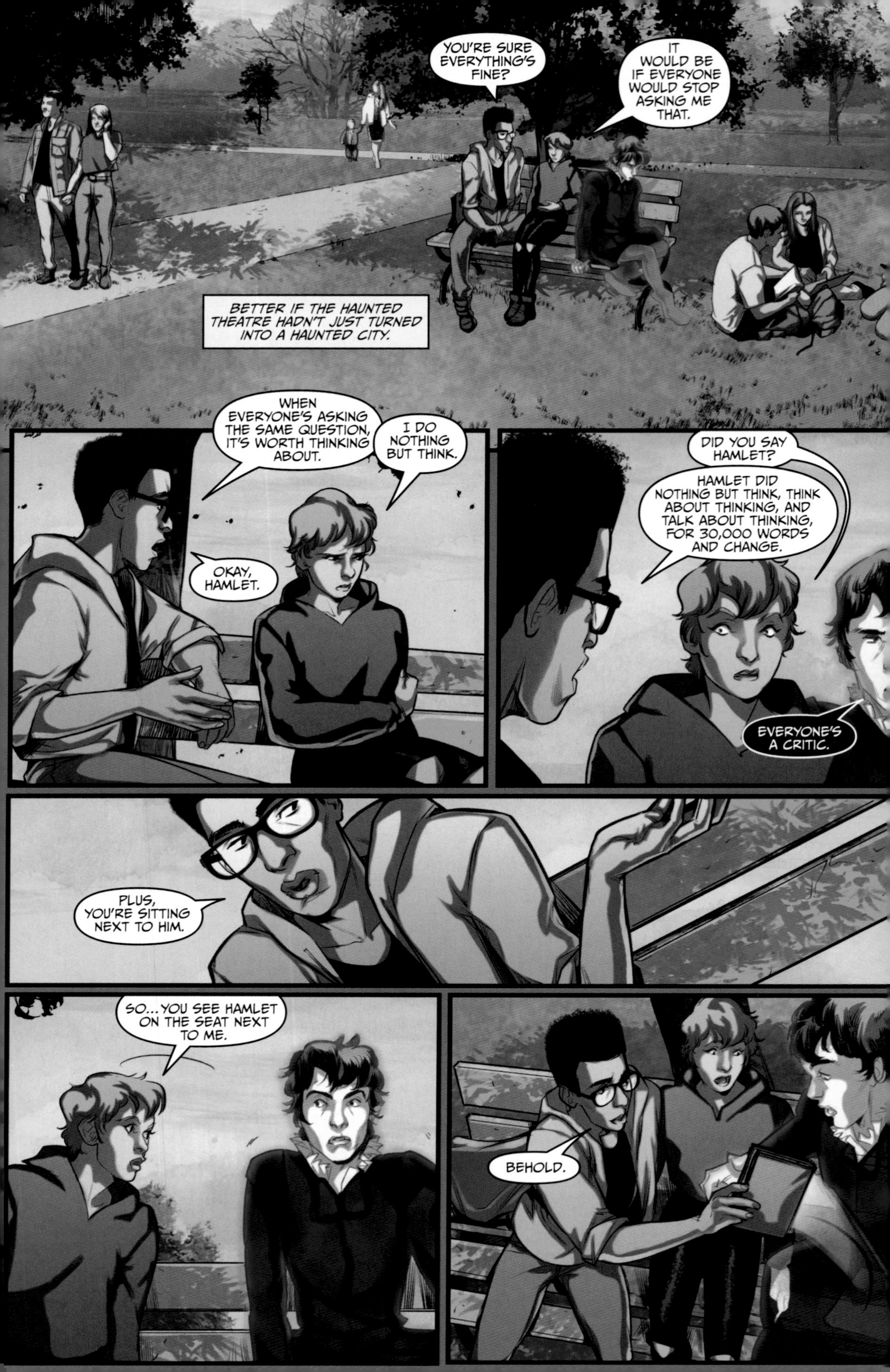
YOU'RE SURE EVERYTHING'S FINE?
IT WOULD BE IF EVERYONE WOULD STOP ASKING ME THAT.
BETTER IF THE HAUNTED THEATRE HADN'T JUST TURNED INTO A HAUNTED CITY.
WHEN EVERYONE'S ASKING THE SAME QUESTION, IT'S WORTH THINKING ABOUT.
I DO NOTHING BUT THINK.
OKAY, HAMLET.
DID YOU SAY HAMLET?
HAMLET DID NOTHING BUT THINK, THINK ABOUT THINKING, AND TALK ABOUT THINKING, FOR 30,000 WORDS AND CHANGE.
EVERYONE'S A CRITIC.
PLUS, YOU'RE SITTING NEXT TO HIM.
SO... YOU SEE HAMLET ON THE SEAT NEXT TO ME.
BEHOLD.

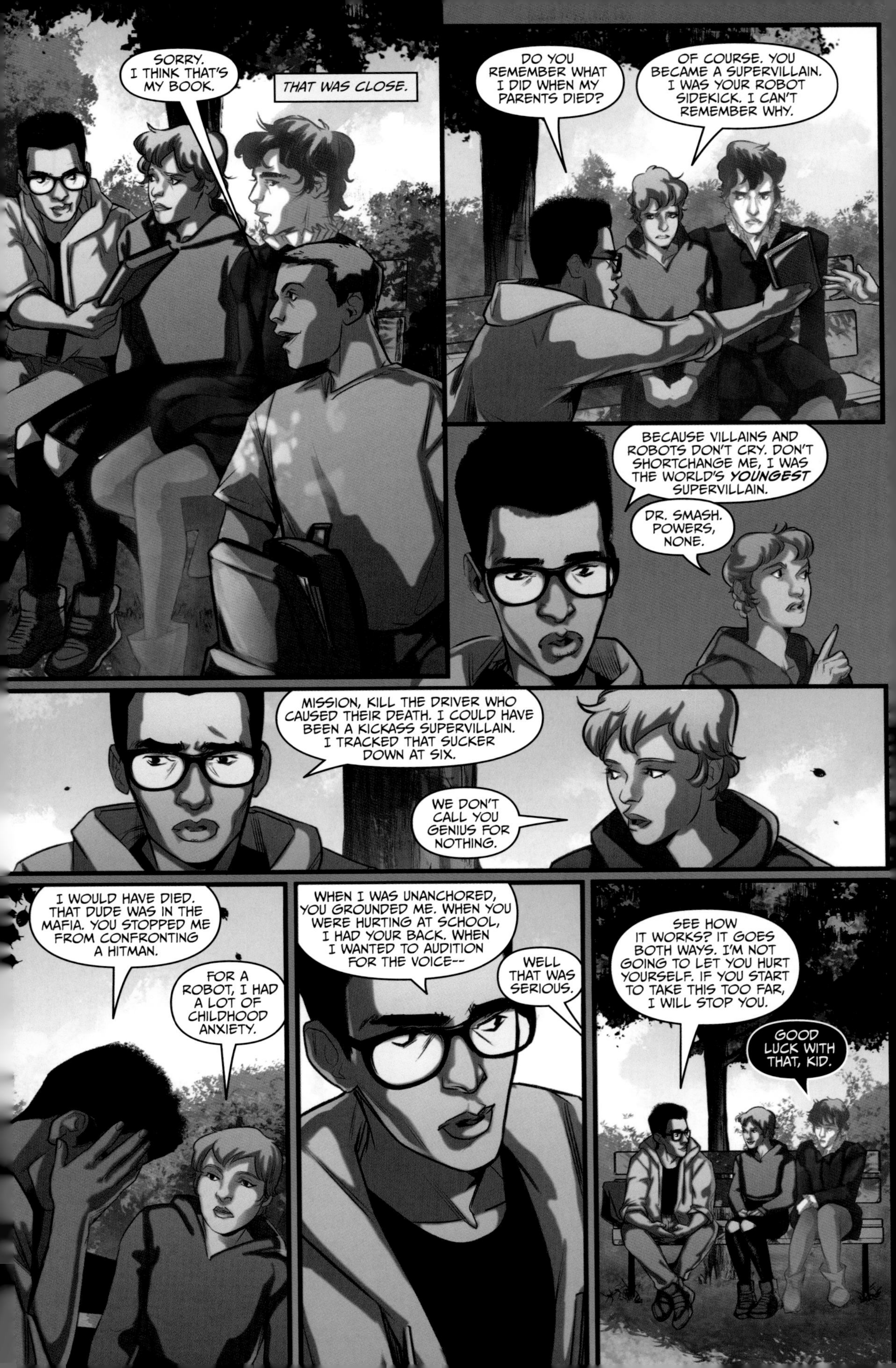
SORRY. I THINK THAT'S MY BOOK.
THAT WAS CLOSE.
DO YOU REMEMBER WHAT I DID WHEN MY PARENTS DIED?
OF COURSE. YOU BECAME A SUPERVILLAIN. I WAS YOUR ROBOT SIDEKICK. I CAN'T REMEMBER WHY.
BECAUSE VILLAINS AND ROBOTS DON'T CRY. DON'T SHORTCHANGE ME, I WAS THE WORLD'S *YOUNGEST* SUPERVILLAIN.
DR. SMASH. POWERS, NONE.
MISSION, KILL THE DRIVER WHO CAUSED THEIR DEATH. I COULD HAVE BEEN A KICKASS SUPERVILLAIN. I TRACKED THAT SUCKER DOWN AT SIX.
WE DON'T CALL YOU GENIUS FOR NOTHING.
I WOULD HAVE DIED. THAT DUDE WAS IN THE MAFIA. YOU STOPPED ME FROM CONFRONTING A HITMAN.
FOR A ROBOT, I HAD A LOT OF CHILDHOOD ANXIETY.
WHEN I WAS UNANCHORED, YOU GROUNDED ME. WHEN YOU WERE HURTING AT SCHOOL, I HAD YOUR BACK. WHEN I WANTED TO AUDITION FOR THE VOICE--
WELL THAT WAS SERIOUS.
SEE HOW IT WORKS? IT GOES BOTH WAYS. I'M NOT GOING TO LET YOU HURT YOURSELF. IF YOU START TO TAKE THIS TOO FAR, I WILL STOP YOU.
GOOD LUCK WITH THAT, KID.

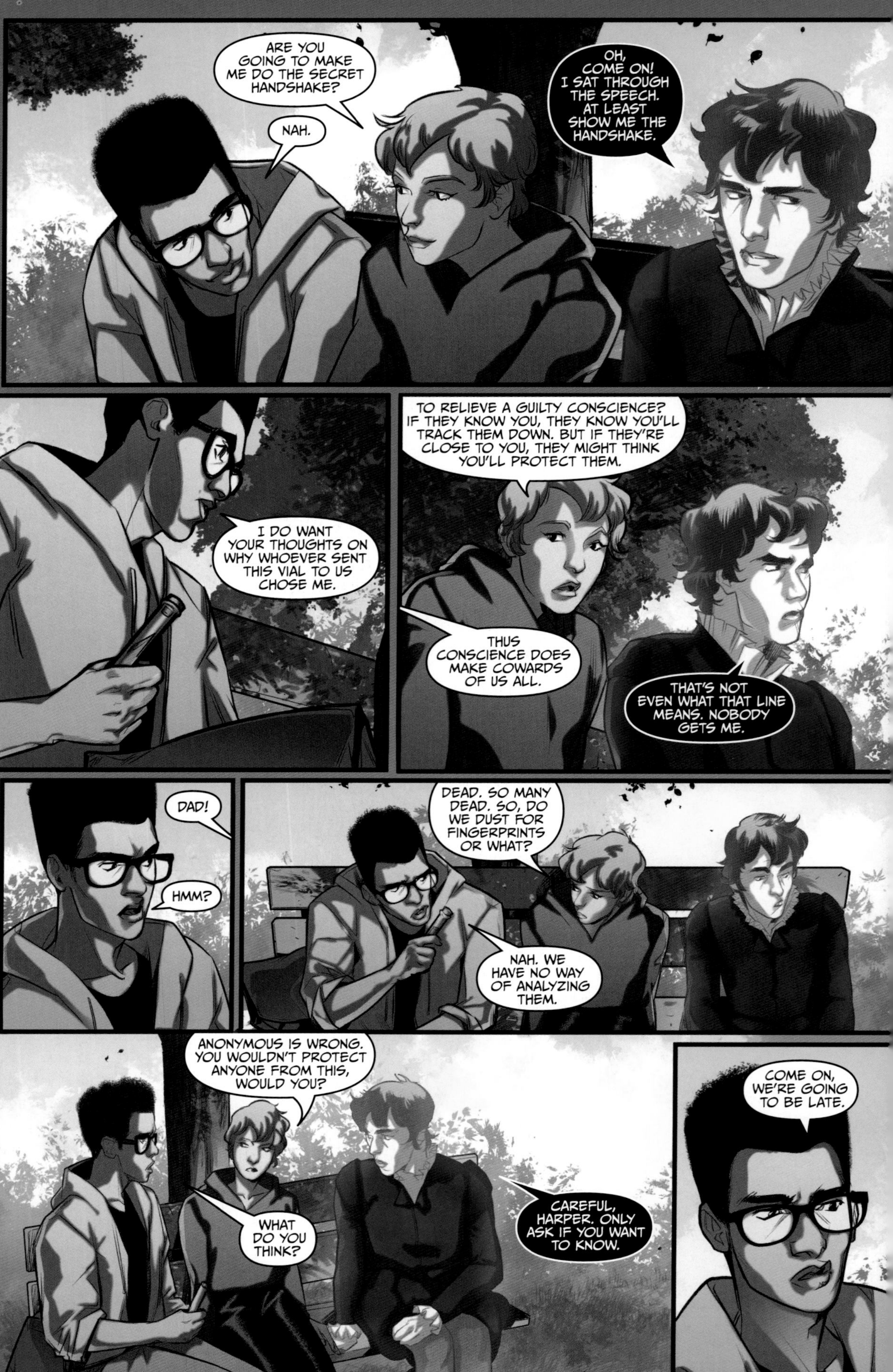
ARE YOU GOING TO MAKE ME DO THE SECRET HANDSHAKE?
NAH.
OH, COME ON! I SAT THROUGH THE SPEECH. AT LEAST SHOW ME THE HANDSHAKE.
I DO WANT YOUR THOUGHTS ON WHY WHOEVER SENT THIS VIAL TO US CHOSE ME.
TO RELIEVE A GUILTY CONSCIENCE? IF THEY KNOW YOU, THEY KNOW YOU'LL TRACK THEM DOWN. BUT IF THEY'RE CLOSE TO YOU, THEY MIGHT THINK YOU'LL PROTECT THEM.
THUS CONSCIENCE DOES MAKE COWARDS OF US ALL.
THAT'S NOT EVEN WHAT THAT LINE MEANS. NOBODY GETS ME.
DAD!
HMM?
DEAD. SO MANY DEAD. SO, DO WE DUST FOR FINGERPRINTS OR WHAT?
NAH. WE HAVE NO WAY OF ANALYZING THEM.
ANONYMOUS IS WRONG. YOU WOULDN'T PROTECT ANYONE FROM THIS, WOULD YOU?
WHAT DO YOU THINK?
CAREFUL, HARPER. ONLY ASK IF YOU WANT TO KNOW.
COME ON, WE'RE GOING TO BE LATE.

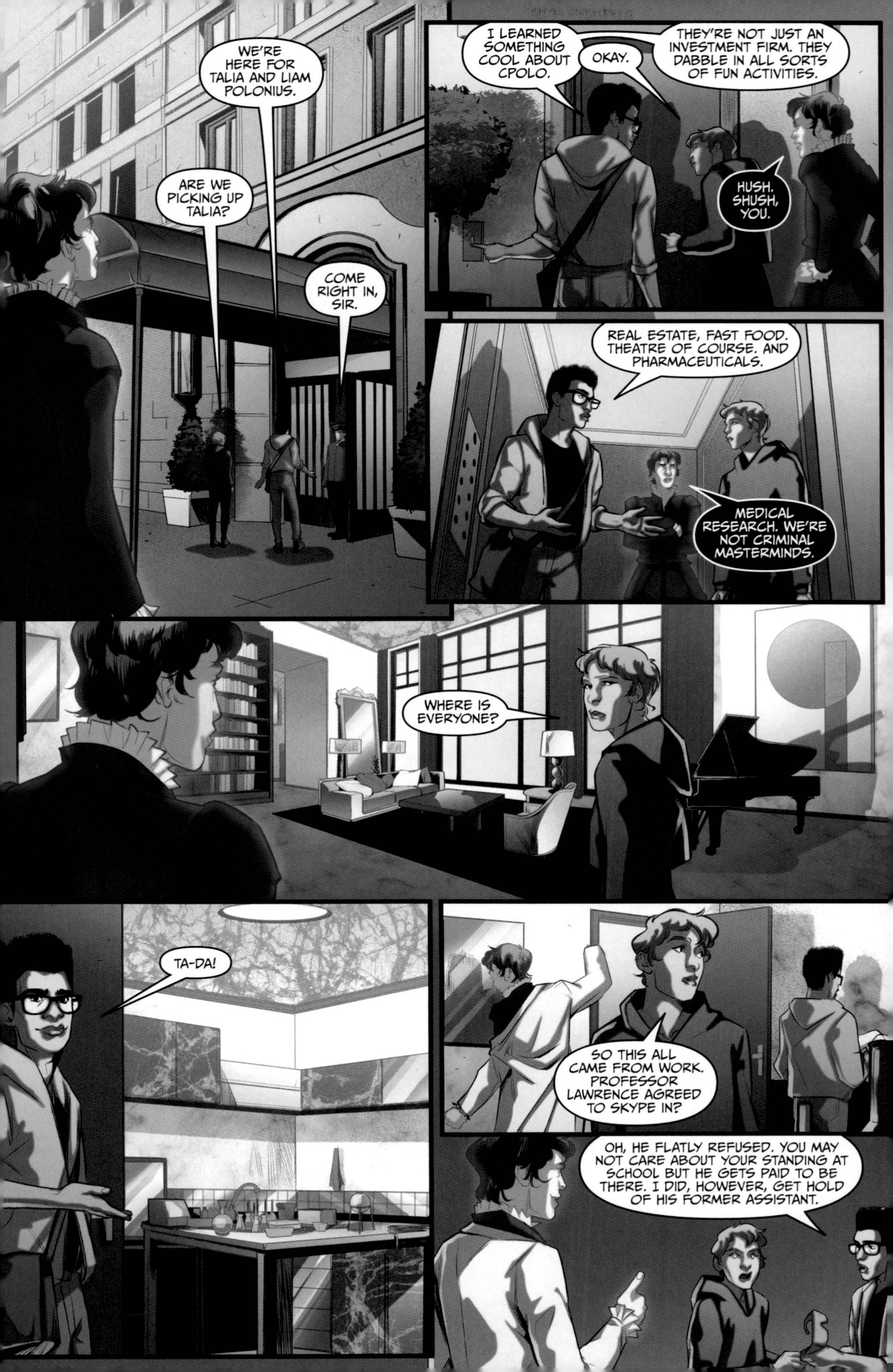
WE'RE HERE FOR TALIA AND LIAM POLONIUS.
ARE WE PICKING UP TALIA?
COME RIGHT IN, SIR.
I LEARNED SOMETHING COOL ABOUT CPOLO.
OKAY.
THEY'RE NOT JUST AN INVESTMENT FIRM. THEY DABBLE IN ALL SORTS OF FUN ACTIVITIES.
HUSH. SHUSH, YOU.
REAL ESTATE, FAST FOOD. THEATRE OF COURSE. AND PHARMACEUTICALS.
MEDICAL RESEARCH. WE'RE NOT CRIMINAL MASTERMINDS.
WHERE IS EVERYONE?
TA-DA!
SO THIS ALL CAME FROM WORK. PROFESSOR LAWRENCE AGREED TO SKYPE IN?
OH, HE FLATLY REFUSED. YOU MAY NOT CARE ABOUT YOUR STANDING AT SCHOOL BUT HE GETS PAID TO BE THERE. I DID, HOWEVER, GET HOLD OF HIS FORMER ASSISTANT.

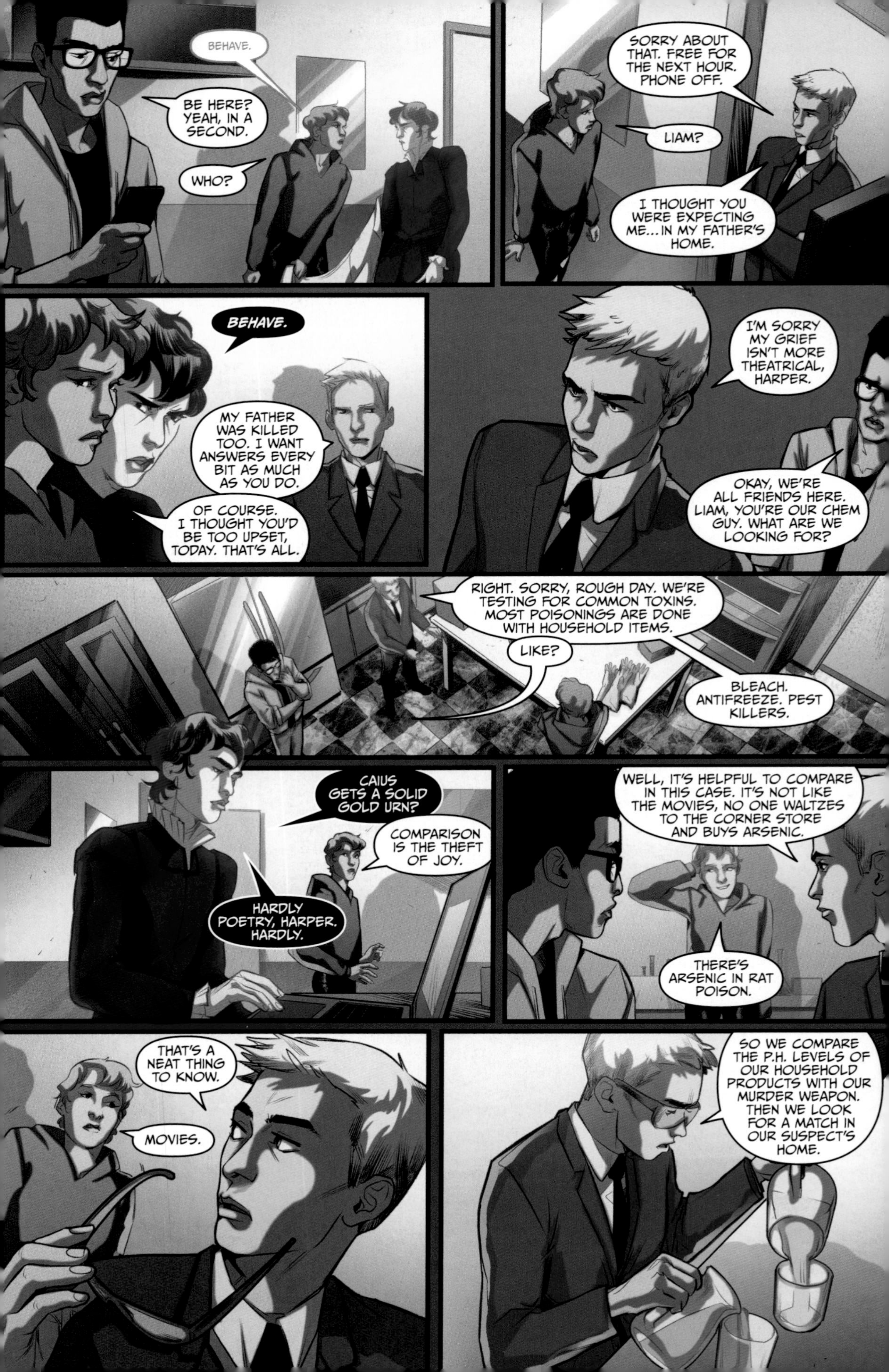
BEHAVE.
BE HERE? YEAH, IN A SECOND.
WHO?
SORRY ABOUT THAT. FREE FOR THE NEXT HOUR. PHONE OFF.
LIAM?
I THOUGHT YOU WERE EXPECTING ME... IN MY FATHER'S HOME.
BEHAVE.
MY FATHER WAS KILLED TOO. I WANT ANSWERS EVERY BIT AS MUCH AS YOU DO.
OF COURSE. I THOUGHT YOU'D BE TOO UPSET, TODAY. THAT'S ALL.
I'M SORRY MY GRIEF ISN'T MORE THEATRICAL, HARPER.
OKAY, WE'RE ALL FRIENDS HERE. LIAM, YOU'RE OUR CHEM GUY. WHAT ARE WE LOOKING FOR?
RIGHT. SORRY, ROUGH DAY. WE'RE TESTING FOR COMMON TOXINS. MOST POISONINGS ARE DONE WITH HOUSEHOLD ITEMS.
LIKE?
BLEACH. ANTIFREEZE. PEST KILLERS.
CAIUS GETS A SOLID GOLD URN?
COMPARISON IS THE THEFT OF JOY.
HARDLY POETRY, HARPER. HARDLY.
WELL, IT'S HELPFUL TO COMPARE IN THIS CASE. IT'S NOT LIKE THE MOVIES, NO ONE WALTZES TO THE CORNER STORE AND BUYS ARSENIC.
THERE'S ARSENIC IN RAT POISON.
THAT'S A NEAT THING TO KNOW.
MOVIES.
SO WE COMPARE THE P.H. LEVELS OF OUR HOUSEHOLD PRODUCTS WITH OUR MURDER WEAPON. THEN WE LOOK FOR A MATCH IN OUR SUSPECT'S HOME.

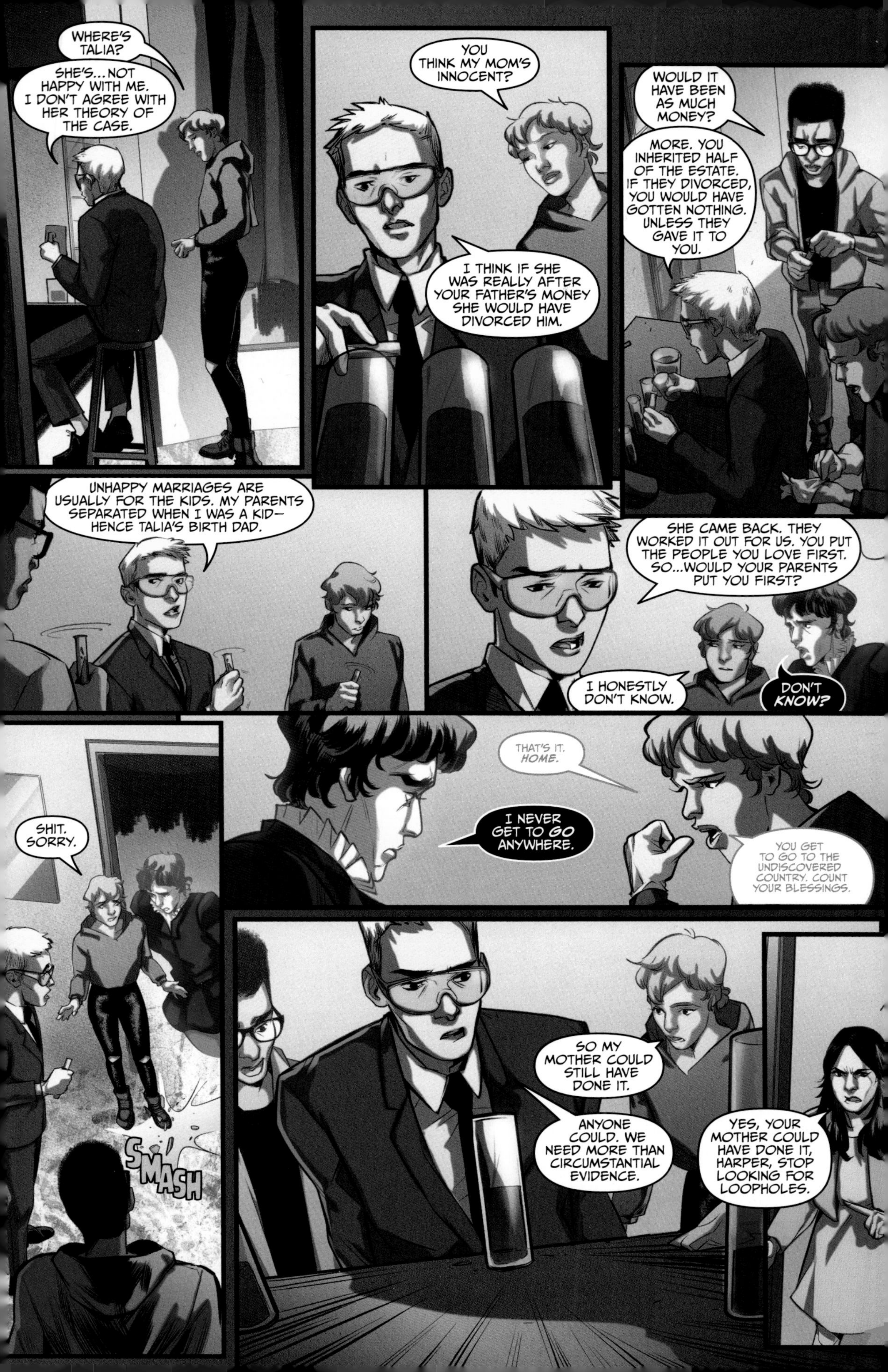
WHERE'S TALIA?
SHE'S...NOT HAPPY WITH ME. I DON'T AGREE WITH HER THEORY OF THE CASE.
YOU THINK MY MOM'S INNOCENT?
I THINK IF SHE WAS REALLY AFTER YOUR FATHER'S MONEY SHE WOULD HAVE DIVORCED HIM.
WOULD IT HAVE BEEN AS MUCH MONEY?
MORE. YOU INHERITED HALF OF THE ESTATE. IF THEY DIVORCED, YOU WOULD HAVE GOTTEN NOTHING. UNLESS THEY GAVE IT TO YOU.
UNHAPPY MARRIAGES ARE USUALLY FOR THE KIDS. MY PARENTS SEPARATED WHEN I WAS A KID— HENCE TALIA'S BIRTH DAD.
SHE CAME BACK. THEY WORKED IT OUT FOR US. YOU PUT THE PEOPLE YOU LOVE FIRST. SO...WOULD YOUR PARENTS PUT YOU FIRST?
I HONESTLY DON'T KNOW.
DON'T KNOW?
SHIT. SORRY.
SMASH
THAT'S IT. HOME.
I NEVER GET TO GO ANYWHERE.
YOU GET TO GO TO THE UNDISCOVERED COUNTRY. COUNT YOUR BLESSINGS.
SO MY MOTHER COULD STILL HAVE DONE IT.
ANYONE COULD. WE NEED MORE THAN CIRCUMSTANTIAL EVIDENCE.
YES, YOUR MOTHER COULD HAVE DONE IT, HARPER, STOP LOOKING FOR LOOPHOLES.

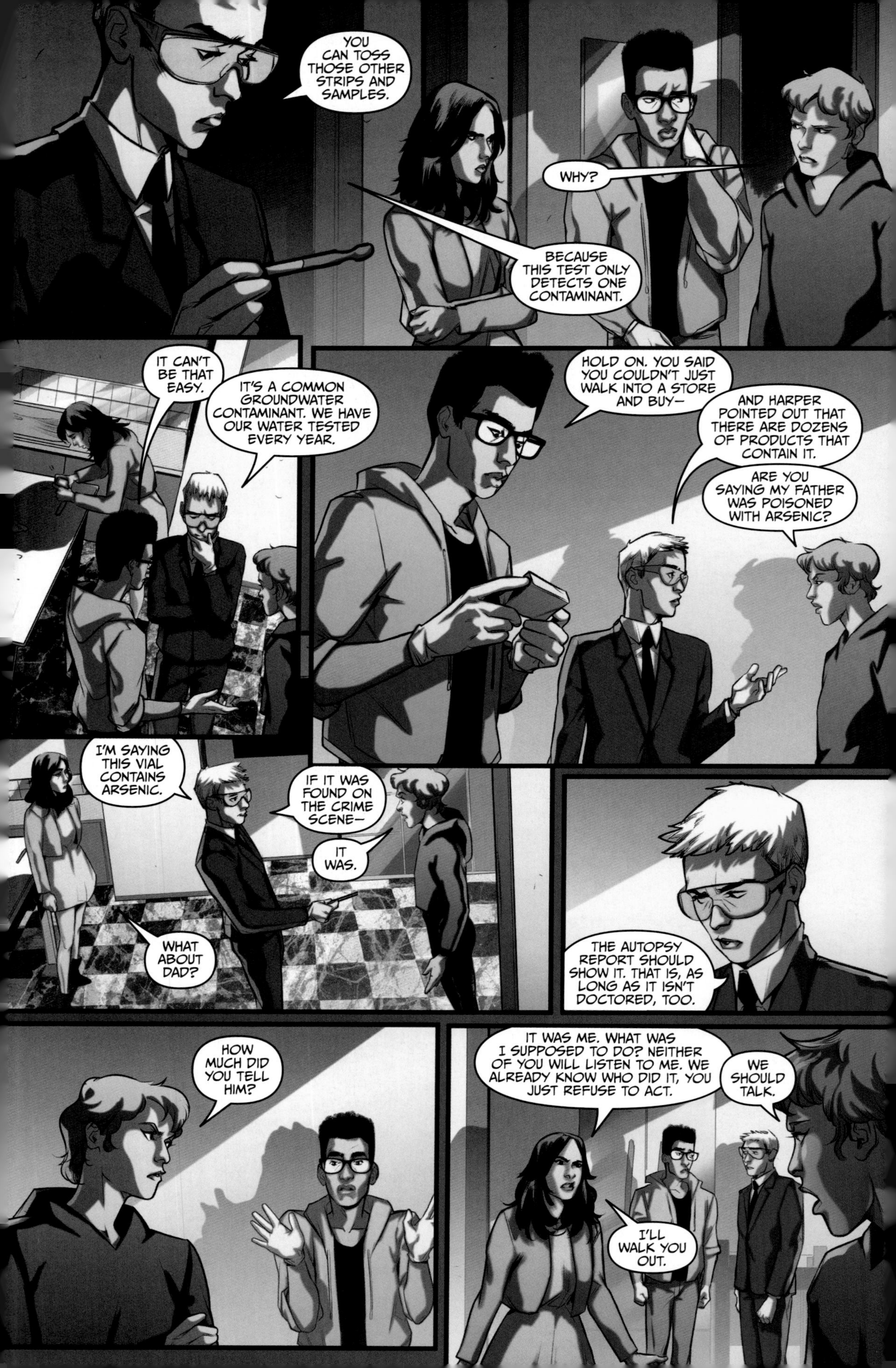

YOU CAN TOSS THOSE OTHER STRIPS AND SAMPLES.
WHY?
BECAUSE THIS TEST ONLY DETECTS ONE CONTAMINANT.
IT CAN'T BE THAT EASY.
IT'S A COMMON GROUNDWATER CONTAMINANT. WE HAVE OUR WATER TESTED EVERY YEAR.
HOLD ON. YOU SAID YOU COULDN'T JUST WALK INTO A STORE AND BUY—
AND HARPER POINTED OUT THAT THERE ARE DOZENS OF PRODUCTS THAT CONTAIN IT.
ARE YOU SAYING MY FATHER WAS POISONED WITH ARSENIC?
I'M SAYING THIS VIAL CONTAINS ARSENIC.
IF IT WAS FOUND ON THE CRIME SCENE—
IT WAS.
WHAT ABOUT DAD?
THE AUTOPSY REPORT SHOULD SHOW IT. THAT IS, AS LONG AS IT ISN'T DOCTORED, TOO.
HOW MUCH DID YOU TELL HIM?
IT WAS ME. WHAT WAS I SUPPOSED TO DO? NEITHER OF YOU WILL LISTEN TO ME. WE ALREADY KNOW WHO DID IT, YOU JUST REFUSE TO ACT.
WE SHOULD TALK.
I'LL WALK YOU OUT.

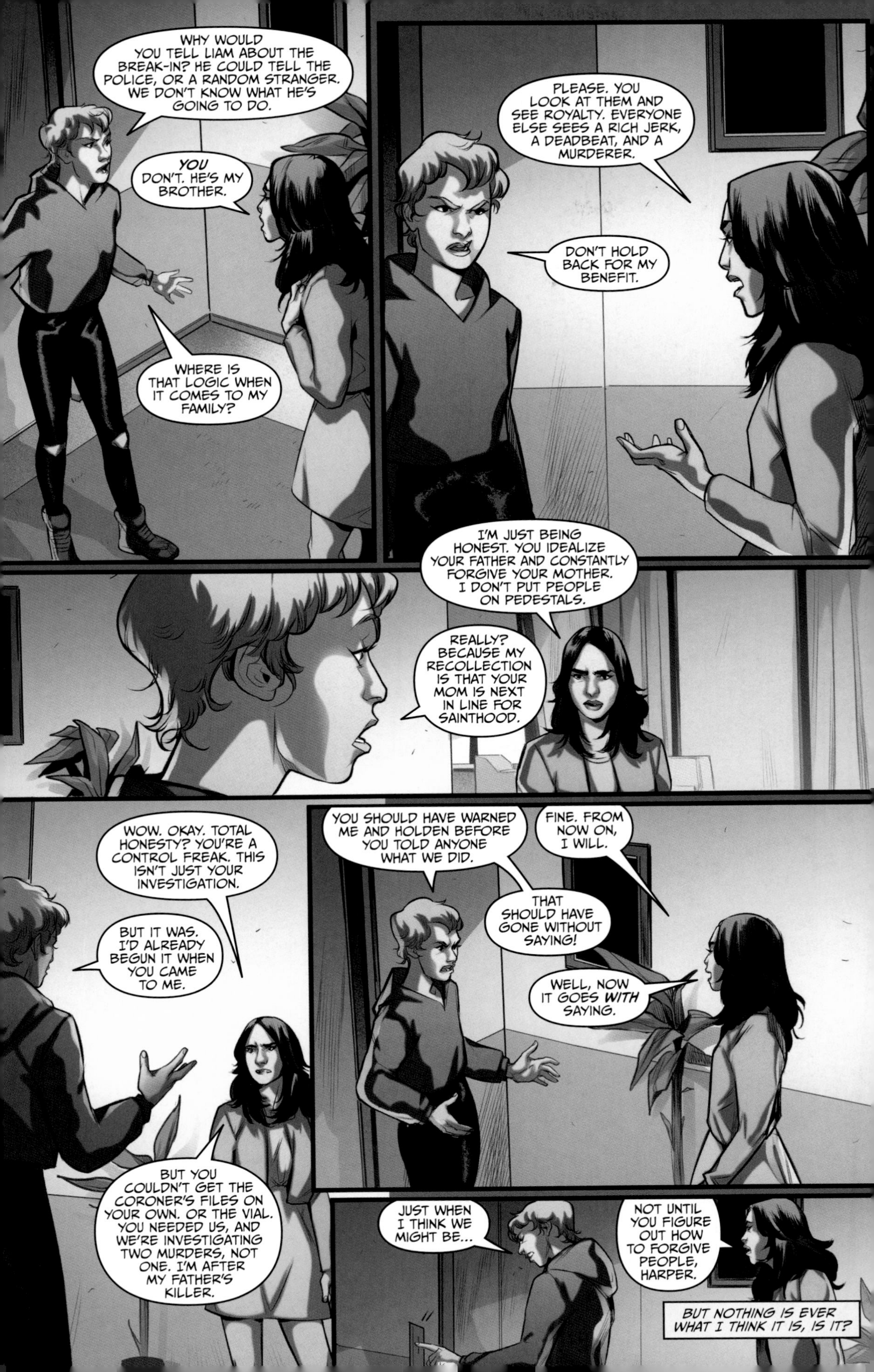
WHY WOULD YOU TELL LIAM ABOUT THE BREAK-IN? HE COULD TELL THE POLICE, OR A RANDOM STRANGER. WE DON'T KNOW WHAT HE'S GOING TO DO.
YOU DON'T. HE'S MY BROTHER.
WHERE IS THAT LOGIC WHEN IT COMES TO MY FAMILY?
PLEASE. YOU LOOK AT THEM AND SEE ROYALTY. EVERYONE ELSE SEES A RICH JERK, A DEADBEAT, AND A MURDERER.
DON'T HOLD BACK FOR MY BENEFIT.
I'M JUST BEING HONEST. YOU IDEALIZE YOUR FATHER AND CONSTANTLY FORGIVE YOUR MOTHER. I DON'T PUT PEOPLE ON PEDESTALS.
REALLY? BECAUSE MY RECOLLECTION IS THAT YOUR MOM IS NEXT IN LINE FOR SAINTHOOD.
WOW. OKAY. TOTAL HONESTY? YOU'RE A CONTROL FREAK. THIS ISN'T JUST YOUR INVESTIGATION.
BUT IT WAS. I'D ALREADY BEGUN IT WHEN YOU CAME TO ME.
BUT YOU COULDN'T GET THE CORONER'S FILES ON YOUR OWN. OR THE VIAL. YOU NEEDED US, AND WE'RE INVESTIGATING TWO MURDERS, NOT ONE. I'M AFTER MY FATHER'S KILLER.
YOU SHOULD HAVE WARNED ME AND HOLDEN BEFORE YOU TOLD ANYONE WHAT WE DID.
FINE. FROM NOW ON, I WILL.
THAT SHOULD HAVE GONE WITHOUT SAYING!
WELL, NOW IT GOES *WITH* SAYING.
JUST WHEN I THINK WE MIGHT BE...
NOT UNTIL YOU FIGURE OUT HOW TO FORGIVE PEOPLE, HARPER.
BUT NOTHING IS EVER WHAT I THINK IT IS, IS IT?

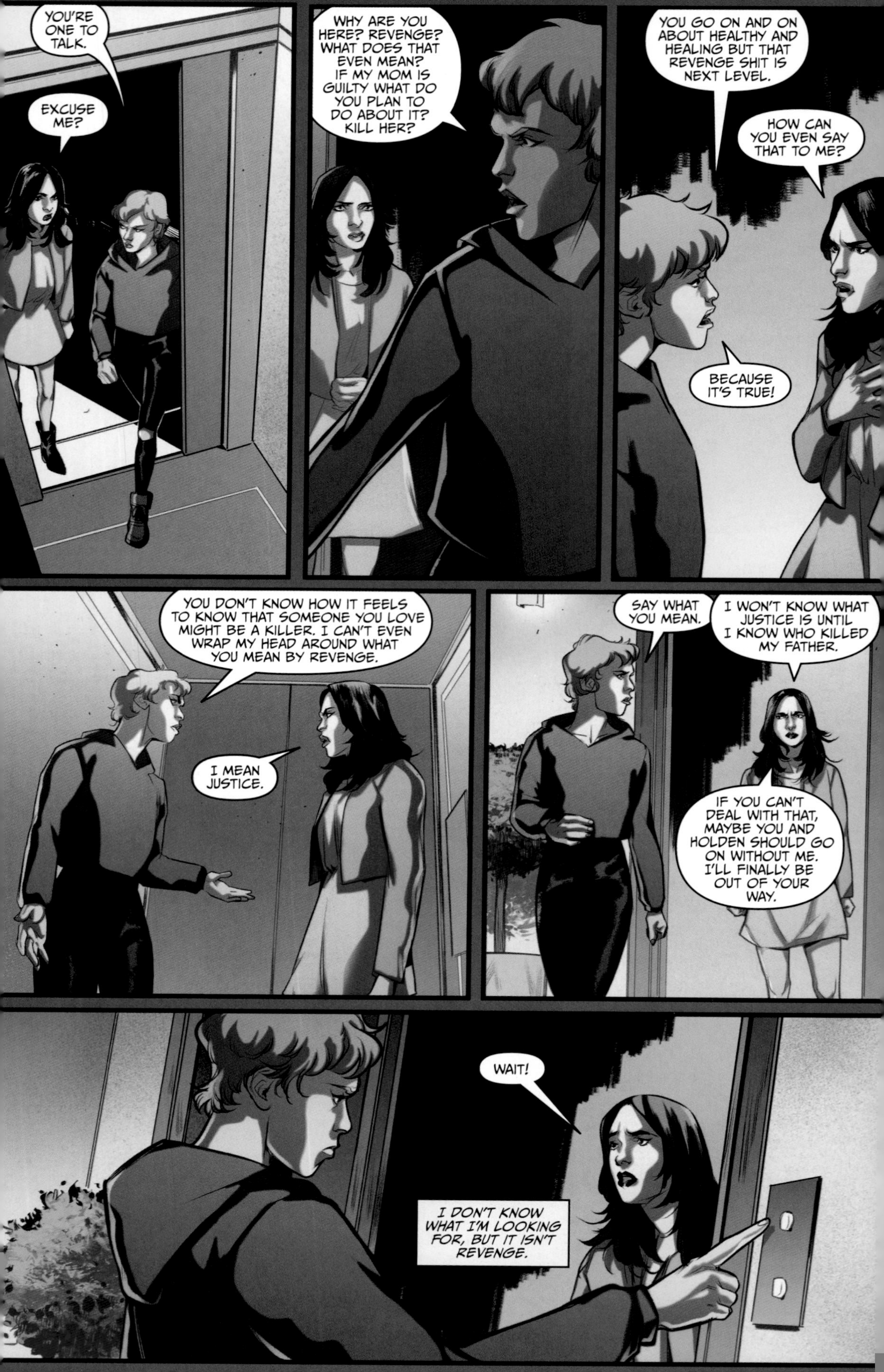
YOU'RE ONE TO TALK.
EXCUSE ME?
WHY ARE YOU HERE? REVENGE? WHAT DOES THAT EVEN MEAN? IF MY MOM IS GUILTY WHAT DO YOU PLAN TO DO ABOUT IT? KILL HER?
YOU GO ON AND ON ABOUT HEALTHY AND HEALING BUT THAT REVENGE SHIT IS NEXT LEVEL.
HOW CAN YOU EVEN SAY THAT TO ME?
BECAUSE IT'S TRUE!
YOU DON'T KNOW HOW IT FEELS TO KNOW THAT SOMEONE YOU LOVE MIGHT BE A KILLER. I CAN'T EVEN WRAP MY HEAD AROUND WHAT YOU MEAN BY REVENGE.
I MEAN JUSTICE.
SAY WHAT YOU MEAN.
I WON'T KNOW WHAT JUSTICE IS UNTIL I KNOW WHO KILLED MY FATHER.
IF YOU CAN'T DEAL WITH THAT, MAYBE YOU AND HOLDEN SHOULD GO ON WITHOUT ME. I'LL FINALLY BE OUT OF YOUR WAY.
WAIT!
I DON'T KNOW WHAT I'M LOOKING FOR, BUT IT ISN'T REVENGE.

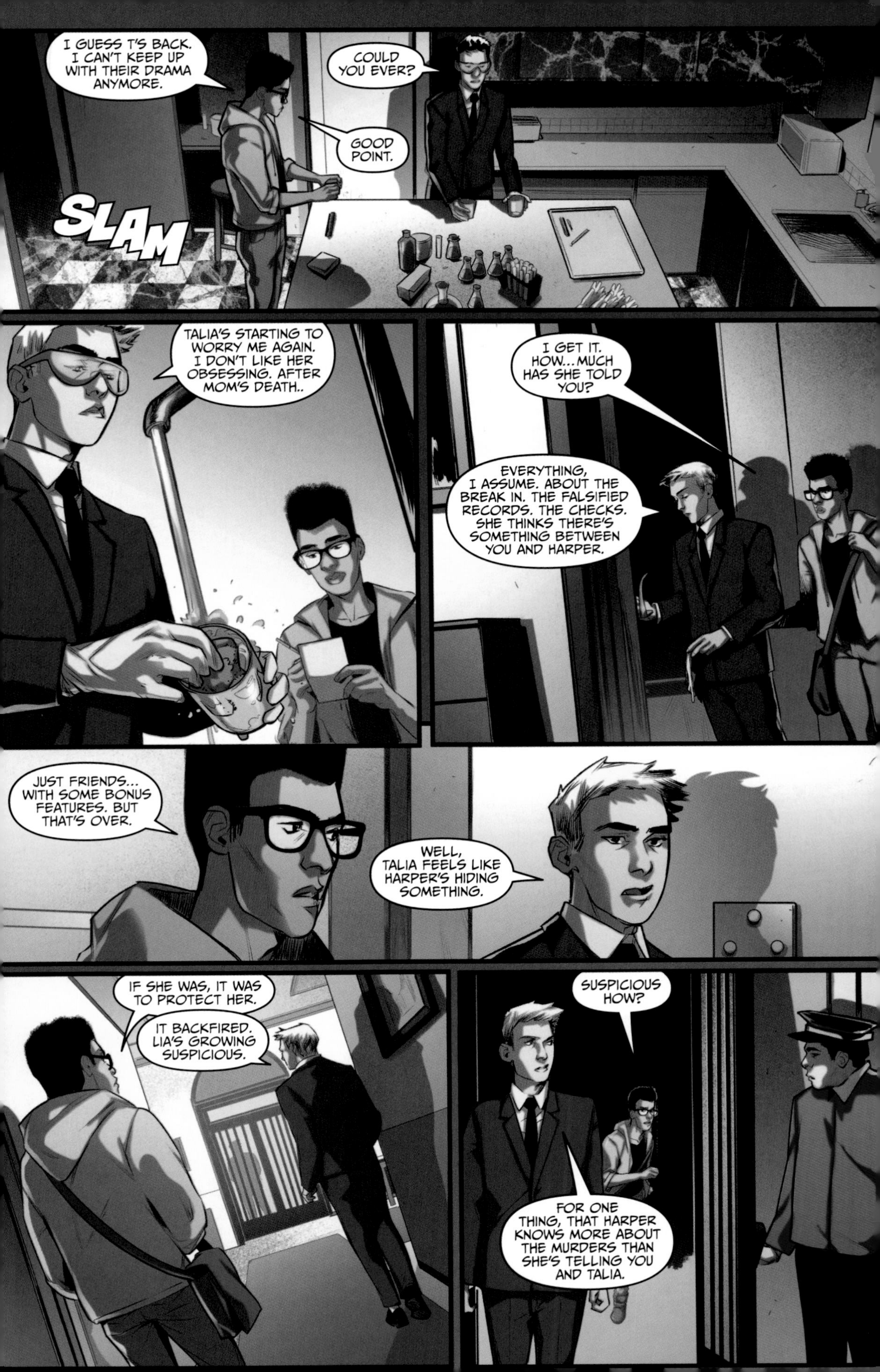
I GUESS T'S BACK. I CAN'T KEEP UP WITH THEIR DRAMA ANYMORE.
COULD YOU EVER?
GOOD POINT.
SLAM
TALIA'S STARTING TO WORRY ME AGAIN. I DON'T LIKE HER OBSESSING. AFTER MOM'S DEATH..
I GET IT. HOW...MUCH HAS SHE TOLD YOU?
EVERYTHING, I ASSUME. ABOUT THE BREAK IN. THE FALSIFIED RECORDS. THE CHECKS. SHE THINKS THERE'S SOMETHING BETWEEN YOU AND HARPER.
JUST FRIENDS... WITH SOME BONUS FEATURES. BUT THAT'S OVER.
WELL, TALIA FEELS LIKE HARPER'S HIDING SOMETHING.
IF SHE WAS, IT WAS TO PROTECT HER.
IT BACKFIRED. LIA'S GROWING SUSPICIOUS.
SUSPICIOUS HOW?
FOR ONE THING, THAT HARPER KNOWS MORE ABOUT THE MURDERS THAN SHE'S TELLING YOU AND TALIA.

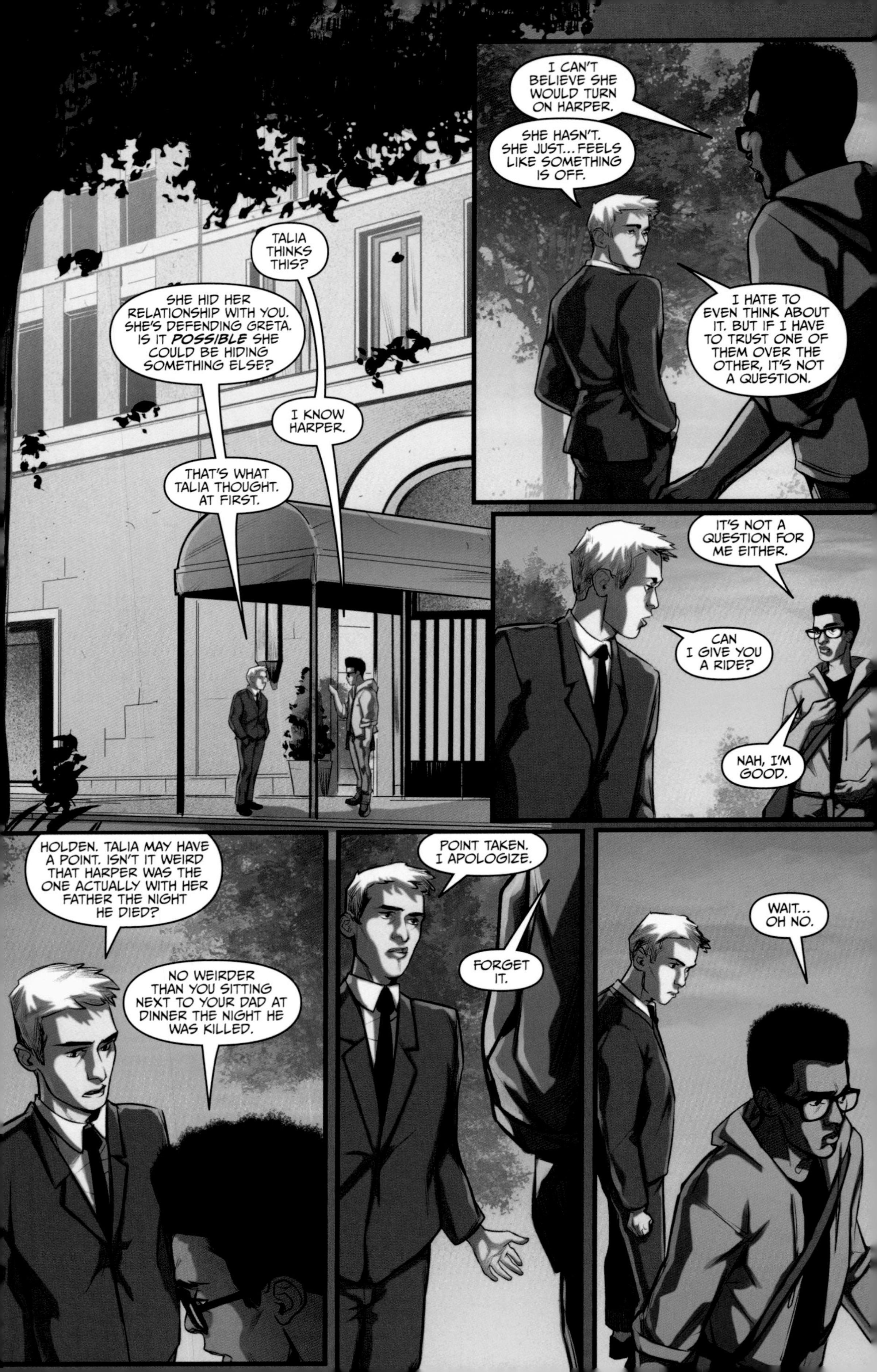
SHE HID HER RELATIONSHIP WITH YOU. SHE'S DEFENDING GRETA. IS IT *POSSIBLE* SHE COULD BE HIDING SOMETHING ELSE?
TALIA THINKS THIS?
I KNOW HARPER.
THAT'S WHAT TALIA THOUGHT. AT FIRST.
I CAN'T BELIEVE SHE WOULD TURN ON HARPER.
SHE HASN'T. SHE JUST... FEELS LIKE SOMETHING IS OFF.
I HATE TO EVEN THINK ABOUT IT. BUT IF I HAVE TO TRUST ONE OF THEM OVER THE OTHER, IT'S NOT A QUESTION.
IT'S NOT A QUESTION FOR ME EITHER.
CAN I GIVE YOU A RIDE?
NAH, I'M GOOD.
HOLDEN. TALIA MAY HAVE A POINT. ISN'T IT WEIRD THAT HARPER WAS THE ONE ACTUALLY WITH HER FATHER THE NIGHT HE DIED?
NO WEIRDER THAN YOU SITTING NEXT TO YOUR DAD AT DINNER THE NIGHT HE WAS KILLED.
POINT TAKEN. I APOLOGIZE.
FORGET IT.
WAIT... OH NO.

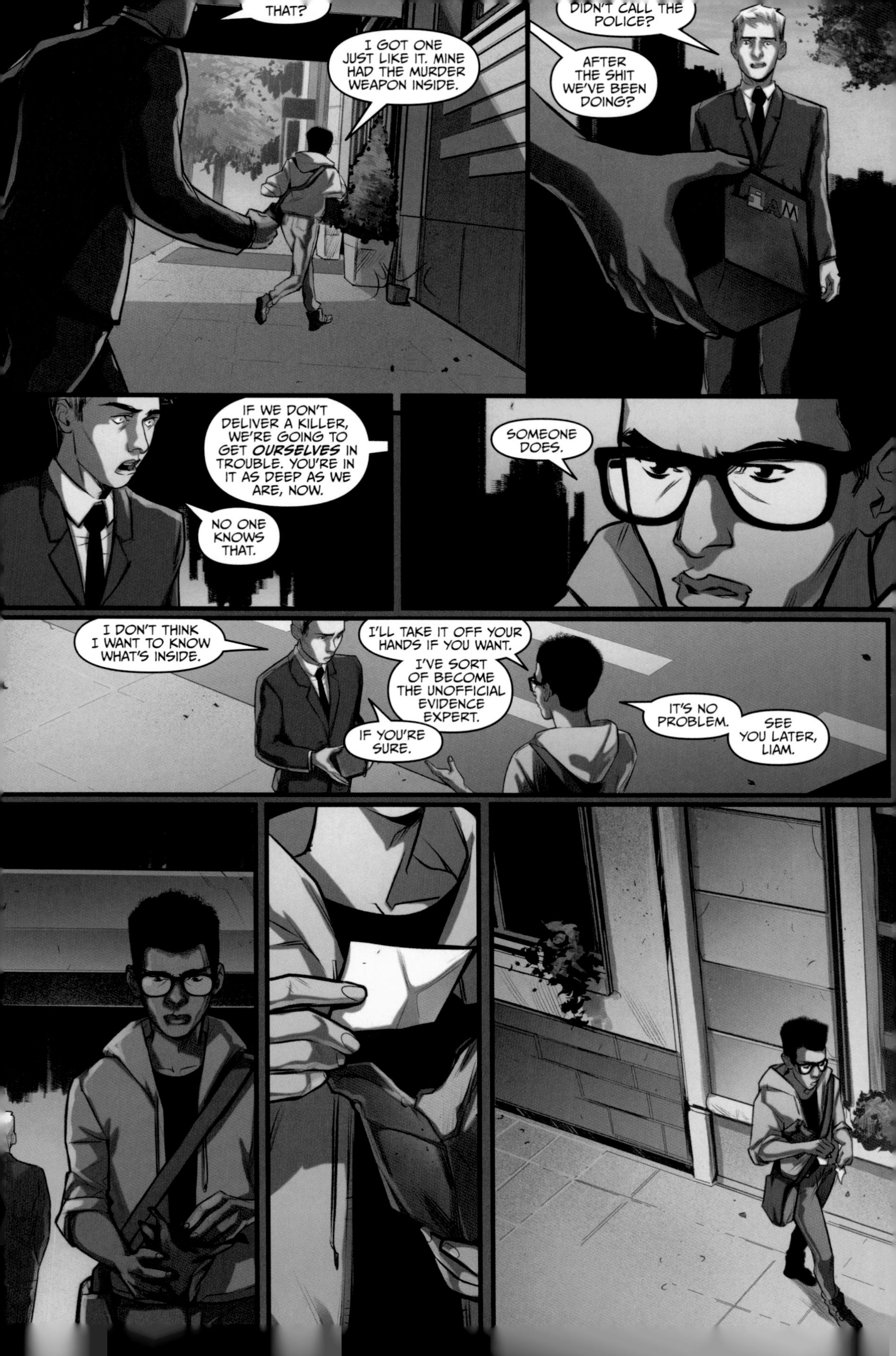
THAT?
I GOT ONE JUST LIKE IT. MINE HAD THE MURDER WEAPON INSIDE.
DIDN'T CALL THE POLICE?
AFTER THE SHIT WE'VE BEEN DOING?
IF WE DON'T DELIVER A KILLER, WE'RE GOING TO GET *OURSELVES* IN TROUBLE. YOU'RE IN IT AS DEEP AS WE ARE, NOW.
NO ONE KNOWS THAT.
SOMEONE DOES.
I DON'T THINK I WANT TO KNOW WHAT'S INSIDE.
I'LL TAKE IT OFF YOUR HANDS IF YOU WANT.
I'VE SORT OF BECOME THE UNOFFICIAL EVIDENCE EXPERT.
IF YOU'RE SURE.
IT'S NO PROBLEM.
SEE YOU LATER, LIAM.

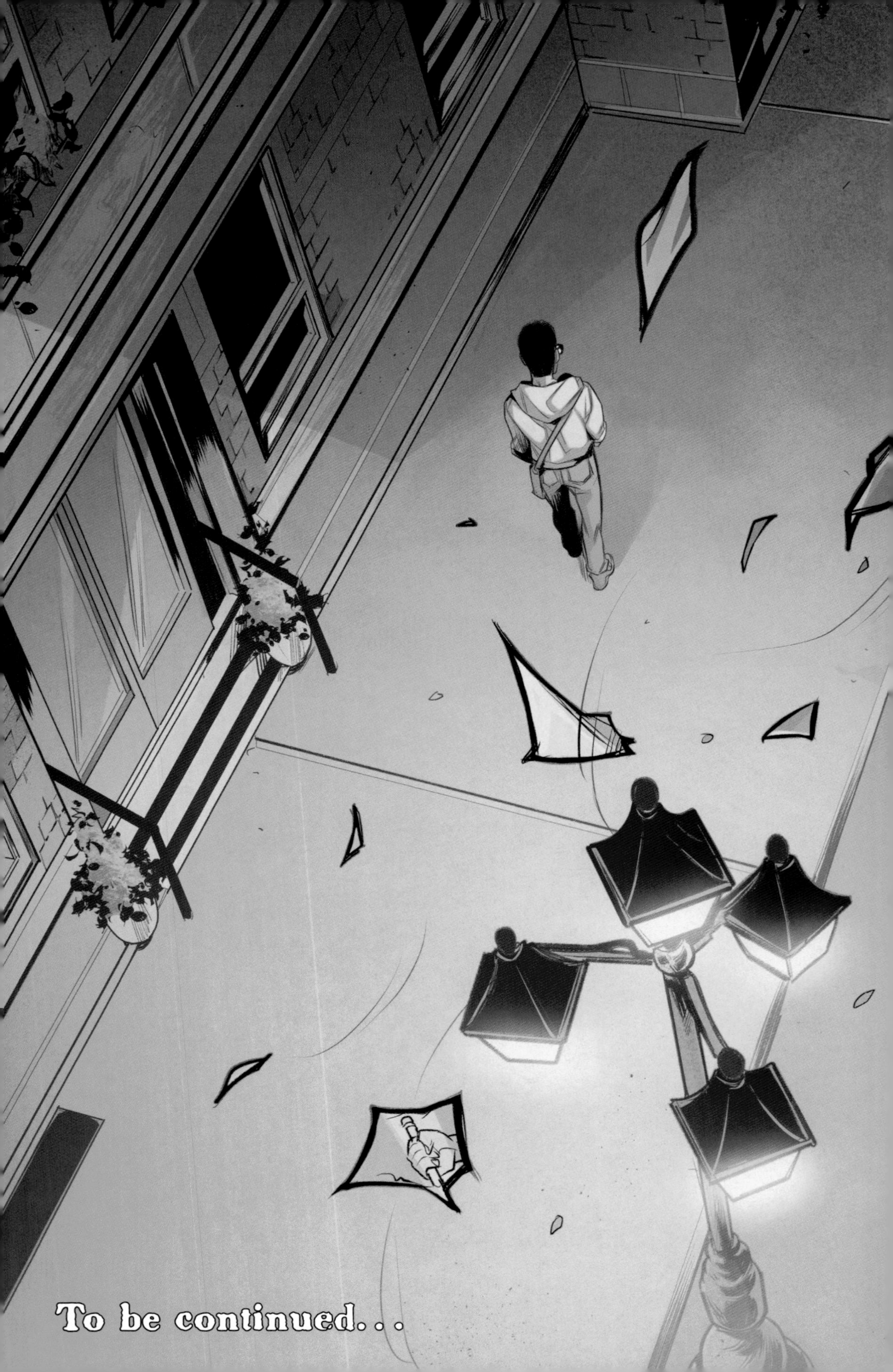
To be continued. . .

Tragic
EXTRAS

Script to Art - Chapter 2, Page 8

PANEL 1.

Clayton looks almost sad as Harper stuffs the paper into her backpack, looking panicked.

CLAYTON:
No. It's a piece of advice from someone with personal experience. Like it or not, I'm your family and I care.

CAP:
A little more than kin, and less than kind.

PANEL 2.

Tears fill Harper's eyes and she begins to look agitated—a hallucination is coming on. The color is beginning to drain from the room except for little accents of red—a telltale sign for the hallucinations.

HARPER:
Don't d-do that. You stopped being family the d-day you turned on D-Dad.

CAP:
My father's brother, but no more like my father
Than I to Hercules.

PANEL 3.

Clayton shakes his head.

CLAYTON:
You don't know as much as you think you do, kid.

CAP:
It is not nor it cannot come to good.

From Dana

The transitions to the hallucinations in *Tragic* incorporate Hamlet's soliloquys into the story. In this scene, I wove in excerpts from Hamlet's first words in Act I, scene II. "A little more than kin and less than kind" is Hamlet's first line of the play, an aside about Hamlet's uncle who's married to his mother. In *Tragic*, Harper is referring to her uncle Clayton who is involved with her mother. In both cases the line reflects the character's unhappiness with the inappropriate relationship. It makes the uncle more than family, kind of a jerk, and not equal in kind to Harper's father. Harper doesn't want her father replaced, and she rationalizes her feelings about it by finding specific faults with Clayton. Harper then quotes from the Act I, Scene II soliloquy: "My father's brother, but no more like my father than I to Hercules." This reinforces the idea that Clayton doesn't measure up to Hamilton while taking a knock at herself—she's no hero, an idea that repeats itself throughout Tragic. The transition ends with "it is not nor it cannot come to good," half of Hamlet's soliloquy closer, and a predictor that the situation will end in tragedy—at least, unless something intervenes.

From Valentina

From the first moment I read the script, Harper and her world of hallucinations fascinated me greatly. Hallucinations creep into Harper's reality and consequently into the page, allowing me to play with the grid and the panels and somehow "twist" the pages where hallucinations appear. An example of this is page 8 of Chapter #2: we can tell from Harper's terrified look in the first panel that something is wrong and we gradually see hallucinations appear, like black tongues or tentacles that penetrate the page and gradually take over Harper's reality. To increase and emphasize the effect of the delirium that Harper is experiencing, I added some elements in gray (on some pages even red) and especially chose to give the panels a different, curved, distorted look, to move them as far away as possible from their usual features, just like Harper turns away from reality. My goal was to have these elements, which are perceived as painfully real, encompass everything and take over Harper, the other characters, and not least the page itself.

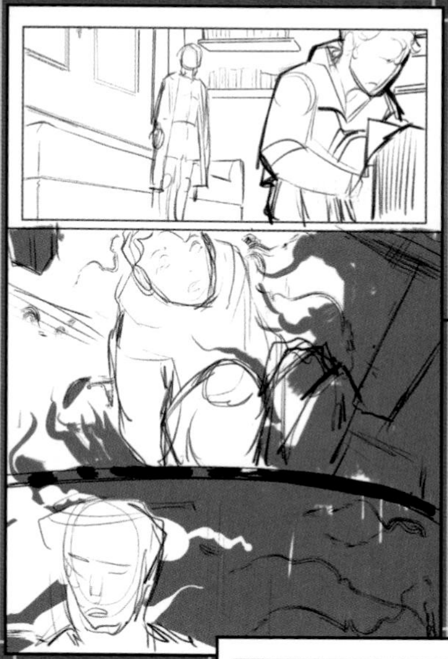

Layouts

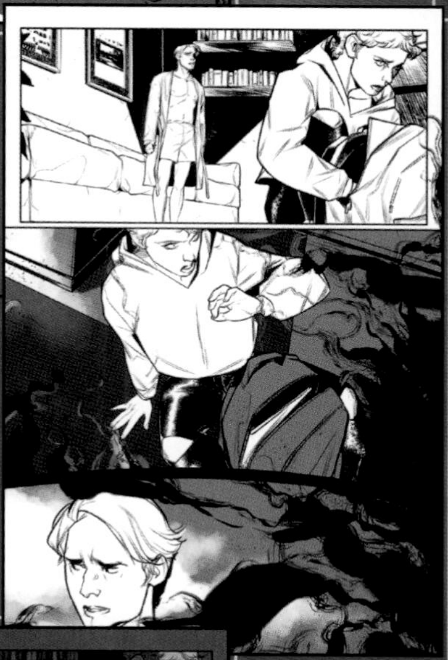

Inks

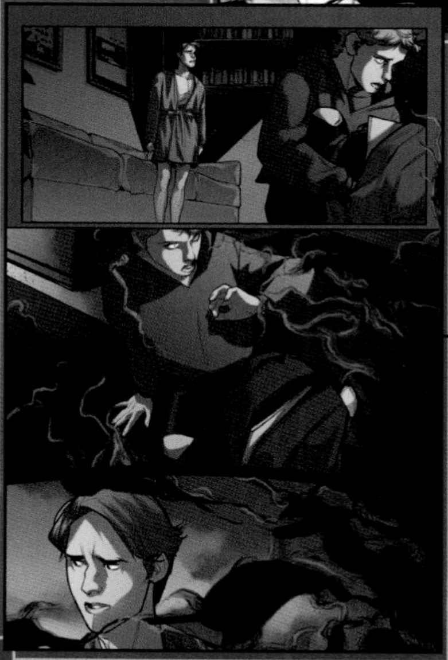

Colors

From Chiara

After I receive the inked pages, the first step in the process is to give flat colors, and then general lighting and shadows. In doing all this I get to start thinking about mood lighting, which obviously depends on the result I want to achieve. Page 8 of Chapter #2 shows a particular moment of transition: in the previous pages we saw a highly dramatic scene - Harper confronts Clay after finding the coroner's report. In this page, from the second panel on, a hallucination is about to take over. Colors need to emphasize this transition. So, the cool night blue that characterized the entire previous sequence contrasts with the coloring of the tentacles that creep across the page and the bright red of the hallucination, a visual conflict that increases the dramatic vibe of this moment.

Caius

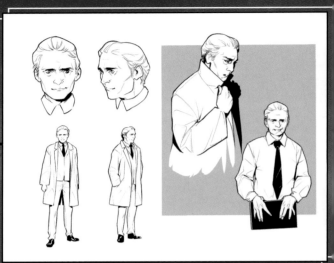

Clayton

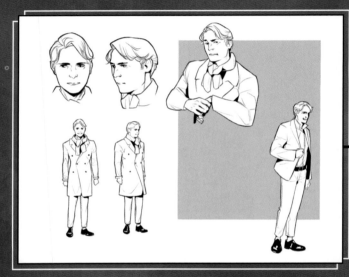

Ghost

Greta

Hamilton

Harper

Holden

Liam

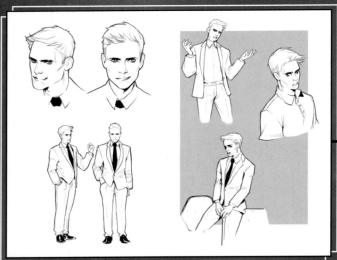

Talia

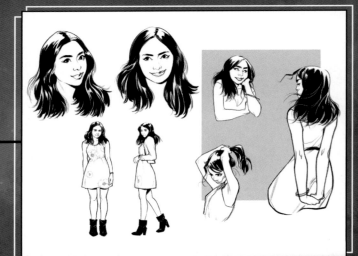

TRAGIC Shakespeare Connection

Tragic is a contemporary interpretation of Shakespeare's *Hamlet*. One of the challenges was trying to preserve not only the spirit of the story, but key plot points and snippets of dialogue within the confines of a graphic novel and the cadence of a young adult novel. One thing I experimented with was bringing in wisps of Hamlet's soliloquys in the transitions to Harper's hallucinations. The moments are surreal and otherworldly, and the poetic dialogue is a bridge to an alternate reality unlike her everyday world, so I was able to play with the language and tone a little bit. In the world of the graphic novel, Harper is familiar with *Hamlet* because it was very important to her father, so the text is floating around in her subconscious.

Most key *Hamlet* characters are present in *Tragic*. Hamlet's corollary is Harper, who also struggles with balancing duty, resentment, and indecisiveness; Hamlet's mother Gertrude is represented by Greta, who has ultimately prioritized herself; and his uncle Claudius appears as Clayton, who is equally ambitious and entangled in a fraught relationship with his late brother. Ophelia's double is Talia, Harper's childhood sweetheart that Harper still has feelings for after a bad breakup. Ophelia's doting brother Laertes is present as Talia's brother Liam, and her doomed father Polonius appears briefly as Talia's father and the business partner of Harper's dad. Hamlet's closest companion and confidant, Horatio, appears in the form of Holden, Harper's lifelong best friend with whom she recently had a brief romantic entanglement.

On that note, a queer reading of *Hamlet* suggests a potential romantic relationship between Horatio and Hamlet, and it was important to me to preserve this aspect of Hamlet's character. While I'd like to take credit for queering Hamlet, the theory has been around for decades. However, I'd never consider writing a *Hamlet* adaptation without prioritizing Hamlet as a queer figure. One reason I chose to change Harper's gender was actually because Hamlet projects a lot of his anger at the women in his life, and I didn't want to carry that aspect of the story forward.

Most of the changes I made were updates related to setting and character. Hamlet's father is a king; Harper's dad is a former actor who now runs an artistic empire. Hamlet is a prince; Harper an heir. They live in a lavish estate in a major metropolitan area rather than a castle in Denmark.

What remains are the key plot points. Major relationship conflicts and deaths, the play within a play, and of course, the ghost. There are several big changes, but they're huge spoilers. But the ghost of Hamlet/Harper's father plays a much bigger role in *Tragic* than in *Hamlet*, where he makes brief appearances throughout the play to give Hamlet his mission to avenge his death. In *Tragic*, he's just as pushy but less terrifying. He still serves as a sort of angel or devil on Harper's shoulder, urging her forward, and she's still not sure which one, but in a less literal sense. While Hamlet genuinely questions whether the ghost might be a demon, Harper questions the reality of the ghost. They both ultimately accept it and in both cases it serves as the catalyst to verify that their father was murdered and by whom. *Hamlet* isn't thought of as a thriller, but the ingredients are in the text. His father dies mysteriously, he's haunted by a ghost; he spends a good chunk of the play attempting to elude a bounty placed on his head, and he has a mystery to solve—did his father die of natural causes as everyone insists, or can he prove he was murdered, and who did it? I tried to capture as much of that in spirit in *Tragic*, with dozens of Easter eggs for Shakespeare fans. It was so much fun to write— I hope it's half as fun to read.

Dana Mele

Dana Mele is a Pushcart Prize–nominated writer based in upstate New York. A former bookseller and lover of pomegranates, Dana is the author of the YA thrillers *People Like Us* and *Summer's Edge*. *Tragic* is Dana's debut graphic novel. Follow Dana on Twitter at @danamelebooks and Instagram at @danammele.

Valentina Pinti

Born in 1989, hailing from Italy, Valentina Pinti studied painting at the Academy of Fine Arts, before turning to comics and illustration. Since 2017 she has been collaborating with several publishers, in Italy (Noise Press, Star Comics), France (Petit-à-Petit, Editions Soleil), the UK (Rebellion Comics) and the US. For the American market, she drew three issues of "Buffy the Vampire Slayer" (BOOM! Studios), and is currently working on the upcoming "Red Sitha" (Dynamite Entertainment).

Chiara di Francia

Chiara Di Francia (1984 – Turin, Italy) has been working as an illustrator and comic artist since 2010. She illustrated books for Hachette Livre, Sigil Entertainment Group, Yil Editions. In 2020, she drew a volume of the "Mary Shelley Presents" series (Kymera Press), which won a Bram Stoker Award for Superior Achievement in a Graphic Novel. Since 2018, she has been collaborating with Arancia Studio as an illustrator and color artist, working for the French market (Jungle, Dupuis, Les Humanoïdes Associés and many more), then landing on the US market. She's currently coloring "Red Sonja by Mirka Andolfo" and "Red Sitha" (Dynamite Entertainment).